PRAISE FOR
DEAD MAN'S CREEK

'A commanding, consuming and outright thrilling mystery. Chris Hammer's first-class series goes from strength to strength.' **Chris Whitaker**

'My favourite Australian detective is Nell Buchanan. *Dead Man's Creek* is a richly textured novel.' **Ann Cleeves**

'Utterly brilliant, a darkly simmering mystery – an Australian *Where The Crawdads Sing*.' **Dervla McTiernan**

'Chris Hammer is at the height of his power here. *Dead Man's Creek* is a superb piece of storytelling – a dark and compelling saga brilliantly rooted in a rich Australian landscape.' **William Shaw**

'Dingo noir at its finest. This may well be Hammer's best work yet. Atmospheric and thrilling. I was gripped.' **Victoria Selman**

'Chris Hammer has surpassed himself in *Dead Man's Creek*. I doubt I'll read a better novel this year.' *The Times*

'Hammer is at his best in this panoramic novel' *Sunday Times*

'Exceptional. This is storytelling that grasps the reader like poison ivy, never once losing its hypnotic grip: both compelling and masterful.' *Daily Mail*

'An excellent, multi-layered and atmospheric thriller' *Mail on Sunday*

'A sprawling and gripping new crime novel from the Australian noir master' *Peterborough Telegraph*

'A delight from start to finish' *Irish Independent*

'*Dead Man's Creek* has it all-a vivid setting, characters that live and breathe and feel utterly real, and an epic mystery stretching across decades that thrills and surprises. This is a perfect crime novel.' **Lisa Gray**

PRAISE FOR
SILVER

'Hammer is a great writer – a leader in Australian noir' **Michael Connelly**

'I think this is better than the first' **Ann Cleeves**

'Hammer combines Scarsden's backstory with a vivid portrait of a divided community to mesmerising effect' *Sunday Times*

'Richly descriptive, with a large and well-drawn cast, this is an immersive and enjoyable novel that lives up to the promise of its predecessor' *Guardian*

'Compelling, original and brilliantly executed – an excellent thriller' **Charles Cumming**

'A terrific story . . . This is an excellent sequel; the best Australian crime novel since Peter Temple's *The Broken Shore*' *The Times*

PRAISE FOR
SCRUBLANDS

'Shimmers with heat from the sun and from the passions that drive a tortured tale of blood and loss' **Val McDermid**

'An almost perfect crime novel . . . Intelligent, thought-provoking, great narrative energy, a central character who's imperfect but self-aware, and of course that amazing setting . . . I loved it' **Ann Cleeves**

'A dark and brilliant thriller, one that lingers in the mind' *Mail On Sunday*

Chris Hammer

COVER THE BONES

WILDFIRE

First published in 2023 by ALLEN & UNWIN as *The Seven*

First published in Great Britain in hardback in 2024 by
WILDFIRE
an imprint of HEADLINE PUBLISHING GROUP

1

Cataloguing in Publication Data is available from the British Library

Hardback ISBN 978 1 4722 9571 2
Trade paperback ISBN 978 1 4722 9572 9

Map by Aleksander J. Potočnik

Printed and bound in Great Britain by Clays Ltd, Elcograf S.p.A.

MIX
Paper | Supporting
responsible forestry
FSC® C104740

Headline's policy is to use papers that are natural,
renewable and recyclable products and made from wood
grown in well-managed forests and other controlled sources.
The logging and manufacturing processes are expected to conform
to the environmental regulations of the country of origin.

HEADLINE PUBLISHING GROUP
An Hachette UK Company
Carmelite House
50 Victoria Embankment
London EC4Y 0DZ

www.headline.co.uk
www.hachette.co.uk

FOR FARMSY—LEGEND!

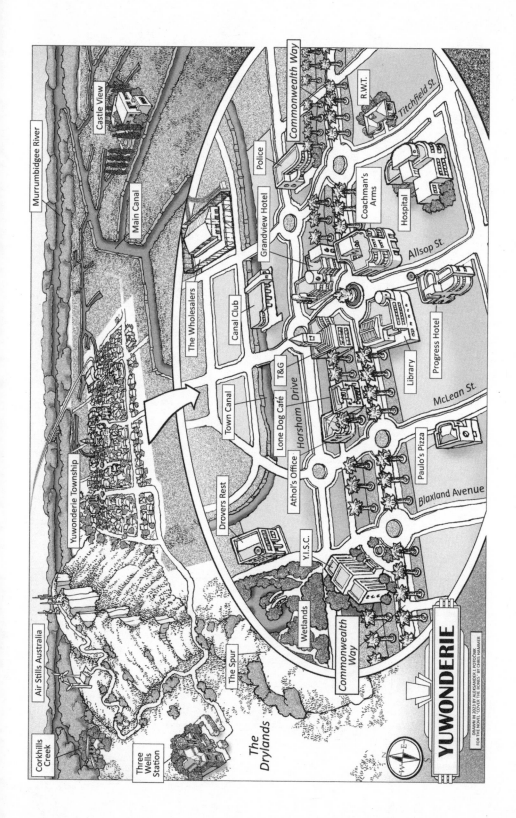

YUWONDERIE

DRAWN IN 2023 BY ALEKSANDER J. POTOČNIK
FOR THE NOVEL 'COVER THE BONES' BY CHRIS HAMMER

Our lands, our lives, and all, are Bolingbroke's,
And nothing can we call our own but death;
And that small model of the barren earth
Which serves as paste and cover to our bones.
– *Richard II*, William Shakespeare

prologue

THE IRRIGATION CANAL STRETCHES INTO THE DISTANCE, PERFECT FOR WATERSKIING: two kilometres long, ten metres wide, ruler-straight, almost as large as Yuwonderie's main canal. There's a gentle breeze wafting in from the north, enough to ripple the surface. Eggs splashes water onto his face, then eases himself into the canal, feeling its sun-warmed embrace. It's Sunday, and his supervisor at the Wholesalers has let him off early. The others were already here waiting, preparing, Eggs keen to go first, his friends happy to let him. And now all is ready for this summer's challenge: the curve. He has the ski, the towrope handle. He wriggles his feet into the soft rubber toe pieces, leans back, pushes the tip of the ski above the surface, curling himself into a ball, an astronaut on a launch pad.

On the bank, Johnny Titchfield is driving the farm truck, while Pete Allsop is the go-between in the back tray. Eggs gives the thumbs-up, Pete yells, 'Take the slack!' and Johnny edges the vehicle forward, along the path above the right-hand bank, the tightening rope emerging from the water. 'Gun it!' yells Pete, and Johnny floors it. The truck lurches into motion, and Eggs is all concentration: the wrench to the shoulders, the pressure on his legs, pushing ever so slightly to get up and stay upright in the narrow canal as the truck gathers speed, hanging on, edging the ski to counter the rope's sideways pull. Avoiding the banks. And then he's up, in equilibrium, accelerating down the canal, Pete yelling his encouragement, Johnny struggling to keep the speed constant on the runnelled track.

Eggs feels the thrill of it, the exhilaration, water spraying and wind in his face, tearing down the canal, orange trees to his left, grapevines to his right. Now they're moving fast, the truck reaching cruising speed, and there's not a lot to it, the narrow canal allowing no room for slalom. He enjoys the moment, taking a hand from the crossbar to wave to Pete, to demonstrate his mastery. A family of ducks sees him coming and bursts into flight as he slices through them, laughing.

So far, so easy, but now they are almost at the curve; it's time to concentrate. He can see it approaching, and then it's almost upon him, Pete yelling, 'Two hundred!' The canal angles to the right—not by much, twenty degrees at most, but the turn will take precision: carve too early and he'll clip the apex; too late, and he'll swing wide and career into the left-hand bank at fifty kilometres per hour.

'One fifty!'

Time is starting to slow. Eggs can see the red flag, the sighter they've planted at the bend.

Johnny is backing off on the speed, letting Eggs's momentum carry him forward. They've debated this, thought it through, how best to take it. The trajectory is self-evident: go wide to the left, cut across the top of the turn, giving himself the width of the

2

canal to straighten again. It's the speed that's tricky. If the truck slows too much, the rope will slacken and Eggs will lose impetus, ski sinking below the surface—but if Johnny doesn't back off enough, then as the truck takes the curve ahead of him, it will impart a slingshot effect as he rounds the curve, propelling him uncontrollably towards the outside bank. None of them knows yet what speed is optimal. They've talked and talked, but this is the first time they've tried it.

'One hundred!'

He's told Johnny and Pete to take it slow, this first run. Better to run out of steam and fade into the water than to hit the bend too fast. If he feels himself being slung wide, if the speed is too much, he'll need to bail, strike the water, not the earth, but he has no idea if that's possible, if there would be enough time. And now, as time slows even more, the narrowness of the canal presses in on him: so easy to negotiate in a straight line, so difficult to take a turn. A split second, that's all he'll have.

He's in position, close to the left-hand bank, feeling the rope tighten, the acceleration.

'Fifty!'

The countdown is redundant; he barely hears it. Johnny is still going too fast.

The apex, the red flag.

A thought: Johnny is speeding on purpose, putting him in his place.

Resolve comes to him: he won't pull out, he'll defy them.

The rope thrumming now, as if with malevolence.

And still he hangs on.

Do or die.

'Now!'

He carves into it, feeling the ski responding, the power coming through beneath him, his shoulder close to the water, pushing on his thighs, the acceleration growing. The truck is around the corner, the energy flowing down the rope, through his arms, into him, the force elemental, past the point of no return. And through the apex, his head and shoulders floating for a split second over dry land, lifting his head ever so slightly to avoid hitting the flag, the rope still pulling, no slack in it, Johnny not easing off enough, Eggs carving so hard his shoulder is clipping the water.

'Yes!'

And he's around, the canal stretching out for another dead-straight kilometre. The rope's tension is back to normal and he lets go with one hand, pumping the air with his fist, Pete yelling in victory, Johnny blasting the horn. Satisfaction. Fulfilment. Accomplishment. Victory. Eggs takes a look over his shoulder, the red flag waving its own congratulations. He turns back, sees it too late, the shape in the water, the white sack.

Too late to turn. He jumps, leaping sideways, out of the ski, just before it ploughs into the sack, lifting and tumbling as he hits the water, closing his eyes, shoulder first, going under. But not too deep, not too awkwardly, some water up his nose, nothing more. Not hitting the bottom. No damage done, the exhilaration still with him. Treading water, stitching the unforeseen obstacle into the narrative, an embellishment to an already compelling story. His mind is moving quickly, rehearsing the version he'll recount at the pub, as he begins to stroke back to retrieve the ski, waving to the truck, showing he's uninjured. It's stopped some ways down the track. Pete is out of the tray, sprinting towards him, slowing as he sees Eggs is unharmed. Eggs turns, searching for the ski, sees it a little way further along, floating towards the bank, not far from where it struck the sack. Curious now, he swims towards the object, wonders what it could be. Something solid: he remembers the thwack of the ski colliding with it as he hit the water. Solid, but buoyant enough to float. Where did it come from? He needs to get it out, can't believe they didn't see it when they reconnoitred the course, planted the flag, did their dry run.

It's mostly submerged, barely breaking the surface. He's about to reach out, to touch it, then stops. It's not a sack. The white is a shirt. White smeared with mud. And streaks of blood, drifting. The back of a head, brown hair wispy in the water. Holy shit. A body—he's hit a body. He treads water, recoiling, then slowly starts to back away. It's real. A dead person.

chapter one

Miss Bessie Walker
Castle View
Via Narrandera

Mrs Elizabeth Walker
Worthington Point Mission
New South Wales

September 1913

My dearest Mother,

So I have arrived and am found acceptable. I believe I detected a sense of relief as I dismounted from the carriage: my clothes respectable, my teeth intact, my hair restrained. Their eyes swept my face, keen to detect any sign of my lineage, pleased when they saw that, like my hair, it is subdued. They complimented me: on my posture, on my diction, on my cleanliness. On the lightness of my skin. I smiled, demure, speaking softly with my head bowed. They asked if it were true that I could read and write, and seemed pleased, if a little perplexed, when I confirmed it. The mother set me a task, a test, to demonstrate my ability. Afterwards, she declared my work passable and herself satisfied. She assigned me an additional duty there and then: that of her secretary, so that she might dictate her correspondence to me. She blames rheumatism for her inability to write, and her failing eyesight for her struggle to read. She is fooling no one, but I have no wish to embarrass her.

She is a tiny thing, worn down by life. Her name is Madeleine, and she informed me with pride that it was French, while in the same breath forbidding me from ever using it to address her. I must call her Madam, as if she is some great lady, this is some other century, and I am her possession. None of that is true, not legally: she is no more an aristocrat than I am a chattel, but the relationship at times is not so very different. It is her house and it is she who provides my food and my board. She is my mistress and I am her servant.

For a while, I found myself at something of an impasse, not sure exactly how to approach her and how to calibrate this new station of mine, until I realised what it was that she truly wanted from me: not obedience, not subservience, but gratitude that they should take me in. I was initially a little taken aback by this. I had thought it a work contract, nothing more, nothing less: they would give me food, board and payment in return for my cooking, my cleaning and, so it would seem, my 'secretarial' duties. I am indeed grateful for the work, but I feel as if she believes my gratitude should run deeper and be demonstrated more effusively, as if she has sacrificed something, as if her generosity in employing me deserves some greater declaration of loyalty. Having deduced this, I put it into practice, declaring aloud the debt I owe her. It sounded hollow to me, yet no matter how ambivalent I felt in uttering the words, they worked and she relaxed. Her sacrifice has been acknowledged, our relationship defined.

In truth, it is not so very bad. It is clear she is not used to having a maid. She works at the house herself and smiles and jokes, before withdrawing as if remembering she is meant to be playing a role, but I suspect her nature is not so very aloof: she has spent too many years engaged in domestic toil to rise too far above it, no matter what her ambitions or the expectations of her son.

He had barely sized me up and voiced his approval than he was away again, out with the sheep, mustering. His mother tells me he has barely been at home these past few weeks, for he has been camping with the men, herding the flock, bringing them to the shearing shed in preparation for their clipping. It was only on my second day that he returned once again in the evening, badly in need of washing, feeding and sleeping. His name is Horace and he is now the man of the house. Madeleine tells me he intends to marry, have children and live on the property. She is thrilled by this, by the prospect of grandchildren, and has suggested my role may soon enough transform into one of nanny and, later, governess.

He visited me in the cookhouse, checking to see if I was settling in. I'm not sure he was so much checking on my welfare as coming to inform me that this year's wool clip will be prodigious, to boast that the Titchfields are growing wealthy, that they have planned a new house as grand as any in the district, that now his father is dead he can set the family on a better trajectory. There will be more servants, more qualified and more experienced; I represent just a first step. He is a hearty young man, so full of his plans and enthusiasms that he cannot help but share them as they come bursting out of him.

The land hereabouts is very flat and dry, the grass brittle brown even before summer's onslaught, with few trees to offer shade. The graziers have cleared most of them away; I cannot say why. The sheep gather under the survivors, wandering back and forth between their shelter and the creek's waterholes. The river proper is some miles to the north. Out of this featureless plain rises a high and rocky hill, known locally as the Castle. It still has some trees upon it, although near its peak there is a cliff of sheer rock. It is a strange and wonderful sight, as if it carries some unspoken portent. Our people must have a name for it; I wonder what it might be.

The house itself is more solid than grand, no squatter's mansion, but by no means poorly constructed. It is a single storey, with sash windows and elevated floorboards, and a lovely parlour, from which I am banned except to clean. There is a separate dining room with an imposing table; Madeleine was quick to inform me it is made of cedar from the coast. There are three bedrooms: one for her, one for her son and one for her daughter, away at school at present but due to return soon. There is a small study at the end of the house, the office from where Horace administers the farm business. There is a series of sturdy outbuildings set back from the main house: a cookhouse, a washhouse, a little shack for me. These are where I will spend the majority of my days. A tad further in one direction is a killing shed, and further yet twin outhouses. They have built a new one for the family and I am to have the old one. It would seem that, according to some unknown rule of society, servants should not void down the same hole as their betters!

Will I be happy here? I am not so sure.

This evening, after I helped clear the table, Madam came to me in the cookhouse, where I was washing the dishes. I do feel she is lonely out here, starved of feminine company. She confided in me a great secret, one that I am not meant to know and that I am forbidden to share: nothing is settled yet, but some local families want to bring water to the district, and prosperity with it. An irrigation scheme, they call it, similar to that being developed north of the Murrumbidgee.

She said her husband was the visionary who first saw the potential in the pan-flat country of the district, so similar to the landscape north of the river. 'Why should we not have something like that?' he had asked. Madeleine spoke of this scheme in reverent tones, as if reciting the Scriptures, or recounting some heavenly vision set out by her late husband, the prophet of the Riverina: the rail line extended, small landholders invited to share the bounty, a town rising from the plain, with halls and shops and schools and churches. There would be cricket teams and football clubs and an annual agricultural show and visiting theatre troupes. The desert made green; the land drought-proofed. She said I was indeed fortunate to be here at the beginning of this new epoch, that I might witness his dream become a reality.

She left me there to finish my chores, telling me she didn't want me to read to her after all, that she was too tired. I don't mind her. For all that she tries to elevate herself and put on airs, I think there is a kind soul residing within her.

I trust all is well with you, and I look forward to your letters.

Your loving and obedient daughter,
Bessie

chapter two

DETECTIVE SERGEANT IVAN LUCIC LOOKS ALONG THE CANAL, TRYING TO VISUALISE
what has happened, whether the murder took place here or it's
merely where the body was dumped. Probably the latter, but he
doesn't want to count anything in or out. The local police have done
a good job of taping off the area, preventing contamination, but
the body has gone and he can understand why: the heat. He
wipes the sweat from his face with a handkerchief, glances at the
sky, the power of the mid-December sun uninterrupted by cloud
cover. It would have been unrealistic to leave the remains in situ.
Just one of the many differences between being a big-city cop and
covering the whole of regional New South Wales: the vastness of
the territory and the time it takes to get anywhere. The victim—a
local accountant, Athol Hasluck—had been discovered the day
before, about midday Sunday, but it wasn't until the evening that
the head of Homicide, Dereck 'Plodder' Packenham, assigned the
investigation to Ivan. He and Detective Constable Nell Buchanan
left Dubbo first thing in the morning, driving straight to the crime
scene, a six-hour drive; Yuwonderie closer to Melbourne than

to Sydney. And so twenty-four hours have passed between the discovery of the body and their arrival; it's already in the morgue and they'll have to rely on the photographs taken by the local police.

At least the locals had thought it through, retrieving the body from the opposite bank, having concluded it almost certainly entered the water from this side, the one with car access. Good thinking on their behalf, something to be acknowledged, to be commended. He makes a mental note.

He looks, but doesn't try to move past the tape and get closer to the canal. Crime scene investigator, Dr Carole Nguyen, is on her way from Sydney, and she won't want him trampling evidence. There's not a lot to see anyway: a few scuff marks on the bank; a couple of small triangular flags planted by the police; the canal stretching into the distance, curving slightly in the other direction. Innocuous. The boys' ski sits next to the water, abandoned. He looks skywards, the cloudless dome confirming the forecast: no rain on the horizon. No chance of evidence being washed away. He wonders if he can justify getting in police divers. If it were Sydney, there would be no debate: the investigator and the divers would have been here yesterday. But the capital is a seven-hour drive, or a chartered flight, and his budget is limited.

He walks back to where Nell stands talking with the local copper, McTosh. What sort of name is that—Ernst McTosh? The sort that got you bullied at school, maybe. Why not change it to Macintosh, make life easier? The sergeant is small for a policeman and whippet-thin, receding red hair cropped close. Not an ounce of fat. A marathon runner or a cyclist. Ivan knows the type: a competitor, not a contemplator. A bloke with something to prove. He can see it in the officer's don't-mess-with-me stance: legs spread wide, arms crossed, a small man trying to look larger. Ivan has no problem with that: the bloke is doing everything he can to help, including preserving the crime scene.

'Anything?' asks the local man.

'Nothing you haven't already noted.' And then, remembering: 'You the one who thought of retrieving the body from the opposite bank?'

'Aye.'

'Good thinking.'

'Thanks.'

'Tell me, this place,' Ivan says, looking around, gesturing with arms wide. 'Why here?'

'Don't know,' replies McTosh. 'Out of the way. Out of sight of the road, once they were around the curve in the canal.'

'They?'

McTosh shrugs. 'Him. She. They . . . Sorry.'

'You're probably right.' Ivan turns back to the canal. There is a red flag down on the curve, different from the police markers. He gestures. 'What's that? Is it a farmer's?'

'No. The boys. A sighter for their waterskiing.'

Ivan nods. 'So you interviewed them?'

McTosh looks unsure, perhaps wondering if he's exceeded his authority, whether Ivan is about to praise him or reprimand him. 'A preliminary statement, yes. Not much to it. They found the body. Called it in.'

'That's useful,' says Nell, smiling reassuringly. One of her many skills: putting people at ease.

'Ta,' says McTosh. 'I've sent Constable Simmonds to fetch the boy who found the body. You can ask him yourself.'

'Thanks,' says Ivan, swatting at a fly that's been circling persistently, irritated that the sergeant is taking liberties with his investigation. He tells himself to relax, that the man is only trying to help. 'So the main road is, what, around the curve there and about another two kilometres or so along the canal?'

'Two-point-three,' says McTosh.

'No gate, right? Accessible to anyone?'

'There's a gate, but no lock. Boys were almost certain it was open when they got here. Thought it a little unusual, but nothing extraordinary. There's no stock, just the trees and the vines, so no real need to keep it shut. We've dusted it for prints, got a few impressions. Nothing matching on the database. We'll check against known users: owners, workers, irrigation company.'

Nell is smiling again. 'Excellent. You're right on top of this.'

'We do our best,' says McTosh, not quite able to disguise his pleasure.

'This land,' says Ivan. 'Same owner both sides of the canal, or is it a boundary?'

'No, same owner.'

'You know who they are?'

'Everyone in the district knows that. The Titchfields. Very prominent.'

Ivan sees Nell raise her eyebrows. 'As in Otto Titchfield MP?' she asks. 'Country First?'

'That's our boy,' says McTosh, a touch of irreverence in his voice. 'Not so very happy with having bodies deposited in his canal. Let me know that. As if we have some say in where they get dumped.'

Nell laughs, and Ivan smiles. He's beginning to warm to McTosh after all. He lets the moment linger before returning to the serious stuff. 'What about the boys—the waterskiers? He doesn't have a problem with them being here?'

'One of them is his son. Johnny Titchfield. He was driving the truck. Finished boarding school, back in town for the holidays. Off to uni, so I believe.'

'Fair enough,' says Ivan. 'The dead man—identified as Athol Hasluck. Any doubts about that?'

'None whatsoever. Formally identified by his wife Jacinta. I recognised him myself.'

'So you saw the body?'

'Aye.'

'Cause of death?'

McTosh frowns, perhaps not happy at the memory. 'Stabbed. Once through the heart. Also marks on his hands and lower body. Not cuts, though. They looked like burns to me. The post-mortem will tell more. Scheduled for this afternoon.'

'What do you know about him?'

'A respectable guy. Forty-nine years old. Local accountant. Grew up here. Went away to uni, worked in Sydney and Wagga. Moved back about ten years ago. Most of his clients are small growers, local businesses, that sort of thing. Did my tax every year.'

Now it's Ivan who raises his eyebrows. 'You knew him?'

'Sure. Mostly through that: getting the tax done. But you'd see him around. Not into footy, but a keen cricketer.'

'Any connection between him and the Titchfields?'

A shrug, eyebrows speculative. 'No idea if it means anything, but the victim's wife, Jacinta, she's the younger sister of Lucretia Titchfield, Otto's wife. But you know, town this size, coincidences like that abound. Athol and Otto must be about the same age. So there's that.'

Ivan thinks about Yuwonderie. Seven hours south-west of Sydney, five hours north of Melbourne, five hundred kilometres inland. The middle of nowhere. Without the irrigation, it wouldn't even exist. Just the sort of town where everyone knows everyone else, where half the town would be related to the other half.

'What about a professional relationship between Otto Titchfield and Athol Hasluck?' Ivan asks.

'Doubt it,' says McTosh.

'Why not?'

'Oh, nothing against Athol. But he's a retail accountant. Mums and dads and small businesses. And not back in the district all that long. The Titchfields are old money. Here for generations. One of the Seven.'

'The Seven?' asks Ivan.

'Toffs, or so they see themselves.' There is a hint of resentment in McTosh's voice, some remnant of the working-class Celt. 'The original landholders, from back before the irrigation scheme was put in a hundred years ago. Made them rich. The bunyip aristocracy.'

'Millionaires, then?'

'Certainly. Many times over.' McTosh looks like he's about to say something more, then pauses as if reconsidering. 'Athol's family, the Haslucks, they're Seven as well, but he's a junior member.'

'So not a multimillionaire?'

'Not him.'

'Titchfield. Hasluck. Who are the other five?'

'Blaxland, McLean, Heartwood, Horsham, Allsop,' McTosh fires back.

'Know them by heart,' observes Ivan.

'My job—important I understand the lay of the land,' says McTosh.

Nell looks towards Ivan; he nods, giving her the go-ahead.

'When Athol Hasluck did your tax, was he straight down the line, or was he into pushing the envelope?'

'Straight down the line. Knowledgeable, but risk-averse.' McTosh pauses, then cracks a knowing grin. 'Then again, I'm a copper; unlikely he'd be bending rules for me.'

'True,' says Nell.

'You knew him,' says Ivan. 'You know the town. Any theories about who might have done this?'

McTosh shakes his head. 'None. Completely out of the blue.'

Ivan looks up, alerted by the flash of sunlight off a windscreen. A police car is coming along the track beside the canal. A second fly has joined the first, flying circuits around Ivan's head. Two years in the bush and he still finds them infuriating.

'That'll be the boy now,' says McTosh.

'Give us a moment,' says Ivan. 'We'll be right over.'

The sergeant walks towards the approaching vehicle, leaving Ivan and Nell. Ivan watches him go, wondering why a man with such a fair complexion isn't wearing a hat in this heat.

'Thoughts?' Ivan asks Nell.

'Why here?' she asks. 'If he was killed here, why this location? And if he was dumped, was it just a convenient spot, or was it designed to send a message to the Titchfields, or make some sort of statement about them? Or about Hasluck?'

'Anything else?'

'No real attempt to hide the body. If the boys hadn't found him, a farm worker would have.'

'Why in the water?' Ivan muses.

'Hoping to wash off DNA or fibres?'

'Possible.' Ivan looks out across the fields. Three crows fly above the net-covered vines, cawing loudly, emphasising the stillness of the day.

Nell is staring down at the canal, concentrating. She looks up, sharing her thoughts. 'Seems an unusual way to kill someone. A single stab wound to the heart. Confronting. Difficult. Deliberate. Up close and personal.' She sighs. 'We're in the country; no shortage of guns.'

Ivan agrees. 'If they *are* burns, and he got them at the same time he was stabbed, this seems an unlikely location. More likely he was killed elsewhere, dumped here.'

Ivan can see Nell's disquiet and understands why. More questions than answers.

'Good they got us in straight away,' she says. 'Didn't leave it with the local detectives.'

'Titchfield,' Ivan responds, eliciting a wry expression from his partner. 'He's a big deal, right? Lots of sway in Sydney. See him on the news all the time. Mover and shaker.'

'Yeah. Popular in the bush. Leader of Country First.'

'Enough to attract media attention?'

'Body found in his canal? I'd say so.'

'That's what I think.' Ivan pauses just a moment more. 'We need to pull out all the stops, Nell. See if we can get the divers down.'

'You sure?'

'Yes. We need to get on top of this. Politics and the media. All the makings of a shitstorm.'

'Done.'

He has a bad feeling about this. Bloody Plodder. The Homicide boss must know about the Titchfield connection; it is almost certainly why he assigned Ivan and Nell to the case. Either the police minister or the commissioner requested investigators who could be trusted to be discreet, or Plodder assigned them on his own initiative. But why hadn't he told Ivan about Titchfield?

Ivan walks over to the police car. A young man is standing talking to a female officer, presumably Constable Simmonds; she's taller than the youth and a good head taller than her boss. The lad looks late teens, shedding the last signs of adolescence, sandy hair, well built, slouching, struggling unsuccessfully to look relaxed. That's not what catches Ivan's attention, though. The boy's face is bruised, a nasty colour around his eye. It looks recent.

'Detective Sergeant Ivan Lucic,' Ivan says, shaking the lad's hand.

'Benedict Bright. Everyone calls me Eggs.'

Ivan can't help smiling. 'They used to call me Lucky. Lucky Lucic.'

'Were you?'

'Not very.' He cuts the small talk. 'Benedict, thanks for coming back out. Trust it's not too confronting.'

'No, it's okay,' he replies, but glances sideways at the canal, nevertheless.

'Your face? That from when you collided with the body?'

'Nah. Fell off my dirt bike. Went out this morning, trying to clear my mind.'

'No helmet?'

The boy shrugs. 'Private property.'

Ivan says nothing, but lets his scepticism bridge the gap. A split lip from coming off a bike is fair enough, not so much a black eye. He changes the subject back to the murder. 'Show me what happened.'

'Straightforward, really,' says Eggs.

They head back past the curve in the canal, walking along the track where Johnny drove the truck, Eggs recounting his story. Coming around the bend, concentrating so hard on staying upright, hitting the sack, discovering it was so much more. It's the same story McTosh recounted, but told with more immediacy.

By the time Eggs has finished, they're almost back with the others. The boy's eyes are on the canal, looking past the crime scene tape; he appears troubled.

Ivan chooses his words carefully. 'When I was a kid, my father used to beat me black and blue. With a belt when he was sober, with his fists when he wasn't.'

Eggs looks at him, staying silent, but there's understanding in his eyes. Then he looks away, back to the canal. 'At least we're still breathing. Not like that poor bastard.'

chapter three

1993

THE WEATHER WAS BENIGN AS SUMMER OFFICIALLY BEGAN. HOT OF COURSE, this being Australia, and nowhere more so than at Yuwonderie, baking out on the great inland plain, five hundred kilometres west of the coast and two hundred and fifty from the mountains. Yet the days remained in the mid-thirties rather than the low forties, and no one complained about the cloudless skies. The irrigation scheme basked in sunlight, basked in an abundance of water, basked in prosperity. No one imagined the long decades of abundance could ever end.

And by a canal, three friends, three young men who had known each other their entire lives, were reunited. Davis was the last to arrive and he grinned, which extended into a smile, which in turn birthed a deep, infectious laugh, even as he shook his head. 'You fucking idiots.' He was looking at the truck, the rope, the waterski. 'Who's the genius?'

'Not shit-for-brains here, that's for sure,' said Craven.

Otto took no offence. 'My truck, my ski, my canal.' And then he too laughed. 'Ideas are overrated.'

'Your old man?' Davis said to Otto. 'He's okay with this?'

'Sure. Compared to Craven's last stroke of genius.'

Davis turned to Craven, who smirked as if being paid a compliment.

Otto continued, 'A bit of circle work down on the lake. Few wowsers got upset. You know how it is.'

'Circle work?' Davis asked Craven.

'Jetski. Lake Yuwonderie.'

Davis shook his head. 'You idiots.' A jetski, noisy as hell, on a lake which was more like a pond, the size of three or four football fields, with a narrow band of grasslands separating it from surrounding houses. Davis had no trouble imagining the reaction, the upswell of resentment: mutterings about rich kids, entitlement and the Seven. 'Why not use the jetski here? Be perfect.'

'Can't,' said Otto. 'The wash could damage the canal banks. But the truck should work.'

'Should?' asked Davis. 'You haven't tried it out?'

'Three-man job. Driver, bloke in the back, plus the skier. That's you. The guinea pig.'

'You blokes are all heart.'

—

Later, at the Coachman's Arms, sitting in the beer garden with his mates in their board shorts and muddy t-shirts, sandals and sunnies, it was as if Davis had never been away. The place felt like home: the long trestle tables, the shade cloth, the sound of Hunters and Chisel and the Oils pumping out of the speakers and mixing with the chitter-chatter staccato and laughter of a dozen conversations. Along the walls were murals of Cobb and Co coaches, of teams of horses, of farriers and grooms. Of a large man with a large beard, holding the reins of his horse, waving to the patrons. The coachman himself. A fabrication, Davis realised for the first time: there was no coachman; there couldn't have been. For when the pub was built in the 1930s, the coaches and the horses would have long given way to trucks and buses, cars and trains. And yet, even for Davis, the budding historian, there was something engaging about the image, as if a lie told for enough decades might become the truth, a benign myth to be embraced.

Certainly he liked the pub, liked its familiarity. The farm workers and tradies, the small landholders and attractive young retail workers, all sharing the same space. Davis loved that about Yuwonderie: none of the social boundaries of Melbourne. The beer, the sun, the clean air, the lack of urgency. The old patterns of banter, fast quips, put-downs, good-natured backhanders, of conversations that touched on nothing important and nothing too personal, merely words playing on the surface of a late summer afternoon.

The three friends recounted the afternoon's exploits once again, and with each retelling the exaggerations grew a fraction more: the speeds attained, the precariousness of near-misses, the truck's erratic steering, the flock of water birds so narrowly avoided.

The conversation only turned serious when Davis announced his intention to study another year in Melbourne.

'Bullshit,' said Otto. 'Waste of time.' Verdict delivered, he drew deeply from his third schooner, as from the well of all knowledge.

At a nearby table, an old man was having a coughing fit as if he had somehow overheard Davis's proposal. Davis watched as the man hacked up a gob of phlegm and sent it, with nonchalant accuracy, on a parabolic arc into the base of one of the beer garden's palm trees. The man gave him a nod of recognition, drank from his beer and reached for another cigarette. Davis nodded back. Old Joe Marney, skin roasted brown by the sun, had worked on the family property for years before retiring to a bush block out by the river. Davis wouldn't mind going over, having a chat, asking about how the pub got its name. Joe would know; he could remember back to the early days of the irrigation scheme. But Davis's friends wanted him to explain himself.

'I enjoy it. I'm good at it,' he told them. 'The honours year is their idea, not mine.' Davis shrugged. 'It's just one more year. No big deal.'

'But history? What's the point?' asked Craven, himself having just completed an accounting-finance degree at Sydney University. 'Not in general—I don't mean that—but for *you*? You're not just part of the Seven; you'll be head of your family sooner than anyone.'

Otto agreed. 'Craven and me, we can fuck around all we like; our parents are still alive. Same with Eric Hasluck: he spends half his time in Europe, but his father and grandfather are both hale and hearty.' Which was true, except that Otto, two years older than Davis, was already deeply enmeshed in the family business, having returned to the district a year ago with an ag science degree. 'Your grandfather won't last forever.'

'Thanks for that observation,' said Davis dryly. He drank some more beer, but he was now on his third glass and the thirst built up waterskiing had loosened its grip. He didn't want to be half-cut when he saw his grandfather. 'Place runs itself, as far as I can see,' he said. 'Pops leaves the day-to-day stuff to Flax Fairfield; he's a better manager than I could ever be.'

Craven sipped at his beer, and when he spoke there was a rare seriousness in his voice. 'Have you told him? Your grandfather?'

'Tonight.'

——

Davis revelled in driving his sports car, his Alfa Romeo. It was eighteen years old, almost as old as he was, but it still went like the clappers. It looked old, a classic car, but he'd had the interior restored, the engine reconditioned and the mechanics returned to near new. He barely used it in Melbourne, but now he was back in town, he relished its low-slung style, the way it hugged the corners, how it responded immediately to a touch of the brakes or tap of the accelerator. No air-conditioning, of course, but he loved the roar of the wind, almost blocking out the music from the tape deck. He loved the gears, loved knocking it back into third, listening to the throaty pitch of the engine, the responsive acceleration. And he loved the way it got up Otto Titchfield's nose. His friend would look at it with unbridled contempt, call it a wog car and tell him to buy a ute, a Holden, even a Ford, anything instead of a posturing import. Out of Otto's earshot, Craven Allsop admired it, but also questioned aloud how practical it would prove to be hundreds of kilometres from the nearest dealer, from the nearest mechanic who understood the intricacies of such European exotica. Davis didn't care. Besides, such decisions were about to be pushed another year into his future.

Davis drove the Alfa from Yuwonderie, over the Spur, into the drylands and the Heartwood family seat. Three Wells Station was as grand and proud as ever it was, from the stone-walled gateway, the oak-lined driveway, past the white fences of the horse paddocks. He breathed it in, this sense of belonging. He arrived at the homestead itself, a statement of wealth reaching back a century and a half: a two-storey rural manor, with deep verandahs and iron lacework, elevated in status above similar homesteads by a central stone tower, topped by a turret. The gardens were like something displaced from England, an oasis in the brown monotony of the surrounding paddocks.

Davis knew the view from the tower by heart, all three hundred and sixty degrees of it, looking out from Three Wells' island of green: the low rise of the Spur to the east, the looming presence of the Castle to the north-east, the tree-lined river to the north, the brown and featureless plain extending to the horizon to the west and south. Out here, it was as if the irrigation scheme didn't exist. Unlike the rest of the Seven, the Heartwoods had not moved their family seat inside its boundary, hadn't built a new mansion, hadn't updated and upscaled into Italianate or Art Deco or, in the case of the Blaxlands' most recent iteration, concrete brutalism.

Davis was grateful his family had remained here on the dusty plains, removed from the town. He thought that perhaps this was where his sense of history came from: this house, built by his family and synonymous with it ever since. When people spoke of the Heartwoods, their thoughts would turn to the house, and when someone mentioned Three Wells Station, the family was immediately connected, so that the two terms were rendered interchangeable. 'Three Wells is chipping in for the relief fund,' people would say, when they really meant the Heartwoods, or, 'The garden at Heartwoods is looking splendid,' when what they really meant was Three Wells.

He parked his sports car in the garage, part of the old stable block. At the house, he let himself in. The door was not locked; it never was. He went up to his room, finished unpacking, then went to find his grandfather.

That evening the family ate out on the verandah: Davis, his elder sister Krystal and their father's father Clemence, their grandfather, instinctively taking the head of the table, his two grandchildren on either side.

'Very good, Krystal,' said Clemence to Davis's sister, who had cooked. 'What do you call this?'

'Stir-fry. The same as I make every week.'

'Well, I like it,' said Clemence. 'I like the spices.' And then to Davis: 'Not quite the fatted lamb for the prodigal, but a hell of a lot tastier, wouldn't you say?'

'Better than college, that's for sure.'

'Well, that's in the past now, my lad.'

Davis stole a look at his sister, who nodded her encouragement.

'About that, Pops . . . They've invited me to do an honours year.'

'I see,' said the old man. He chewed slowly before extracting a piece of well-worked gristle from his mouth and setting it aside. 'Honours.'

'Didn't you do honours, Pops?' asked Krystal, her tone innocent.

Davis blinked his gratitude; his sister would not ask a question like that without knowing the answer.

'You know I did,' said Clemence, sipping from his glass of white wine. 'We all did.'

'Really?' asked Davis. 'I never knew that.'

Davis did know his grandfather had gone to Oxford, as had his father before him and his father before that. Such was the tradition in some squattocracy families well into the twentieth century. Until Davis and Krystal's father had broken the chain, opting for ag college in Victoria instead.

'Not exactly honours,' said Clemence. 'A ranking. A first, a second, a third, a fourth.'

Davis thought of asking which his grandfather had received, but didn't. If it had been a first, then Krystal would already be asking the question.

'A reasonable second,' said his grandfather, unprompted. 'Which was about as good as you could get if you weren't wasting all your time studying.'

'Did it make much difference?' asked Davis. 'Afterwards, I mean.'

The old man snorted. 'Not a jot. Not out here. I guess people were impressed that you'd been to Oxford, God knows why, but they never thought to ask about actual grades or even what you'd learnt.' He picked up the bottle of wine, studied the label. 'What do you think of the house wine, Davis?'

'Excellent, considering the weather that year,' his grandson replied. The 'house wine' was from Heartwood Estate, with the grand house adorning the label, even though the vineyards and winery lay back within the golden circle of irrigation.

'Better than what they serve at college?' asked the old man playfully.

Davis laughed. 'You know it is.'

'Then you must really want to do this honours year.'

Davis smiled. 'I do.'

'And what do you think, Krystal? I can see your brother has already consulted you.'

'Sure. Let him do it. What harm can there be?'

'My thoughts . . .' said the old man, placing his chopsticks on his bowl.

Davis held his breath: the patriarch was about to deliver a verdict.

'History is a fine degree, and a fine profession,' said Clemence. He lifted his glass, examined the colour of the wine, but didn't drink. His grandchildren knew better than to interrupt. 'You are the eldest son. The *only* son. At some stage, you must return and run the estate.' The old man looked down at the centre of the table, as if he had laid the subject before them, like some material object.

'Flax does a brilliant job,' said Davis. 'Hard to improve upon.'

'He does indeed. But in saying that, you reveal your own ignorance of how an estate this size actually works. Think of the government and the public service. The public service keeps the country running. The government could disappear up its own fundament for years on end, and the bureaucracy would keep the wheels turning over. Happens all too often. But the big decisions, the big calls, the ones that shape the country? They come from ministers, the cabinet, the prime minister.'

'It's one year, Pops,' said Davis.

'But is it?'

Davis wasn't sure how to respond.

'Otto and Craven and Athol all took gap years,' said Krystal, coming to his defence. 'Davis went straight through.'

But the old man hadn't taken his eyes from Davis, not distracted by his granddaughter. 'That's the crux of it, Davis. Is it one year?'

'That's all it will take,' he replied truthfully.

'Is it though? You're bright. Capable. What happens when they offer you a place for a PhD?'

'I haven't considered that.'

'You should,' said Clemence, picking up his chopsticks and taking another mouthful, waiting until he has chewed and swallowed before turning once again to Krystal. 'It really is very good, you know.'

'No need to patronise me, Pops,' she said, with enough grit to make her point, but enough lightness that the barb remained good-natured.

Davis was only half-listening, his eyes having returned to his own meal. He'd been thinking so much of this next year, and whether he could persuade his grandfather to support him, that he hadn't thought beyond it.

The silence held for a good few minutes, interrupted by the mad squawking of cockatoos coming in low over the roof, catching the final rays of the setting sun, as they flapped and screeched and whirled about before alighting in a pine tree.

'Wonderful, aren't they?' observed Clemence. 'Sodding pests that they are.'

'Yes,' replied Davis. 'I miss them. I miss it.'

His grandfather placed the chopsticks back on the table. Sighed. 'Our family has held this country for almost one hundred and sixty years. The 1830s we came here, stole it from the blacks, held it against all comers until the government formalised our claim. One hundred and sixty years. Seven generations, counting you. A fair heft of time. I'd rather like it to continue. Life's work and all that.'

Davis exchanged a frown with Krystal. Such an exposition was out of character for the old man.

Clemence looked first at Krystal and then to Davis, as if assessing them, weighing them in his mind. 'We do become rather hidebound, though, don't you think? You young people?'

Krystal smiled. 'What are you cooking up, Pops? What deviousness?'

'Primogeniture,' stated the owner of Three Wells Station.

'What of it?' asked Davis.

'The inheritance of the entire estate by the eldest son. We've always practised it. So have all the Seven. Might be time for a change.'

Krystal lost her smile. She was sitting perfectly still, eyes widening, voice dropping. 'What are you suggesting?'

'That you inherit the estate when I die. You are the elder, after all. And I suspect your heart is in it. More than Davis's.'

'I have a fine arts degree,' protested Krystal. 'How is that better than history?'

'You would need to retrain, of course. Go back and do something useful. Business and financial management, something along those lines. Agriculture, if you feel it in your blood. I'm not about to drop off the twig anytime soon, but I would need to start mentoring you. I was planning to begin with Davis this year.' And only then did the old man turn to Davis, and Davis could see some element of pain in the old man's eyes. 'What's your opinion, Davis? I won't act unilaterally. We can only proceed if we all three agree.'

Davis felt astonished, then confused, and then hurt: his birthright was being pulled from him. He looked about him, at the verandah, the garden, the fields beyond. The house. In his mind he saw again the view from the turret, the wide brown plains, and imagined an even larger estate, reaching into the very heart of Yuwonderie. It had always been his destiny, and his alone. He had grown up with that assumption, had it instilled into him, impressed upon him, until it had become part of who he was, a defining trait, shaping his view of the world and of himself. And now, in between mouthfuls of his sister's stir-fry, his grandfather was suggesting he relinquish it.

'It's one year, Pops,' he repeated.

'If only I believed that,' replied his grandfather, with sadness in his voice. 'Of course, you would receive an allowance, a very generous one, as in generations past—as was planned for Krystal. But the ownership and the decisions would reside with your sister.' He took up the bottle once again, scrutinised the label with its picture of the house, then turned back to Davis, and spoke with weight in his voice. 'The estate would pass to her children. Not yours.'

Davis looked to Krystal for guidance, and he saw concern in her face and compassion in her eyes, not thinking of her own prospects, not yet: still thinking of him. It had been the two of them all these years, for almost as long as he could remember, since their parents died young. Their grandfather had been harsh and distant in those early days, leaving it to his wife to care for them. When she had grown frail and ill, he'd employed a governess, a fierce and judgemental old battleaxe who had reigned over them with absolute authority, until the day she went too far and beat Davis. Clemence had sacked her on the spot. After that it had been boarding schools and summer camps and university colleges.

Only in recent years had the old man mellowed, begun to take them into his confidence.

Davis thought of his sister. The fine arts degree, followed by adventuring: skiing, sailing, flying planes, preparing for her own predestined future. And yet there was also the truth his grandfather had alluded to: her heart was here; she was attached to the place.

Davis stood, walked to the verandah railing. The light had turned golden, bathing the garden, the cockatoos now chatting happily among themselves as they chewed at the pine, a steady stream of twigs and needles and cones showering the ground. The wonderful thing about animals, thought Davis: they always knew where they belonged.

And in that moment, an epiphany. A freedom. A burden lifting; a new life beckoning. He turned, saw Krystal's eyes on him, her forehead creased with concern, his grandfather considering him with wisdom and affection.

'I think it's an excellent idea,' Davis heard himself saying. 'After all, we're heading towards a new century. A new millennium. But only if Krystal wants it. I don't wish to burden her.'

Clemence turned to his granddaughter, not speaking. Davis saw her squint as she regarded their grandfather, a sign that she was thinking deeply. 'How could you know?' she whispered.

Their grandfather smiled, a tension easing from his shoulders. 'Oh, I've walked this earth a fair old while.' He looked from Krystal to Davis and back again. 'But let's not be hasty. Davis doesn't need to return to Melbourne until the new year. We'll give it a month, make sure that we're certain before we announce it. It will cause quite a ruckus among our peers.'

'Fair call,' said Davis, 'but between us let's work on the assumption that Krystal will inherit.'

'Well,' she said, 'if I am to be mistress of Three Wells, perhaps we can tap the cellar for something more appropriate than the house wine. So we can toast you, you canny old coot.'

And Davis laughed, and any remaining tension was washed away, and the matter seemed settled. Worlds had shifted, new orbits dictated, the shape of the universe contorted into a new reality. And yet it seemed such a slight alteration. They were still there, the three of them, united. So not such a very big change after all. Simultaneously momentous and minor.

Some time later, when the sun was down and the lights were on, the smoke from mosquito coils wafting and the mood genial, a satisfied languor upon them, Clemence Heartwood asked his erstwhile heir a final question. 'This honours thesis—what's your subject?'

'The founding of Yuwonderie. How the Seven built the scheme.'

'Oh my,' said his grandfather. 'That should stir the pot.'

'How do you mean?' asked Krystal.

'The Seven, my dear. We do take ourselves ever so seriously. Who knows what skeletons our budding historian might find?' The old man raised a speculative eyebrow. 'And in whose cupboards he might find them?'

chapter four

YUWONDERIE IS DIFFERENT. IVAN REALISED THAT THE MOMENT HE AND NELL
drove from the sun-bleached flatness of the Riverina and entered
the boundaries of the irrigation district on their way to the crime
scene. They'd passed from encroaching drought into verdant
abundance, the perimeter a clear line: dry and brown and El
Niño-blasted to the north; green and abundant to the south. Now
he finds the town centre is different too: planned and impeccable,
twice winner of the Tidy Towns of Australia award. There are
palm trees along the main street, Commonwealth Way, rather than
the straggly and haphazard gum trees typical of a country town.
Yuwonderie didn't just happen, Ivan concludes: it was planned
and built, its vision laid out before any sod was turned.

Ivan had initially resented the bush, as if it were the landscape's
fault he'd been banished from Sydney. Now, two years into his tenure
as head of the Regional Homicide Squad, he's found his attitude
evolving, gradually becoming more positive, a growing admiration
supplanting his initial disdain. And while he's learnt to appreciate
the large and prosperous centres like Tamworth and Mudgee and

Dubbo and Bathurst and Wagga, it's the smaller towns that have captured his imagination, the ones fading away, overcome by the new economies of the bush, their dwindling populations absorbed by the bigger towns. But big or small, growing or contracting, most of the country towns share a common feature: they'd all started from nothing. They'd been seeded by a hotel or a river ford, by a crossroads or a railway crossing, by the discovery of a gold nugget or an elevated spot above the flood plain, or even just being a day's ride from the next settlement. Many faded back into the landscape almost as soon as they were founded, others struggled, a rare few flourished. None of them were planned, not at first, not back in the nineteenth century. And so there is a commonality between them: the streetscapes are similar, the architecture the same: pubs with wide verandahs and corrugated-iron roofs; stone Anglican churches facing off against the redbrick of their Catholic rivals; CWA clubs of white weatherboard and community halls of fibro sheeting; main street service stations falling into disrepair, replaced by highway monoliths; a caravan park by the river; a footy oval; a takeaway serving fish and chips hundreds of kilometres from the sea. Evolving and growing, declining and disappearing.

Yuwonderie has none of that. There's a cleanliness to it, lawns mown, no litter. Even the air smells different: a hint of moisture, a lack of dust, the sense it's a degree or two cooler than the surrounding plains. There are Art Deco buildings that could be from Southern California and roundabouts that wouldn't be out of place in Canberra. Nell steers the four-wheel drive round a central statue-cum-fountain, frothing water, locating a place to park along Commonwealth Way. The shopping strip is festooned with Christmas decorations.

They find the Lone Dog Café in time for a late lunch of toasted focaccia, coffee and iced water, Ivan ravenous after the long drive and the visit to the canal. He and Nell have the place to themselves, the kitchen about to close, the owner checking with his watch before deciding to serve them as if the decision is not his own but dictated by the clock. He's an old bloke with grey mutton-chop whiskers, who talks to himself incessantly as he busies himself moving chairs in from outside while his wife, a decade younger and chirpy with it, takes over the preparation of their lunch. The cafe has managed to mix the old and the new. The wood-framed windows look original and the floorboards are broad and worn, although buffed and oiled back to life. The art on the walls is colourful, random splotches that conspire to suggest familiar shapes: the figure of a woman, the profile of a face, the intimation of eyes, all framed in weathered grey wood. There's lots of space between the tables, something else Ivan has come to value in country towns.

They eat in silence, lost in thought, while mutton-chops gives himself instructions on the storage of the chairs—*this lot, over there* and *let's squeeze a few more in here.* Ivan feels a sense of anticipation: these are the investigations he lives for, the ones that aren't obvious. All too often, there is no mystery, the murders brutal, the killers obvious. The perpetrator is the husband or the boyfriend, sometimes the wife or the girlfriend, or a business partner out for revenge or motivated by greed, but acting in the moment, unable to cover their tracks. Part of Ivan wishes that will be the case here: a quick and easy resolution, justice served. But another part of him hopes for something more challenging, like the case up at Finnigans Gap, or down in the Barmah-Millewa Forest. He thinks of McTosh. The man knows the town, knows its people. And yet he can't nominate a suspect; Ivan wonders about that.

After lunch, Nell drives them to the Progress Hotel a block down on the right, glowing in the mid-afternoon sun, looking simultaneously modern and heritage-listed. They leave the vehicle in the shade of a tree-lined car park and push through ornate doors of brass and glass. The reception counter, adorned with Christmas bunting, has three clocks on the wall behind it and black-and-white photographs dating to the hotel's opening almost a century ago. The clock on the left shows the time in Perth, three hours behind, the one in the middle is labelled *Yuwonderie/Sydney/Melbourne,* and the one on the right, two hours ahead, has the time in Auckland. Nothing as pretentious, or ironic, as Paris, London and New York, but still placing Yuwonderie at the centre of something.

After being checked in by a smiling and efficient clerk dressed in knickerbockers, suspenders and a flat cap, Ivan finds his room tastefully updated: a replica ceiling fan complemented by air-conditioning, the bathroom retiled and fitted with a huge shower rose, water no problem here. He likes this town with its pride and its neatness and its ambition. Now, however, it has a stain and it's their job to remove it: to catch the killer, and return Yuwonderie to unblemished normality.

— —

Not all autopsies are the same. Sometimes, the bodies are close to pristine. At such times, the opportunity to delve inside the complexities of a human machine is a privilege, to glean the answers from a person who can no longer speak their own truths. At other times, the cadavers are so badly decomposed that near freezing conditions, nose plugs and the most powerful extraction fans cannot alleviate the stench. There is no mystique then, and often no answers.

Ivan doesn't like any of them. It's not the state of the bodies that troubles him: it's the finality. Whatever he and Nell and the pathologist might discover, they can't bring the person back. And whatever revelations a corpse may silently impart, it cannot compare to a living breathing human being. There are no souls in a body, and precious little personality. Just remnants of a life ended too soon. He and Nell are always too late: a day, a week, half a lifetime, but always too late. That's what troubles him: the burden of the homicide detective.

Yuwonderie Hospital is an odd affair, another Art Deco building, ninety years old, its concrete render bathed yellow, a little mottled in places. It would make a good museum or a hotel, thinks Ivan, as he and Nell enter the crowded foyer, where the stylish motifs and stonework inlays seem out of keeping with the bustle and practicalities of modern health care. A kindly-looking old man at the information desk directs them towards the morgue, at the end of a long corridor where the retrofitted air-conditioning is groaning as if to plead its case.

The surgeon, down from Griffith, comes out to meet them, removing her gloves, then her mask, revealing a tanned face, eyes bright, a fit-looking fifty-something. 'Jane Seabridge,' she says, shaking hands. She's smiling with her mouth, but the lines on her forehead suggest it's merely politeness. 'I'm sorry. I don't think I should proceed. Not sure I'm qualified.'

Ivan frowns. 'You've done them before?' he asks.

'Many times. And I'll do this one, if you insist. But you might be better waiting for a full-time pathologist.'

'Why?' asks Nell.

'Come through. I'll show you.' She replaces her mask and leads the way into the morgue, pausing to put on new gloves.

Ivan feels the temperature drop and draws a final breath before putting on his own mask. He takes in the stainless steel and ceramics and instruments, smells the antiseptic and embalming fluids and the cloying undercurrent of death, all too familiar. The body is laid out under a sheet, silent and unmoving yet the centre of attention.

Seabridge lifts the sheet from the face. Athol Hasluck. Looking peaceful, eyes closed. 'At first glance, it seems straightforward.' She pulls the sheet back further, exposing the torso down to the waist. The stab wound low in the chest is barely evident, an incision, with its red edges. Who would think such a small mark could prove so fatal?

Seabridge looks at Ivan, then Nell, eyebrows raised. 'A single thrust from a blade, upwards into the heart.'

'Was death instantaneous?' asks Ivan.

Seabridge appears pained. 'It's possible he was already dead.' She lifts Athol Hasluck's hands from beneath the sheet: first one, then the other. There are burn marks on the palms, red and black and charred. 'Not chemical. Not heat. Electricity. High voltage.' She moves down the table, pulling back the covering, revealing the soles of the feet, similarly disfigured. 'The current went straight through him. Like being struck by lightning.'

'But not lightning?' asks Nell.

'I don't think so. Not directly. That would enter the head or torso, exit through the feet. I believe he was holding on to something—say a metal rail or a cable, something like that. The charge entered the hands, exited the feet. Could be lightning, or the source could be something else entirely: a high-voltage power line, an electricity substation.'

'Not a domestic supply?' asks Ivan. 'Two-forty volts?'

Dr Seabridge is apologetic. 'I don't know. I'm a surgeon, not a full-time forensic pathologist.'

Ivan persists with his questioning regardless. 'So electrocuted and stabbed. Can you work out the sequence, which came first?'

'No. But the wounds suggest they happened in quick succession. Almost simultaneously. We might discover more when we open him up.' The surgeon sighs. 'There is another possibility. I can't discount drugs or poisons. I've taken samples for the lab.'

'What are you suggesting?' Nell asks. 'First drugged, then killed?'

'I have no evidence of that. Just informing you that I'm checking.'

Nell sighs. 'It could be all three. Administered at the same time.'

They stand for a moment without speaking, respectful. Ivan can't help but imagine Hasluck's last moments, the violence of his death, the electrical charge thrusting the life out of him, the knife piercing his heart, perhaps toxic substances pumping through his system.

'Someone definitely wanted him dead,' says Nell, as if following the same line of thought.

'We don't even know that,' says Ivan. 'Say he's accidentally electrocuted. Someone panics, wants to get rid of him, the evidence. Stabs him to make sure he's dead before dumping the body.'

Nell nods, conceding his point.

Ivan thinks of Otto Titchfield, of the media. 'Dr Seabridge is right: we need the expertise of a full-time pathologist. The manner of Hasluck's death may shape the whole inquiry.'

'You should also see this.' The doctor raises the remaining segment of sheet, exposing the thighs and then the genitals. There are small red welts, angry burns, on the thighs and on the scrotum. Another on the shrunken penis.

Nell exchanges a look with Ivan.

'Cigarette burns?' he asks.

'No, not that,' says the surgeon. 'I'm no expert, but it looks like hot metal. Like a brand.'

Ivan leans in closer, but can't be sure. 'Maybe a piece of wire.'

'Was he tortured?' asks Nell, and Ivan can hear her breath catching.

'Possibly,' says Seabridge.

'How long prior to death?'

The doctor grimaces, as if unsure of herself. 'Minutes. Hours. Same day.'

'But not contributing to death?'

'No.'

'And not electricity?'

'I don't think so.'

Ivan takes a last look. And then: 'Thanks. You can cover him. I've seen enough.'

'One more thing,' says Nell. 'Time of death?'

The surgeon shrugs. 'Best guess? Night before last. Three or four hours either side of midnight. Late Saturday, early Sunday.'

'An eight-hour window, then?'

'Yes. Being in the water confuses it, especially if we don't know how long after death he was placed there. Let me see if I can narrow it down.'

chapter five

YUWONDERIE POLICE STATION IS ANOTHER PRIME EXAMPLE OF ART DECO: DOUBLE storey, honey brick, with curved corners and a vertical line of circular windows, lending it a nautical feel, the modern standard-issue blue-and-white police sign looking incongruous. By the building's door there's a plaque declaring its provenance, opened by the mayor in 1928. Inside a second plaque declares the station is heritage-listed. And another acknowledges a 2008 refit funded by the Yuwonderie Progress Association, supported by the federal and state governments. McTosh has allocated them space upstairs, an airy room with a high ceiling, elaborate cornices and sash windows of varnished wood looking out over Titchfield Street. The ceiling fan, slowly revolving, has wooden slats. Dust motes dance in and out of rays of sunlight created by venetians. There are two desks on opposing walls, backs to each other, with a table at the centre of the room with four chairs. The light switches are bakelite and the light fittings are leadlight, like Tiffany lamps. Evidence of the twenty-first century is limited: a flat-screen television mounted on one wall; ethernet connections in the walls; a smoke detector blinking.

He and Nell carry their gear up from the four-wheel drive, helped by Constable Simmonds. Two years in, and it's a well-practised drill. Laptops, cables, monitors, a charging station, a wireless amplifier.

He sees Nell check her watch. 'What do you think?' she says. 'Call it a day?'

'Let's see the widow. Get it out of the way.'

——

The exterior of Athol Hasluck's home is modest, neat and well maintained: a nice house on a nice street, more 1970s than 1920s. To Ivan it looks ordinary, but he knows that there is nothing ordinary about being visited by homicide detectives. Another part of the job he dislikes. It's as if he can feel the anguish and heartbreak leaking out of the home into the late afternoon air, the sense of lives gone awry, even before he rings the bell.

Hasluck's widow looks haggard, eyes bloodshot and hollow as she opens the door. She's in her mid-to-late forties, but right now she's looking a decade older. The house is quiet, just the sound of a television.

'Yes?' the woman says.

'Jacinta Hasluck?' asks Nell, as if the grief-ravaged face could possibly belong to anyone else.

'I am.'

'We're so sorry to disturb you at this time, Mrs Hasluck. I'm Detective Constable Nell Buchanan. This is Detective Sergeant Ivan Lucic.'

A flash of Athol Hasluck, naked on the gurney, comes to Ivan. He represses the memory; it's not what he needs as they engage the widow.

'I already spoke—' Jacinta Hasluck stops mid-sentence. 'Detectives? Homicide detectives?'

'Correct,' says Ivan.

A look of relief, or maybe gratitude. 'So they listened after all. I was worried they might not want outsiders interfering.' She brushes her hands down the front of her apron, as if tidying herself, touches her hair. 'Come in. Please come in.'

Ivan stands back, lets Nell enter first. He's become aware during his time in the bush that he can be insensitive at times, overly formal. Nell has a warmth to her, a natural empathy. And a knack for asking the right question, pitched in exactly the right way.

Inside, off a small entry hall, the lounge room is a mess. Washing is piled high, awaiting sorting. A Christmas tree stands in the corner, swathed in tinsel but with its fairy lights extinguished. There's a dining table, yet to be cleared from lunch, the detritus of takeaway containers. Two boys, on the cusp of adolescence, curly-headed and evenly matched enough to be twins, are sitting on the couch, staring at the wide-screen television, still except for their fingers moving rapid-fire over the gaming controls. The boys must know the detectives are there, but they don't look up.

'We can talk on the deck,' says Jacinta. 'No point disturbing them.'

'How are they?' asks Nell.

'Not good. None of us.'

Outside, the wooden deck is spacious and elevated. The heat of the day has moderated and a low breeze is gusting relief. In other circumstances, it would be a pleasant place to converse.

47

There is a table, chairs, but before they reach them Jacinta stops. 'I see him everywhere,' she says. 'Evidence of him.'

Nell reaches out, places her hand on the woman's shoulder. 'It takes time. Give it time.'

It's all the invitation Jacinta needs. She turns and falls into Nell, sobbing. The constable wraps her arms around the crying woman, murmuring, 'There, there,' as if to a child. Ivan looks on, wonders again at Nell, how people instinctively trust her.

The tableau lasts a moment before the grieving woman rallies, pulls herself free. 'I'm sorry,' she says. 'Please sit down. We should talk while the twins are occupied. Before their sister comes out of her room.'

Nell and Ivan exchange a look.

'Thank you,' says Ivan, taking a seat at the table, indicating a spot for Jacinta opposite him. Nell sits at the side of the table, between the other two.

'I'm sorry,' Jacinta says again. 'Would you care for tea? Something to eat?'

'We're fine,' says Nell.

'I'm so glad you're here,' says Jacinta. 'Professionals.'

This time, Ivan picks up on the comment. 'You were worried they wouldn't call us in?'

She seems as if she is about to say something, then recalibrates. 'We're a long way from anywhere. Used to managing our own affairs.'

Ivan feels as if he's missing some nuance.

Nell takes up the slack. 'We'll be doing everything we can to catch the killers,' she says, her voice reassuring. 'We're treating it as homicide, but we need to hear from you.'

Jacinta wrings her hands, considering them as if deciding what to say, then she looks Nell in the eye. The overt emotions have been replaced by the furrowed brow of determination. 'This last month or so, Attie was upset. Worried. Stressed. It was really obvious. He even lost his temper at the boys once. He never did that. Made me realise how often I do.'

'And what was he worried about?' asks Nell.

'I don't know. I asked him, but he wouldn't say.'

'Work-related?'

'Yes. Almost certainly. If it was anything else, something to do with the kids or with our friends or something socially, then I would have heard. That's how it is in small towns.'

'I'm from a small town myself,' says Nell. 'Boonlea, down on the Murray.'

'Oh good. You understand then.'

'Tell us about your husband's work,' Nell suggests.

Jacinta holds her palms open, a gesture of transparency. 'He's an accountant. Was an accountant. Studied at Wagga Wagga, worked at a practice there. We got married, travelled a lot. Moved back to Yuwonderie about ten years ago, a few years after we had the boys. Thought it was time we settled down, built something. He saw an opportunity to start his own business.' She smiles, a sadness in her eyes, perhaps evoked by some fond memory.

'And how has business been?' asks Nell.

'Good, as far as I know. Nothing flash. Local irrigators, small businesses, helping people with their BAS and their company tax, income tax. Tough at first, but Athol built it up over the years, got a reputation for reliability. We live pretty modestly, but the business was doing well. Just recently he got in an assistant.

He said he was getting to critical mass, that he might even hire a second accountant.'

'So it's been just him until recently?'

'He's always had a receptionist who helps with some of the paperwork. Billing and chasing up payments, that sort of thing. His assistant, Alice Figtree, started the beginning of November. No qualifications, but she's very competent, very thorough.'

'And she and your husband, they had a good working relationship?' Nell's tone is light, but Ivan can hear the subtle insinuation.

So can Jacinta. 'He wasn't having an affair with her, if that's what you're wondering. She's a lesbian.'

Ivan hears no judgement in her voice.

'Right,' Nell says. 'Is there the possibility of any other liaisons? I'm sorry, but I do need to ask.'

Ivan understands where his partner is coming from: the marks on Athol Hasluck's genitals. Maybe torture, maybe not.

The widow appears to take no umbrage. Instead, she's shaking her head. 'I don't believe so. I believe my husband loved me. And I know he loved our kids. He was devoted to them.' She looks at Ivan as if to convince him as well, as if this would be more meaningful to a man. 'And he was open about the fact he was stressed, that he was bothered. He just wouldn't tell me why.'

Now Ivan does interject. 'Did he ever talk about his work? Make observations that such-and-such was doing well, or an irrigator was having a tough year—the sort of innocuous comments that any professional might make to their spouse?'

But Jacinta is shaking her head even before Ivan finishes the question. 'No. He was super discreet. He always said he wanted to keep work and family life separate, and he was true to his word. He didn't ever work from home.'

'Unusual,' observes Ivan.

'Easy enough in Yuwonderie. His office is just a five-minute walk, no time in the car. Sometimes he'd go back in after dinner. More so recently.'

Again, it's Ivan who asks the next question. 'Mrs Hasluck, did your husband hold life insurance?'

She looks at him hard, knowing why he's asking. 'Yes. He was a financial planner. Recommended it to all his clients.'

'Can I ask how much?'

'Not enough. How could it be?'

Ivan nods. 'If you can give us the details, we'd be grateful.' He takes a breath, knowing it's better that the tough questions come from him. 'This is difficult to ask, and I'm not suggesting anything by it, but it should be asked just the same. Was there any indication your husband might have been involved in anything untoward, anything illegal?'

Jacinta stares at him. 'I'm told that's what people are saying. He's dead and the rumour mill is at him already.'

'We're not interested in the rumour mill,' Nell says, leaning forward, taking back control. 'We're interested in facts. In finding who did this to him. There must be a reason he was killed.'

Jacinta gestures at the house. 'Check our bank accounts. If there are any criminal proceeds washing around, I'd like to see them. You can have full access. We're comfortable, but not much more. If this is about money, then it's about someone else's.'

'Do you know of anyone who might have wished to harm your husband?' asks Nell.

'No. He was well liked. Ask Sergeant McTosh. He knows the town, its people.'

'And when did you last see your husband alive?'

'The night before last. Saturday. He'd enlisted the kids, put the tree up. We had dinner here. He read a book to the boys. A nightly ritual. Then he said he was going back into work, that he had a lot on.'

Nell looks at Ivan; he gives her the slightest nod of affirmation.

'You know where your husband's body was found. We're trying to establish why there. Did he have any particular connection to Otto Titchfield or your sister?'

'No. We didn't really socialise with Lucy and Otto.'

'You're not close to your sister?'

Jacinta looks a little sad. 'No. They're Seven, we're not.'

Ivan frowns. 'I thought Athol was from one of those families.'

'He is. But a younger son. His brother Eric helped when we first got back, with an interest-free loan, but that's it.' She sighs. 'It's a different world.'

'Can you think of any reason why his body might have been left in the Titchfields' canal?' asks Ivan.

'No. None.'

'Do we have your permission to enter your husband's workplace and conduct a search?'

'Of course. Please do. I'll fetch you some keys and the code for the alarm.'

Nell stands, followed by Ivan and Jacinta, who goes to get the keys.

When she returns, Nell asks, 'And Alice Figtree? Do you know how we can contact her?'

'Let me find my phone.'

After Nell and Ivan have everything they need, including some recent photographs of Athol, Jacinta shows them to the door. The boys are still on the couch, still engrossed in their game. Their mother draws a deep breath.

'Would you like me to talk to them?' asks Ivan gently. 'In case they have questions?'

The look of gratitude on Jacinta Hasluck's face tells him he's said the right thing.

— —

Afterwards, when they're back in the car, Nell touches his shoulder. 'That was kind of you. Considerate.'

'She's floundering.'

'Yes,' she agrees. She starts the engine. 'You think his death is related to his work?'

'Could well be. I'm thinking we should get Kevin down to help out.'

'Kev? I thought you wanted him minding the shop in Dubbo.'

Ivan shakes his head. 'I'm worried. This whole thing could blow up if the media get hold of it. The body on Otto Titchfield's property. We need to make progress. And Kev's done that course in forensic accountancy, remember? He can get into Athol's files, maybe see what we can't. Jacinta just gave us permission.'

He can feel her eyes on him. 'Should we enlist the help of Athol's assistant?' asks Nell. 'She'll have all sorts of background knowledge. Help sort the wheat from the chaff.'

'Not a bad idea. If Kevin is there supervising,' says Ivan. 'We'll need to talk to her tomorrow anyway.' But he can see his answer has elicited a look of concern from Nell, as if she is reconsidering her own suggestion. 'What?'

'These records,' she says. 'If Athol Hasluck was killed because of something he knew, we need to be careful. We don't want to put her in danger.'

chapter six

September 1913

My dearest Mother,

It is a fortnight now, and I am finding myself more settled here at Castle View. These past few days we have been working hard, scrubbing and mending and washing, in preparation for the coming summer. A spring-clean, Mrs Titchfield calls it. There is a strange satisfaction to be had from such physical work. It is only in the evening, when the day's tasks are done, that I get to read, but some evenings I am so tired that I only manage a page or two.

And now the daughter has arrived back from boarding school in Albury and she is a delight. I had feared a snob, some pretentious debutante, some embodiment of her mother's aspirations and her brother's ambitions. Instead she is a natural girl, freewheeling and unafraid. The first thing she did was to strip off her school dress and don breeches and an old shirt, like a tomboy, tying up her hair in a bun. Her smile is infectious. She's genuinely delighted that

I am here; I know because she told me so. She had feared isolation, with only her brother and his boorish friends for company. She has brought a trunk of books with her to while away the long days. She is very happy to share with me, is delighted that I am literate, that the burden of reading for her mother doesn't fall upon herself alone.

Her name is Elaine. You would not describe her as a great beauty, but neither is she entirely plain. Her nose is a little long, her mouth a little small in repose, her teeth a little crooked when it is not. Yet her hair is thick and blonde and glorious, and her blue eyes radiate humour and kindness and mischief. And it is her eyes that draw you in, so that you overlook and quickly forget any other deficiency. For her eyes express her hunger for life and all it has to offer.

She is still at school, yet a full year older than me at seventeen. She seems younger at times, having not yet been forced to confront the cruelties of the world. She was surprised to learn I had left school at twelve, that attending the big school was denied me. So I told her of you and Pa, how you are a schoolteacher and continued my education at home, of your insistence on learning, on the importance of reading and writing, how spelling and correct grammar is a better indication of refinement than all the airs and graces and fashion and money combined.

She chides me, saying my written expression is old-fashioned and overly formal, but I'm sure she means nothing by it. She attends a private school in Albury; of course her turn of phrase is more contemporary. The important thing is that Elaine is a reader; we have bonded over it. She adores the Brontës and Mrs Gaskell and Jane Austen and Wilkie Collins, although she isn't much taken by poetry and despairs of Shakespeare, whom she is forced to study in class. She says the best sort of books are those where you lose yourself in the story, and I think I agree. She held my hands and whispered that perhaps someday we too should be writers. And then she laughed, and the idea blew away, like dandelion fluff. I do think she finds it difficult to take anything seriously for too long. Perhaps that is the secret to her charm.

But while Elaine is like an open window, her brother can be like a closed door. Horace is gruff, and there is something of the bully in him. Not violent, yet his words are sharp. His mother, who had attempted in those first few hours to lord it over me until her better nature shone through, is subjugated by him. Not out of fear or intimidation, but by a mother's love. I'm not sure he even sees it, merely feels that is his rightful place, head of the family, now that the father is dead. He tells me that it was his idea to get me in, to help his mother, to assist the womenfolk, although I suspect it was just as much to do with elevating his own status. At times he can be almost convivial, but mostly he continues to play the master to my servant, even while his mother only manages to maintain it intermittently, and Elaine, God bless her, has never even attempted it. There are times when he catches himself treating me as a fellow human being and, as if to remind himself more than me, he mentions my antecedents. At other times I catch him running his eyes over me. I know what that look means, and I make sure not to be alone with him. Perhaps I misjudge him, perhaps I don't, but I will not risk the consequences. He might hold himself aloof, but he has more in common with some of my cousins than he would ever care to admit.

He is to be married, a local girl, daughter of a neighbouring family, also graziers, the Allsops. Elaine doesn't think much of her and makes cruel asides to me. Her name is Faith, and I haven't met her, so I can make no judgement. But I do feel a tad sorry for her. I can't imagine being married to Horace will be a life of laughter and joy; he is too self-important for that. Although he is determined to be successful, I can see that about him, and there is something in his single-mindedness that inclines me to believe he will indeed forge a fortune.

They are all excited by the grand plan, the irrigation scheme first touted by the now-dead father, the proposal they assert they dare not mention while talking of little else. Their imaginings are agitated by the scheme taking shape north of the river, with new towns planned and now being built; Griffith and Leeton, with farms fed by irrigation water from the Murrumbidgee. The Titchfields propose forming an alliance with neighbouring farmers to create a parallel scheme south of the river. Horace was happy to explain it to Elaine and myself, to demonstrate his grasp of such matters. He said there are similar plans for the Murray, but they can't proceed until the states come to an agreement over who owns the water. There is no such problem here, he claimed, the Murrumbidgee being the sole preserve of the New South Wales government. He said the design is simple: a weir will be built across the river to raise the height of the water, which will then be diverted south-west along a purpose-built canal following the contours of the land. The canal will then split into a series of smaller and smaller canals, supplying all the farms of the district. Like the system being constructed north of the river, the scheme will be gravity-fed, the land so flat that no pumping will be required.

'Will it make such a difference, all this water?' I asked, playing the innocent, as he had piqued my interest. 'Is the rain not enough?'

He laughed at that, at my ignorance. 'Not nearly enough. We have huge parcels of land, thousands of acres, but while it is fit for grazing sheep and cattle, cropping is risky. That rain of which you speak is not dependable; we are too far from the mountains. But if we have reliable access to water, then we can grow wheat, barley, maize even. Perhaps cotton, perhaps rice. Even fruit trees and grapes. The value and profitability of the land will increase a hundredfold. It will be a latter-day garden of Eden.'

When I expressed my admiration for the elegance of the scheme, he seemed very pleased with my choice of words.

'We will clear the land, get rid of the remaining gums. No room for animals if we are cropping. But that is not the real magic. Not by a long shot.'

'And where is the magic then, if not in the design?' I asked, feeling sorry for the animals and the trees.

'In the financial structure: it is a marvel—but you might not follow it, being a creature of poetry.'

'My arithmetic is excellent,' I retorted, and immediately felt ashamed that I had risen so easily to his goading, but it was enough for him to continue. Either that or he liked the sound of his own voice, and explaining the scheme aloud helped make it real in his own mind.

'The scheme north of the river is being developed by the government. They are calling it the Murrumbidgee Irrigation Area. They've bought up all the land, acquiring it by an act of parliament, and are selling it off to landholders by lottery. All sorts of carpetbaggers and adventurers are flowing in. Migrants and whatnot. Small landholders and socialists, people with not the first idea of modern agriculture. Many will fail, mark my words. But we have a different model.

We will develop our own scheme, keep the land, or most of it, and reap the benefits.'

'Why would the government allow that? Did you not say they own the water in the river?'

He looked at me then, his eyes narrowed, as if he had seen something unexpected in me. 'That is very observant of you,' he said at last. 'But governments are run by men. And men can be influenced. By logic and persuasion and clear thought.'

I thought of asking more, but I could see in his countenance that his pride in the plan had been sated and he wanted to talk no more.

Elaine is not convinced. She says the scheme may eventuate, it may not, but it is as likely we will be old women by the time any spade is sunk into the earth.

Your loving daughter,
Bessie

chapter seven

IVAN JOGS THROUGH THE MORNING, FEELING GOOD, FEELING ALIVE, THE AIR
still cool, the day still young. It's Tuesday and, two days after Athol
Hasluck's body was discovered, there's still been no mention of
his murder in the metropolitan media; Ivan and Nell still have
clear air. The sun is not long up, but already there's a bustle to
the place, cars and trucks navigating the main street, a peloton of
cyclists humming down Commonwealth Way. It's a wide street, its
planners declaring their ambition for the town in it, their confidence in Yuwonderie's future. It stretches along a low ridge between
small hills, the town elevated ever so slightly above the surrounding
farmland. It's a street grown into itself, its width brought back to a
human scale by the nature strip dividing it in two, with grass and
flowerbeds and curved wooden seating amid low bushes, spaced
between squat palm trees placed at precise intervals.

Ivan jogs down this nature strip; under the cloudless sky, the
palms lend the town a Mediterranean feel, or perhaps that of an
attenuated Los Angeles; without the traffic and the smog and
the guns and the crime. *The Truman Show* version, adorned with

Christmas tinsel. Both sides of the street are lined with shops, the long collaborative awnings of an Australian country town hanging from the Art Deco buildings, cement-rendered and pastel-painted, or their yellow-brick equivalents.

The nature strip comes to an end. The centre of town is marked by a roundabout and, at its centre, a stylised fountain of polished stone topped with the heroic figures of what could be a trio of gods: a muscle-bound Zeus holding aloft a bunch of grapes; a youthful hero with a corn cob in one hand and a pumpkin in another; a chunky Aphrodite, gravity-defying breasts bare to the elements, cupping an orange suggestively in one hand. All three are gazing over Ivan's head, eyes fixed on a distant horizon, some promised land. Water, the source of the town's wealth, spews out around them, rollicking and foaming into the dry air of the interior. Ivan thinks of the other towns he's visited during his two years in the job: communities with clock towers at their hearts, or war memorials, or often enough the two melded together. Not here, no mention here of the glorious dead, no memorialisation of the fallen. Perhaps Yuwonderie was founded too late; had sacrificed no heroes of its own. Or maybe Yuwonderie's founding fathers had their eyes so resolutely set upon the future that there was no time to ponder the recent past, to reflect on such sacrifices.

Surrounding the fountain and its roundabout, all four corners of the intersection are marked with large structures, revealing a pleasing architectural symmetry. There is something precise here, something measured and confident. On one corner is a pub, the Grandview Hotel, boasting an impressive facade of brick, glass and sandstone cladding. There is a former T&G insurance building, with its distinctive tower; there are council chambers and a library, all in one building; and another pub, the Coachman's Arms. Ivan keeps running. At the top of Commonwealth Way he reaches the Yuwonderie Irrigation Scheme Company building, two wings flanking a grand entrance. Almost a hundred years old, it remains steadfastly modern, not part of frontier Australia but the vanguard of modernity.

Rising behind it, there's a huge outcrop of rock: a small mountain, dominating the town to the west, a couple of hundred metres high. He recognises the shape, a severe drop-off facing the town but with the suggestion of a gentler slope on the far side. He's seen similar formations dotting the plains all across the southern Riverina, ancient outcrops dating back to the beginnings of the continent. This one has a telecommunications mast supporting microwave dishes and a mobile phone tower, so there must be a road. Probably a lookout, no doubt some walking paths. It appeals to him: not just the challenge of ascending it, but what it offers, a view out across the landscape, an overview of the town. A way of understanding. He checks his watch. A challenge for another day; perhaps tomorrow morning's run.

Ivan turns right, descending the ridge, through some back streets before coming across a canal, stretching through the town, straight and peaceful. If the water is flowing, he can't see it. This early in the day there is still mist, low and ephemeral, like a dusting, floating by the banks, already burning off as the sun continues its ascent. Instead of crossing the road bridge, he goes down stairs to a path running alongside the waterway. Here are cyclists and dog walkers, even an elderly couple with matching walker frames, all out before the sun turns punitive. Ahead of him a brown lab, off its leash, plunges into the canal, barking incoherently at some ducks. The birds take flight, in on the joke, honking with amused derision. The dog struggles out. Its owner stands hands on hip, laughing ruefully.

'Top dog,' says Ivan as he passes.

'Completely hopeless,' says the woman, taking no offence, even as the dog sprays her with water as it shakes itself dry.

Ivan crosses a bridge, heads back along the canal in the direction of the rocky outcrop. He reaches a diversion from the canal, feeding back into parkland closer to the town centre. He follows the path, coming to a pedestrian bridge across an inlet. MEMORIAL WETLANDS, proclaims a sign. He takes the footbridge. A large rock guards the entrance to the swamp. A plaque mounted on the rock states: IN LOVING MEMORY OF JESSOP TITCHFIELD, CLEMENCE HEARTWOOD AND VAN DYKE ALLSOP. MARCH 2001. Nearby is an explanatory sign:

> The Memorial Wetlands were established in 2001, returning the area to its natural state and replacing the artificial Lake Yuwonderie. The reserve honours the memory of the three prominent community leaders who died here in a boating accident in early 2000. Erected by the Yuwonderie Progress Association and funded by their loving families as a gift to the community of Yuwonderie.

The name Titchfield catches Ivan's eye. No doubt Jessop was a relative of Otto. Heartwood and Allsop, also members of the Seven families. Ivan finds it intriguing: the men drown, but the families fill the lake, as if to punish it. He keeps moving, the gravel paths crunching underfoot with a satisfying sound. They wind back and forth through the rushes, almost a maze. He takes one, ends on a small island with a green birdwatching hide. He retraces his steps, tries another route, emerging from the far side of the maze, feeling a vague sense of satisfaction, as if he has somehow solved a riddle.

In front of him is a pub, the Drovers Rest, looking out across the wetlands, its paintwork no longer immaculate as if the moisture from the ponds has crept up the slope. Beyond it lies a new housing estate: modern bungalows, suburban. He thinks of his small unit in Sydney, rented out nowadays, his weekend trips to the capital becoming too infrequent to justify leaving it untenanted. On a busy road, full of traffic and noise and fumes, nowhere near parkland or wetlands or any green space, at all. But worth more than these modest bungalows, with their driveways and garages and yards.

He starts heading back, jogging around the perimeter of the wetlands this time. He thinks of Nell. He enjoys working with her. She's smart and motivated, well balanced, a bit impetuous at times, a bit too attracted to wild men, but always supportive, a team player in a way he never was. In Sydney it's large teams, multiple investigations conducted simultaneously, an emphasis on procedure, on process, on hierarchy, with forensics and specialists on tap, with lawyers and prosecutors to be consulted and appeased. Easy to stay remote, to not engage on a personal level. He remembers his own mentor, Morris Montifore, and how he rescued the angry young officer who was drinking too much, arguing too much, and definitely gambling too much. Who saw his potential, pulled him back into line, gave him purpose. He's lucky to work with Nell, to have her support, with her lightness and humour, quick with a quip, happy to prick his seriousness. And she's a good investigator, seeing things he overlooks, picking up on the body language, the subtle shifts in mood that he tends to miss. He promises himself to be the best possible mentor to Nell, to help her as Montifore helped him.

He's almost back in the town centre, crossing the bridge over the canal. It appears to mark a boundary between the older commercial centre and the newer suburbs. As he jogs, his mind returns to the case. Most likely Athol Hasluck died elsewhere, his body dumped in the canal but definitely murdered. And this will be the day that helps determine the flow of the investigation, whether it quickly resolves itself, with eyewitnesses coming forward or clear forensic evidence emerging, or if it will be longer and more challenging.

He's agreed to meet Nell at the Lone Dog Café. As he returns along Commonwealth Way, he passes an elderly busker a couple of storefronts along from the cafe. The grizzled man is performing a grizzled rendition of a Neil Young song. He looks out of place in the neat, clean town; Ivan wonders why he hasn't been moved on, sent down to the Drovers Rest, or cleaned up and put to work as a Santa Claus. He drops a five-dollar note into the musician's open guitar case and is rewarded by a nod of appreciation.

Nell is waiting at an outside table. 'You seem to be in a good mood,' she observes.

'Must be,' Ivan says, smiling.

He pays for a large flat white and a blueberry muffin at the counter inside. The owner with the mutton-chops tells him he'll bring the order out, and then repeats the same thing to himself: *I'll bring it out.* Outside, Nell is scanning her phone, looking fit and eager, back from her martial arts routines.

'You just missed McTosh,' she says. 'Getting a soy latte on his way to the office.'

'Soy latte? I thought he'd be more of a deep-fried kippers with Worcestershire sauce man.'

'We'll have no ethnic profiling here, Sergeant,' she chides.

'He have anything useful to say?'

'He did. There's CCTV on the main street. Athol's office is just around the corner on McLean Street. McTosh has put Constable Simmonds on it. She's already located vision of Hasluck walking towards his office the night he died, about the time Jacinta Hasluck gave us. But there's nothing to show him leaving again, or anyone else leaving. Apparently, the office is on the second floor and there's a second set of stairs out the back, leading down to an alley and parking, so the assumption is that Hasluck left that way.' She pauses. 'Or was taken out.' She breaks off a piece of pastry, but finishes what she is saying before popping it in her mouth. 'They've sealed the office, treating it as a potential crime scene. Same with the back stairs. McTosh wants to know whether they should search inside, lift prints and hunt for fibres. He can get a team from Griffith—they've had more forensics training and have better kit—or leave it for a specialised team. But there's no sign of a struggle, and there's no blood.'

'Electricity?' asks Ivan.

'According to McTosh, just the normal two-forty-volt supply you'd expect in any office.'

Ivan is impressed. The local sergeant would make a good detective; he's happy to take the initiative, unlike some small-town officers. 'Carole Nguyen is on her way. The Griffith team can help, but they should wait so she can supervise.'

'So what next?'

'Two-pronged. Athol's movements on Saturday night, and trying to work out who might want to kill him.'

'You think his wife is a suspect?' Nell asks.

'What's your view?'

'No,' she says. 'Not this time. Three kids, he's the breadwinner, not much insurance. Hard to see her dumping the body.' She closes her eyes for a moment, opening them again as she speaks. 'And just her level of distress. Her grief.'

'No, I can't see it either.'

'Has Sydney agreed to send a specialist pathologist?' she asks.

'Blake Ness, here by lunchtime. Flying into Griffith, getting a car. Coming down with Carole Nguyen.'

— —

Instead of walking back to the hotel afterwards, he takes a small detour. He wants to see Athol Hasluck's accountancy practice, even if it's just from the outside, place it in the context of the town. He finds it located above an internet cafe. It has its own street-level entry, a frosted-glass door with gold lettering, the font in keeping with the building's heritage: ATHOL HASLUCK, CHARTERED ACCOUNTANT. There is police tape, and a sign inside the door has been flipped to 'Closed', diffused but still legible through the frosted glass. He'd like to get in there, to get upstairs, get a feel for the place, take the measure of the man. He will, when Carole gives him the okay.

His phone rings as he's walking away. It's an old number, still remembered by his handset. Uncle Milos. His mother's half-brother. He hasn't heard from him in years. Decades.

'Hello, Ivan Lucic,' he offers tentatively, and then: 'Is that you, Uncle?'

'Yes, it's me,' says the man, and Ivan can hear the age in his voice, a frailty. And something else: trepidation.

'What is it, Uncle?'

'Have you heard?'

'No. What?'

'Your father. He's being released.'

Ivan stops walking. Stops breathing. 'When?'

'Soon.'

'How?'

'He was sentenced to thirty years, but they're giving him time for good behaviour. They say his health isn't good.'

'I see.' Ivan doesn't see, but he doesn't know what else to say, how to respond. 'Thank you for telling me. I didn't realise.'

'Ivan, there is something else.'

'Milos?'

'I heard, I don't know if it is true, but they say he will come back here. To Australia.'

Ivan stares. A young man walks past, so Australian, with thongs, a blue singlet, a tattoo on his arm. 'No. They won't let him in. Surely he'll have to go to Croatia.'

There's a pause at the other end of the line, as if his uncle is unwilling to continue. A moment passes before he speaks. 'Ivan, your father has never been to Croatia. Just Bosnia. Just the war. He's not a dual citizen; he was born here. An Australian. Dinky-di.'

'Shit,' says Ivan. He knew that; shouldn't have needed to be reminded by Milos.

'You don't have to see him,' Milos says. 'You don't have to have anything to do with him.'

'No, I don't. Thank you for telling me.' He pauses. 'Are you okay, Milos?'

'I'm good. In Adelaide. I don't want to think about him. I think if I saw him, I might try to kill him.'

'Promise me you won't.'

A bitter laugh comes down the phone. 'Ten years ago, maybe. But no, I'm too old, too past it. But I never want to see him again.'

'Same here.'

The call ends, and Ivan is left staring into space. The sheen has come off the morning. The sun is up, and the mist has gone from the canal. The rock looks down, imperious. The joggers and dog walkers are at work; the kids are at school. At last he moves. What's he been thinking, running through wetlands, daydreaming? Justice is waiting; waiting for him to deliver it. A man is dead; his wife is grieving. Better Ivan get moving, get into his suit, get to business.

chapter eight

1993

THE WORLD DAVIS LOOKED OUT UPON THE NEXT MORNING SEEMED DIFFERENT, as if he had been gifted new eyes. The previous day, he'd woken as the heir to an estate; now he was a university student, career uncertain. His future, previously so clearly delineated, had overnight become nebulous and ill-defined.

After breakfast, he drove his Alfa into Yuwonderie, passing through a landscape both familiar and novel; the sky appeared larger, the trees seemed taller, a filter of nostalgia and loss bathed the fields even as a sense of excitement paved the road ahead. The looming bulk of the Castle looked to be considering his decision, sitting in judgement. It was an exciting world, a world without obvious boundaries. Perhaps he would become a historian, perhaps he wouldn't, and the uncertainty thrilled him.

Davis changed the tape in the sound system, realising he could pick a new trajectory as easily as selecting a new cassette. And that was the wonder of it: he didn't know what he wanted to be, and yet that decision now lay entirely within his own control. He relished the thought that he was now like most other twenty-one-year-olds: he wasn't sure what lay ahead.

He moved across the Spur, that low ridge of land extending out from the base of the Castle, and entered the irrigation zone. A few minutes later and he was in Yuwonderie township, driving to Commonwealth Way and parking directly outside the Yuwonderie Irrigation Scheme Company headquarters. The building dominated the town from atop a small hill, authority reinforced by the Castle rising behind it. It was an imposing two-storey edifice, Art Deco, more austere than its contemporaries. The two wings that flanked a central entrance were businesslike: there were no curves here, no Art Nouveau flourishes, none of the roundings of streamline moderne. Ornamentation was minimal. Only at its centre, between the wings, was there room for softening, with a semicircle of stone steps leading up through columns to a round portico, with a stylised image of a water wheel inlaid in stone on the floor. The building spoke of authority, a statement of functionality and progress, embracing the optimism of the 1920s. Davis climbed the steps, seeing it with his new eyes, those of a tyro historian, and pushed through the double-brass doors of the entry.

The foyer was light, stone-lined but with an airiness to it, the ceiling two floors above, stairs on both sides leading to a balcony bridging the two wings against the back wall. A fresco of water and crops and men and women toiling industriously together was mounted on a wall across from a reception desk, the same sort of imagery deployed in that era by everyone from Stalin to the New Deal.

At the reception desk, he asked if he might meet with the general manager, a man named Maurice Gotson.

The receptionist frowned. 'You have an appointment?'

'I'm sorry—I wasn't aware I needed one,' replied Davis, feeling foolish. 'Could I arrange one now, please?'

The receptionist looked at him doubtfully before coming to a decision, her smile calculated. 'Here, let me put you through to his executive assistant. He can deal with you.'

'I can go up and see them, if you like,' offered Davis.

'Better on the phone, I think.'

Davis was feeling more uncomfortable by the moment. How stupid of him to simply arrive, expecting people to be available.

The receptionist handed him the receiver, eyebrows raised in scepticism, lips curled in amusement.

'Hello, can I help you?' asked a man at the other end, voice rich with irritation.

'Good morning. My name is Davis Heartwood. I'm very sorry to bother you, but I was wondering if I could make an appointment to meet with the general manager, please? Just for a few moments.' And then adding, as an afterthought, 'It doesn't have to be today.'

The irritation had left the man's voice when he replied. 'Mr Heartwood. I'm sure that will be possible at some stage. But perhaps I can help? Is there anything in particular you wish to address?'

'I was hoping to access the company's records. I'm doing an honours degree at Melbourne University and am planning to write a thesis on the establishment of the company and the development of the irrigation scheme.'

A pause. 'How fascinating. And you're in the foyer now? Give me a few minutes to speak to our records section and then I'll be right down.'

'Thank you.'

Davis returned the phone to the receptionist, her gaze no longer superior, her eyes wide with curiosity. He offered her an apologetic smile and made his way over to an island of chairs and low tables beneath the mural. There was a bronze plaque.

THE YUWONDERIE IRRIGATION SCHEME COMPANY BUILDING, OPENED BY THE RIGHT HONOURABLE THOMAS BAVIN, PREMIER OF NEW SOUTH WALES, THE 3RD OF MARCH 1928. CHAIRMAN: WILLIAM HEARTWOOD. GENERAL MANAGER: HORACE TITCHFIELD.

His great-great-grandfather William, here at the opening, the inaugural chairman, the year after the old Parliament House in Canberra was opened. Davis wondered which of the two buildings was the more impressive.

He hadn't seen the plaque before, not this one, not that he remembered, but he'd seen plenty like it. The town was dotted with them. He'd always found them vaguely embarrassing: the seven families big-noting themselves at every opportunity. But now he considered an alternative interpretation: the founding families were conscious that they were creating something new and bold, that they were blazing a trail. And so they were keen to mark it, believing they were making history. A confidence that people would want to remember them, for their vision and for their industry, for building a town and a district and an economy out here, in the middle of nowhere. It made him ask himself why a proper history of the scheme had never been written.

A man emerged, trotting down the stairs and across to him, nimble on his feet, like a dancer. He was wearing a lightweight suit, the silk kerchief in his top pocket matching his tie, and his shoes were leather slip-ons. Davis smelt cologne. 'Mr Heartwood. I'm Hilary Housego, Mr Gotson's executive assistant.'

They shook hands, the man's grip firm without being ostentatious.

'It is always good to meet with our major shareholders. Tell me more of this thesis of yours.'

'It's for my history degree.' And Davis explained more fully the proposal for his honours dissertation and how the company's records might assist him.

The man watched him closely as he spoke, eyes sharp with intelligence. 'I can't see why that would be a problem,' said Hilary. 'It's all here in the archives. The founders were proud—and thorough.'

'Sounds promising,' said Davis, smiling.

Hilary beamed. 'Come with me. I've spoken to our records department; let's see how they might help you.'

The well-dressed man led him past the reception desk, through a door, almost to the end of a long corridor, then down some stairs to a basement Davis had never suspected existed. They headed back along another corridor towards the building's centre, arriving at a door marked REGISTRY, the sign painted in gold leaf.

They entered the room, lit by a bank of fluorescent lights. A bright-eyed young woman was waiting behind the counter. 'Ah, Lucretia,' said Hilary. 'Enright still not in?'

'Running a little late, sir.'

'Well, I'm sure you are more than up to the task.' And he added with a cunning smile, 'So good of you to pop on a bit of lippie for me. I'm honoured.'

Davis thought he saw the young lady blush, yet she gathered herself and looked him in the eye. 'I'm very pleased to be of assistance, Mr Heartwood.'

'Davis.'

'And I'm Lucy. I was in the year below you at school.'

'At primary?'

'Yes.'

Hilary interrupted. 'You are in good hands with Lucretia, Mr Heartwood. I must be getting back. But please let me know if there is anything else I can do to help. And if you do want to meet with the general manager at any stage, I'm sure it can be arranged. An interview, perhaps. He would certainly be able to put the achievements of the scheme into perspective.'

'Thank you. Thank you very much,' said Davis, even as he was thinking he was capable of shaping his own opinion on the history.

Once the man had left, leaving a lingering suggestion of lavender behind, Lucy smiled at him, eyes shining. 'We're not really an archive, you know. We just keep the day-to-day transactions. All the records. I've got no training; I just put things in files.'

'But you have documents going back to the company's foundation?'

'I guess. They just accumulate, pile up year after year. There's enough room in the sub-basement for half-a-dozen squash courts— unless someone has been through and tossed them out, but I've never heard of anyone doing that. Come on, I've found a place for you down the corridor.'

Lucy led him to a small meeting room. There was a table of blond wood surrounded by six chairs, and a row of windows set high in the wall, abutting the ceiling, light wells providing natural illumination. 'You can get comfortable while I burrow into the records, if you like.'

'I'd prefer to come with you. Is that okay?' Davis said.

'That would be fun. But here, have a look at this first while I work out where we need to go. It might give you an overview. What happened when, that sort of thing.'

She handed him a book titled *Yuwonderie 50 years: 1924–74*. 'It's a bit naff, but see if it helps.'

The volume was large and weighty, expensively produced with a cloth cover and glossy paper and full-colour printing, more photos than text, resolutely upbeat, a piece of public relations. He glanced at the contents, read the chapter headings:

Foundations
A better model
The desert turns green
The green revolution
Smallholders
Yuwonderie township
The present
The future

He flipped to the first chapter, 'Foundations'. The text was heroic—full of 'taming the wilderness' and 'subduing nature' and 'imposing order'. No mention of any Indigenous people, no mention of how the Europeans had come to the district, no mention of any pre-existing ecosystem. But that in itself might prove useful: the document reflecting bygone attitudes, still alive, maybe even more so, by the 1970s.

He found a handy timetable, worth photocopying:

1900—Samuel McCaughey buys North Yanco station on the north bank of the Murrumbidgee. Develops a private irrigation system covering 40,000 acres.

1903—The NSW government announces its intention to construct a publicly funded irrigation scheme north of the Murrumbidgee—genesis of the modern-day Murrumbidgee Irrigation Area (MIA).

1904–1912—Graziers south of the Murrumbidgee propose their district be incorporated into the scheme. The government rebuffs their approach.

1910—The NSW government resumes majority of McCaughey's Yanco property.

1912—Murrumbidgee Irrigation Area (MIA) formally declared by the NSW government.

1914—Southern graziers led by the Seven families—Allsop, Blaxland, Titchfield, Hasluck, Heartwood, Horsham and McLean—establish a company to explore the feasibility of building a privately financed irrigation system south of the Murrumbidgee.

1914—The towns of Leeton and Griffith in the MIA formally declared.

1916—The NSW government declares the MIA must have priority access to water from the newly constructed Burrinjuck Dam, undermining the viability of the Yuwonderie proposal.

1918—The NSW government reverses its decision, guaranteeing Yuwonderie a proportionate share of Burrinjuck water.

1918—Yuwonderie Irrigation Scheme Company (YISC) formally incorporated.

1919—The Seven founding families release land to be auctioned to small landholders, raising capital to help finance construction. The auction is vastly oversubscribed.

1920—Earthworks begin.

1921—Yuwonderie township laid out.

1923—Lake Yuwonderie and weir constructed.

1924—The scheme officially opened.

1928—The company headquarters opened.

1930s—The Depression. The NSW government recognises the growing success of Yuwonderie, helping to finance expansion of the private scheme and extending the railway from Leeton south across the river.

Davis considered the timetable. He'd need to verify it from primary sources, of course. A coffee-table book would gloss over some facts, ignore others, inevitably get some wrong. But it offered him a chronological framework for his thesis. The starting date could be 1900, when McCaughey first brought irrigation to the Murrumbidgee. It could cover the establishment of the Yuwonderie scheme, contrast its private structure with the government-led scheme in the MIA, and end in the 1930s, with the smallholders firmly entrenched, the town constructed and the region set to prosper in the years ahead.

Lucy returned. 'Any use?' she asked.

'Good starting point,' he said, looking up, surprised to see a transformation in her. Her hair was brushed back, mascara applied to her lashes. She was wearing earrings, and he couldn't remember if she'd had them on before. It struck him that she was rather pretty, with her open face and shining eyes.

'Come on,' she said. 'Let's go exploring.'

'Are you sure it's okay?' he asked. 'I'd hate to get you in trouble. If you're short-staffed, I mean.'

She laughed at that, a light and breezy exhalation. 'Mr Housego has given the all clear,' she said. 'And what Housego says goes. Besides, you're one of the Seven.'

'You think that's why he's given me access?'

She looked at him quizzically. 'Don't you?'

chapter nine

WHEN IVAN ARRIVES AT THE POLICE STATION, NELL IS ALREADY UPSTAIRS, IN the room McTosh has allocated them. She has the monitors up and running, the computers working, has commandeered a whiteboard from somewhere. Now she is setting up a video recording device on the central table.

'Expecting someone?' he asks.

'Alice Figtree—Athol Hasluck's assistant. I called her to line up a meeting, but she wanted to come in. Be here in about fifteen minutes.'

'Good stuff,' says Ivan. 'Saves us going to her.'

'She sounded a bit flustered.' Nell gestures at the table. 'Thought this might be less confrontational than an interview room.'

'Good thinking.'

Alice Figtree arrives, escorted upstairs by Constable Simmonds. She seems agitated, looking around the room as if it might harbour some menace. She looks about forty, but it's hard to tell. Her dress is conservative: a pleated skirt and a loose silk blouse, polished shoes with heels neither too high nor too low. But her hair is side cut, the tips bleached and pink, and Ivan can see the piercings where she has removed metal from the rim of her left ear. There are rings on most of her fingers, including what might be a gold wedding band. The hint of a tattoo edges from under the sleeve of the blouse. Her face is youthful, make-up restrained, anxiety in her eyes. Or is it grief?

Ivan introduces Nell, then himself. 'Please take a seat.'

She sits at the table; Nell offers her tea. Alice accepts, and Constable Simmonds heads back downstairs with their orders. Ivan wishes he'd had a bit more time to prepare, but he can't think what else he would need to know. He runs through the formalities. 'Alice, we'd like to record this interview. We have your consent?'

'Of course.'

He starts the recording. He is sitting opposite Alice, Nell between them at the end of the table, the same as she had done with Jacinta Hasluck the evening before. Ivan understands why: it makes the interview feel more collegiate, not two against one.

'Alice, how long have you been employed by Athol Hasluck?'

'Only about six weeks.'

'And how did you come to work for him?'

'I was looking for a casual job, and I heard he was looking for a part-time assistant. I got in touch, and he put me on a trial. It was working well.'

'He said so?'

'Yes.'

'We believe Athol Hasluck was murdered on Saturday night. You're aware of that?'

'Yes.'

'Can you tell me where you were that night?'

Alice stares at him, unflinching. 'I was in Wagga. With my wife. At a wedding. We drove back Sunday morning.' She looks at Ivan, then Nell. 'People saw us there. The hotel will vouch for us.'

'That makes it easy,' says Nell. 'You understand we had to ask?'

'There's no money—nothing,' says Alice abruptly.

'Sorry?' says Ivan.

'I've been going through the accounts. Athol's accounts. There's nothing there. He's drained them.' She sounds more distressed than when she acknowledged the murder of her employer.

'Can you explain that?' asks Nell.

'He was teetering on bankruptcy.'

'How can you go through his accounts?'

'He gave me access. That was part of the reason I was hired. To streamline the record keeping. To organise the client files. Once he was dead . . .' Her voice trails off.

'You've been in the office?' asks Ivan. 'It's been taped off.'

'No,' says Alice. 'Before. I was there on Sunday afternoon, after I got back from Wagga. He'd given me Friday off to go to the wedding, so I'd gone in to pick up some files so I could work at home that evening. I was there when the news came that he was dead, so I took copies of the accounts and spent yesterday examining them.'

Ivan decides against pursuing why she was looking at the records; the important thing is that she did, and has volunteered the information. 'Okay, Alice. His debts. This might be important. Please tell us exactly what you've found.'

The woman draws a deep breath, begins. 'Athol wasn't very good with tech. I'm not sure if he meant for me to, but I could also gain access to his personal accounts, his and his wife's. I would never have looked at them, except when he died, I thought it might help. I thought I could let Jacinta know where she stood financially.' She turns to Nell. 'That's why I called. Why I wanted to see you.' She turns back to Ivan. 'They have a large mortgage, payments due on their car, and Athol's credit cards—all three of them—are maxed out. He's cancelled their private health, and his income protection has lapsed. He only narrowly avoided having the power and water to the house cut off, he was so late with the payments.'

'What about his life insurance?' asks Nell.

'That's good. Renewed eight months ago, before the debts got serious.' She grimaces. 'It's not very much, though. Not enough.'

'Does Jacinta know any of this?' asks Nell.

Alice shakes her head, and now she seems truly distressed. 'Not as far as I'm aware.' She looks at Nell, as if seeking guidance. 'I don't know what to do. But Jacinta will be finding out soon enough.' Alice frowns, concern carving lines in her forehead. 'I had no idea. She'll need to be told.'

Ivan considers this. 'Where has the money gone?'

'I don't know. Yet.'

'You can find out?'

She shrugs. 'Hope so. Depends if he tried to cover his tracks.'

'So you have digital copies?'

'Some.'

Ivan pauses. This could be key to finding the killer. 'We'll need a list of all the people he owed money.' And then: 'You're not aware of him receiving any threats? Angry clients turning up at the office? Anything like that?'

Alice shakes her head. Voice apologetic, as if she should have seen something, 'No. Nothing like that.'

'Okay, let us talk to Jacinta Hasluck. We should get her permission before examining their personal files. Don't be surprised if you get a call from her.'

'Of course.'

'Have you full access to his business accounts as well?'

'Yes. I've started going through them. I hope I can salvage something for his family.' She swallows. 'I've never met them, but he had photos on his desk. Twin boys. A girl.'

Ivan gives her a moment. 'And the client files?'

'They're in the office. In filing cabinets.'

'Paper files?'

'Mostly.' She grimaces. 'They're a bit out of control. That was a large part of what I've been doing: culling and digitising.'

'Okay, it's probably best to leave them for the moment. We'd need to get permission from the individual clients, or a warrant.'

'A warrant?' asks Alice. 'Is that necessary?'

'Depends.'

She nods. 'You'd need warrants for the client files if you wanted to use them to build a case, right? To use in court?'

'Correct,' says Nell.

'But I could look,' says Alice.

'We can't authorise that,' says Ivan.

'I'm already authorised,' says Alice. 'That was part of my job.'

Ivan turns to Nell. Her forehead is furrowed. He looks back to Alice. 'Concentrate on his personal files and the business, okay? At least for now.'

'Sure.'

'We've an officer on his way here. Kevin Nackangara. He has training in this area. We'll need him to work with you.'

'Is that necessary?'

'You must understand the implications if you tamper with evidence or withhold information from us, no matter how ugly. This is a murder investigation.'

Alice looks at him as if she has smelt something bad. 'I liked Athol. He was good to me. I'll do everything I can to help you catch his killer.'

'We're grateful,' says Ivan. 'But for now, stay away from the office and the client files. Work from home on the digital copies until Kevin gets here. Don't tell anyone you have them. And back up everything.'

'You think I'm in danger?'

It's Nell who answers. 'Whoever killed Athol might not want you poking around in his affairs. You need to be extra careful.'

chapter ten

October 1913

Dear Mother,

Two days past, Horace declared we were to have guests here at Castle View, that we would entertain. His mother and Elaine and myself immediately set ourselves to work, cleaning and washing and tidying. Madeleine Titchfield revealed herself to be a master baker, expert at the cookhouse Metters. I had only used the top of it, that and the cast-iron pot above the fireplace, but she showed Elaine and me how to use the oven: how to chop the kindling, how to set the fire, how to assess the oven temperature by sprinkling a little flour and seeing how quickly it browned. It seems to me more an art than a science, and she the artist. She made a tea cake and a pudding and fine white bread, all in readiness for the next day.

I'm not sure what I expected. Grand men with monocles and grey beards, waistcoats and fob watches. Instead, it was the neighbours, two rough-hewed men, Noel and Jack Marney, who arrived not by carriage but on horseback. It immediately struck me how young they were—younger than Horace: Noel in his mid-twenties, Jack twenty-one and looking barely out of his teens. They swung from their horses with such practised ease, nonchalant in their movements and interaction with their animals. Not so with people. They seemed awkward, not quite knowing how to look at Elaine and myself. They were freshly shaved; I could see the rashes and the nicks. They wore suits, clean and respectable, but their hats were the hats of the bush, battered and sweat-stained, as if they were so used to wearing them that they were unaware of the clash with the rest of their attire. Off the horses and on their feet, they held the hats before them, whether out of embarrassment or politeness I could not say. But when Horace emerged to greet them, Noel laughed and Jack smiled, and the creases by their eyes suggested that these were men who laughed and smiled as a habit and not just for show. The two are back from droving, bringing sheep and cattle through from South Australia and the drought lands of the west.

Noel is the larger of the brothers as well as the elder. He carries himself with assurance, as if he is well glued to the earth, bringing its gravity within him. Jack is lighter on his feet, more quick-witted, constantly on the move, a smile on his lips and a glint in his eyes. He teases Noel, but with such good spirits and affection that his brother takes no offence. The first time he did it to me, it took me a moment to recognise it for what it was. For once I was glad of my complexion, lest he see my blush. Afterwards, as I helped in the kitchen, I reflected on how he'd lifted my mood simply by including me in the banter, as if I were among equals. And it made me think for the first time that I might be happy here, that it might feel more like a home than a job, provided there are people like Elaine and Jack nearby.

It seemed all the bother of the preparations had been unnecessary, for Noel and Jack were clearly the type who would never stand on ceremony. And yet I am glad we went to the effort. The brothers were so complimentary of the meal overseen by Mrs Titchfield, and particularly her baking, that I thought she might pop a button, so much did she swell with pride.

I did not eat with them. Instead, I waited upon the table, a dutiful servant. But while Horace and Mrs Titchfield pretended to ignore me, the brothers and Elaine from time to time directed a comment towards me, or even a question. I believe it was deliberate, in part to deflate Horace's balloon, in part out of kindness to me. The men drank wine. I sampled a little in the cookhouse and was entirely unimpressed. And yet, in the heat of the day, it had a mellowing effect on them, and Horace's attempt at high manners gave way to humour and laughter. Mrs Titchfield did not drink, but it was pleasing to see her relax as the success of the meal and the day were assured. As I served pudding, Jack winked at me and I needed to retreat to the cookhouse to regain my composure. And yet, later, when I was serving fruit, I saw him regard me with a sadness in his eyes that I did not understand.

The conversation was all of the great scheme, this plan of Horace's to build an irrigation system south of the river. This was the real reason he had invited the brothers: to enlist their support, for their home, Jolimont, and their land lies within the boundaries of the canal development. They were all for it, vocal in their support, and I'd suggest it was this as much as the wine that was behind Horace's more convivial demeanour.

'No more droving,' said Jack at one point. 'I guess it's about time.' But he sounded a little wistful and not so sure.

Another man arrived, in a small black buggy: an older gentleman with grey mutton-chop whiskers and a top hat. He was aged at least fifty years, perhaps older. His name is Augustine Chaulker, another landholder and a friend of Horace and Elaine's late father. The younger generation's deference towards him, echoed by Mrs Titchfield, gave me fair warning that this was not someone to be trifled with. He had a chilling effect on the gathering, with Horace and even Elaine becoming more formal. As he took a place at the table, I found myself returned to the station of servant girl, delivering him tea and cake. He informed me scornfully that he did not imbibe alcohol.

However, despite his initial haughtiness, it would be incorrect to say that Mr Chaulker was in any way hostile to the scheme proposed by Horace. Just the opposite: he declared himself a keen supporter. And once the talk went to the proposal, which it almost immediately did, he exhibited all the enthusiasm of a convert. Indeed, he declared it divine providence.

They discussed politics, how important it was to have the local representatives onside, on the council at Narrandera, in the state parliament in Sydney and the federal parliament in Melbourne.

I was listening as I cleared dishes from the table, and Jack must have noticed my interest, because he asked, 'And who shall you be voting for?' His tone was playful, and also curious.

'They don't call it a secret ballot for nothing,' I replied.

'You can't vote,' asserted Augustine Chaulker, a tightness in his voice.

'Not until I am twenty-one,' I said.

'And not then, surely.'

'Surely I can,' I said, and I know it to be true, for I carry my father's name and his legacy as much as I carry yours and your mother's.

I could see Horace shift, uncomfortable with the direction of the conversation, which was a diversion from the scheme.

It was Jack who eased any tension with a quick barb about the local member, moving the subject of the conversation away from me. Noel laughed at his brother's assessment, but I felt Horace's eyes upon me, as if reassessing his opinion.

It was almost dinner time, the sun lowering, when the three guests departed. By then, Mr Chaulker was entirely supportive of the irrigation plan and the Marneys were a little unsteady on their feet, as was Horace. But once the brothers were mounted, their assurance returned, their horses more than capable of carrying them home. Before mounting, Jack had taken the hand of Mrs Titchfield and kissed the back of it, like some London gallant, and she beamed at the flattery. He then did the same to Elaine, telling her what a pleasure it was to remake her acquaintance, and then to me: a light brush of the lips on the back of my hand. And I found myself a silly girl, beaming every bit as much as Mrs Titchfield.

Horace was in a jolly mood, elated at the support he had won from Chaulker and the Marneys. He took a glass of port and settled himself on the verandah to record his thoughts in his journal. Mrs Titchfield, too, was pleased with the success of the day, but she was entirely exhausted and retired early to bed satisfied she'd done her best for Horace. I must learn how to bake. Elaine knows a little, but her mother is reluctant to teach her, wanting her to have servants instead, to rise above. But she wasn't there to disapprove as Elaine helped me wash the dishes and clear the table. I am already dreading the day when she returns to her school and I am left alone to support Mrs Titchfield and cater to Horace and his whims.

While we cleaned, Elaine explained to me that the Marneys hold the key to Horace's scheme, that their property lies at the very core of the area that Horace believes to be suitable. She said their father had been sceptical, delaying progress, believing that either the proposal would prove unviable and they would lose their money, or that the government would see its worth and confiscate their land. But the family had been hit by tragedy: the mother, the father and a sister had died the previous year in a flash flood. Not long after, the brothers had gone droving, and this had been the first opportunity, after a respectful interlude, for Horace to revisit the proposal.

I mentioned to Elaine, as we polished the good cutlery and returned it to its storage, how lightly the brothers wore their grief. She suggested that was due entirely to the two of us. When I asked what she meant, she said they had arrived expecting Horace and maps and survey reports and the austerity of Augustine Chaulker, and instead they had found two pretty young girls. 'Careful,' she said to me. 'Drovers.' But she was laughing.

Oh, Mother, I do think I might be happy here. Oh, reading back, I see I have already mentioned that. No matter. Pray that it is true.

Your dutiful daughter,
Bessie

chapter eleven

IVAN IS BEING FORCED TO WAIT, AND HE DOESN'T LIKE IT: WAITING FOR ALICE
Figtree to trawl through the financial records of Athol Hasluck;
for Sergeant McTosh's team to collect and sift through any
CCTV footage; for Blake Ness and Carole Nguyen to arrive from
Sydney and Kevin Nackangara from Dubbo. He paces the floor
in the detectives room, prodding his imagination, trying to think
of some way to find Athol Hasluck's killer. Momentum is something his old mentor Morris Montifore used to talk about: how
investigations can generate their own impetus. Back then, Ivan
hadn't fully understood what his boss meant, but now he does:
that intuitive sense of whether a case is progressing, whether the
pieces are coming together or flying apart. He's conscious, as are
all homicide detectives, that the first forty-eight hours are crucial.
It's not that the killer is necessarily identified and caught in that
time, but that progress is being made, that the investigation is
beginning to define itself. It's almost forty-eight hours since the
waterskiers found Hasluck floating in the canal and his team is

nowhere near that stage. He reckons he and Nell deserve an extra twenty-four hours to compensate for travelling time, but even so, they can't afford to sit on their hands waiting.

As he paces, he racks his mind, searching for the next step, but instead an unwelcome fact imposes itself: his father, being released, coming home. He quashes the intrusion, not allowing it to grow. He doesn't need distractions, not now. As soon as Nell returns from showing out Alice Figtree, he suggests they get moving.

In the four-wheel drive, he reiterates his theory of momentum for her benefit. She's heard it all before, of course, but she listens silently. He recounts another of Montifore's dictums: detectives must propel investigations, push them hard, until with luck and perseverance they reach the point when they start driving themselves. That's what they need to do now: push hard, reach the tipping point.

'Eliminate suspects, narrow the field,' says Nell as she steers the police vehicle around one last circle, past a vast petrol station and onto a road heading out of town.

'Exactly.' He smiles, knowing she's repeating one of his own maxims. 'Eliminate those with alibis and then concentrate on those remaining.'

—◆—

Castle View, surrounded by vines and orange groves, is having nothing to do with Art Deco or anything else so tasteful. It's ostentatiously modern, made of stone and cement rendered to imitate stone, with arched windows of plate glass, making the most of its metre or two of elevation. It's home to Otto Titchfield, political brahmin, leader of the Country First party and head of one of the Seven families.

'Built to impress,' says Nell as they emerge from a gum-lined drive. The house itself is framed by pencil pines, as if transplanted from Tuscany. There are lush green lawns and ranks of roses.

The door is opened by a small woman, bird-like, eyes downcast and manner diffident. For a moment, Ivan mistakes her for a maid. Only when she meets his gaze does he see the resemblance to her sister, Jacinta Hasluck.

'I'm Detective Sergeant Ivan Lucic,' he says. 'We phoned ahead.'

'Lucy Titchfield,' says the woman with a tentative smile. 'And you?' she addresses Nell.

'Detective Constable Narelle Buchanan,' says Nell.

'Please come in. We've been expecting you.'

She shows them into a beautifully appointed drawing room, with a bow window framing a view over the town to the Castle, a vaulted ceiling, two ostentatious chandeliers and a white marble fireplace. 'I'll fetch Otto,' she says.

Ivan sits, watching Nell as she moves about the room, examining the oil paintings, the glass-doored bookcase, the subtle wallpaper.

She turns, smiles. 'Absolutely loaded.'

Lucy Titchfield returns, not with her husband but pushing a trolley topped with a silver coffee service and bone china crockery. The woman offers refreshments. Ivan takes a coffee, Nell has tea. Lucy serves them with quiet efficiency, her slippered feet making no sound. She must be only about fifty, but she's moving with the care of someone more elderly, as if her back is stiff or her joints are sore.

By contrast, Ivan can hear Otto approaching down the hallway well before he reaches the room, boots echoing off hardwood floors. He enters, red of face and wide of belly, gut held tight in a blue cotton shirt and underpinned by a straining belt of plaited leather. His RMs are simultaneously well-worn and well-polished. Titchfield plants himself in a chair, arms plonked on the armrests, legs spread, not offering a handshake or an introduction. 'No idea why you want to talk to me. Haven't seen the bloke in months.'

Ivan doesn't respond immediately, and Nell follows his lead. Ivan's not about to succumb to bluster. Lucy inserts herself into the silence, serving her husband coffee. Ivan has a sip of his own, complimenting Lucy on its quality, before introducing himself and Nell. He places his phone on the table. 'I'll record our interview, Mr Titchfield,' he says. 'A formality.'

The politician frowns. 'Is that necessary?'

'Hard to say in advance. Any reason why we shouldn't?'

'Any reason why I shouldn't insist on having my lawyer here?' The man's voice is gruff, and one of his nostrils has lifted in a sneer.

'That's your prerogative, and we're happy to accommodate you,' says Nell, voice deceptively pleasant. 'We can arrange for a time for you to come to the station.'

Titchfield stares at her, as if noticing her for the first time, but she holds his gaze and he concedes. 'Record away. I'll let you know if I need representation.'

'Thank you,' says Ivan, giving Nell a quick look of gratitude. He sets the phone app to record. 'First question. Entirely routine, we ask everyone. Where were you Saturday night? Say, from seven o'clock onwards.'

Titchfield harrumphs. 'Some routine. Is that when he died?'

'So we believe.'

'I was here. With my wife. At home.'

'He was,' pipes up Lucy. 'We both were.' She is sitting to one side, hands clasped, expression attentive, as if ready to jump at a mere suggestion from him.

'You can check our phones if you like,' adds Titchfield.

'Thank you,' says Ivan. 'We will inform you if we do indeed seek tracking information.'

The big man is frowning, as if the seriousness of Athol Hasluck's death is only now occurring to him.

'You said before we started recording that you hadn't seen Athol Hasluck for months,' says Ivan. 'But you obviously knew him well enough?'

'Why do you say that?'

'He's your brother-in-law.'

'Of course.'

'You don't socialise?'

'Not so often. I have a demanding schedule.'

It's Lucy who explains. 'Athol is—was—fine. But my sister and I don't really get along.'

'Any reason for that?' asks Ivan.

Lucy sighs. 'I think she resents all of this.' She gestures to the room, the obvious wealth.

Ivan returns his attention to Otto, who is frowning, as if the interview is not what he expected. 'You'd agree with that, Mr Titchfield?'

'Yes. Never had a problem with Athol. His family. One of the Seven. A younger son.' He looks from Ivan to Nell and back again, comes to some internal decision, relaxes his shoulders, steps down the aggression in his posture. Leans forward, engaging. 'We all grew up here. Used to be part of the same friendship group. More or less the same age. But he moved away. University, whatever. Probably at Jacinta's instigation. Welcomed him back when they returned, of course, but you understand how it is: friends drift apart. Life carries you in different directions. I see more of his elder brother Eric. At the club, on various boards. Sterling chap.'

'Head of his family? Like you?'

'Indeed.'

Nell addresses the wife. 'And you, Mrs Titchfield?'

'Me?'

'Did you know Athol Hasluck?'

'When we were young, yes. We were quite close. And more recently, he was a member of the local party branch.'

'He was indeed,' adds Otto, apparently back on safer ground. 'I'm told he had aspirations. I can ask around, if you like.'

'Aspirations?' says Nell.

'Politics,' Titchfield replies. 'I'm moving to federal politics, expanding Country First. No secret about that, been in all the papers. Means that my seat in the state parliament will be vacant. People are manoeuvring for preselection. I heard Athol Hasluck was considering throwing his hat in the ring, but I don't know if that's true or not. Hadn't approached me for support. I've had a few people sound me out, see if I would endorse them. He wasn't one of them.'

Now it's Ivan who finds himself leaning forward. 'How would you have rated his chances of success?'

'Hard to say. Lucy?' He defers to his wife, somewhat to Ivan's surprise.

She seems unsure. 'There's a couple of the others who are already serving on the local council. More experienced.'

'So not a frontrunner?'

'No.' She looks at her hands, then across to her husband, before speaking. 'I had heard he was part of a ginger group. Reformist.'

'In what sense?'

'Wanting more grassroots input. That's their sales pitch.'

Otto laughs, a barrel-chested sound. 'My wife is being overly coy. They say I exercise too much power, that I run the party as a personal fiefdom.'

'Do you?' asks Ivan.

Titchfield guffaws, but then turns serious so quickly that Ivan wonders if the laughter was ever genuine. Now the politician's face has turned hard, the subterranean aggression resurfacing. 'No. This is a democracy, and Country First is a democratic party. The most grassroots of them all.' And then a playfulness returns to his eyes, so that Ivan is unsure whether he has heard the man's honest opinion or a political line. A memory comes to him: a case he investigated early in his career as a detective, still learning the ropes of homicide alongside Morris Montifore. A murder in a theatre group in Sydney, a tabloid feeding frenzy. He recalls how difficult it was interviewing the actors. Some of them were very good: their sincerity and their tears and their earnest avowals. And, as it later transpired, their lies. He wonders if politicians might not possess a similar skill set.

Nell breaks in, her question directed at Otto Titchfield. 'Any reason why Athol Hasluck's body would be dumped on your land?'

Titchfield is not perturbed by the change in subject. 'No. As I said, I haven't seen him for months.'

'And you have no business dealings with him?' asks Ivan.

'How do you mean?'

'He was an accountant.'

'That's right. But no. He hasn't been back in town for that long, only set up the business when he returned. That's my understanding. My family have been prominent here for more than a century. We've been with the same accountants for generations.'

'Locals?'

'Not likely. Sydney. Family enterprises can get complex. Tax-wise. Inheritance. Holding companies and subsidiaries and family trusts and whatnot. No disrespect to Athol Hasluck, but probably a bit out of his league.'

Nell turns to the wife. 'And you, Mrs Titchfield? Have you had any recent contact with Mr Hasluck?'

'A little. Athol did the bookkeeping for the local branch and for the Watermen's Foundation. Pro bono.'

'The Watermen's Foundation?'

'A fundraising body for Country First. All the big parties have them.'

Ivan looks to Otto. 'You knew about this?'

The big man appears insulted. 'Of course I knew. But I don't have anything to do with it—not directly.'

Lucy quickly adds to her husband's answer. 'It's normal practice. You don't want members of parliament or candidates too closely involved with fundraising. They need to stay at arms-length, to avoid the appearance of compromise or undue influence. It's not just Country First; all the major parties do it. You understand?' She glances at Otto, then back at the detectives. 'We used

Athol to demonstrate our support for local business and for a party member.'

'I thought you said his work was pro bono?' says Nell.

Lucy smiles. 'True. But it's a vote of confidence. If people knew we trusted him, so might they.'

'And we needed to keep it totally separated from our private concerns,' Otto chips in.

'I see,' says Nell. 'But you're involved?' she asks the wife.

'I do what I can, yes.'

Otto laughs, another of his basso profundo guffaws. 'Don't be so modest, my dear,' he says. 'My wife is the president of the local branch and chief executive of Watermen's.'

It makes Ivan wonder about the definition of arms-length, but it's Nell who continues. 'So you have seen a fair bit of Athol recently?' she asks.

'Together with the rest of the branch committee,' Lucy says. 'We've been meeting once a fortnight. We'll step it up to weekly in the new year, as the election approaches. I saw him the week before last. Wednesday night.'

'And did you notice anything unusual about his demeanour?'

'Nothing at all.'

'And his administration of the accounts?'

Lucy Titchfield shrugs. 'Fine. It's just basic bookkeeping. Ticking boxes.'

Ivan is about to pose another question, but Otto speaks before he can. 'Can I take you into my confidence, detective?'

'Of course.'

'As I said, I have no idea who killed Athol or why his body was dumped on our property. But I fear it's politically motivated. Country First is a new force in Australian politics, challenging the old order. It could be the start of some sort of smear campaign.'

chapter twelve

1993

A WEEK HAD PASSED SINCE THE HEARTWOODS FIRST DISCUSSED ALTERING THE family's succession plan, and Davis found himself embracing the decision more and more. There was a tingling in his limbs, a surge in his heart, an anticipation front of mind. He could barely wait for whatever was coming next, even as he immersed himself in the present.

He felt a growing awareness that this might be his last summer in the district—for who knew where he might head after his honours year?—so when Otto and Craven mentioned a party down by Lake Yuwonderie, a twenty-first, he was keen to go, to reconnect with some of his friends from primary school, the start of a long goodbye.

Davis drove in from Three Wells, alone in his sporty little Alfa Romeo, windows down, an old Rolling Stones compilation tape belting away, and it wasn't until he pulled into the car park by the lake that he realised he didn't know whose twenty-first it was. No matter, Otto and Craven were invited, had urged him to come along. He wished he'd thought of a present, but it was too late to worry about that now. He had brought a bottle of vodka; that would do. It was one of the things he loved about Yuwonderie: if someone had a party, all sorts of people were welcome to roll up, because everyone knew each other, or if they didn't, they knew someone who did; two degrees of separation, that was Yuwonderie.

The party was at a picnic area built by the Progress Association with free barbecues and a couple of open-air shelters, next to an artificial beach, river sand trucked in, with a pontoon fifty metres out into the lake. As Davis got out of his car he realised he was early. The sun was only thinking about setting, the Castle still bathed in golden light. Under one of the shelters a couple of families were still packing up their picnic dinner and herding children. It was not yet eight o'clock and most partygoers were still at home or drinking at the pub. There were only about half-a-dozen people setting up under the other shelter, yet he figured it would be awkward to turn around again. So he walked up, fully expecting to know at least one or two people. A boom box was set on low, pumping out the familiar sounds of The Church.

'Hi there,' said a young bloke, beer in a stubby holder. 'Want to give us a hand?'

'Sure. I'm Davis.'

'Good on you, Davis. Tezza.' And they shook hands.

Tezza led him to a ute. There was a firepit in the back, a forty-four-gallon drum sliced in half lengthways, welded to footings. It was well-used, covered in soot.

'Careful,' said Tezza. 'Get it all over you if you don't watch out.'

Davis could see his companion had come prepared. As well as the firepit, he had a load of wood, pre-cut and ready to go. Tezza clambered up into the back of the vehicle, and they eased out the drum, Davis on the ground, taking the weight. Tezza rested his end on the back of the tray, jumped down, and lifted it again. They carried it towards the shelter, Davis attentive, not wanting to mark his moleskins. Tezza was wearing board shorts, a t-shirt and sandals. Davis wondered if he was overdressed with his blue collared shirt and RMs.

'Where do you want this?' Tezza asked a pretty girl, her hair crimped blonde and her jawline ruler-straight, wearing cheap John Lennon sunglasses, a party affectation by the look of them. She directed them to a spot just down from the shelter, towards the water. 'Just there, I think,' she said, and Davis and Tezza complied.

'Hello,' she said to Davis, as he was examining his blackened hands. 'Have we met?'

He saw her properly then for the first time, realising he didn't know her. 'No. I'm Davis.' He gestured, demonstrating his inability to shake hands.

She frowned. 'You new around here?'

He smiled at that. 'No. Away at uni. Back for summer.'

'Well, thanks for helping,' she said, flicking her head towards the firepit, where Tezza was scrunching newspaper pages and placing them in the base of the drum.

'Happy to help,' said Davis. 'Whose party is it?'

'Mine,' said the girl. 'Nice of you to come.'

Davis didn't know where to look. 'I'm sorry. Some friends invited me, said it would be okay. But I'll leave if you like.'

'No. Stay. You've helped out.'

'Thank you,' he said. 'What's your name?'

'Stella. It's my twenty-first.'

'Well, happy birthday. I brought some vodka.'

'How sweet.' She laughed. 'Keep helping Tezza, will you?' And she turned and walked back towards the shelter.

—–

By the time the sun had set and the first stars were emerging in the eastern sky, the alcohol and music had begun to take hold, with the celebration growing to an amoebic whole, wobbling back and forth under its own internal forces, as more and more revellers arrived. Davis was feeling completely at home. Otto and Craven had finally turned up, well juiced, having eaten steaks at the pub, and the three of them had fallen into the old patterns of banter and bullshit. He told the story of his arrival, turning it into an amusing anecdote, playing up his embarrassment when he'd met Stella. 'You could have told me whose party it was,' he said.

'Don't fuck with her,' said Craven, slugging on his beer, raised eyebrows emphasising his teasing tone. 'Copper's daughter.' And they all laughed.

The night wore on, the fug of dope smoke wafting and the chug of booze flowing, the warmth of the night like an invisible rip, tugging people towards the water. Otto and Craven started stripping off, encouraging Davis to join them. He remembered Tezza's board shorts and wished he'd thought to wear something similar. Otto and Craven were naked, so he quickly undressed and followed them, running headlong into the water. Once in, they swam to the pontoon and climbed its ladder, dripping wet.

The pontoon was swaying, people were laughing and chatting excitedly, last remnants of the sunset gone, the Castle a black presence against a star-filled sky. There was a couple with glowstick necklaces, their faces turned Halloween-eerie. Otto was complaining about a lack of drink when above the western horizon lightning flared, unexpected, and then again, sheet lightning, illuminating the darkness, revealing their nudity. No one cared. Someone had had the foresight to swim a wine cask out, and people were passing it round, holding it up above their mouths, taking goon shots. Davis took his turn, the wine gushing, surprising him, almost choking, the wine warm and sweet. Feeling himself about to cough, he turned, spat it out, aiming for the water but spraying a couple sitting on the pontoon's edge, dangling their feet in the water.

'Watch it, fuck-knuckle,' hissed a bloke, voice disembodied.

'Shit, sorry,' said Davis, stepping towards them. And at that moment, lightning flared again, catching him in motion.

'Get your dick out of my face,' said the young woman, and her companion was scrambling to his feet.

'Get the fuck off,' he said.

Davis hesitated, and Otto took it upon himself to interject. 'He said he was sorry.'

'Just fuck off,' the unidentified youth repeated. 'Not your party, not your pontoon.'

'Pretty sure it is,' said Otto.

Davis reached out, took his arm. 'Come on, Otto. Let's go. My mistake.'

But it was too late: the youth had heard the inflammatory words, Otto's claim of ownership, compounded by Davis using his name. 'Oh, if it isn't the Seven, indulging in a bit of slumming. Their pontoon. Their lake. Their swinging dicks.'

'Fuck you,' said Otto.

And it was on, the youth a darkened blur, shoving, Otto swearing as he tumbled from the pontoon, the splash as he hit the water, the laughter at his expense.

'I'll have you cunts,' managed Craven, full of piss and wind, before being silenced by the cracking sound of something, perhaps the wine cask, connecting with his face.

'Enough,' said Davis, feeling a hand reaching for him, diving from the pontoon before it could get a hold. Surfacing. 'Craven, come on.' Another splash, another body entering the water, hopefully Craven escaping the pontoon.

'Craven?'

No reply. And a fear struck Davis. His friend hit. Drunk as a lord. Hit hard and now in the water.

'Craven?'

'Yeah. Here.'

Davis swivelled, the voice behind him.

'Oh, Craven, wherefore art thou?' came a mocking voice from the pontoon.

But Davis hardly heard, overcome with relief.

More lightning, the storm approaching fast, the flash enough for Davis, treading water, to see Otto's bare bum as he attempted to climb the ladder back onto the pontoon, only to be repelled by a foot to the chest and mocking laughter.

Davis could see Craven treading water, darkness on his face. Two strokes and Davis was next to him. 'You okay?'

'That cunt hit me.'

'My fault,' said Davis. 'Otto, let's get out of here.'

And they swam to shore. Davis was hoping to sneak onto dry ground, hoping the sound of the pontoon brawl had been drowned out by John Farnham singing 'You're the Voice'. But someone had taken their clothing. Otto was first out, and after a short and futile search, he was standing, legs spread, fuming, oblivious to his nakedness and the impression he was creating. 'Fucking bastards,' he fumed. A flash went off—not lightning, but a camera, accompanied by tittering. Otto swore at the giggling shadows, but Davis found himself laughing.

'Here.' A voice. It was Lucy, the girl from the irrigation company. She was holding a bundle in her hands: their clothing.

'Thanks,' said Davis.

'Bastards,' said Otto, reaching for his pants.

'It was just a joke,' said Lucy, sounding confused at Otto's anger, no doubt unaware of what had occurred out on the pontoon. She turned to where Davis was examining Craven's face. 'He okay? What happened?'

'Bit of a tiff. Nothing serious.' Back in the light coming from the shelter, he could see no blood, but his friend was breathing hard and looking a little dazed. Davis wondered if he had copped a mouthful of lake water.

Once they'd dressed, Otto left in a huff, leaving Craven sitting quietly by himself, still unsure of what had happened. Davis found himself with Lucy, talking about nothing very much. They were enjoying the sight of the approaching storm, now almost upon them, the Castle a black presence one moment then daylight bright the next. The wind dropped away to nothing, as if drawing breath before the onslaught.

The girl Stella appeared, talking directly to Davis. 'I think you should leave. Take your friend,' she said, looking across at Craven.

'It was a mistake,' said Lucy, coming to their defence.

'Just go,' Stella said to Davis, ignoring her. 'Everyone's had a skinful. So have you. Go before it happens again. Before someone calls my dad.' And she turned, decision made, and walked back to her friends.

'Bitch,' said Lucy.

'Her party, her call,' said Davis. 'You going to stay?'

'Not much left for me here,' said Lucy. 'Won't last much longer anyway. The rain will see to that.'

The first drops started to fall as they made their way to the car park. And as if to emphasise the point, a sheet of lightning engulfed the sky, much brighter, much closer.

'Wow!' said Lucy, and any further words were drowned out by a mighty peal of stereophonic thunder, starting at one horizon and rolling across the sky above them.

Davis looked back towards the shelter, people dancing, the boom box booming. Once the rain hit, everyone would be squeezed in together, sheltering from the storm. Stella was right: with them all trapped in there, it could get nasty. Time to leave.

A few cars along, Craven fired up his truck and headed off, having forgotten to turn on his headlights.

'It's going to bucket down. You want a lift?' Davis asked Lucy.

'I can walk.'

'Thought you said you lived on a farm?'

'It's only a kilometre or so.'

'You'll get soaked. Get in.'

She hesitated, and then the decision was made for her. Another massive sheet of lightning, blinding in its intensity, split the sky, dazzling his eyes, followed immediately by thunder so close and so loud he could feel it in his guts.

Lucy got in the car.

They were just out of the car park, heading towards the main street, raindrops smacking the windscreen, fat and heavy. The temperature dropped; Davis's ears popped. He got as far as Commonwealth Way, the wind whipping old newspapers and an empty drink can along the street.

'You can just drop me down the end there, past the fountain,' said Lucy.

'No way. Not in this.'

A dog ran out in front of the car, coming from who knew where, crazed by the thunder. Davis swerved, almost collecting the median strip, only just managing to correct and straighten the car.

'Holy shit,' said Lucy.

But before Davis could express his own relief, there was the flash of lights. Red and blue. The police.

Davis pulled over. The cop car came to a rest directly behind them.

'How much have you had to drink?' whispered Lucy.

'Dunno. Plenty.'

The cop reached the car. Davis wound down the window.

'What was that?' asked the cop.

'Dog ran in front of the car,' said Davis, keeping his diction clear and slow. 'I almost hit it.'

'It's illegal to swerve to avoid an animal. You know that?'

'Sorry. Reflex.'

The cop nodded, letting Davis know he was being assessed. 'You had anything to drink this evening, son?'

'One or two. Not too many.'

'Is that right?' And the cop smiled: not a smile of warmth or civility, but the opposite. 'Licence.'

Davis arched his back, retrieved his wallet, extracted the document.

The cop examined it, frowning. 'Davis Heartwood? Three Wells Station?'

'Yes, sir.'

The officer handed the licence back, crouched, looked through the open window at Lucy. More lightning, turning the cop into a horror film extra. 'Where you heading, Davis?'

'Dropping my friend off, then driving home.'

'Well, take good care. Drive slowly. If the storm hits, pull over. Let it pass.'

And the cop walked back to his car before Davis could thank him.

'Fuck. How lucky was that?' said Davis, breathing deep with relief. 'He didn't want to get drenched.'

That made Lucy laugh. 'Sure.'

The rain came in hard and fast and furious then. The wipers worked frenetically, but the blades were old and the headlights were weak. Davis pulled over.

'You have a girlfriend?' asked Lucy. 'Down there at university?'

'I did. She's gone back to the States now. She was on exchange.'

'Not coming back?'

'No.'

'You must miss her.'

'I guess.'

She leant across, kissed him quickly, before retreating again. 'I'm sorry you and your friends were treated so poorly.'

The non sequitur threw Davis, the gesture and the words. 'Reckon we deserved it.' And then, as an afterthought: 'Comes with the territory.'

She laughed again at that. 'You poor thing,' she said, gentle mockery in her voice.

Davis liked her laugh.

This time when she leant across and kissed him, he kissed her back. Her hand on his leg, the rain pounding on the roof. And then, as quickly as it started, a lull.

'We'd better go,' said Davis. 'While we can.'

The rain was building again as, following Lucy's directions, they reached the end of her driveway, down on the flatlands, among a group of smallholdings. 'Seriously, you can drop me here,' she said.

'Why would I do that?'

He took it carefully down the drive, slaloming past potholes filled with water, the sump on the low-slung car bottoming out more than once. Another burst of lightning, the storm receding but still close enough to illuminate a field of fruit trees, leaves scarce. And at the house, the headlights caught a derelict car up on blocks, a tractor with a deflated tyre. The house with a single bare bulb above the porch.

'Thank you so much,' said Lucy, kissing him again, then leaping out of the car, running through the rain to the door.

Davis was careful turning the Alfa, careful to avoid getting bogged. But he still saw the peeling paint of the house, the rusting water tank. And he couldn't ignore the trees, their branches spindly in this summer of plenty.

chapter thirteen

IVAN IS ALONE AT THE POLICE STATION, BACK FROM INTERVIEWING THE
Titchfields, and he's again feeling a type of pressure in his guts:
the need to build momentum. Nell's dropped him off and gone
on to the Progress Hotel to meet pathologist Blake Ness and crime
scene investigator Carole Nguyen. Blake can make his own way to
the morgue while Nell takes Carole to the irrigation canal where
Athol Hasluck's body was found. Ivan rings Plodder Packenham,
head of Homicide.

'Ivan. What news?'

'We spoke to Otto Titchfield.'

'And?'

'Athol Hasluck's body was found on his property.'

'Tell me something I don't know.'

'Hasluck was mired in debt. Not good for an accountant. He
did the books for the local branch of Titchfield's political party,
Country First, and a fundraising body, the Watermen's Foundation.'

Ivan can hear Plodder breathing, but it's a moment before his boss replies. 'So what's the theory? Hasluck ripped him off, so Titchfield killed him?'

'Can't ignore the possibility.'

'Why you telling me?'

'Could get sensitive.'

'No shit.' A sigh down the line. 'What do you want, Ivan?'

'A forensic accountant to go through Athol's books. Maybe get someone in from the Fraud Squad.'

'No.'

The immediacy of the response and its brevity surprises Ivan. 'Any particular reason?'

'You know what Watermen's is, Ivan?'

'A fundraising body. Works at arms-length from Titchfield and Country First. That's what they told me.'

'It doesn't just raise donations; it disguises them. That's the whole purpose. All the major parties run them. The Electoral Commission calls them associated entities—a polite term for a dubious system. Nevertheless, we can't have police rummaging through the accounts of a political slush fund without good reason. The whole political establishment would be screaming blue murder, not just Country First.'

'So what are you saying? Ignore it?'

'Of course not. But before we go down that route, you'll need evidence, not just suspicion. Needs to be bulletproof. With warrants, by the book. And even then, you'll have to consider if it's worth the grief.' Plodder gives it a beat. 'We don't have many job vacancies west of Dubbo.'

'There's an alternative.'

Plodder responds with a grim laugh. 'Do I need to know?'

'Covering my arse, boss. I like it in Dubbo.'

'Smart lad.' Another laugh. 'Let's hear it.'

'Athol had an assistant, Alice Figtree. Authorised by him and his clients to work the accounts. She's the one who discovered his debts.'

There is a long moment as Plodder calculates the implications. 'Okay. But play it close. And if she turns up something more substantial, then we'll still need to go through proper channels.'

'Thanks, boss.'

'Anything else?'

'Budget is a little tight.'

'Not anymore,' says Plodder. 'Not for this. Spend what you need. If Titchfield is implicated, you need to nail him before he can muster political support.'

'I've asked Senior Constable Nackangara to come down from Dubbo to help.'

'Kevin? Good idea.'

'I've requested police divers. Thought they might have come in today with Carole Nguyen.'

'Leave it with me. They're up on the Hawkesbury. Murder-suicide. Car in the river. Need to recover the bodies before they can move on.'

'Understood,' says Ivan. 'Any sign of media interest in what's happening here?'

'A few hounds sniffing. I'm doing my best to put them off, giving them plenty of access to the Hawkesbury.'

After the calls ends, Ivan finds Constable Simmonds downstairs at a desk in the squad room, headphones on, glasses on, concentrating so hard on the screens in front of her that she doesn't notice his approach. Ivan can see what's captivating her: low-res images from CCTV cameras.

'Anything?' he asks.

She doesn't respond.

He taps her on the shoulder, and she jumps with surprise.

'Jesus. You gave me a fright,' she says, removing her headphones.

'Sorry,' says Ivan. 'What have you got?'

'Found him,' says the constable. She pulls up a file, plays it. It's a wide-angle view of a street, from a camera mounted inside the window of a shopfront. 'Electrical goods store. McLean Street. Across the way from Athol Hasluck's office.' She spools through. 'Here. Saturday night.' The picture is clear, a higher resolution than most CCTV and in colour, although the night-time lighting renders it close to monochrome. The frame rate is low, making any movement jerky. A car passes through the frame like a ghost. Simmonds points to the screen. A tiny figure enters the frame from the left on the far side of the road, the wide-angle lens making him too small to identify. But it looks like a man to Ivan, a dark silhouette. The figure stops at Athol's business, opens the door with a key and enters. A light goes on, and a few moments later another light appears upstairs. 'Athol's office,' says Simmonds, pride in her voice.

'What time?' asks Ivan.

'Three minutes past eight, Saturday night.'

That matches what Jacinta Hasluck told them. Ivan recalls Jane Seabridge's estimate: time of death between eight pm Saturday night and four am Sunday morning. He looks back at the image on the screen: no movement, just the light burning in the upstairs window. Athol Hasluck, with under eight hours to live. 'You have him leaving?'

'No.'

'Anyone else entering?'

'No.'

'The light?'

'Still on when dawn comes.' She looks up at Ivan. 'I'm searching other cameras, seeing what else I can find.'

'Thank you—excellent job,' he says and leaves her to it.

It takes just a few minutes to walk to McLean Street. He sees the electrical goods store, heads over to it, can see the camera up inside the window, peering out through Christmas tinsel. He turns back, sees what the camera would see: an everyday street, people going about their business.

He walks across to Athol's workplace. The police tape is still there, forbidding entry. But it's not the front entry Ivan has come to see. He walks further along the street, past the internet cafe, to a laneway running the length of the block behind Commonwealth Way. He walks down it, finds a small dead-end alley leading back in the direction of the main street. Three doors along, Athol's building is easily identified by more crime scene tape. There's a flight of concrete stairs leading up to a rear entry. They are cordoned off by tape, and Ivan can see where the railing has been dusted for fingerprints. McTosh and his team, not waiting for Carole Nguyen, knowing the stairs are exposed to the weather. More good work. Ivan doesn't bother going any further; he doesn't have to. This is how Hasluck left, either alone or with his killer, still alive or already dead.

Ivan looks about him. There are no signs of CCTV: probably not in the laneway, certainly not in this alley. He walks along to the end, to a gate at the back of one of the main street shops and a sign: DELIVERIES—THE LONE DOG CAFÉ. There's a phone number; Ivan takes a photo, just in case he needs it in future. He looks around, and there, tucked into the shelter of an alcove in the wall, just outside the gate, is a crude bed made from cardboard boxes, together with a few empty bottles and scattered takeaway containers. A doss spot for the homeless, abandoned now. He takes a closer look, finds an empty carton of flavoured milk. The use-by date is today. He sniffs at it, the smell faintly curdled, any residual liquid evaporated.

Back on Commonwealth Way, prosperous and brimming with civic pride, the idea of Yuwonderie harbouring a homeless population seems unlikely, but Ivan isn't fooled. The homeless are everywhere: in the cities, in the big towns, in the smallest hamlet. Yuwonderie might present itself as different, but there's no escaping high rents and low welfare.

He walks to the Lone Dog Café. The cafe is shut, but when he peers through the window, he sees movement. He taps on the glass.

'We're shut, mate,' says the man with the grey mutton-chops, opening the door just a crack.

Ivan flashes his badge. *Police,* the man informs himself and opens the door further, his face furrowed. 'Yes?'

'Can I come in? Just a few questions.'

The man acquiesces, standing aside to let Ivan enter. *Won't take long,* Ivan overhears the man whispering to himself.

Ivan explains that he's investigating the murder of Athol Hasluck. 'Your back entrance opens onto an alleyway. You don't have security cameras, do you?'

The man shakes his head.

'There are signs of someone sleeping rough out there. Any idea who?'

Again, the man shakes his head. *Sleeping rough?* he says to himself before clearly addressing Ivan. 'If they are, I haven't seen them.'

'What about the old geezer who was busking a bit further up the street this morning? You think he might doss out there?'

'Bert Kippax? Not sure he'd be sleeping rough.'

'He might know who does sleep there, though,' Ivan says.

'Could do at that,' says the man. 'Nice enough bloke when he's not blotto. One of yours.'

'Sorry?'

'Used to be the town cop. Before the sauce got hold of him.'

'What happened?'

'Don't know,' the owner says. 'Before my time.' And to himself: *They say he lost his daughter.*

— —

Ivan meets Blake Ness in the bistro at the Coachman's Arms. Nell is still with Carole Nguyen; she's texted, saying they've moved on from the canal, are now meticulously searching Athol's practice. Ivan has replied, suggesting they meet him and Blake at the pub for dinner when they're done. Blake orders some chips to go with his schooner to 'keep the wolf from the door' and offers to share them with Ivan. They taste hot and salty and good with Ivan's low alcohol beer.

'I've examined Athol Hasluck,' says Blake, popping a chip into his mouth. 'Opened him up, had a thorough look. Hope you didn't want to be there.'

'No need for that,' says Ivan. 'I trust you.'

'Funny. All you coppers say that.' The pathologist drops the banter, becomes serious. 'Dr Seabridge was quite thorough with her initial measurements. She sent them through, and I studied them on the way down. I can narrow the time of death to two hours either side of midnight, Saturday night going into Sunday morning. Also, he was definitely dead before he went in the water.' Blake has an open expression, as if inviting inquiry.

'And?'

'He'd imbibed alcohol and painkillers. Most probably oxycodone. Quite a bit.'

'Oxycodone? He'd need a prescription, right?'

'Certainly would. Opioid.'

'And it's pretty heavy-duty.'

'Yes. A step up from codeine. Mixing it with alcohol like that would make him drowsy, at the very least. People can die from that combination. Rock stars do.'

'I'll check with his wife or doctor. See if he had a script.'

Blake nods. 'Hard to say, but it's possible he had lost conscious-ness when he was killed. Or was semiconscious.'

'But the drugs and alcohol didn't kill him?'

'No. He was still alive when the knife went into his heart. No accident about that.'

'The electrocution. Before or after death?'

'Oh, before.' Blake sighs. 'Can't be definitive, but I'd say electrocuted then stabbed to death.'

'And the other burns? On the thighs, the genitals?'

'Intriguing. Shortly before his death, I'd say. Between a few minutes and up to an hour or so. I think Dr Seabridge was right. Hot metal. Wires. White-hot, some red-hot. Like being branded.'

'Is it possible he was drugged with alcohol and oxy, then tortured? Someone trying to extract information?'

Blake frowns. 'Pretty amateurish way to go about it. Doesn't make much sense to give painkillers to someone you're inflicting pain upon. He'd be befuddled, for sure, but there are much better drugs around to get people talking. Rohypnol, that sort of thing.'

Ivan takes this on board. 'Anything else I should know about the timing?'

Blake picks up a chip, stares at it without seeing it. 'The drugs and alcohol were well metabolised. Been in his system for at least two hours. Some alcohol still in the gut, but not much. The burn marks, the minor ones, were definitely administered while he was alive. The electricity and the knife, more or less simultaneous.'

'You say knife?'

'Yes—a thin one. Very sharp. Cutting edge on one side.'

'Like a filleting knife?'

'Just so.'

'Not a switchblade? Or a stiletto?'

'No. They typically have double edges.'

'Length?'

'Eighteen centimetres. If the killer drove it all the way to the hilt.'

Ivan considers that, the graphic nature of the killing. 'A knife like that—fairly commonplace?'

'Yes, unfortunately. A kitchen knife, or a fisherman's knife.'

'And the electrocution: could a domestic supply do that sort of damage?'

'Possibly. Perhaps three-phase.' Blake answers while watching a woman pass by carrying a dessert from the bistro, then looks down at his near empty plate of chips as if making an unfavourable comparison. 'An electric shock like that contracts the muscles quite violently. Touch an exposed wire with the back of your hand and you get repulsed. But if you're grasping the wire, the muscle contraction tightens your grip. By the look of it, he was holding a wire or a cable or a railing or whatever with both hands. Huge shock. Blacks out, power disconnected, knife finishes him. That's perhaps the most likely scenario.'

Blake is looking over Ivan's shoulder. Ivan thinks the pathologist has recognised someone, but when he turns to look, all he can see is the bistro counter and the desserts in a display case.

Blake's attention returns to Ivan. 'Also, he was barefoot in the canal.'

'Doesn't mean he was like that when he died, does it?'

'I think it might. I couldn't detect any foreign material. That amount of electricity, those sorts of burns. Socks, shoes, whatever would have melted or burnt, left a residue.'

'Even after submersion?'

'Yes. The canal water isn't flowing. Not strongly.'

'And the significance?'

'Why would he be barefoot? You see, without shoes, if he was standing on a conductive surface, like metal or a wet floor, the current would flow that much more easily.'

'So not accidental?'

'That's for you to determine. The knifing was definitely deliberate.'

The chips are gone and the men are onto another beer by the time Nell and Carole arrive. Just the presence of Carole and Blake instils confidence into Ivan: they are the best in the business, real team players, and they've solved tough cases together in the past.

After Nell has sorted drinks and they're seated, Blake repeats his findings from the autopsy for the benefit of the two women.

'I wish I had as much to contribute,' says Carole. 'There wasn't a lot to see out at the canal, certainly nothing to suggest that Athol Hasluck died there. I'll go back out tonight before the moon rises and search for traces of blood with Luminol, but I don't expect to find much. There had been some foot traffic inside the taped-off zone: scuff marks, nothing distinguishable. Some tyre marks— again, nothing identifiable. My working theory is that he wasn't killed there but at some unknown location. Two people drove his body there, carried him to the canal in some sort of covering—a tarp or blanket or plastic sheet—and lowered him into the canal.'

'What about his office?' asks Ivan.

'No signs of blood stains, although I'll give it the once-over with Luminol after I get back from the canal. But a stabbing like that, there would be a lot of blood. I would have found something. And nothing to explain the burn marks or the electrocution.'

'So he didn't die there and he wasn't tortured there,' says Ivan, a statement not a question.

'I'd agree with that. There was no sign of a forced entry, no sign of a struggle, no sign anything was taken.'

'So nothing of any use?' asks Ivan, unable to keep the disappointment from his voice.

'Early days,' says Carole. 'I've lifted plenty of prints, got a variety of fibres, and there are the prints the locals gathered outside the back entrance and on the gate by the canal. Plenty to get on with.'

'I had a look round the back of Athol's,' says Ivan. 'There are signs someone has been sleeping rough at the end of the alley. It's a long shot, but maybe they saw something. I'll check it out with McTosh and his team; see if they can find out who uses that spot.'

Nell nods slowly, turns to Carole. 'You say no forced entry. You think Athol knew his killers? Maybe he invited them there.'

Carole offers up a half-smile. 'He opened the door.'

chapter fourteen

December 1913

Dearest Mother,

It has happened so quickly. I am in love. There, I have written it, like casting a dream and finding it suddenly real. And now I shall place this paper in the envelope that sits beside me, lick the stamp and take it with the other mail, walk the long track to the road and leave it there for collection. It shall sit there awaiting dispatch, no different in appearance from any other of the letters of duty and mundanity that I have transcribed for Mrs Titchfield these past three months, the inhabitants of Castle View ignorant of what it is I have committed to paper. It looks no different from my previous weekly missives to you, and yet these words are different, so very different. For Jack Marney is different. And so this envelope, so light in the hand, carries within it the weight of my world.

Let me recount it for you, Mother, this waking dream of mine, this unfolding novel of a life.

We went to Yanco, Horace and Elaine and I, staying over at a hotel. A real hotel, with chandeliers and a dining room and ice for the drinks. I shared a room with Elaine, as her maid. The occasion was a cricket match, and Horace was down for the district team. He wasn't at all interested in the contest, but he realised that it was the perfect opportunity to promote his scheme to his teammates. Yanco is the property of the famous irrigationist Sir Samuel McCaughey, and it is upon his private scheme that the plan for the Murrumbidgee Irrigation Area scheme is based.

We visited his house, a most grand affair, truly like something from an English novel, with gardens so green and wide they could be a park.

I have little understanding of cricket, except that it goes for a very long time, with nothing much happening for extended periods until, well past the point when the attention of even the most ardent observer has wandered into conversation and conviviality, and the polite applause has dried up, a tremendous cry goes out and all the players are leaping about shaking hands and slapping each other on the back. I understood there were two teams, one from north of the river and one from the southern banks. I was told that the team with the most runs would be the winner, but only if there was enough time to secure a result. I thought to ask more, but then refrained. I am mindful that in such company, even with the support of Elaine, my words are rationed and my entitlement to questions even more severely so, and I was not inclined to waste them on cricket.

Besides, I was not able to keep my eyes on the game—or not on the ball, a shiny thing of red leather. For I found my attention drawn again and again to Jack. He looked so dashing in his white clothes, his trousers secured not with the plaited belt of his visit to Castle View but with a blue sash, matching his cotton necker-chief. He waved to me once, but I was too embarrassed among that company of ladies and old men to wave back. At bat, he hit the ball to the rope—a 'boundary', I was told—and I fear I cheered a little too loudly. I didn't see him after the game; the men retired to drink beer and smoke their pipes. I am told it was an excellent contest and closely fought, but I am taking the word of others in that regard.

While the men celebrated, Elaine and I took the carriage and retired to our hotel, for that night there was to be a grand dance to mark the harvest. It was called a bachelors' and spinsters' ball and was for all the eligible young people of the district, and I was to help Elaine to ready herself. Of course, I had no expectations of attending; I was not invited and I could not afford it. So imagine my surprise when Elaine insisted that I should accompany her as her guest. She said the ball wasn't just for people of property, that I could come as her friend. Her mother wasn't with us, and Horace was preoccupied with his lobbying and machinations. And if he should challenge my right, we would simply say that I was there as Elaine's companion, that we wanted to relieve him of his filial obligation to play chaperone, so that he might better advance his proposals. And so I agreed; how could I not?

Elaine looked beautiful, like an angel made corporeal. She had a new dress of fine silk in a modern style. Clearly, she had planned this all ahead of time, for she had packed an old dress of hers for me and had even had it altered so that it might fit, me not being as fine-boned as her. I brushed her hair, and she brushed mine, chat-ting and laughing and conspiring, like we were sisters.

'What an impression we shall make,' Elaine said. 'The fair and the dark. Like complementary twins.'

The dance was held outside, in the gardens of the great house at Yanco. Sir Samuel himself was there, overseeing it like a patron saint. There was the largest tent I have ever seen—a marquee, they called it—with a specially laid floor of polished wood and a band. Chinese lanterns hung from the trees and there were electric globes strung about, Yanco boasting its own power station down by the river. It was one of those perfectly still summer evenings, where the heat has drained but the warmth remains. Away from the lights, the whole spread of the stars was there, so clear that one might touch them. I felt myself Cinderella; I felt myself transported.

Jack asked me to dance. Walked straight up to us, barely taking his eyes from me long enough to acknowledge Elaine. She greeted him warmly, but then made some excuse or other—someone she had spotted in the crowd with whom she really must discuss some matter of urgency. I told Jack I knew less about dancing than I did about cricket, but he said it didn't matter in the least, that all I needed was to follow where he led.

I wonder if it was the same for you, Mother, when you first met Father, him a white man, you with your blended blood and dark complexion. Did it matter more in those times? Were people more predisposed to judgement? If they were on this night, I was not aware of it. How could I have been? For I only had eyes for him and, I believe, he for me.

The first dances were group efforts, ensembles. I didn't know the steps, and I was becoming more and more embarrassed with each new partner, until I came back to Jack and he smiled so broadly that I determined to keep going, that all the awkwardness was worth it to see that smile. How I wished I could dance, so as to do him proud. I have my accomplishments. Reading, writing, arithmetic, yes. A little philosophy. My ability to read the weather, to trap a fish or skin a rabbit, is as valued here as everywhere in the country, but at a ball you are expected to leave all that behind, to be refined. I did my best. My tongue is quick and my mind alive; I can trade quips and observations, although I am lost at gossip. And, I fear, at dancing.

The music changed in a way I didn't perceive at first, and some people left the floor and others joined it. Around me the dancers were moving as couples. 'A waltz,' said Jack, and I froze. He told me again to follow his steps. I tried, but it was terrible. And so, sensing how truly inadequate I was, he simply lifted me, the strength in his arms undeniable, until my feet were only brushing the floor, no more. I felt I was gliding, flying in time with the music. But to gain the necessary leverage, he was required to hold me close. I can still feel him, smell him, hear his laughter and joy. For that waltz and another, we circled in our own private orbit.

At the end of the second waltz he offered to get me punch. I was standing there, breathless. And then the foulness. A matron descended upon me, and at her back I could see Augustine Chaulker, scowling, and next to him Horace, fidgeting and looking out of sorts.

'A word, my dear,' said the shrivelled witch. 'Outside.'

Her voice brooked no argument. I followed her from the tent.

Once separated from the crowd, she launched straight in. 'You are not here to dance. You are not a lady of the district. Your type is not welcome here.'

I opened my mouth to protest, but no words came.

'Leave,' said the shrew, pointing off into the darkness. 'Now.'

I was so shocked; I didn't know what to do. I went to re-enter the tent, but she stepped into my path, pointing once again. 'That way.'

And what did I do? I felt so shattered, I simply followed her command, Icarus in a ball gown.

I had no idea where I should go. Not back to our room at the hotel, for Elaine had the key. I could not enter the bar there, an unaccompanied girl, and where else could I go in my finery? It mocked me now, that beautiful dress.

I thought then that perhaps there might be a camp by the river where I might shelter. I knew all I had to do was mention your name, or your mother's, tell them mine, and I would be accepted and safe.

But before I could decide, Jack found me. His eyes were full of pain. 'I am so sorry,' he said. 'I should not have put you through that.'

That confused me, for I couldn't see how any of this was his fault, and I said so.

He smiled that lovely smile of his. 'You really are sweet,' he said. And I could hear in his voice that he was genuine.

He walked me back towards the ball. He had a quiet anger about him, a determination, and wanted us to return to the dance, declaring that he would stand by me, stare them down. But I didn't want to embarrass Elaine or jeopardise Horace's advocacy. And so I convinced him to desist. He left me there for a moment, re-entered the tent for long enough to tell Elaine I was safe, and then joined me once again.

The ball went for some hours more, and all that time we sat together in the warmth of the evening, and the anger went out of him and the despair left me. He told me of his life droving, and I recounted mine at the mission. And for all the wonder of that ball, the Chinese lanterns and the food and the dresses and the fine orchestra with their wonderful tunes, I would not have gone back into the marquee for a minute, so complete were those hours outside. We could hear the music, and it was as if the band played just for us; when we saw a shooting star, it was as if it was sent for us and us alone. When a bell rang for food, Jack went inside, loaded two plates and returned to me. By the end of the evening, we were holding hands. When the others finally emerged, before they could see us sitting off to one side in the shadows, he leant over and he kissed me. Just the once, but it felt as if it went forever.

And so you have it, the evening on which my life left one course and embarked on a new one.

Your dutiful and happy daughter,
Bessie

chapter fifteen

IVAN HEADS OUT FOR HIS MORNING JOG, PASSING THROUGH THE TOWN, THROUGH the wetlands, sun glancing off water, ducks afloat in the low mist, to the base of the rocky outcrop, the Castle, towering above him. Getting up it will be a challenge, but the reward will be the view. From the top, he will be able to survey the town, check it against the internal map he's been sketching in his mind. The idea appeals to him, superimposing the investigation onto the landscape.

Jogging over a wooden footbridge, he finds a trail winding around the base of the hill. He follows as it passes behind a few outlying houses and then heads into bushland, box scrub. There is a sign, letters carved in wood. SUMMIT. 45 MINUTES. MEDIUM DIFFICULTY. He glances at his watch. Still before seven. The sign will be a conservative estimate, he knows that. Walking, it will be more like thirty minutes. Running, he should be able to cut that in half. He speeds up, setting a punishing pace. That's what he needs: running hard enough to hurt. Hard enough to push the memory of this morning's online article from his mind: OZ WAR CRIM SET

FREE. Just a small story, six sentences, cutting like a knife. He runs faster.

The trail is well-maintained at its steepest, with stairs of treated wooden sleepers cut into the ascent. He lifts the tempo, so that his thighs are on fire, his calves threatening to cramp. He gets to a flatter section, tries to accelerate, but there is erosion here, the trail not stable. His foot slips on gravel; he starts to fall, grabs at a tree branch. It snaps and he tumbles, nothing serious, breaking the impact with his hands. He lies for a moment, panting. Then he stands, brushes the dirt from his palms. No harm done. Nevertheless, he needs to take it easier, walking where necessary, jogging where safe. Concentrate on the job at hand; there is nothing he can do about his father.

He starts walking as the gradient increases again. He must be three-quarters of the way up. There's a bench here, with a view out over the town, even better than he expected. Like SimCity, he thinks, all laid out in front of him. Above him, there is a sheer cliff of rock. Maybe thirty metres. The summit promises an even grander panorama.

From the small lookout, the trail folds back through the bush, away from the view of the town, leading to the far side of the hill, the gentler slope. Here it joins an access road. Off to one side he sees the top of a windmill, blades slowly revolving as it picks up the first of the morning breeze, and a sign: AIR STILLS OF AUSTRALIA. There's a locked gate, a logo depicting a smiling water drop.

He runs up the road to the summit. There's a mobile phone tower beside a service hut, both encircled by a fence topped with barbed wire. TELSTRA says one sign, letters in black, a second, letters in red: AUTHORISED ENTRY ONLY—TRESPASSERS PROSECUTED.

A few metres further along is another fence, another shed, a tower supporting microwave dishes and more signs: DEPARTMENT OF COMMUNICATIONS and VIDEO SURVEILLANCE. Sure enough, up on the tower, a serious-looking camera.

Ivan continues past the towers to the end of the road, finding a walking track marked by a vandalised walkers cairn, and on to a lookout. He's surprised to see a young man sitting there. Benedict Bright. Eggs.

'You looking for me?' asks the youth, turning around at the sound of his approach.

'No. Just running. You?'

'Couldn't sleep. I like it here.'

Ivan sits next to the boy, observing to himself that seven twenty is indeed an early hour for a teenager. The bruising around the youth's face appears worse if anything, no longer a uniform blue but breaking down into yellows and reds and purples. 'Nice view.'

'I thought he was a sack,' says Eggs.

Ivan doesn't need to ask what he's referring to. 'Did you know him? The victim?'

'No.'

Ivan studies the lad, who's frowning, staring out at the town, expression troubled. 'You okay?' asks Ivan.

The lad meets his gaze. 'Just a bit freaked out, you know. Finding him like that.'

'Don't take it to heart. You blokes did the right thing, alerting the police, giving us every chance of finding the killer.'

'So it's true—he was murdered?'

'We think so, yes.'

'Shit.'

Ivan glances at his watch. The ascent took longer than he'd anticipated and he needs to get going, but he feels uncomfortable leaving Eggs alone. 'Tell you what, while we're up here, could you do me a favour?'

'What?'

Ivan gestures towards the town. 'Explain it to me. Who owns what. Which way the water flows.'

The lad examines him intensely and then, from nowhere, comes a smile. 'Which way the money flows?'

Ivan smiles back. 'That could be even more useful.'

'Always is.' The smile grows. Eggs points towards the horizon. 'That way's north. See the line of trees, that grey-green line? That's the river. The Murrumbidgee. That's where the water comes from. And the money. Everything, really.'

'So no farming without irrigation?'

'Yeah, there is. Dryland farming, but mostly grazing on the non-irrigated land. Property worth a fraction of the irrigated land.' He stands, points to the south. 'Here, you can see it.' Sure enough, the delineation is clear between the verdant green of the irrigation district and the bleached paddocks surrounding it. The scheme itself is shaped something like an inverted funnel: narrow where it leaves the Murrumbidgee, widening as smaller canals branch out either side, until the funnel leads into a large, vaguely circular swelling of green. At the centre, the town itself, on a low ridge, the main street straddling two hills.

Eggs points out the canals, explaining the flow of the water, and the properties lining their banks, identifying the different crops on the green squares surrounding the town and stretching to the river. He indicates some of the town's more prominent buildings.

'Very comprehensive,' says Ivan. 'Your family—you're farmers?'

'Not anymore. My dad went broke years ago and shot through. Mum's latest boyfriend is a tradie.' Eggs grimaces, a gesture of helplessness. 'We've still got a little bush block down by the river.' He points off to the north-west, away from the scheme. 'Belongs to my mum. She'd sell it, but it's not worth anything. Too scrubby, too flood-prone.'

'Pity,' says Ivan.

'No. I like it there.'

'Get away from your mum's partner?'

Eggs doesn't speak, but Ivan sees the affirmation in his eyes.

He changes the subject. 'What's the big place back that way?' Ivan points to a patch of green to the south-west, also well outside the boundaries of the scheme, a large house set amid a small forest.

'Three Wells Station. Owned by the Heartwoods. One of the Seven. Wrong side of the Spur.'

'The Spur?'

'See it? Running down off the Castle?' Eggs points it out: an elevated ridge, an extension of the Castle reaching south from the base of the outcrop, not high enough to be called hills but high enough to stop the flow of water. To the east, the land is green, irrigated and tamed, to the west it's brown and wild.

'The boundary of the scheme,' says Ivan. 'Water can't get over it.'

'Correct.'

Ivan surveys the panorama, trying to commit it to memory. 'So, the Seven, point them out for me.'

'Too easy.' And the boy does. The Heartwoods at Three Wells Station are outliers. The other families all own large houses within the irrigation district itself: the Titchfields, straddling the canal where the body was found, the Allsops, the McLeans, the Haslucks, the Horshams and the Blaxlands.

'Impressive. You know them by heart. Where they live.'

'Everyone does.'

'Am I right: the Seven own more than half the land?'

'Yeah, and probably more water than land.'

Ivan frowns. 'That's possible?'

'Sure. Water ownership and land ownership are two separate things. There are people who own water without owning any land at all. Hedge funds, day traders, speculators. Like the stock market, or derivatives, or a casino.'

'Sounds like you've studied this.'

'I want to go to uni. Do economics.'

'Not a farmer then?'

'No way.'

Ivan turns back to the view. 'What does the water trading mean for the farmers? The small landholders who actually use it to grow things?'

'On average, they probably end up paying more for water than they otherwise would.'

Ivan scrutinises the landscape. Athol Hasluck had been losing money when he died. Or siphoning it off, funnelling it else-where. He realises the aspiring university student might be more useful than he first thought. 'So you make money in Yuwonderie through irrigation and water trading—does that sum up the town's economy?'

'That's the base of the financial pyramid. All the other stuff, real estate and retailing, the stock and station agents, the schools, the engineering companies, the doctors and lawyers and the hospital, all the rest is built on that foundation. The Seven own a lot of that base, but they own some of the residential and commercial property too. And they control the other big money-spinner as well: Yuwonderie Wholesalers.'

'What's that?'

Eggs points. 'See that huge complex down by the railway line?'

Ivan can. There are trucks coming and going like Matchbox cars from a warehouse boasting the scale of an oversized aircraft hangar. 'It's massive.'

'It is. Pretty much a monopoly. All the stuff that gets grown here has to get to market. So back in the day, all the irrigators got together and set up a co-op. Common story. It sells in bulk—the fruit and veg to the markets in Melbourne; a bit through to Sydney if the prices are right. Off to Leeton with the rice for processing. Wine grapes are sorted and sold to different wineries. Flowers and some high-end horticulture air-freighted.'

'It all goes through the Yuwonderie Wholesalers?'

'Pretty much. There's no compulsion. Anyone can sell to anyone else. But a smallholder selling to Coles or Woolies is ripe for the plucking, so they stick with the Wholesalers. The place has its own trucks, the lot. Vertical integration.'

'So everyone's happy then?' asks Ivan.

Eggs laughs out loud, the first time. 'Can tell you're from the city.'

'What do you mean?'

'Farmers are never happy.'

'Not even the Seven?'

The lad snorts at that. 'Well, they're not really farmers, are they? More like aristocrats. Or robber barons.'

'What about you? What do you think of the Wholesalers?'

Eggs shrugs. 'Makes sense to me. Cut out the middlemen, more money for all the farmers. Provided it's managed right.' He smiles. 'I've been working there three years now: after school, weekend shifts. Saving for uni. Saving to get away. So I can't complain.'

'When do you plan to leave?'

'A couple of weeks. The new year. Get to Melbourne well before uni starts. Get a job, find somewhere to live.'

'You've decided then?'

'Nothing keeping me here.'

———

Running back down the trail, Ivan stops at the lookout with the bench and surveys the town once more, seeing it in an entirely different light. No longer SimCity, more a medieval city-state, with the homesteads of the Seven like castles and the houses of the small landholders like those of vassals.

He's glad that Eggs is getting out, getting away from the town, getting away from a violent home. And all the way back down the Castle he feels the weight of his own childhood heavy on his shoulders, wondering if the others have seen the news report: his father in prison in The Hague but not for much longer.

chapter sixteen

1993

IN THE BASEMENT ROOM AT THE YUWONDERIE IRRIGATION SCHEME COMPANY, Davis made halting progress. The sunbeams streaming down through the lightwells seemed to come from far above, a celestial illumination of his newfound freedom. Most of the records, Davis soon learnt, were purely transactional, records of services rendered and invoices paid and, later, once the scheme was beginning to operate, of water supplied and receipts for payment. All important in their time, no doubt, but of little use to a budding historian: they told no story.

The one document of interest that Davis secured early on was the initial constitution of the company, or at least the company that gave birth to the scheme: the South Murrumbidgee Irrigation Company. It gave him two valuable pieces of information: the date the company was legally incorporated—1 May 1914—and a list of shareholders, the founding families: Titchfield, Allsop, Pratt, Hasluck, Horsham, Heartwood, Chaulker, Marney and Blaxland.

It sparked his interest. Nine founding families, not the seven he knew so well, with no mention of the McLeans. And what had happened to the other three? He'd never heard of the Pratts and the Chaulkers, and the only Marney he knew was old Joe, who'd worked on their property as a roo shooter and rabbit trapper.

He studied the document further. Each of the families bought equal shares for two hundred pounds apiece. The stated purpose of the South Murrumbidgee Irrigation Company was not to build the scheme or to make money but 'to determine the viability of a privately developed and operated system of irrigation and drainage south of the Murrumbidgee River downstream from Yanco. This analysis should encompass engineering and financial structures, as well as assessing political support.'

It wasn't much, but it gave him his first piece of primary source information and the hint of a narrative. He could imagine the southern graziers watching with interest and envy the development of the government-run MIA north of the river and taking the initiative, setting up their own company. He was intrigued by the three challenges identified: engineering, financial and political. In his mind he was already ranking them: political first, financial second, engineering last, for he sensed the political story would be the most compelling. He felt a pulse of excitement. As far as he was aware, there was no similar thesis on the subject, not at honours level nor a PhD. He'd found his starting point.

Lucy was attentive. She visited frequently from her office along the basement corridor, and their relationship, born in the storm of the lakeside party, blossomed. They took to eating lunch together. To flirting. To stealing kisses. This was different from his flings at college, falling into bed at the end of a drunken night. One of those had then developed into a longer relationship with his American girlfriend, but this was something new. Davis enjoyed the slow pace of it.

At lunch one day, as they sat across from each other at a park table, they laughed once again about the night of the party, when the storm had thrust them together. He recalled how he'd dropped her at her house, and he mentioned the condition of her family's farm: the trees without leaves or fruit, the grass long.

Lucy grimaced. 'Let's not talk about that,' she said. 'It's embarrassing.'

That sparked his curiosity. 'Why?'

'Leave it, Davis. It doesn't concern us.'

He frowned. The researcher in him was curious. 'I can't take any credit for the success of Three Wells Station. It's entirely the work of my grandfather and his forebears, not me. So if that has nothing to do with me, I can't see why the condition of yours should reflect on you.'

'Oh really?' And there was a little fire in her voice, as if he had hit a nerve. 'So you take no pride in the achievements of your family?'

'I guess I do.'

'Then I can feel disappointment in mine.'

He saw her point, silently upbraiding himself for his insensitivity, bringing up Three Wells Station, of all things, as a tool for comparison.

He reached across the table, took her hand. 'If you ever do want to talk about it, I'm here.'

She pushed his hand away and glared at him. 'I'd better get back to work.'

— —

It was Craven who explained, a couple of days later at the Coachman's Arms. It was steak night, as it was twice a week, and Davis, Otto and Craven had decided to eat together. Otto was chiacking him about the research project, but Craven seemed more interested.

'It's a great idea,' said Craven. 'I'll be keen to see what you find out.'

'Why?' said Otto. 'It's a hundred years ago. Who gives a shit?'

'Seventy-five,' said Davis. 'And it's interesting.'

'Also useful,' commented Craven. 'After all, one day it will be us making those decisions.'

'If you say so,' said Otto, eyeing a passing backpacker. He drained his beer and wandered off after her.

'Tell me one thing,' said Davis to Craven. 'I was talking to our manager the other day. He reckons interest rates are on their way down, the effects of Keating's recession are passing, and it's shaping as a good year. Our estate is doing well. Few too many grasshoppers apparently and the cost of fertiliser on the rise, but otherwise looking rosy.'

Craven shrugged. 'That's the beauty of irrigation; it's always a good year. How's the dryland part of the property?'

'Could do with more rain.'

'My point exactly.'

'So how come I see some farms not doing well? Irrigation farms. Smallholdings. Thirsty trees, vines getting bulldozed.'

Craven gave a little laugh. 'My guess? Shortage of money or water. Probably both, made worse by interest rates. They've been crippling to anyone carrying debt.'

'How can they lack water? It's an irrigation scheme.'

Craven looked at him, staring hard, as if Davis should already understand this. 'You thinking of any place in particular?'

'Not really.'

Craven smiled. 'You want me to tell you what's happening at your girlfriend's farm?'

Davis grinned back. 'Am I that transparent?'

'Always.' Craven checked about him, as if to make sure they weren't being overheard. 'She hasn't told you?'

'I don't want to pry.'

Craven laughed. 'You mean you do want to pry, you just don't want to be discovered doing it.'

'Fair call.'

'Works like this,' said Craven. 'All landholders used to have guaranteed access to water. It came with the land. If you sold your land, you sold your water. But a few years back, the government separated ownership of water from land. You can buy and sell water on the open market. If you need a bit more, you buy it, if you have excess you can sell it. Your manager will be doing that all the time with your winery and irrigated blocks. Big part of his job nowadays.'

'Really?'

'Sure. He trades through us.'

'Your company? Riverina Water Traders?'

'Who else? But your manager is only trading temporary water, and that's the only water he's ever selling. Your grandfather is canny, knows how to play the long game. He's kept his permanent water and bought more on the market.'

'Permanent? Temporary? What's the difference?'

'Permanent water is an annual entitlement, held in perpetuity. But holders of permanent water don't have to use it. They can sell this year's allocation, or part of it. That's temporary water. Next year they'll still get their permanent allocation. And once again, they can use it, sell it or buy more.'

'Seems logical. Market forces. So you think Lucy's dad has decided to sell this year's water instead of using it?'

'Maybe,' says Craven, frowning. 'But you can also buy and sell permanent water. I'm guessing that's what might have happened with him. He sold some permanent water—perhaps to finance improvements, like planting more trees, or to service debt—and became reliant on temporary water. Might have worked well at first, when temporary water was cheap. But then prices started rising, debt with them. Interest rates a few years ago were nudging twenty per cent. More crops going in up and down the river, year after year, greater demand and higher prices for water, lower income from crops. Maybe his debt built up, so he sold more permanent water, bought temporary water on the market, and it didn't end well.'

'You think he's in debt?'

'Could be. Could be Lucy's father has no more permanent water left. And surviving on temporary water is hand to mouth; sooner or later you'll hit a wall. There'll be a drought, less water will be released from the dams, and prices will go up. You'll be caught between a rock and a hard place. Bad enough if you're growing an annual crop like rice or cotton or irrigated wheat. You can bite the bullet and not plant that year. But if you've put in grapes or citrus or avocadoes or whatever, you're fucked. It's not just a matter of this year's crops; it's keeping the plants alive. Take away the water, and this climate is brutal. A desert.'

'I had no idea. What do you think he'll do?'

'Mate, I only know a bit about his water, not the rest of his affairs. That said, my guess is that sooner or later he'll sell the property. It's valuable, with good access to water. But whoever buys it will need to own permanent water, or they'll find themselves in the same situation.'

'What about us? The Seven? Could we buy it?'

'Sure. Happens already. We can buy a block without water, shift some of our water onto it. Easy.'

He was about to ask more, but Otto announced that their turn at the pool table had come around, and that was the end of the conversation. And when Lucy turned up at the pub with a couple of girlfriends, he decided not to spoil the evening by broaching the subject with her.

—–

It wasn't so very long after this that Davis and Lucy made the local newspaper, the *Yuwonderie Wonder*. The editor, who was also the photographer, the reporter, the subeditor and the classified ads salesperson, put them on the front page, a photograph of the two of them squinting into the sun in front of the company's commanding facade.

COMPANY SECRETS UNCOVERED
By Esther Brinks
All the world knows that the Yuwonderie Irrigation Scheme Company was founded by seven prominent families.

But now a young member of one of those families, Davis Heartwood, has uncovered long-lost documents that cast doubt on that accepted wisdom.

Mr Davis, 21, is undertaking an honours year at the University of Melbourne before returning to the district permanently.

His thesis will explore the establishment of the scheme and its early years.

'The precursor company, the one that got the ball rolling, was founded by nine families, not seven as is commonly thought,' he told the *Wonder*.

'It's not clear why the other families, the Marneys, the Chaulkers and the Pratts, didn't end up participating in the final scheme. It's just one of the things I hope to discover.'

Mr Heartwood has been given full access to the archives of the YISC. 'I am extremely grateful. I wouldn't be able to progress my research without it,' said Mr Heartwood.

The company has even offered Mr Heartwood the assistance of archivist Ms Lucretia Fielder.

'It's very exciting,' she told the paper. 'It's like being in *The Raiders of the Lost Ark*.'

Davis had never known anyone to pay attention to the *Yuwonderie Wonder* before, but it seemed everyone saw the article. Lucy cut it out and kept it, Otto and Craven teased him about it, and his grandfather read it with wry amusement.

'Who were the Marneys, the Pratts and the Chaulkers?' Davis asked him. 'Do you know?'

'Chaulkers are still around, dryland farmers,' the old man replied. 'Not sure what happened to the Pratts and the Marneys.'

'What about old Joe? Used to work out here?'

His grandfather shook his head. 'Not from a prominent family, or any family that I know of. Good worker, but he had barely two shillings to rub together.'

It was shortly after this that Davis was invited to dine at the Canal Club, which he knew all about but had rarely visited. His grandfather was a member, but seldom went. Its name derived from its location, next to the town canal, providing members with a view over the liquid wealth flowing in from the Murrumbidgee. It was housed inside an understated building, single storey, rendered cement, Art Deco. From the street, most of it was hidden behind an impeccably groomed hedge and framed by squat palm trees. He drove into a car park guarded by a sign written in polite cursive: *Please, Members and Guests Only.* Inside, the building was quiet, the deep-carpet hush of a funeral home. He knew membership was reserved for the elite of the district: graziers from nearby stations, doctors and solicitors and accountants and, of course, the Seven families. It had two wings: dining and bar facilities to the right; accommodation to the left, seven suites, there to cater for more far-flung members if they were in town for the night, or for the show, or the picnic races. Membership was open to men only, though women were allowed as guests to the dining room.

Davis had been there when he was young, on family days with his parents, and occasionally to eat in the wood-panelled dining room. But this lunchtime, he was to be a guest in the board-room. He had dressed for the occasion in a sports jacket, clean moleskins, a new shirt, polished boots. It wasn't enough. The doorman provided him with a tie, asking him to put it on before he could be led into the inner sanctum.

He was greeted by two of the patriarchs, family heads the same generation as his grandfather, Jessop Titchfield and Van Dyke Allsop. Titchfield looked uncomfortable in his suit, an ancient thing smelling of moth balls, while Craven's grandfather was the opposite, dressed in a bespoke suit, chalk-striped navy. He seemed to have taken his name to heart and grown a goatee together with a waxed moustache.

'My dear boy, so pleased you could join us,' said Van Dyke, shaking Davis's hand and indicating he should occupy the seat at the head of the board table. The old men were positioned one either side of the table, which was large enough to accommodate a dozen people in comfort.

Davis tugged at his tie nervously.

'Yes, sorry about that. Feel free to remove it if it bothers you,' said Jessop. 'The staff are sticklers for propriety. Sometimes I wonder who's running the place, them or us.'

'We used to dress for dinner,' said Van Dyke, as if this were a counterargument. 'Once a month. The family heads, in here. Dinner suits. Shame we no longer do it.'

'We do, you know, but only once per year,' said Jessop. 'How's your grandfather? I was hoping he might come along, but he sent his apologies. Arthritis playing up, is it?'

'Awful. But he's a tough old bloke,' said Davis, knowing his grandfather didn't have arthritis.

There was small talk as an obsequious waiter took drink orders: weather, crops, markets, Melbourne, the test series against the West Indies.

It was only over the meal that the purpose of the meeting became clear.

'We have a proposition for you,' said Van Dyke, his voice casual. 'It's the scheme's seventieth anniversary next year. We're planning some events. A festival, perhaps some public art, some good works, some plaques, that sort of thing. It occurred to us your research might be timely. We would like to publish it.'

Davis wasn't sure how to respond. 'It's a thesis. Academic. Dry and boring.'

'But is that all you want for it? To be seen by a handful of examiners, then sit forever gathering dust on some shelf? Unread and under-appreciated? Why not make the most of it: two birds with one stone. The last time we did something like this was for the fiftieth. What we're thinking is a coffee-table book, a sumptuous affair. You'd provide the text; we'd have someone source all the photos. Get in a proper designer, an experienced editor. We'd pay for it, of course; pay you. Pay for a researcher to help you, if you had someone in mind.' Van Dyke looked across the table to Jessop, who grunted and nodded his approval. 'What do you think?' Van Dyke asked Davis.

'Certainly worth exploring.'

'Agreed then. We'll get a contract drawn up. Perfect.'

Davis looked from one patriarch to the other, their smiling faces. 'I'm not entirely sure I'll need an editor. It's imperative that the thesis is entirely my own work.'

'Naturally,' said Jessop. 'The thesis is yours alone. But the book is what the public will see.' He smiled. 'We sometimes forget what a remarkable achievement the scheme is. Not just the engineering and agriculture and prosperity, but the way the entire town, the entire community has been lifted. We're one of the most affluent regional communities in the country. One of the most united. That comes from those days, when the Seven established the scheme, welcomed the smallholders in with open arms. We are all the beneficiaries. The entire town.'

'Hear, hear,' said Van Dyke, raising his glass.

Davis smiled. 'Tell me, what happened to the Marneys, the Chaulkers and the Pratts?'

There was silence for no longer than a heartbeat.

'No mystery there,' said Van Dyke. 'The Chaulkers are still in the district. Graziers. The Marneys sold up, moved up near Cootamundra. Don't know about the Pratts. Those families were involved at the beginning, their land close by but not suitable for irrigation. Too far out, or not flat enough, or too high. Wrong side of the Spur. Couldn't get water to them. When that became evident, they dropped out.'

'Makes sense,' said Davis. But he couldn't help but wonder how it was that Van Dyke Allsop knew what had happened to the Marneys when his grandfather didn't.

— —

That evening, when he returned to Three Wells, Davis took a walk. Out past the stables and the old workers cottages and past the first of the three wells, covered over now, the windmill still there but an electric pump tapping the aquifer coming down from the Castle. Up the rise, not so high but high enough, the view out over the plains, over their private landing strip with its windsock and hangar. And back the other way, the isolated grandeur of the Castle, the green smudge of the scheme beneath it. He climbed to the little family cemetery, with its sheltering oak, fenced behind wrought iron. It struck him as entirely in keeping: paddocks had barbed wire, and houses had picket fences, but something about a graveyard demanded wrought iron. He entered. It was well-maintained, the grass always mown, dead now in the summer heat. He walked to his parents' graves. A memory came to him of the funeral, his sister in tears, him feeling removed, his grandfather, hair grey only at the temples back then, rigid with grief.

He walked to them, bowed his head, greeted his mother, apologised to his father for renouncing the inheritance, wondering how he might have reacted. Angry? Envious? Supportive? There was no way of knowing. But he didn't feel so bad; he felt as if his father would understand.

Further along, he found the grave of his grandmother, whom he remembered better than his parents, the plot next to her awaiting Clemence. And the generations before: Douglas and Elaine, William and Mary, Joshua and Elizabeth, back to the first William and his two wives, Charlotte and Mathilda. There were other graves as well: of younger brothers and sisters, the ones who had left, gone out into the world and forged new lives, yet had returned in death, back into the family fold, indistinguishable at last from the family patriarchs. And there were the children: the ones who had died young, so many of them, collected together in the little graveyard.

It gave him a feeling of melancholy, as cemeteries will, but he also found it strangely reassuring. If he went through with it, renounced his inheritance, his family wouldn't be renouncing him. They would still embrace him. No matter which road he took, he would join them in eternity, here in the family plot. He'd always known death was waiting, the lesson learnt by all children whose parents die young. His grandfather would be buried here, next to his wife. And Davis imagined that someday he too would lie here. Krystal would own Three Wells Station, but he would not be banished.

chapter seventeen

IVAN IS RUNNING A FEW MINUTES LATE, SO HE DOES THE RIGHT THING, BUYING coffees and pastries at the Lone Dog Café. But when he gets to their office on the second floor of the police station, he finds not just Nell but Alice Figtree waiting. He looks down at the tray and up again.

'Alice,' he says. 'Coffee? I have a latte here.'

She shakes her head. 'That's kind, but I don't drink milk.'

'I saw a coffee machine downstairs. One of those pod things. You want one of those?'

Alice smiles. 'No, I'm good.'

Ivan, released of any beverage-related obligations, passes Nell her coffee and a paper bag containing a raisin spiral, before settling at the central table.

'What news?' he asks Alice. Now he looks at her properly, he can see she has lost some of the previous day's sheen: her silk blouse has been replaced by a black t-shirt bearing a red-and-white design, the short sleeves revealing the Celtic tattoo on her left arm, and yesterday's skirt has been traded for work pants. Her make-up is less meticulous, and she looks tired, her eyes bloodshot.

'They let me back into the practice,' she says. 'I made some more digital copies, spent a good part of the night at home going through them.'

'Find anything useful?' asks Ivan.

'I think so,' says Alice.

There's something in the way she says it that stops him from sinking his teeth into his almond croissant. Instead, he places the pastry back on its paper bag.

Alice continues. 'I've been able to construct an overview of Athol's personal accounts and the business accounts.'

'And?' Nell prompts.

'Athol's debt was worse than I first thought. A lot worse. He'd gone through all of his and Jacinta's personal money, blown out the mortgage, maxed out the credit cards. The lot.' She swallows. 'He also plundered his trust account.'

Ivan becomes rock still, mind working, eyes focused on Alice.

'Explain what that means,' says Nell.

Alice looks pained. 'Accountants are like solicitors. They hold money in trust for their clients. Matters to be settled, tax owing, all sorts of things. Athol was also a financial adviser, and many of the investments went through his account. It is absolutely forbidden to access those accounts except to act on behalf of your clients.'

'Fraud?' asks Nell. 'Larceny?'

Alice dips her head, sorrow in her eyes. Clearly, she was fond of her former boss. 'Yes. Criminal. He could have gone to jail. He'd have been struck off as an accountant, lost his financial planner's licence. Been exposed to civil action as well.'

'And he was able to keep it secret?'

Alice is shaking her head. 'Not for much longer. The trust accounts are audited once a year. No auditor could miss this. There's a couple of hundred thousand dollars missing.'

'When was the audit due?' asks Nell.

'In six weeks,' says Alice. 'He might have been able to delay it for a while, but not forever.'

There is a silence. The two women must be thinking the same as Ivan: hundreds of thousands of dollars missing is a pretty good motivation for murder. He recalls the burns on the dead man's thighs and genitals. Tortured by someone who wanted their money back? He keeps the thought to himself; no need to distress Alice.

'The money he took from this trust account, is it possible to identify which of his clients it belonged to?' asks Ivan.

Alice grimaces. 'No. It doesn't work like that. It's pooled together.'

'Any sign where the money was going?' asks Nell. 'Was he a gambler?'

Ivan senses her sideways glance at him and feels a jolt of shame, but he can't complain: she knew about his poker machine addiction and had helped him work his way through it. And it's an obvious question.

Alice leans forward, as if confiding something personal. 'That's what kept me up so late. Finding out the level of his debt wasn't so hard; he wasn't trying to disguise it. It's there in black and white. It would be even more obvious to a trained auditor.' She pauses for a moment before continuing. 'Finding out where it's been going was trickier. That he did disguise. Up until about a year ago, his personal record keeping was immaculate even if the client records were a bit shoddy. It's only these past twelve months, as the debt started getting out of hand, that he began muddying the waters. It becomes more difficult to separate investments being made by him and those he was making on behalf of his financial-planning clients. So I still have plenty to do, but I can already tell you there were a couple of places where he was investing money beyond the stock market, mutual funds and property trusts. A fair amount of money went through a local company here in town: Riverina Water Traders. Another recipient was a Melbourne-based company that has operations up on the Castle: Air Stills of Australia, or ASA. And then, just a month ago, he bought a block of land about five kilometres out of town. There's no record of where he got the money from. The ultimate ownership is disguised, held through an offshore trust, so I can't say for sure whether he's the beneficial owner, but he's certainly been involved with all the transactions.'

Ivan has been jotting down the information as Alice speaks. Now he looks up. 'This land—where is it?'

'Other side of the Castle. Across the Spur. There's a surveyors map in among the paperwork.'

Ivan recalls Eggs's geography lesson. 'So not irrigated land?'

'Not out there. But he paid half a million for it.'

'I thought land out beyond the irrigation area was all but worthless,' says Ivan.

'Not if you own enough of it,' says Alice. 'But you'd really need to ask someone who knows more about that.'

Ivan switches topics. 'The investments made through Riverina Water Traders—I spoke to someone who compared the water trade to a casino.'

Alice takes a deep breath. 'I hear there's a speculative side to it. The front bar at the Coachman's is full of conspiracy theories about market manipulation, Pitt Street farmers and Wall Street spivs, but I'm not sure there's much proof.'

'So was Athol playing the market?' asks Nell.

'I don't know. He used to talk about water a lot. It was a bugbear of his. He'd be trying to set out savings and investment plans for small landholders, but it was always complicated by not knowing how much they would be paying for water. So he was definitely investing on their behalf. But if he was building up debt, then my guess would be he was playing the market.'

'And losing,' says Nell.

'And losing,' Alice echoes.

Ivan moves on. 'And Air Stills of Australia? I saw their premises up on the Castle. Or their front gate, at least. What's that all about?'

'No idea. I hadn't even heard of them until last night. I googled them. A private company, a start-up. Developing technology to extract water from the air.'

Ivan almost laughs. It sounds preposterous. 'Athol was putting money into that?'

'Yes. His money. I suspect his clients' as well.'

'Air to water. What's stage two: water into wine?' Nell says flippantly.

Alice gives her a wry smile. 'That's a fair description of irrigated vineyards.'

'Air stills. How does it work?' asks Ivan.

'No idea. There's an explanation on the website, but it's just an overview. However, I can tell you this much, it's still at the experimental stage. So no sales, no revenue, no dividends. Just the promise of big returns if it comes to fruition.'

It doesn't make sense to Ivan. 'This bloke was an accountant, a financial planner, not some naive punter. He would understand the ebb and flow of money. And risk, and how to assess it. And yet you're saying he went into massive debt, including putting his career in danger, his livelihood, his freedom, by plundering his trust account. And for what? To spend half a million on a block of land without access to water, to invest in a start-up with no revenue in sight, and to play the water-trading market?' He looks at Alice. 'I don't know half as much as you do, but that sounds like financial suicide to me. A fiscal death wish.'

Alice's eyes cloud, and Ivan remembers a moment too late that she knew Athol well, liked the man. 'I think that's a fair summary,' she says, her words formal but the emotion not far below the surface.

Ivan attempts sympathy as he responds. 'Alice, I don't know what any of this means. But it's informative and extremely useful, and certainly gives Nell and myself plenty to work with. So thank you.'

'Yes,' says Nell. 'Thank you.'

Alice nods, a weak smile working its way through. 'There's something else.'

'Really?' asks Ivan.

'This.' She reaches into a folder, pulls out a photograph, hands it to him. 'It was in the front of his diary, which was sitting on his desk.'

Ivan looks at the print. There is something about the quality of the paper, the faded colour, that dates it, takes it back before the era of digital printing to the days of film and chemicals. It is a picture of eight young people: four couples, grinning broadly at the camera; five standing, three seated; the men in dinner suits, the women in party dresses. Athol Hasluck, smile ablaze, is standing at the centre of the back row, easily recognisable, a younger version from the photos his widow lent them on their first day in Yuwonderie. In this image, his hands are on the shoulders of a seated girl: pretty, with crimped blonde hair and an engaging smile. Sitting on a chair to the right of the girl is a handsome young man with a mat of honey-coloured hair and dimples, a dark-haired girl draped across his lap, one arm around his neck. Her face is partly obscured by the champagne glass with which she is toasting the camera, but her twinkling eyes are clear enough, full of joy. Behind the seated couple, standing next to Athol, is a very tall young man with dark hair and broad shoulders, his arm around the waist of a petite girl next to and slightly in front of him. The other couple, standing on Athol's other side, are laughing, faces turned slightly towards each other, as if they have just shared a private joke. Ivan looks at the photo closely, flips it over. *January 1994* is written on the back. He hands it on to Nell.

'Why show us this?' he asks Alice.

'It was taken thirty years ago,' she says. 'Yet it's right there in the front of his diary. It struck me as odd.'

'Who are they?' asks Nell. 'There's Athol, but do you recognise any of the others?'

'I do. Most of them are members of the Seven.' Alice smiles, as if the police should be more observant. 'The tall man next to Athol is Otto Titchfield, our local MP.'

Nell hands Ivan the photo so he can see for himself. The man in the photo looks young and fit and lean, displaying none of the girth of the present-day politician. 'And the young woman? Otto has his arm around her waist. She looks familiar.'

'Jacinta Hasluck. Jacinta Fielder back then.'

'My God,' says Ivan. He realises why he didn't immediately recognise her: in the picture she is beaming in the lightness of the moment; the woman he met two nights before was shredded by grief. 'Who's the young woman in front of Athol, his hands on her shoulders?'

'Stella Kippax,' Alice replies.

'And the other seated couple, next to her?'

'The man with blond hair is Davis Heartwood. The girl on his lap with the champagne glass is Lucretia Fielder, Jacinta's elder sister.'

'Now married to Otto Titchfield.'

'Correct.'

'And the other couple?' asks Nell. 'Standing on the other side of Athol?'

'The man is Craven Allsop and the woman is Krystal Heartwood. My wife.' She checks their reaction before continuing. 'Craven is the CEO of Riverina Water Traders.'

Ivan studies the photograph again. He can almost feel his neurons firing, trying to find connections. He summarises, hoping it might nudge his thought processes, or those of Nell and Alice. 'So back then, none of them were married, and they were with different partners. Athol, later married to Jacinta, was with this Stella. Otto, later married to Lucretia, was with Jacinta. And Lucretia was sitting on the lap of this blond-haired bloke.'

'Davis Heartwood,' Alice reminds him.

'Let me guess: your brother-in-law. From one of the Seven families.'

'He was, yes.'

'Was?'

'He's long dead. Murdered. Years ago. Probably not long after the photo was taken. I never met him.'

Ivan meets Nell's gaze, neurons now firing like a small reactor. He turns back to Alice. 'What happened?'

'Shot dead. The killer was never caught. Krystal would know more, but she doesn't like to talk about it.' Alice blinks a couple of times. 'I think she still misses him.'

Ivan stares at the woman standing next to Athol, Krystal, her face turned to the man next to her, Craven Allsop. He looks again at Davis Heartwood, Lucy Titchfield draped across his lap. 'And Athol Hasluck kept this photograph in his diary?'

'Right inside the front cover,' says Alice.

'Jesus,' says Nell.

'That girl in the front,' says Alice, 'Stella Kippax. She disappeared the same time Davis was murdered. She's never been found. They think she was probably killed as well.'

'Kippax . . .' For a moment he struggles to recall where he's heard that name before. Then he has it. 'Related to Bert Kippax? Former police officer?'

'Yes,' answers Alice. 'I believe so. Her father.'

Ivan takes a moment to assimilate that before moving the conversation along. 'Athol's files. The filing cabinets with the paper records. Let's shift them here. You can work out of this office.'

Alice's eyes widen. 'Why?'

'Keep them safe. You and the files.'

Nell interjects, addressing Alice. 'You can walk away, you know,' she says. 'There is no obligation on you. We can collect the files. Work through them ourselves.'

Alice frowns, shakes her head. 'I'd like to continue, if I can.' And then, by way of explanation, 'Athol helped me. Gave me a job. I feel I owe it to Jacinta and the kids.'

'We'll get some uniforms to move the files over,' says Ivan. 'Don't examine them until they're secured.'

Alice looks momentarily uncertain before agreeing. 'All right.'

With that settled, Nell escorts Alice out, then returns upstairs to where Ivan has started on his almond croissant. 'Are you fucking mad?' she asks.

'Possibly,' says Ivan, trying to appear unperturbed.

There is passion in Nell's voice as she responds. 'She's a civilian. No qualifications, no clearance. You've invited her into the heart of a murder investigation, giving her access to a secure section of a police station. You're entrusting her with the files that could crack this case wide open. How do we know she isn't involved in fraud? That she won't use the opportunity to destroy evidence? Why are you taking that risk? Not to mention endangering our careers.'

Ivan sips his coffee before answering. 'Everything you say is correct.'

'So what am I missing?'

'Politics. Watermen's. Millions of dollars. Disguised political donations. Potential corruption. Potential shitstorm. I talked it through with Plodder. He doesn't want anyone to know what we're probing. Not the Fraud Squad, not anyone. No warrants, no prosecutors. Not yet. We keep it in house until we find something concrete. If Otto Titchfield or the government or the commissioner's office get wind of what we're up to, we risk getting closed down.'

Nell just stares, as if she can't quite believe what she is hearing. 'If Alice double-crosses us, the blowback will be enormous.'

Ivan laughs. 'Kevin will be supervising her. Plodder has authorised it.'

Some of the passion drains from Nell, but she sounds a long way from being convinced. 'Shit doesn't flow uphill, you know that.'

'Kev's driving down tonight. Alice can only get access while she works through him, here in the station. No destroying evidence, no manipulation.'

Nell sighs, sits down. 'What next?'

'The money trail. Riverina Water Traders and Air Stills of Australia. I want to know why Athol was funnelling money in there.'

'What about the photo?' asks Nell, flicking her head towards the print, still lying on the desk in front of Ivan.

He glances at it, can't see any immediate relevance. Nevertheless, it's intriguing: eight young people, two murdered, one vanished. He looks back to Nell. 'Pull the records on Davis Heartwood and Stella Kippax. See what you can find. And see if McTosh has had any luck tracking down Bert Kippax—the old bloke who was busking near the cafe yesterday morning. And ask Constable Simmonds if he shows up on any CCTV on Saturday night or Sunday morning.'

When Nell has gone downstairs to see the constable, he finds himself looking again at the photograph. They all look so happy, so blessed. He tries to remember what he was doing at that age. Not getting dressed in a dinner suit to go to parties, that's for sure.

chapter eighteen

February 1914

Oh, Mother!

I am so sorry I have not honoured my commitment, that I have not written these past several weeks, that you felt compelled to write to Mrs Titchfield.

The truth is that I have not been ill of body, but of soul. Sick at heart. I was so happy there for a week, floating, barely conscious of the concerns of Elaine and her mother, the sideways glances of Horace, the laughter from the workers. A week in a lifetime. I wonder: is that my ration? Is that all I get?

He is married, Mother. He is married!

It fell to Elaine to tell me the truth, to destroy my hopes. I can't blame her; she was doing me a service. The image I had of him, that kind gentleman from the night of the dance, was stripped from me and left in tatters. I cried and could not stop. I was inconsolable. I couldn't eat; I felt I was barely able to breathe. Even Mrs Titchfield took pity on me. She resumed cooking herself, brought meals out to me in my little shed; meals I couldn't stomach.

He came to the house. More than once. I refused to see him. How could I? He had humiliated me, broken me, lied to me. Here I was, fearful of Augustine Chaulker and the censure of Horace, yet it was Jack Marney who treated me as the inferior, the one who thought I was not worth the truth.

Elaine explained that he married some three years ago, but his wife had lost her mind and was now locked away for her own safety. I said I didn't care; he should have told me. Eventually Elaine convinced me I should see him, if only to tell him to his face to cease his pursuit of me.

I played it over and over in my mind, how I would confront him, flail him with words and leave him empty of hope and full of regret. The reality proved to be much harder. Elaine led me to the tree by the brook where he waited with his horse. She was meant to stay, but of course she didn't.

He looked terrible, his face blotched, eyes red. I was glad to see it.

'I should have told you,' he said, looking at the ground, this brave man not brave enough to look me in the eye. 'I thought you knew.'

I said nothing. Not trusting my words, not trusting my temper; the cutting words were on my tongue, but I lacked the icy resolve needed to launch them.

'She is gone, Bessie. Lost. I don't think she will ever be coming back.'

'Lost?'

'Lost to me. To the world. To herself. She is in Goulburn. At Kenmore, the asylum.' And he had pain in his eyes then; no tears, but a kind of suffering.

I wasn't sure what to say. Elaine had told me something of it, but I'd been so consumed by my self-pity and my anger that I had been unable, or unwilling, to hear. Now I could witness Jack's misery, his pain.

'We had a child,' he said. 'That was why we married. I needed to take responsibility.'

'You loved her?'

And he said nothing, his eyes still on the ground, twisting his hat in his hands. 'Not like you.'

That fired my anger again. How dare he make the comparison? 'But the child was yours?'

'It was mine.'

And then I better understood the pain in his eyes. 'Where is the child now?'

'Dead. Born dead. He came early, unexpected. She was there alone for almost a week. She nearly died herself.'

'And you?'

'Droving.'

I walked away then to stand by the creek, watching the water bubble by. He didn't move; just waited until I returned to him.

'What is your wife's name?'

'May. Short for Maybelle.'

It was my turn to look at the ground, to wonder why I persisted, why I hadn't already left him, or called Elaine back to dress me again in propriety and resolve.

'You had me believe you were in earnest. That you were available.'

'I am in earnest. I believed you knew.'

Mother, I couldn't keep the anger from my voice, my opprobrium. 'A most convenient belief.'

'I can't divorce her, Bessie.' He looked me in the eye as he said it.

'Ah. The honourable man, to stand by his demented wife. But not so honourable as to resist deceiving me. You plucked me from the crowd, waltzed with me, held me so close, swinging me about the dance floor like a trophy, for all to see. And here I thought it was the colour of my skin that saw me ejected by that old witch and Mr Chaulker, their prejudice. But it wasn't, was it? They all believed I knew, that I didn't care, that I condoned your infidelity.'

'It is the law,' he said, eyes sad but voice measured.

'What law?' I almost spat the words, such was my contempt.

'Her illness, her insanity, it is not grounds for divorce. I must wait five years. That is what the statute dictates.'

I said nothing.

'I sought an annulment well before I met you. But it wasn't possible, not with the child.'

I said nothing. My words were exhausted. And to be honest, I could not help but feel some seed of sympathy.

'It was three and a half years ago, Bessie. I was just eighteen. I have not looked at another woman since. At every chance I got, I went droving, out where there is nothing but mulga and eagles and thoughts.'

'What are you saying?'

'I am saying wait. Wait for a year and a half.'

'And then?'

'And then, well, if you have found it in yourself to forgive me by then, then perhaps you and I will take our chance after all.'

Am I a fool, Mother? For in that moment, while my expression remained full of disdain, the smallest spark was lit within my breast.

And so I find myself hoping. I find myself able to leave my quarters, to repay Mrs Titchfield for her kindness, to work harder and longer in her service. And to hope once again that eventually it will not be a solitary week of happiness the gods might grant me. And, of course, I have recovered the ability to write to you.

They have all gone now, over to a meeting at Jolimont, all the families of the district planning to unite in support of their scheme, and I am left in peace.

I promise that, whatever may transpire, I will always write. At least once a week. You have my word.

Your loving daughter,
Bessie

chapter nineteen

IVAN LEAVES NELL TO ORGANISE THE TRANSFER OF ATHOL HASLUCK'S FILING cabinets to the police station and heads out, walking up Titchfield Street towards Riverina Water Traders. He thinks again of his mentor, Morris Montifore, and his maxim that detectives must run investigations until they reach a critical mass; then they start running the detectives. Ivan can sense this case approaching that pivot, where the investigation will assume a life of its own. And he feels a growing conviction that the inflection point is money: where Athol was getting it from, where he was sending it to, whom he upset in the process.

They need to trace the flow of funds: Alice and Kevin establishing the paper trail, while he and Nell scrutinise the conduits already identified: Riverina Water Traders, Air Stills of Australia, the Watermen's Foundation. That's where the money has gone, one way or another. Next, Alice and Kevin must drill down into the client accounts, work out where the cash came from, identify who has been robbed. That might be where they find their killer.

As Ivan goes to cross over Commonwealth Way, his thoughts are disrupted by a truck, a B-double, ventilating its air brakes as it negotiates one of the roundabouts. It belches smoke as the driver changes down a gear. The truck's canvas flanks are painted with fruit, glowing and healthy, beneath the words *Yuwonderie Wholesalers*. It seems simple: water flows in, produce flows out, money flows back. The town appears to be so prosperous, so tidy. And yet in the back alleys, the homeless sleep rough. Not so very different from any other town, really. Just better presented.

His eye follows the truck as it passes along the main thorough-fare, ruffling Christmas decorations in its wake. He sees the buildings, their pleasing symmetry and consistency: the Grandview Hotel and the Coachman's Arms, the council buildings and the T&G tower, all the way to the Yuwonderie Irrigation Scheme Company headquarters, sitting on its own rise, elevated ever so slightly above the other buildings and framed by the Castle. He ponders the names of the streets: Blaxland Avenue, Horsham Drive, Allsop Street, McLean Street and Titchfield Street. The Seven families. Everywhere.

He walks down from the ridge, reaching the Water Traders' offices. It's a plain enough building, unusual in that it's freestanding and only one storey, set back a little from the footpath, a cross between a domestic residence and a doctor's surgery. Yet even here the branding is apparent: ALLSOP 1928, it says high up under the eaves; RIVERINA WATER TRADERS PTY LTD, CRAVEN ALLSOP, CEO, says the sign by the door.

— — —

Craven is pencil thin, with a Zapata moustache. Ivan wonders if he has an eating disorder, or a two-pack-a-day habit. When he smiles, Ivan can see his gums have receded and there are gaps between his teeth. Ivan recalls the photo Alice Figtree found in Athol Hasluck's diary. Compared to Otto and Lucy and Jacinta and even Athol, Craven is the one that Ivan has the most difficulty reconciling with that thirty-year-old image. If Otto has grown larger and more imposing, Craven seems to have hollowed out.

He leads Ivan through a small anteroom into a large open-plan office. The exterior of the building might be heritage-protected, but the entire interior has been gutted and refitted in sleek modernity. Half-a-dozen people are seated at a row of desks, most of them on phones, typing as they speak, huge screens on the wall in front of them. To Ivan, it looks like a bank's foreign exchange floor or a stockbroker's trading room. The monitors are awash with data, yellow and green figures, blue and red graphs, constantly changing, constantly renewing. It's incomprehensible to Ivan, except for a large electronic map on one wall, a stylised depiction of the southern rivers, looking like a subway map, with dams and weirs like stations, numbers flickering.

A door to a back room opens, and a technician in a white coat emerges. Ivan catches a glimpse of a row of computer racks, lights flashing like a telephone exchange, and he hears the hum of electricity and the purr of air-conditioning. The door closes, and relative silence returns to the trading room.

'What's through there?' Ivan asks Craven.

'We run our own data centre. More efficient.'

'To trade water?'

'Fractions of a second can count.'

'Must use a lot of electricity.'

Craven frowns. 'Got to spend a dollar to make a dollar,' he says.

The businessman takes Ivan to a far corner, where there's a small glassed-in office. They enter, and Craven shuts the door after them.

'I'm investigating the death of Athol Hasluck,' says Ivan.

'So I assumed.' Craven offers the same smile he used to greet the detective. 'I am completely at your service. Anything I can do to help.'

'Just a few questions. I won't keep you long.' After obtaining the water trader's permission, Ivan sets his phone recording. 'You knew Mr Hasluck?'

'Oh yes. Very well. We were at school together. Business associates here.'

'And still friends?'

'Very much so.'

'Members of the Seven,' observes Ivan.

'Not unusual. Half the town is related in one way or another.'

'When was the last time you saw Athol Hasluck?'

'Oh, about a fortnight ago.'

'How did he seem?'

'Stressed.'

'How so?'

'He told me he was experiencing some cash-flow issues.'

'Meaning?'

'He wanted to borrow money.'

'How much?'

'A considerable amount.'

'Meaning?'

'Six figures.'

Ivan feels a prick of annoyance. 'You care to be a bit more precise?'

'Sorry, I can't. He was the one who used that term. Six figures. We didn't get any further than that. I said I couldn't put my hands on that sort of money, not at short notice. I lent him twenty thousand dollars.'

'Can you substantiate that?'

'Yes. He signed a receipt.'

'You were confident he would repay you?'

The smile starts to dissipate, and for the first time Craven Allsop pauses before answering. 'Athol was a friend. If he couldn't repay, then he couldn't repay. We called it a loan, but if it turned into a gift, so be it.'

Ivan considers Craven's generosity. 'So when you told Athol you couldn't get your hands on a six-figure amount, you weren't actually telling the truth, right?'

The last remnants of the smile leave Craven's face altogether, replaced by the beginnings of a scowl. 'I'm not sure I appreciate your characterisation, but yes, I could have accessed the money if necessary.'

'But you didn't like the chances of getting it back?'

'It was too much money to lend without collateral, even to a close friend.'

Ivan decides to back off. 'I'm not here to judge you, Mr Allsop. I think most people would act in a similar way. Indeed, I'm sure the majority of us would not have offered the twenty thousand if we didn't think it was coming back.'

Craven says nothing, but dips his head as if in appreciation, and some tension comes out of his shoulders.

'Tell me, though,' Ivan continues, 'when you told Athol you couldn't access six-figure amounts, do you think he would have believed you?'

The smile returns, but a facsimile, lacking warmth. 'No. He was an accountant. He knows this town, its financial landscape. He knew what I was saying. It was just easier, for both of us, for me to say I couldn't access the money rather than saying straight up that I didn't want to lend it to him.'

Ivan nods. 'Knowing that, how did he take it?'

'He wasn't angry, if that's what you're thinking. More like resigned.'

'I see,' says Ivan.

'Can I ask you something, officer?'

'Try me.'

'Did Athol kill himself?'

The question surprises Ivan; he'd thought by now the manner of Athol's death would be common knowledge. 'We believe he was murdered.' Ivan uses Craven's silence to move the conversation on. 'You did a lot of business with him?'

'Through Water Traders?'

'Yes.'

'I did. I can talk about most of it, but I'm not sure about some of his clients. There may be privacy concerns. Privilege. That sort of thing.'

'Let's start with what you can tell me. An overview.'

Craven steeples his hands. 'Right. What do you know about water trading?'

Ivan thinks of Eggs's exposition. 'I know water can be bought and sold. That it's an active market. That there are not just irrigators involved, but speculators and hedge fund, too.'

Craven looks impressed. 'That's a fair summary.'

'And Athol?'

'Athol was involved in water trading in a number of ways. You know he was a financial planner as well as an accountant?'

'I do.'

'So he would invest his clients' money. We offer a number of products. Everything from permanent titles to pooled funds to trading instruments. Different timelines, different risk profiles. So up until about a year ago, that's what we did: he'd come to me, seek advice; we'd invest the money. Win for him, win for me, win for his clients. But about a year ago, Athol started trading on his own account, mostly on the higher-risk markets.'

'And how were they performing?'

'Fairly solid. Nothing spectacular. It's been a couple of wet years, so no scarcity. Prices are low.'

'So he was losing money?'

'No—not making much, but breaking even.'

'You've checked?'

'Of course. He told me he was having cash-flow problems, remember? Trying to borrow six figures. Of course I checked.'

'And found?'

'The investments on behalf of his clients seem sound enough. Some up, some down, but overall tracking well. I advised on those investments so there were no surprises there. And his trailing commissions were flowing as expected.'

'He collected on an ongoing basis?'

'It can be a good business, financial planning.'

'What about his own investments?'

'Up until a year ago, all good. A few losses when La Niña set in and the dams filled up, but nothing disastrous. And again, he was acting on my advice.'

'So what changed?'

'He started trading on his own. Through our trading platform, but without my advice.'

'That's possible?'

'Oh sure. Irrigators do it all the time. Not as traders, although some do. Some are quite sophisticated. But most will just want a bit more water to finish off a crop, or to sell a little extra. They watch the market online, then trade when they want to. They know what's in the mountain dams, what the season is looking like, when they require the water, when other irrigators will want water. They don't need me.'

'But that's not what Athol was doing?'

'No. He wasn't a farmer. Increasingly, he was playing the market. Speculating. The last thing he wanted was water; he was an accountant chasing profits. But it can be a bit like musical chairs, some of the derivative markets. You could end up taking title of physical water with nowhere to store it.'

'Is that what happened to him?'

'On at least one occasion.'

'What happened to the water?'

'When the music stopped playing? He had to pay someone to take it.'

Ivan contemplates that. 'So someone made a killing. Free water, with a cash bonus for good measure.'

Craven smiles once again, and this iteration is no more attractive. 'That's an interesting way of depicting it.'

Ivan changes tack. 'He also invested in a block of land. Half a million dollars. Out past the Castle. Not irrigated. Is it possible he was trying to get water to develop that block?'

Craven stares at him, mind clearly working. From the look on his face, this is news to him. 'Over the Spur? Are you sure?'

'You didn't know?'

'He never mentioned a thing.'

'Is there something significant about that location?'

Craven is shaking his head in apparent disbelief. 'Not that I can see. It's beyond the legislated boundaries of the scheme. And the land there is higher. You'd need to pump the water. And the soil is bad. Plus, there are regulations about taking water out of designated irrigation areas.' Craven ponders it for a moment more, before shaking his head conclusively. 'No. He couldn't move water there. Impossible.'

'So no connection at all?'

'No. When did he get this land?'

'In the past year.'

Craven looks as if he has heard something absurd. 'So why was he coming to me, asking for a six-figure loan, when he's squandering money on worthless land?'

Ivan has no answer, so he again switches the direction of the interview, bringing out a plastic evidence bag containing the group photo Alice found in the front of Athol's diary. 'This familiar to you?'

Craven examines it, and this time the smile appears to be genuine, the recognition apparent. 'Yes. That's me, on the right there.' And then, the smile turning into a frown: 'Why show me this?'

'To an outsider like me, the photo appears to be of four couples. Davis Heartwood with Lucy Fielder on his lap. Otto Titchfield with his arm around Lucy's sister Jacinta, the same Jacinta Fielder who went on to marry Athol Hasluck. Athol has his hands on the shoulders of Stella Kippax, and you're next to Krystal Heartwood. Is that how it was, or is that just the way the photo turned out?'

Craven is looking at him intently, as if mesmerised. It takes a moment for him to gather himself and answer. 'That's pretty accurate, although Krystal and I weren't a couple, just friends. My memory is that Davis and Lucy had just started dating, Athol and Stella seemed pretty tight, I'm not so sure about Otto and Jayce. I don't think that lasted long. I'm not sure any of them did.'

'What was the event, do you remember?'

'There were a lot of twenty-firsts back then, but us blokes are in dinner suits, so I'm pretty sure that was a B&S. Out at Bandaville.'

'B&S?'

'Bachelors' and spinsters' ball. Country institution. Once designed for eligible young people from far-flung properties to meet prospective partners. Nowadays, they're piss-ups.'

'Do you know why those couples split?'

Craven looks perplexed. 'Not really. Davis and Stella started seeing each other, then they disappeared.' He shrugs. 'People realigned. I assume you know what happened to Davis and Stella?'

'Davis was murdered.'

'We didn't know that at the time. They just vanished. We thought maybe they'd eloped.' Craven looks away, eyes focused as if on some memory, before returning his attention to Ivan. 'How is the photo relevant?'

'It probably isn't. Just being thorough. Athol's assistant found it inside his appointments diary.'

'Alice Figtree?'

'You know her?'

'A little. You know who her wife is, don't you?' And now Craven is wearing a strange kind of smile, as if he's unsure of what emotion he should be communicating.

'I do. Krystal Heartwood. Davis Heartwood's elder sister. The owner of Three Wells Station,' says Ivan. 'The woman standing next to you in the photograph.'

The smile has gone again. 'I heard your forensics person examined Athol's office. Searched for fingerprints, that sort of thing.'

Ivan is puzzled. 'That's correct.'

'Yet it was Alice who found the photograph?'

'What are you suggesting?'

'That Alice and Krystal are more interested in what happened in 1994 than what happened last weekend.'

chapter twenty

1994

AS SUMMER EXTENDED AND DECEMBER TRIPPED OVER INTO JANUARY AND A NEW year, Davis found himself falling into a pattern. Otto had returned to work on the Titchfield estate, and Craven was embedded in the Allsops' recently established company, Riverina Water Traders. Lucy worked nine to five, so he spent his time in the basement room at the Yuwonderie Irrigation Scheme Company headquarters. The light still flooded in, the fan continued its slow revolutions, Lucy remained positive and attentive, but that first flush of enthusiasm, the sense of freedom and momentum, was beginning to leach from Davis. Christmas had taken a toll, as it often did: a lonely occasion, the three of them overly cheerful but unable to ignore the empty seats. Increasingly, Lucy was the attraction, not the work. The documents they extracted from the archives were stupendous in number, overwhelming in detail, but notably lacking in revelations. His initial euphoria was gradually replaced by a restless boredom.

He felt perhaps he was playacting, pretending to be a historian, a researcher, that he really had little idea of what he was looking for and where he might find it. This was different from his first three years of university: sitting in lectures, debating in tutes, writing standard essays about standard texts, studying for standard exams. Now he was out on his own. Lucy told him he was being too hard on himself, that the university year hadn't even started, that he'd already stolen a march on his contemporaries. She brought him more and more files, finding new and potentially interesting topics deep within the filing cabinets and compactors and shelves and tea cabinets of the vast underground chambers of the YISC. It was as if, in her efforts to please him, she thought only of quantity. And it was true, every time she delivered a new document, he was profuse in his thanks and generous with his kisses, but that didn't make the records any more enthralling. Water delivered and invoices paid, maintenance programs planned and implemented, technical studies of water seepage and evaporation debated by the board. The piles built up on his desk, a skyline of paper, a Manhattan of bureaucracy.

The first time Lucy had taken him into the catacombs, it made him feel like Howard Carter in the Valley of the Kings, but gradually he began to realise that these documents weren't so much buried treasures as the landfill of yesteryear. He couldn't work out why the company had bothered to keep most of it: was it laziness or an overwrought sense of self-importance, or was there simply a vast space in the sub-basement with little incentive to cull the archive? Who would have predicted that the paper trail deposited by a company dealing in water could itself prove to be so dry? He realised what he was missing: a story, a story with blood and flesh and emotions and humanity. And conflict. The truth was important, of course, but how to frame it into a narrative? Wasn't that what Manning Clark had done, Geoffrey Blainey, all the great historians of left or right? Weave a tale, supported by the facts, a bewitching story of explanation, of why things had come to pass, determining what was choice and what was inevitable in the march of time? Davis wasn't interested in ideology, but he desperately desired a narrative; without it his history would be nothing more than a chronological recitation of facts. But where could he find this elusive story?

He consulted once again the coffee-table book, and whereas before he had been dismissive, he now found it commendable. Its anonymous author, some gun-for-hire ghostwriter, had indeed created a narrative, one of heroism and valour, of visionary men taming nature, turning the desert green, setting out in black and white the centrality of the Seven. It wasn't his narrative—it belonged to the Canal Club—but at least it was *a* narrative, at least the author had found a through line.

He couldn't just create one; he wasn't a fiction writer, he knew that. He needed a true story, but where to find it? And that was when he concluded it would never be found in the YISC archives. Corroboration, perhaps, but not the story itself. This thought came to him as he studied the early minutes of the board meetings of the precursor business, the South Murrumbidgee Irrigation Company.

The minutes were cursory, simply recording the decisions made, containing nothing of the debates that had fired around the table eighty years before. A proposal to build a secondary channel flowing east from the main canal was rejected, while one flowing west was approved. But why? At most, such decisions were justified by a curt word or phrase: 'cost' or 'engineering' or 'topography'. They gave no indication of who was on what side of the debate, nor of the arguments they had made. Looking at these abbreviated records gave him as much insight as visiting the cemetery and interviewing the participants' gravestones.

—–

The days wore on. He was finding it increasingly hard to concentrate, to focus his mind, so that his eyes passed over a document without comprehension, so that he found himself at the bottom of a page without re-calling a thing he had read. At other times he would find himself re-reading a sentence for the third time, while his mind wandered elsewhere. But he didn't have much choice. If he abandoned the work, Lucy would be disappointed and his grandfather would conclude his bid for freedom was insincere. So he stuck with it, even as he began to watch the clock, wait for the end of the day, so he could join his mates at the pub or drive Lucy to the top of the Castle in the Alfa. He realised, if nothing else, he knew something of the drudgery experienced by those faceless men and women who had created the records in the first place.

And then he found the minutes of a board meeting of the South Murrumbidgee Irrigation Company dated September 1916, and his perseverance was rewarded.

At first glance, the two-page document seemed as innocuous as all the rest. Typed notes on yellowing paper, brittle with age. The first thing that caught his eye was the list of those present—Hasluck, Allsop, McLean, Titchfield and Horsham—and those absent: Messrs Heartwood, Pratt and Blaxland. Eight families now, no longer nine: the Marneys and Chaulkers not mentioned, replaced by the McLeans. The meeting must have barely made a quorum, and Davis made a note to himself to learn what a quorum was for a board meeting of a private company back then.

The first four items seemed routine:

1) Authorisation of expenditure on new plant and equipment;
2) Agreement on a wage increase for staff;
3) Funding for a delegation to state parliament;
4) Flood impact, recovery and mitigation.

It was only over the page that he found the item which pricked his interest, and only on a second look. Initially, the title seemed as mundane as the rest:

5) Acquisitions and disposals, inclusions and exclusions.

He only read it a second time because he didn't immediately understand what it referred to. He dug deeper. According to the minutes, land within the proposed irrigation scheme had been bought and sold, but not who had sold and who had bought. The minutes merely noted that all landholders within the boundary of the scheme remained committed to its success. As for inclusions and exclusions, the meeting noted that the limits of the scheme area had been modified, based on the latest surveys and hydrological assessments, with some land now included and some excised. There were no reasons given, nothing of the boardroom debate, but there was a map. It was an elegant thing, expertly drafted. It showed the new boundaries of the scheme and the design for the canal ways. A thought illuminated itself within his head:

winners and losers. Maybe here was the flesh-and-blood story he was seeking—or at least its skeleton.

It took Lucy the rest of the afternoon to find it, but by that evening he had the 'before' map in his hands, detailing the shape of the scheme and the layout of the proposed canals before that decisive board meeting of spring 1916. He could see the changes, where a canal had been eliminated and another inserted, and he could see the perimeter of the irrigation scheme, but neither map showed who owned the land. He wondered if that was deliberate: that the board did not want decisions made on commercial and engineering grounds to be influenced by the knowledge of who owned which land and, thereby, who would benefit or lose from their decisions. But he realised that was not credible. The board members were all landholders, would all know the extent of their own holdings and no doubt those of their neighbours. The maps might not spell it out, but they would be all too aware. And these decisions had been made with three of the families unrepresented, including his own.

Flush with newfound enthusiasm, Davis returned to the room the next day to find it lighter, as if the sun were more powerful and the fan-pushed air fresher. He asked Lucy to return the files to their places in the archive. He was no longer fishing; he had an objective. He asked for all the correspondence between landholders and the board in the months leading up to the 1916 meeting. Here he might learn who was for and against the changes. The arguments might again be couched in terms of costs and engineering, of mutual benefit and cooperation, but he should find it easy enough to establish who believed themselves to be losing from any proposed changes.

But Lucy couldn't find it. He joined her and helped scour the records, but to no avail: the correspondence had not been kept.

'God, they've kept everything else,' he exclaimed. 'There's mountains of correspondence.'

'Only after the formation of the YISC, though,' Lucy pointed out. 'This company wasn't so fastidious. They didn't keep the correspondence.'

'Why not?' asked Davis.

Lucy shrugged. 'They hadn't decided whether or not to go ahead. They didn't have a headquarters. Only a skeleton staff. They wouldn't have kept anything if the proposal went nowhere, if the scheme was never built.'

Davis sat then, on the hard concrete floor among the compactors, head in hands. Was it possible the truth was no longer accessible, that the crucial records were no more? That the documents telling the story of the scheme's establishment were gone, while every last detail post-establishment was stored in perpetuity? Lucy was no doubt correct: the board had thought their correspondence inconsequential and had disposed of it. Only in retrospect was its importance apparent.

And then another interpretation came to him: perhaps the board had indeed recognised the correspondence as consequential—enough to order its destruction.

'Sydney,' said Davis. 'Let's go to Sydney.'

'Whatever for?' asked Lucy.

'To check the public records. Land records.'

'When?'

'No time like the present.'

And Lucy laughed at such a ridiculous idea, that bright trill of hers, until she saw he was serious.

By the next day, Lucy had warmed to the idea: warmed to it very much. She liked the prospect of driving there, of spending time in the city. Not in the archives, but in the shops and at the beaches and by the harbour. She'd told him she'd thought it impossible, but when she had asked Hilary Housego permission to take Thursday and Friday off work, he had not only authorised it but told her they could count as working days, for, after all, she was assisting Mr Heartwood, whose family was a major share-holder and who was writing a bold new history of the company, as commissioned by the YISC and Canal Club. Housego had even granted her a small per diem. She hugged Davis and kissed him and told him she could not have been happier.

——

They drove in his Alfa, the engine purring, the exhaust throaty, the windows open. It was hot, but Davis didn't mind. It felt somehow glamorous, heading off with Lucy beside him, like he was on a quest. He figured it would take nine hours each way, so they set off early and drove the Great Western Highway instead of the Hume, and stayed overnight at Katoomba. Cliff Views was a lovely hotel, dilapidated and well past its heyday, but full of character. They walked in the evening to Echo Point and ate at an old cafe and made love for the first time in their Victorian hotel, and Davis was content. He thought he'd had a taste of the future, a small sample.

The next morning he looked out over the cliffs and deep valleys of the mountains and felt destiny rising with the wind.

A late-season Christmas beetle alighted on his hand with its wings of shifting colours, and he took it as a good omen.

Driving into Sydney was gruelling, the traffic along Parramatta Road as thick as horseflies. The smog was heavy and the heat was rising. Diesel belched from trucks, horns sounded and brakes squealed. Every intersection had traffic lights that conspired against them, turning red as they approached. It was not the image of Sydney he'd carried with him. But Lucy remained upbeat, armed with a brand-new Gregory's street directory, advising him of which lane he should be in, while pointing out even the most obscure landmarks. Eventually they entered the city, limped down the canyon of George Street, and emerged into the sun and the blue, out across the bridge, the glorious bridge. Davis was relatively unfamiliar with Sydney so had sought the advice of Craven, who had studied at Sydney University. Craven had recommended staying in the CBD until he'd learnt that Lucy was going as well. Then he recommended Manly instead.

It was like a postcard: the sea, the lifeguards, the Norfolk Island pines. Lucy clapped her hands and did a little dance, a bodily expression of her pleasure. They walked along the beach, shoes off, swam in the ocean, and sat above the promenade and ate fish and chips for dinner.

Next day, they caught the ferry into the city and, leaving Lucy to explore it on her own, Davis walked up the hill a block from Circular Quay. Anyone else might have been intimidated by the Lands Building—a grand structure of honeyed sandstone and Empire—but not Davis. For imposing though the building undoubtedly was, it had been built to service the landholders of the colony and house their records, and Davis's family were and had always been prominent among landholders, dating back to the early years of the colony. To his eyes, all the columns and all the archways and all the balustrades and evocations of Rome and Athens existed only to recognise the importance of land and, through that, the landholders. He didn't hesitate; he entered through the front door.

He had called ahead and been told that all records of land transactions in New South Wales dating back to 1863 were held in a central registrar within the Department of Lands. The records themselves were contained in bound volumes, too valuable to be accessed by the public. For that, he would require letters of introduction from his professors at Melbourne. However, there were microfiches available, detailing maps and boundaries and lot numbers, exact copies of the bound volumes. He would be able to access those, identify the holdings he was interested in, then order photocopies of the relevant folios. The turnaround could be some weeks, and payment would be required. Bank cheques preferred.

It took him a while to work out the system, to identify what he was looking for, but soon enough he understood it. Each parcel of land had its own title, and each title had its own record. The record was updated each time the property changed hands. For Three Wells Station, he knew, the record would be simple, recording no sales, just the orderly inheritance from one generation to the next: a thin volume for a very long story. The next entry would be ownership passing from his grandfather to his sister Krystal. The thought made him momentarily sad—his own role in the history of his family would not be recorded here. But then again, it may well be embossed elsewhere, on the spines of books and in the indexes of learned works, places where his sister's name would not be found.

He also learnt that Three Wells Station was unusual. Not all titles continued uninterrupted. Land could be divided into smaller titles, at which point the old record would be closed and a new record for each parcel would begin, keeping to the system of one record per title. Less commonly, land could be consolidated into a single title, also necessitating the creation of a new record.

This knowledge gave him a starting point, and he knew which maps to seek. The first he located was dated 1890, and it covered the region south from the river, with Worthington Point to the west, Narrandera to the east and large grazing claims to the south, with the boundaries between individual titles clearly delineated. As he understood it, the maps themselves were not updated when titles changed hands, only when boundaries were significantly altered. The next map he located was 1912, marking land titles and boundaries as of that meeting of September 1916. The map had no names attached to the titles, just folio numbers, but he was familiar enough with the lay of the land that he could identify some of the holdings, even eight decades later. One feature that intrigued him was Hasluck Creek, leading south into what was labelled Hasluck Lake. But there were property lines running through the lake. Waterways could not be privately owned, he knew that, so it must have been an ephemeral lake. He double-checked his contemporary map and saw the correlation—the main canal a straightened version of the creek, Lake Yuwonderie more or less superimposing itself on the old lake, if only a quarter the size. Smaller, but deeper.

Spooling further through the microfiche, he discovered the next map, drawn in January 1917. He could see it was essentially a copy of the older maps, with new lines inserted. He felt a surge of discovery, a Eureka tremor. The lines were dramatically different. He looked closer. One of the properties—holding half the lake and the area that must now be the town itself—was gone, carved up among the three neighbouring properties. And then a 1924 map: the same land consolidated into a single title. He wrote it all down. The microfiche machine was connected to a photocopier. He reeled off copies, immersed in the hunt. The final thing he did was seek out the most recent maps. The large-scale one covering the region had been redrawn in the 1950s, but with little change; the ones of the town and the irrigation area depicted limited consolidations in the small landholdings; the one of the town revealed new subdivisions, but otherwise the old centre remained remarkably unchanged, still dominated by one large holding.

Afterwards he sat at a table, examining the printed-off maps. He went to the counter and ordered copies of the folios, the ones of the big landholders. The story he'd been seeking felt closer, even though the clerk warned him the summer break meant it might be two or three weeks before he received the records in the post.

As he left, he looked back. In the late afternoon sun, the building's sandstone was aglow, a physical embodiment of the centrality of land. Ownership might pass from one family to another, yet the land itself endured. He thought of the coffee-table book and its narrative: how the Seven had transformed uncultivated fields through irrigation, making their holdings simultaneously more productive and more valuable. A story of cooperation in which everyone emerged a winner; the story promoted by the Canal Club. But, as if illuminated by the light of the setting sun, he saw that the Lands Building hosted a parallel story, one of competition, in which property was bought and sold, in which the Seven had fought backroom battles among themselves to acquire more and more of it: a story in which there were losers as well as winners. He had his narrative.

That evening, Lucy and he walked barefoot on the beach at Manly. He was in a good mood, and she was laughing, dancing about, skipping in and out of the shallows, kicking at the foam. She told him she had only ever seen the ocean twice before: once on a family holiday when her mother was alive and once on a school excursion. She had bought postcards to send to all and sundry.

They dined at an Italian restaurant on the Corso, and she made another confession: it was her first time in a proper restaurant, one where a waiter brought menus and returned to take their orders and poured their wine. Her eyes were wide, and Davis caught a glimpse of how lean her teen years must have been, and how gilded his own had been by comparison.

And yet that night they fought for the first time. It started innocently enough, the enthusiasm of his discoveries bubbling to the surface.

'There were other families, Lucy. Other landholders. One right in the centre, where the town is now.'

'Who was it?'

'I won't know until I get the records. My guess would be the Marneys or the Chaulkers or the Pratts—those families that were part of the initial push for the scheme.'

'They must have taken the money. Been bought out. It happens.'

'True. But when I asked about it during that lunch at the Canal Club, they told me those families' land fell outside the scheme, that it was too elevated or the ground too uneven. But the land in the map was right at the heart of the present-day scheme.'

Lucy was shaking her head. 'It's so long ago. What if you're right? There was some sort of wrongdoing and it ends up implicating your own family, or friends like Otto and Craven.'

He regarded her with astonishment. 'What are you suggesting? I just leave it?'

'Why not? If all it might do is damage the people you care about?'

He was speechless. He'd been convinced they shared a common purpose.

Lucy saw his dismay, tried to reason with him. 'Your grandfather won't live forever, Davis. You must think of the future. You'll have to sit with those men on the company board, dine with them at the Canal Club. You shouldn't antagonise them.'

He looked at her, thought he saw her assumptions, her hopes . . . and felt repelled by them. He told her the truth. 'I won't be sitting on the board—or dining at the Canal Club.'

It was her turn to look astonished. 'What do you mean?'

'My grandfather intends that Krystal should inherit Three Wells Station. She's the elder, after all, and more interested and capable than I'll ever be.'

Now Lucy's face gave nothing away. 'You seem remarkably calm about that,' she said.

'I support it. She'll own Three Wells, but I won't starve. I'll have an annuity. I can live the life I choose.' He gestured around the restaurant, with its candlelight, linen tablecloths and attentive waiters. 'This. Travel.'

Lucy's emotions started to reveal themselves. 'Provided she doesn't balls it up, like my father. We have land, but it makes us no money. Not enough for me to study, not enough for Jayce to finish school. Stuck in my shitkicker job in the basement. That's what happens when land is left untended, when the future is left to drift. When you entrust your future to someone else.'

'My sister is not the same as your father.'

'Is that so? She spends her time flying planes and skiing and sailing the Mediterranean. What does she know of farming? Didn't she go to art school or something?'

'Fine arts,' said Davis coolly, trying to tamp down his own rising anger.

'Yes, I heard she was very inner city.'

'What does that mean?'

'Never mind,' said Lucy, as if sensing she might have overstepped the mark.

But Davis, riled, didn't let it go. 'What's it to you, anyway, what I choose to do?'

And she looked at him, knowing full well his unspoken allegation: that she was more interested in his land and his status than she was in him. 'Fuck you,' she said, and stood up. Before stalking out, she glared down at him. 'My first time in a restaurant. Ever. You prick.'

chapter twenty-one

THE DAY IS PICKING UP HEAT AS IVAN WALKS BACK TO THE POLICE STATION. HE can feel the power of the December sun on his brow, feel the sweat beading, and is glad it's just a couple of blocks. He needs to pick up the car to drive to Air Stills of Australia, up near the summit of the Castle. He pushes through the doors, gives a nod to the duty clerk, mounts the stairs, finds Nell working away in the detectives room.

'Anything?' she asks.

He recaps what Craven has told him about Athol Hasluck being desperate to borrow money. 'And you?'

'I called Jacinta Hasluck.'

'How is she?'

'Not good. Alice had just been there, explained her financial situation.'

'What's she going to do?'

'Take the kids to Wagga. Stay with some friends, seek help from one of Athol's old colleagues.' Nell grimaces. 'I asked her about painkillers. Oxycodone. She says neither she nor Athol used opioids or had a prescription.'

'That's useful. Thanks.'

'I pulled the file on Davis Heartwood and Stella Kippax. McTosh has got one of his constables out searching for Stella's father.'

'What have you learnt?'

'They disappeared early 1994. Just vanished. No sign of them until the body of Davis Heartwood was found in 2009. About ten kilometres north of here, in a woodland reserve near the Murrumbidgee. He was buried in a shallow grave, uncovered by a once-in-a-hundred-year flood. His hands had been tied, and he'd been shot in the head, twice.'

'Executed?'

'Looks like it.'

'No doubt it was him?'

'None. There were remains of shoes, a watch. DNA confirmed it.'

'And the girl?'

'Never found. Her father Bert ran the station here. Led the investigation. He'd been searching for them the whole time. Never gave up. Not until they found the body. They searched the area around Davis's grave, including cadaver dogs, found nothing.'

Ivan whistles. 'Explains a lot.'

'Sounds like it all but finished him. He retired on medical grounds.' Nell shifts in her seat. 'Stella was his only child. His wife died back when she was a kid.'

Ivan is momentarily lost for words; there is only the sound of the fan slowly revolving overhead. 'Davis Heartwood came from a wealthy family,' he says at last. 'Was there a reward offered for information?'

Nell frowns. 'No, not that I can see. Although they paid to extend the search in the woodlands, and hired a private investigator.'

'Anyone we know?'

'No. Melbourne-based. A Dorothy Newing.'

'Worth a call?' asks Ivan.

'Dead three years ago.'

'Inconsiderate of her.'

'An inquest into Davis's death found he'd been murdered, most likely shortly after the couple's disappearance. The coroner surmised that it was reasonable to assume Stella was also dead but didn't make it a definitive finding.'

'Okay. Anything else?'

'A couple of things. There was money missing from a safe at the Heartwood property, Three Wells Station. Approximately two hundred and fifty thousand dollars in cash. Police theorised that Davis and Stella had taken the money and run off together. Sounds like that's what Bert Kippax believed, even though the Heartwood family insisted that such behaviour would be totally out of character for Davis. Then, after his body was found, the money was seen in a different light; perhaps thieves had forced him to open the safe, then killed him and the girl. At any rate, the money was never recovered.'

'What was the other thing?' asks Ivan.

'Davis's car. An Alfa Romeo. It was found parked in the main street here, with the car keys missing. Also'—Nell takes a breath, swallows—'a local doctor gave evidence. She thought Stella may have been pregnant.'

'Jesus. Bert Kippax know that?'

'He was the investigating officer.'

'God.'

Ivan catches himself staring at Nell, that intense gaze he adopts when thinking, peering directly into her brown eyes. She raises her eyebrows at him; after two years she's used to it. He looks away, picks up the photograph, the one that Alice found inside Athol's diary. Davis with Lucy Titchfield on his lap, Stella sitting next to them, with Athol standing behind her, his hands on her shoulders possessively.

'Three decades ago, a young man was murdered and his girlfriend disappeared. Now Athol Hasluck is killed, and he had this photo in the front of his diary. What's the connection? Is there a connection?'

There's a long silence, Nell concentrating. Eventually she speaks. 'You think it should be the focus?'

Ivan shakes his head. 'Athol and his debts have to be more relevant than a thirty-year-old photo. The sooner Alice and Kevin can get stuck into that, the better.'

— —

Unlike the walking track, which climbs from the town side at least as far as the lookout with the bench, the maintenance road ascends the far side of the Castle, where the incline is less steep. It gives Ivan another opportunity to look out beyond the borders of the irrigation district. The boundary is clearly defined: the western edge runs south from the bottom of the Castle below the ridge that Eggs had pointed out to him. The Spur, he had called it. Hardly any elevation at all, not enough to require a cutting for the road to run through—but enough to impede the flow of water. The divide between irrigation and dryland, between the land of plenty and the land of not enough. Beyond the Spur there's a stark change in the landscape, the colour drained out of it. Drought-prone and marginal. Somewhere out there is the land Athol Hasluck purchased just weeks before his death: a man desperately short of money squandering half a million dollars. Why?

Ivan reaches the turn-off to the Castle. The road climbs through sparse trees, getting more and more steep, and then begins to wind its way back and forth across the gradient. He reaches the shoulder before the last rise to the summit, the place where the walking path joins the road. And here's a gate, double-locked and adorned with signs. AIR STILLS OF AUSTRALIA and ACCESS PROHIBITED—TRESPASSERS PROSECUTED and PRIVATE PROPERTY—ENTRY BY APPOINTMENT. As if to emphasise the point, Ivan can see another video surveillance camera. He rings again, talks to the same voice he spoke to when he arranged his visit.

'Oh, that's right. I'll come fetch you.'

It takes a good ten minutes, and Ivan is feeling irritated by the time a small white van arrives on the far side of the gate. There are logos painted on each door: the smiling water drop with ASA underneath. A man wearing a white lab coat and thick glasses emerges, looking like a boffin from central casting. He unlocks the gate with some difficulty.

Ivan joins him. 'G'day.'

'You got ID?' asks the man.

Ivan flicks out his badge.

The man squints at it through his glasses, getting in close. Time for a new prescription, thinks Ivan.

'And you are?' he asks.

'Dr Quentin Ponds.'

'You're a doctor?'

'PhD. Two of them. Electrical engineering and metallurgy.'

'Impressive.'

'Leave your car here. No cameras, no phones,' says Ponds.

The calm abruptness of the statement seems unusual to Ivan, and he wonders if Dr Ponds might not live somewhere on the spectrum. He raises his eyebrows, but realises the expression is beyond the acuity of the doctor's eyes. 'I'm a police officer. I'm keeping my phone. I won't take pictures without permission.'

The scientist looks momentarily bewildered, then says, 'Take it up with the boss. His rules, not mine. Jump in.'

Ivan climbs into the passenger seat. There's steel mesh between the driver's compartment and the back. It's like an electrician's van, full of cabling and tools and drawers and whatnot. Ponds gets the engine going, leaning all the way forward, practically engulfing the steering wheel as he moves his head close to the windscreen, as if this might somehow improve his vision. Ivan almost offers to drive, but thankfully the scientist swaps out his Coke-bottle glasses for an alternative pair: prescription sunglasses. 'That's better,' he says. 'Keep forgetting I have them.'

The track winds around the side of the hill, through some scrubby bushland, until they're facing north-west, away from the town. Ivan glances out the window. From this side of the Castle, the view is of flat swathes of brown and blond, broken in the distance by more buttes, distant cousins of the Castle, and the thin tree line of the Murrumbidgee.

'Any reason you're located halfway up a mountain?' he asks, more as a way of making conversation than anything.

'Altitude.'

'That helps?'

'Of course. A few degrees cooler, the wind a knot or two stronger.'

'Why's that important?'

Ponds is about to answer, then thinks better of it. 'Ask the boss.'

They continue along the track until it emerges onto a plateau, looking almost carved into the Castle. They pass an impressive array of solar panels, at least a hundred of them in two groups, and two windmills, the power-generating kind: not huge, but big enough.

'Lot of electricity,' comments Ivan, an image of Athol Hasluck's hands returning.

'Lot needed,' says Ponds.

There's a large steel machinery shed and a couple of smaller demountable buildings. Ponds pulls up outside one. OFFICE, says a sign. A Range Rover is parked outside: fully optioned, a couple of hundred grand's worth. Victorian plates.

'In there,' says Ponds as they climb out of the van. 'See ya.'

'Thanks,' says Ivan, but the scientist is already scuttling towards the machinery shed, as if relieved to be alone.

Ivan can hear a voice inside the office, and knocks on the door. It's opened by a man of about sixty talking loudly into a phone he's holding out in front of him. 'Not good enough,' he says, as he waves Ivan in. 'Not nearly good enough.' A pause. 'No, it's not acceptable. Put him on.' He shrugs at Ivan apologetically, gestures for him to take a seat. 'Ah, André,' he says, and then continues the conversation in what sounds like French.

He's wearing Bluetooth earbuds, so Ivan can't hear the other part of the conversation. He looks about the room. Desk, chair, computer, filing cabinets, a site map, a whiteboard. There's a display case containing a scale model of the work site and a monitor, mounted on the wall, showing the local weather conditions: temperature, wind speed and direction, relative humidity, as well as other measurements: power output, litres per hour and water storage.

The telephone conversation ends.

'Inspector Lucic, welcome. I'm Toby Fairchild. Founder and CEO. Sorry about that. Some of these suppliers try to get away with murder.' He holds out his hand as he talks; when Ivan goes to shake it, the man envelops the detective's hand with both of his. The handshake of a politician. Or a salesman.

'It's just sergeant,' says Ivan. 'Detective sergeant.'

'Bound for promotion, surely,' says the man jovially, with a twinkle in his eye. He reminds Ivan of someone: a movie star or someone on television—a game show host, perhaps. His voice is booming, as if projecting to a studio audience. His face is tanned, his snow-white hair swept back in a leonine mane. A golden rock of a watch radiates wealth from his wrist. 'What brings you here, Sergeant?'

'A local man died four nights ago. Athol Hasluck. We're investigating his murder.'

'Murder? So it was murder?' The man sounds almost excited at the prospect.

'We believe so.'

The joviality drops away from the man like a beach towel, leaving him suddenly solemn and still. 'My apologies. It's a very exciting time for my company. I get so caught up in it, I forget that there's a world outside. How can I be of assistance?'

'Mr Hasluck invested money in your company.'

'Indeed he did. A considerable amount. An astute investor. I dare say his widow will be thanking him.' The solemnity is beginning to fracture, the enthusiasm oozing through its gaps.

'Can you tell me how much he had invested?' asks Ivan.

'Not off the top of my head. A sizeable amount, I can tell you that much. Not one of our cornerstone investors, not by a long shot, but quite significant for a moderate-income individual.'

'Six figures?'

'Oh, yes. I would say so. But not seven. Or eight.'

'His own money?'

That gives Fairchild pause. 'I believe so. But he was also instrumental in guiding a number of high-net-worth investors from the local area. He was a financial adviser, ran his own wealth-creation advisory service. Fully qualified, fully authorised. We are diligent in checking such matters.'

'Members of the Seven? They're investors?'

Fairchild breaks into a broad grin as if they are sharing a joke, displaying teeth that are Hollywood-white. 'Ah, yes. The Seven. Quaint, aren't they, these small towns? But yes, some of them. I can't give you names, you understand, but I'm sure they would be happy to confirm their stakes should you ask. They're proud of their contribution to the prosperity of this town, eager to see it progress.'

Ivan attempts to puncture the entrepreneur's buoyancy. 'Can you tell me where you were on Saturday night?'

But it only elicits a guffaw. 'Melbourne. Dinner with friends and family. Plenty of witnesses.'

Ivan's finding it hard to get a handle on Fairchild; he seems resolutely upbeat, despite the murder of one of his investors. 'Tell me, Mr Fairchild: what exactly are people investing in here?'

'The future, that's what. A never-ending, guaranteed supply of water. The great Australian dream, the unattainable dream, made real.'

'Is that right?' asks Ivan.

'Ha,' says Fairchild. 'I hear the doubt in your voice. No, don't try to deny it; I've heard it a thousand times before. But give me five minutes and I'll change your mind.'

'I'm all ears.'

'First, consider where we are. Australia. Driest populated continent on earth. A landmass the size of Western Europe or the continental United States, but most of it is desert, or too arid, or with rainfall too unreliable for any sort of cropping. Grazing a head or two of cattle every ten square kilometres, at most. All that potential, lost for want of moisture. Now consider Yuwonderie; see what happens when you can access reliable water.

'Yuwonderie is some of the best agricultural land in the world. Good soil, more blue-sky days than practically anywhere, and water. The soil isn't going anywhere, and neither is the sunlight, but the water remains the limiting factor. Irrigation was meant to drought-proof this land, guarantee never-ending prosperity. But it's failing. For all the dams and weirs, for all of the Snowy Mountains Scheme and diverting rivers inland, the authorities still struggle to satisfy demand. There have been years here when irrigators have received only a fraction of their allowances. Places not far from here have had years when they received none: a zero allocation.'

'Looks pretty good to me.'

'Oh, it is—this year. The dams are full, water is cheap. But people here remember the millennium drought. It's burnt into the collective memory. Many didn't survive; others were left traumatised.' Fairchild leans forward, lowering his voice as if sharing a confidence. 'The water market is failing. Corrupt. Infested—infested, I say—with charlatans and spivs and fast money men. Screen jockeys and smooth talkers. They've cornered the market, manipulating it at will. The money they made during the drought, off the back of those poor farmers . . . utterly unconscionable. A national disgrace. And the government just sat back and cheered them on.'

And now Ivan realises what Fairchild reminds him of, with his booming voice and theatrical appearance: he sounds like a preacher, an evangelist. 'Go on,' Ivan says, as if the man needs encouragement.

'Well, those farmers, those who survived, aren't stupid. They know the good times will end, that drought will come again. People out here used to be sceptical about climate change. Well, no more. The smart ones—and most of the survivors are smart— are trying to find a way to insure against the next big dry. Some are trying to buy more permanent water, higher-security water. Easy enough for those with deep pockets, like the Seven; not so easy for the little bloke. Most of them live hand to mouth. This year, you can buy temporary water for next to nothing. But try to buy permanent water, high-security water, and it'll cost you an arm and a leg, and that's if you can find any for sale.'

Ivan has heard enough. 'Tell me about Air Stills.'

'You know much about science?' asks Fairchild.

'If a grape grower can comprehend it, I'm sure I'll manage.'

'With forensic clarity,' says Fairchild, laying on more charm. 'The thing is this: the air is full of water. See?' He points to the wall monitor. 'Right now, relative humidity is sixty per cent. At one hundred per cent, it would be raining.'

'There's barely a cloud in the sky.'

'Deceptive, isn't it?' says Fairchild, beaming, as if Ivan has made exactly the right observation. 'Here's the nub of it. It's called relative humidity for a reason: it's relative to the amount of water the atmosphere can hold before it starts condensing. That's dependent on a number of factors, the most important of which is temperature.' He turns to the digital display and back again. 'The temperature currently is thirty-one degrees. If it suddenly fell to about twelve degrees, then relative humidity would increase to one hundred per cent; clouds would form, and it would begin to pour down.'

'With the same amount of water in the atmosphere?'

'Precisely. And this is an important point. If climate change drives average air temperature up by two per cent, then the atmosphere will hold vastly more water. This is a two-edged sword for farmers. The higher temperatures mean the atmosphere can carry more water without raining, but if the temperature does drop, the water will quite literally fall out of the sky. And that, in a nutshell, is what we are in the process of accomplishing. Extracting water from thin air—or what will increasingly become fat air. Fat with water vapour.'

'If it's so obvious, why hasn't anyone done it before?'

'Oh, they have, they have. But for drinking water, not agriculture. We're talking large scale. New technology.'

'What's new about it?'

Fairchild smiles. 'Am I looking at a prospective investor?'

Ivan smiles back. 'You never know.'

'You'll have to be quick. We are right at the end of a capital raising. Finishes in two days' time, at close of business Friday. It'll set us up for a stock market listing and going into production. The culmination of years of work. The pay-off.'

'Is that what Athol believed?'

'Correct. Come the listing, his holding would become liquid. He can sell on market. My prediction is that existing shareholders will double or triple their money. Tenfold isn't out of the question. That's if they're unwise enough to cash in.'

'I might be interested,' says Ivan, finding it strangely easy to lie. 'I'm expecting to come into some family money. But you'll have to explain the technology.'

'Right,' says Fairchild, rubbing his hands, the preacher with the prospect of a convert. 'There are three existing technologies. One process is chemical. But that's expensive, and there are all sorts of issues with contamination and waste disposal. So forget that. Leave it for NASA and Mars. The second method is cooling down metal lattices using traditional refrigeration. Water vapour condenses on the lattices and drips down into a reservoir. Works well enough, it's just not cost-effective. Uses a lot of power and the heat pumps are expensive, with limited life spans. Lots of moving parts, expensive to manufacture, expensive to run, expensive to maintain. The third method is the one we're pursuing. No moving parts and powered by renewable energy. It exploits a well-known phenomenon, the Peltier effect. If you pass an electrical current through two plates made of different metals, it can warm one plate and cool the other, forming condensation on the cool plate. So think about that. A simple construction with no moving parts, no maintenance and a life span measured in decades, all powered by renewable electricity.'

'Sounds like a no-brainer.'

'So why hasn't anyone done it before? That's what you're thinking, isn't it?'

'Crossed my mind,' says Ivan.

'Because the effect is weak. Lots of power needed for not much water. But what we've managed to do here is develop new, far more efficient alloys that magnify the effect manyfold, making it cost-effective on a large scale for the first time. Suitable for agriculture. Simple and cheap to manufacture. Some of the exotic rare earth minerals used in the alloys are expensive, that's true, but they increase the yield exponentially. We've also developed a new matrix for the plates. To the naked eye they look the same, but on the microscopic level they channel electricity, air and water in highly effective ways. Our main labs are in Melbourne, but our testing grounds are here.'

'Why Yuwonderie?'

'This is where we are likely to sell our finished product. Arid, inland Australia. Where rain has always been unreliable and insufficient, and irrigation is going the same way. But it's near a developed area, with infrastructure and transport and workers and wholesalers. This site we're on here is ideal. There's a little bit of altitude, so it's naturally a degree or two cooler than down on the plain, and there's plenty of wind for electricity generation.

And any water collected can flow downhill.' Fairchild smiles, arms wide, as if everything is explained.

'And the locals are enthusiastic?'

'Absolutely. Why wouldn't they be? And one more advantage: the water is pure, free of pollutants and salt. Pristine.'

'Can you show me?'

'Well, we keep the technology under wraps,' says Fairchild, but the allure of a prospective convert seems to win him over. 'You will need to leave your phone here. I'm sorry, but some of this technology is highly sensitive.'

'Sure,' says Ivan.

Fairchild leads the way across to the large machinery shed. There are entries for vehicle access, but the retractable doors are shut. Instead, Fairchild punches a code into a lock and they enter through a regular-sized door.

Inside, Ivan can hear a low-pitched drone and smell oil and something else. Ozone. Over a low partition, Ivan can see the tops of huge stainless-steel vats, like in a commercial winery, and air shafts, like air-conditioning ducts.

The entrepreneur leads him over to a machine of stainless steel. It's tall: three times Ivan's height. Fairchild points upwards: the top of the machine is connected to one of the air-conditioning ducts. 'That's where the air is fed through from outside. We're experimenting with some evaporative cooling to drop the temperature a few degrees before it hits the plates. And you see the cables? They're going into the back of the still, bringing in electricity from the solar panels and windmills.'

Ivan can hear the machine humming. 'It uses quite a bit of power?'

'Not an outrageous amount. The process is already efficient, and we're improving it all the time. The Melbourne team is highly motivated.'

'Dangerous, isn't it? All this electricity and water mixing?'

Fairchild laughs. 'No. Not at all; not if you know what you're doing. Come up, I'll give you a look.'

They climb the ladder.

Fairchild opens the door at the front, triggering a light. And there before Ivan is a series of plates mounted in an array, long thin triangles, narrower at the bottom than at the top, glistening with condensation, dripping water.

'World class. Cutting edge. State of the art,' summarises Fairchild. 'Seen enough? I need to shut the door or we'll have Dr Ponds on to us for messing up his measurements.'

'All good,' says Ivan.

They return down the ladder.

'In the base here is the collection vat,' says Fairchild, leading Ivan around to the side of the machine.

There's a tap. A shelf with stainless-steel tumblers. Fairchild grins, raising his eyebrows, and pours a glass of water, passes the tumbler to Ivan, then pours himself one. The container is cold to the touch, and the water cool and clear to drink.

'It's distilled. Naturally, by the sun. Collected by us. One hundred per cent natural, one hundred per cent pure, one hundred per cent renewable.' And Fairchild raises his tumbler in a toast. 'Taste it: the future of Australian agriculture.'

Ivan can't help but be impressed, but he returns his attention to his investigation. 'So what exactly were you promising Athol Hasluck to attract his investment?'

'Same as everyone else. A share in the future. A foundation stake in a transformative technology. All of our processes are heavily patented; the IP is rock solid. We'll apply to list on the stock exchange as soon as we've completed the capital raising. That's if we're not taken over beforehand. There are some very big companies circling. Very big. Global. They see the potential. But I'll tell you the same thing I told Athol: I've spent years on this, devoted my life, my fortune. We won't be selling cheaply.'

'You could get bought out?'

'Sure, if the premium is generous enough. I hold a majority stake.' He shrugs. 'I want to make money, of course, but I also want to help these poor sods who have found themselves exploited by the water traders. And a big company would be able to ramp up to full production, accelerate further efficiencies and bring this to market far more quickly.'

'Did Athol Hasluck at any stage attempt to withdraw his investment?'

Fairchild becomes serious for a moment. 'He did. About two months ago. How could you possibly know that?'

'He was in debt.'

'So he claimed. But I couldn't help him. Every penny I have is sunk into this company. Mortgaged the house, sold the investment properties, tapped the super fund.' Fairchild gestures around the shed. 'This is everything I have. I'm all in. That's the reason for the capital raising: to get us over the line for the stock market listing, to meet the ASX requirements.'

'Sounds risky.'

'Not with this technology. This is like being in on the ground floor at Apple or Google or Microsoft. This is a game changer.'

'Did Hasluck owe you any money?'

Fairchild blinks. 'No. Not me.' And again the entrepreneur extends his arms in a gesture of openness. 'I had no reason to wish harm to Athol. He brought me a lot of solid investments. Not just his own, but money from the Seven and others. I owe him, not the other way around.'

'So he didn't get any of his investment back?'

'No. In fact, just a week or two ago he was inquiring about investing more. He knew he was on a winner. A month from now, two at the most, his debts would be a thing of the past.'

——

Driving back down the mountain, Ivan considers what he knows about Hasluck. If what Fairchild says is true, then that would explain why the accountant didn't try to disguise his debts, why he was prepared to raid the trust account: because he was confident of repaying it well before the audit. And it suggests something else: the rationale for splurging on the purchase of the barren block on the other side of the Spur. Water flows downhill, as Fairchild had said, from the Castle to the blocks surrounding its base, no matter on which side of the Spur they were located.

chapter twenty-two

September 1914

War has come, Mother. I'd heard it spoken of, but dismissed it as nothing more than the men wanting to sound important, to voice their opinions with the same authority as they expound on the weather and the cricket and wool prices, as if anything they might say could possibly have a bearing on events a world away. I had thought whatever might unfold in Europe could never affect us here: a man no one had ever heard of shot over a grievance no one understands in a city no one can pronounce. And yet the men were right: we are at war. Not just any war, either; already they are calling it the Great War, saying we must be part of it, that we should *want* to be part of it, that it will engulf the world and all its empires.

It is a terrible thing, Mother, this war, but for me it has proven a godsend, for it has reconciled Jack and myself. For months we circled each other, neither of us knowing how we might break the impasse, whether we wanted to, whether we dared to, his marriage a seemingly impenetrable barrier, with still a year to run. But his imminent departure has provided the catalyst, the knowledge that our time together is limited, that the horizon of the future is no longer so expansive.

Jack says he must go, he and Noel both. They say Australia is raising an army, and first and foremost they seek horsemen to form a cavalry, the Australian Light Horse, the finest in the world. He claims that the mounted troops of Europe, with their rigid formations and uniform drills, can be no match for the flair of the Australian bushmen and our horses. I smile encouragingly, but what do we know of European armies and their abilities, except that they have had centuries to refine their skills and practise their butchery?

I admonish myself for wasting this past half-year: squandering it, as I see it now. Who knows how long our impasse may have lasted if the war had not put an end to it?

Jack has given me a ring. It's a plain band, unadorned, but made of pure silver. I wear it on my right hand, with pride and disbelief: its meaning is clear, for Jack and myself and for all the world. Jack wears a matching one, unusual in a man. I think it is that, as much as anything, that has allayed Mrs Titchfield's anxieties. She has warned me to be circumspect, not to court scandal. No doubt it's the reputation of her own family she is most concerned with protecting, but I can't help but feel she looks upon me with a generosity of heart. Or perhaps she is cunning, and realises that, come another year, I will be elevated, a lady of the district and a member of their incipient gentry, for without the Marneys, there can be no irrigation scheme.

Jack and I are careful. Having brushed up against public condemnation once, we are at pains to avoid it a second time. Fortunately, the land hereabouts is so empty, populated by sheep and cattle and kangaroos, that it is harder to locate company than it is to find solitude.

He has gifted me a horse, a pony, and is teaching me to ride. I have called her Penny. She is a mild-mannered thing, intimidated at first by Jack and Noel's steeds. I find it strange and exhilarating and not a little scary. Jack says the secret to horses is straightforward: treat Penny with kindness and she will return the favour.

When I could ride well enough, he took me across to their farmstead. Jolimont is its name, and that of their spread. Many of the local farmsteads are built on low rises, a few feet above the plain, a small insurance against the floods that may or may not come again. Jolimont is different; it stands on a real hill, giving a view out over the plain and all the way to the Murrumbidgee forest. The Castle is closer there, even more prominent than here at the Titchfields. I wonder what name we might have for the rock in our language, Mother. Would you know? It can be seen for miles, and such a notable landmark must surely have a name and stories to go with it. In the dawn, whether seen from Castle View or from Jolimont, the rising sun hits it first, so that it glows above the plain, a beacon welcoming the new day. I can see it, in the distance, from the Titchfields', and it comforts me to think Jack might also be gazing upon it from his own home.

The house itself is not grand, but the Marneys have owned Jolimont for less than ten years. Noel said their father bought it from the original settlers, Scots called Stewart, who had purchased it from the local blacks. I laughed when he said it, and was forced to explain that our people would never sell land as the concept of possessing it is foreign to us. He insisted they had taken the payment, becoming somewhat annoyed, and I agreed that was likely, that they would have seen it as a wonderful jape, receiving something for nothing.

Noel looked at me then, anger gone, and he said to me, 'You really are a rare bird, Bessie.' I think it was a compliment, that there was admiration in his voice. I would like to think so. He is a good and loyal brother to Jack, and supportive of our entwinement. 'You are good for him,' he said another time. 'You have returned him to himself and to the world. That is good enough for me.'

The main house, Jolimont, is rightly Noel's, although Jack bunks there most of the time. But when Noel marries, Jack has a little bush block of his own, separated from the main property, about seven miles away on the other side of the Castle, by a little billabong on the flood plain, near a place they have called Corkhills Creek. I don't know who Corkhill was or why the creek is named after him, but there is a rough hut there, down among the trees beside a stock route. It was a drover's cottage. Now that I can ride, we go there on occasion, on my half-day off, and picnic beside the water, away from prying eyes and gossip-laden tongues.

But now that must end, for Jack will enlist; he says he cannot shirk it. I want him to wait; wait until he is divorced, wait until we are married.

'To what purpose?' he asks. 'Are we not already man and wife? What do we care what the world may think, or what formalities they might insist upon? And I will return to you, Bessie, you know that. I will never forsake you. Never.'

Noel will follow as quickly as he can, once he has settled their affairs. The brothers say that all the men in the district will go; they will be the elite, members of this grand Australian cavalry. Horace Titchfield, too, has made his intention clear, much to his mother's dismay, although he will remain behind even longer than Noel, to push the irrigation scheme through before he leaves.

The Marney brothers have come to an agreement with the Titchfields. Once Noel has gone, Horace will care for their property, for the cattle and sheep, for the fences and the sheds. And I am to spend two days a week at Jolimont, cleaning it and keeping it in good order. It is a practical measure, of course, yet I can't but interpret it as an endorsement, the Titchfields acknowledging that I will soon join the Marney family.

Amid the excitement, only Mrs Titchfield seems subdued. She is still mourning her own husband and dreads the thought of being alone; Elaine has returned to school for a final few weeks and now Horace is set upon going to war. Mrs Titchfield is pressing him not to enlist, but he is stubborn and used to getting his way.

I asked Jack to teach me to shoot.

He looked at me hard after I made the request. 'Whatever for?'

'The district is emptying of men, and Elaine has returned to her studies. Mrs Titchfield and I will be left to defend ourselves.'

'From what?' asked Jack, voice laced with concern. 'Do you fear your kinsmen?'

I had to laugh at that, to quell the insult and dampen my pride. He is such a good man, Mother, but sometimes I despair of his ignorance. Yet he relented and taught me to shoot, although I fear I will never be any good at it. Jack himself is as natural with a rifle as he is with a horse, smooth and confident. And yet, as he drew a bead, talked me through it, squeezed the trigger, I could see the cloud come across his eyes. It is one thing to down a rabbit; it is another to end a man.

As the day of his departure approached, we were alone at the little shack down by Corkhills Creek, having ridden out by ourselves, and he once again pressed his suit, voicing his intentions.

Jack told me he had instructed a lawyer in Narrandera to pursue the divorce the moment the five years has passed, even in his absence, so that when he returns, we might marry immediately. And he told me that he had this solicitor, McLean, draw up a last will and testament. His land and his property—his little shack with its bush block—would pass to me and not his wife. She would receive his army pension but would have no claim on the land. He told me Noel knows of the document, that he witnessed it and will be executor. He hung his head and told me that if the reverse were to happen, that if Noel should fall, Jolimont and its lands would pass to him.

He refers to me as his fiancée. It is a comfort. But just as I saw the thoughts that clouded his mind as he drew the bead on the rabbit, I know the same thoughts bother him more generally. He promises with his words that he shall return, but with his actions he prepares for an eventuality in which he does not.

I hate this war, Mother, even though he is yet to leave, even before a shot is fired. First it brought us together again, and now it conspires against us and our future. And what a future it is that he paints for us, Mother. There will be water, and we can have a homestead and children. And you can leave the mission and come stay with us, for a visit or to live. It will be a future as bright as any we could ever imagine. It is so close that I can almost touch it.

Your loving daughter,
Bessie

chapter twenty-three

IVAN DRIVES DIRECTLY TO HIS NEXT APPOINTMENT AT THE CANAL CLUB, HEADING back into town from the Castle and not bothering to call in at the station. Craven Allsop at the Water Traders and Toby Fairchild at Air Stills have both confirmed Athol poured money into their respective ventures and that he was in debt, although if what Fairchild said was true, and Athol had inquired about topping up his investment only a week or two ago, he must have found a new source of money. That would fit with Alice's discovery that the murdered accountant had recently spent half a million dollars buying land. But where had the money come from? Alice said she could find no record of its origins. If Athol had been desperate, maybe he'd done something desperate, something off the books. Something that had got him killed.

Ivan arrives at the Canal Club, parks the car. It's an elegant building by the town canal. The exterior is immaculate, the interior opulent with wood and brass and thick carpets. There is a hush to the place, as if the building itself demands respect. He's come to meet Nigel Blaxland, president of Otto Titchfield's

Country First party. A deferential man dressed like a butler asks him to wait in the foyer while he informs Blaxland. It gives Ivan a chance to consider his approach. He had every reason to interview Craven Allsop and Toby Fairchild: Athol had invested money with them. This is different. Nigel Blaxland is head of one of the Seven families, a man of political influence. Ivan will need to tread carefully.

Blaxland himself appears, waddling towards Ivan. He is a big man, in his seventies, stooped and losing the battle against gravity. His jowls hang below the uppermost of his chins, those chins cascading directly into his cravat without an intervening neck. His eyebrows have run feral, like an unclipped hedge, and beneath them his eyelids are so hooded that to properly survey Ivan he lifts his head and peers down along his bulbous, scarlet nose, giving him an imperious air as they shake hands. The man's eyes float like oysters.

The Blaxland family patriarch leads the way through to a lounge, shuffling slowly with the aid of an ebony cane, wheezing as he goes. His gut, encased in a blue cotton shirt, is overflowing his belt like a meaty sporran. They reach a set of maroon chesterfields facing each other across an antique marble-topped table, and Blaxland lowers himself, spreading out, reminding Ivan of a walrus on a beach. Ivan sits opposite but doesn't speak, allowing Blaxland time to recover his breath.

'Would you like to dine?' the big man eventually asks, hand on his extensive stomach.

The suggestion repels Ivan: being locked into a long meal inside the stuffy confines of the club, watching Blaxland devour who knows what. 'No, thank you—I've already eaten,' he lies, setting his stomach protesting. He realises he's overdue for lunch. Too late now.

'I knew Athol Hasluck quite well,' says Blaxland, not waiting for Ivan to pose the question. 'A very sincere, very diligent young man. The sort the party needs. Next generation.'

Ivan smiles, places his phone on the table. 'Protocol says I should record our conversation, but I'm sure it's not necessary.'

A deep harrumph emerges from Blaxland, as if from an underground cavern. 'You're welcome to. Can't imagine it will be of much use, though.'

Ivan nods his gratitude but doesn't start recording. He wants Blaxland to be candid, and he doesn't want to antagonise someone possessing such political clout. They're interrupted by a waiter, dressed immaculately and displaying the same practised deference as the man at the door. Blaxland orders a port; Ivan agrees to a soda water. He waits for the staff member to recede before asking his first question.

'How deeply was Athol Hasluck involved in party business?'

'Possibly not as much as he would have liked. I believe he harboured ambitions.'

'Such as?'

'The party is relatively new, as I'm sure you know. Otto split from the Nationals eight years ago. First term he was an independent. Thought he might reconcile with the party, that they'd see the error of their ways. When that didn't happen, he ran as a candidate of the Country First Party. It was just a banner at first, but once he was re-elected, he started thinking bigger, beyond his own future. We established a proper party structure. We've had a huge response. Local National Party supporters are sick of the

Queenslanders ruling the roost, doing more for corporate miners than for family farms. They want their own voice and we're giving it to them. Now we're ready to take the next step.'

'Otto Titchfield moving to federal parliament?'

'That's part of it. Not easy, but we're confident we can do it. He has the profile, has the support. So we will need a replacement for his state seat. We'll also run candidates for the Senate and for the state upper house, the Legislative Council. We're in with a chance in both.'

'So Country First has come a long way in a short time. And Athol Hasluck wanted to be part of it?' prompts Ivan.

'Indeed. Offering his services pro bono. Useful chap.'

'What roles did he play?'

'Nothing senior. Not on the party executive. Just rank and file. Helped with the books for the local branch, but not head office. He also did the accounts for the Watermen's Foundation. No doubt trying to curry favour.'

'Did he have any say in where the Watermen's funds were spent?'

'None. That's up to the board.'

'You're on the board?'

'Yes, ex-officio, as party president.'

The waiter interrupts, delivering Blaxland's fortified wine and Ivan's soda water, plus a bowl of olives, some nuts and a bunch of plump grapes. Ivan can't remember Blaxland requesting them; clearly the staff know their clientele. Ivan thanks the waiter; his host doesn't bother.

'How is the money spent?' asks Ivan.

Blaxland plucks a grape, sucks it into his mouth, chews before answering. 'There are three bodies: Country First's national body; the local branch that looks after Otto's campaign and now that of his replacement at the state level; and the Watermen's Foundation. Three bodies with overlapping objectives, but run independently and with different rules. The money we raise as a party is used exclusively for the party. General running costs and to fund campaigns. Watermen's is different.'

'How so? Doesn't the money still go to the party?'

'Not necessarily.' Blaxland eyes Ivan's phone. 'You sure that thing isn't recording?'

'Of course.'

'Thank you,' says Blaxland. 'What I'm about to tell you doesn't sound good coming from a party president.' He takes two or three olives, chews at them, then holds a small bowl beneath his mouth and spits the pips into it. 'Watermen's is a fundraising body primarily established to circumvent donation disclosure laws. You'll see all sorts of other reasons given, but that's the essence of it. Big donors, not wanting to be identified. You follow?'

'Yes. I understand all the parties have something similar. Associated entities.'

'Good. You've done your homework. And because Watermen's is technically independent from Country First, it has much greater discretion over where it spends the money. So we've been seeding third-party activist groups, paying social media mercenaries, hiring preference whisperers, cultivating journalists, getting private investigators to dig dirt on rivals. The dark arts. And helping out like-minded candidates in other parties, often in return for preference deals, or inducing them to defect to us. That sort of thing.'

'A slush fund,' says Ivan.

Blaxland rumbles with mirth, like a trifle in an earthquake. 'You said it, not me.'

'So how did Athol fit in?'

The mirth subsides. 'He didn't. Not in any decision-making capacity. He did the books, that's all.'

'But he could see where the money was coming from, and where it was going. Potentially sensitive information.'

The big man's wild eyebrows come together to form an uninterrupted hedgerow of concern. 'You're suggesting he was blackmailing someone?'

'Is it possible?'

There's a low-frequency rumble of unease and a moment of consideration before the party president answers. 'Difficult to see. There's the potential for some embarrassment, true, but I know of no illegalities, either by the donors or the foundation, nothing you'd pay a lot of money to keep buried.'

Ivan changes direction. 'You were telling me about Athol's ambitions.'

Blaxland grunts, grabs a handful of nuts and feeds his maw, chewing as he speaks. 'I understand he was considering nominating for Otto's vacant state seat.'

'How did you rate his chances?'

Blaxland finishes chewing the nuts, sips some port. The glass looks tiny in his fleshy mitt. 'Difficult to say.'

'I'm told he was part of a reform faction. A ginger group.'

This time the eruption of mirth is tectonic, and Ivan fears momentarily that he's about to be sprayed with nuts. But Blaxland contains his outburst before speaking. 'That's an amusing way of framing it.' The family head shifts forward in his chesterfield, as if to confide some secret, but his girth prevents him and he settles back with a sigh. 'Look, the reality up until now is that Otto and the party have been reliant to a large extent on the Seven. I assume you are familiar with the founding families?'

Ivan looks around the Canal Club before answering. 'I am.'

'Athol and a few of his fellow travellers wanted Country First to become more inclusive, to widen the base of the party to include more small landholders. And more diversity. Women, migrants, small businesses, that sort of thing. As party members, not just voters. So understand, any reform agenda he was promoting was to do with internals, not policy or electoral strategy. He was no more progressive than the rest of Country First. Thank goodness.'

'And what do you think of his proposal?'

'Me? I consider it a distraction. So does Otto. We need to spread geographically, not spend time and effort garnering additional support here in the one place where we already have plenty.'

'Are the Seven families all party members?'

'No. Far from it. But they all donate, which is the important thing.'

'Watermen's or the party?'

'Both. But don't tell them I said so.'

'Did Athol believe the party was captive to the Seven?'

'I doubt it. He was a Hasluck, after all. Otto and Lucy wouldn't have him managing the books if he'd felt like that.' Blaxland peers about him, as if assessing the quality of the Canal Club. 'The Seven

227

bring much to the party, and not just money. History, for a start. Every local member in the state parliament going back to the First World War has come from one or other of the families; Otto is simply the most recent. We enjoy a high profile, a high standing in the community, a reputation for benevolence and philanthropy. Our endorsements carry a lot of weight.'

'I'm led to believe Watermen's has attracted some very generous donations.'

'I believe so. But don't ask me where they all come from. My interest is in spending the money, not collecting it.'

'So who would know about the money trail? Where it was coming from, where it was going to?'

Blaxland frowns, as if he doesn't appreciate the direction of Ivan's questioning. 'Athol oversaw the accounts, so him to an extent. Lucretia and the two other board members: myself and Agatha McLean. Otto will deny any intimate knowledge. That's the theory: candidates and sitting members operate without becoming beholden to donors.'

'The theory. What about the practice?'

Blaxland smiles a knowing smile. 'I'll leave that to your imagination.'

'So, to varying degrees, Athol, the three board members, plus Otto?'

The large man says nothing.

Ivan thinks of the way Blaxland had not acknowledged the waiter earlier, as if the man had been invisible to him. The family head was so used to having underlings look after him, he was almost unaware of their existence. 'If money was missing from Watermen's, who would know?'

Blaxland lifts his head so his oyster eyes can better scrutinise Ivan. 'What are you suggesting?'

'That Athol Hasluck embezzled money.'

But Blaxland merely shakes his head, setting his chins wobbling. 'No. I've heard nothing of that. Nothing at all.' And then: 'That makes no sense. There is nothing illegal about donating to a political party. If someone noticed money missing, they'd tell me. And Lucretia and Otto. And the police. They wouldn't kill someone.'

When Ivan leaves, Blaxland doesn't rise but remains beached on his chesterfield, apparently deep in thought.

——

Ivan returns to the police station and parks the car, considering what he's learnt from Craven Allsop, Toby Fairchild and Nigel Blaxland: nothing conclusive, just the accumulating evidence that it's all about the money. And yet he's still struggling to identify a suspect.

He stands outside the station, but he doesn't enter. He needs to eat, and he needs to think, to work out his next steps. He decides to walk to the Lone Dog Café. The day, like the town, seems too perfect: the sky too clear, the temperature too high. He calls Nell to see if she wants food, but her phone rings out. He wonders how she's progressing. Maybe he should speak to Carole, seek the crime-scene investigator's opinion on procuring warrants for the Water Traders and Air Stills—both seem to have plenty of electricity. But he dismisses the idea almost as soon as it comes to him: the mere presence of power is hardly the basis for a search warrant. Chances are it would be denied and he would be embarrassed.

By the time he gets to the Lone Dog, he's more thirsty than hungry, sweating in the heat, but the cafe is shut. What is it about Australia, that you can't get a coffee after three in the afternoon? He should have eaten at the Canal Club after all. Instead, he retraces his steps, before spotting the Coachman's Arms on the far side of Yuwonderie's central fountain. He recalls the bowl of chips that Blake ate the previous afternoon, and his stomach voices its opinion, an audible rumble. He crosses Commonwealth Way and enters the pub, passing the gaming area—the faint sound of poker machines, their siren call, floating in the air—and keeps going, seeking the bistro. Predictably, its kitchen is closed, lunchtime passed, dinner yet to begin, chips unavailable, but there are a couple of sandwiches and wraps under glass at the bar. He buys a chicken caesar salad wrap and a pint of soda water and heads out into the beer garden, into the fresh air and away from the pokies den. And there, sitting at a table, all alone except for a bottle of wine and a solitary glass, is the busker, Bert Kippax.

Ivan walks over, sits opposite. 'Afternoon,' he says.

'Has been. Up until now,' says the old man. His eyes are blood-shot and his untrimmed beard bears witness to his last meal.

'I've been looking for you,' says Ivan.

'That so,' says Kippax, taking a sip of wine, examining Ivan over the rim of the glass. If he's drunk, he's showing no sign of it; all Ivan can see is calculation. 'Homicide, right? Investigating Athol Hasluck?'

'Ivan Lucic,' says Ivan, offering a handshake.

The old man looks sceptical but shakes regardless. 'Getting anywhere?'

'Maybe. Maybe not.'

'Why you looking for me?'

'Is it true you used to be police here?'

'I was. For twenty-five years. Long time ago now.'

'You'd know a thing or two, then,' says Ivan, 'about Yuwonderie.'

'Always too little or too much.' He takes another sip of his drink. 'How can I help?'

'You been sleeping rough?'

That elicits a laugh. 'Nah. Might look like it, but nah. The police pension, God bless it.' He raises his glass in an ironic toast. 'Keeps a roof over my head. Enough left over for a drop of vino.'

'Others do. Sleep rough, I mean.'

'Of course.' Bert swishes the wine around his glass in a circular motion but doesn't take his eyes from Ivan. 'What do you want?'

'Athol Hasluck was murdered on Saturday night. Earlier that evening, he went into his office. Was seen on CCTV entering off McLean Street. You know where I'm talking about?'

Bert nods.

'Sometime later he left, but the CCTV rules out the front door. He must have exited out the back door, leading to the alleyway there. Might have walked out by himself, might have been abducted. There's evidence of someone sleeping rough back there. Near the back entrance to the Lone Dog Café.'

Bert Kippax is nodding even before Ivan has finished. 'I know the spot. Sheltered from the elements. You think someone might have seen something?'

'A possibility. You know who might have been there?'

'I can ask around. But the weather has been fine for a week or more.'

'And?'

'Much nicer to sleep in a park, or by a canal, or in one of the hides down in the wetlands,' says Bert.

Ivan thinks of the milk container, the use-by date. 'You might be right. But I'd appreciate you trying to find out. There are signs it's been used lately.'

'I'll do what I can. But I don't like your chances.'

'Of finding them?'

'No. Of getting anywhere with your investigation. This town has a way of closing ranks.' There's a touch of bitterness in the man's voice, and Ivan thinks he knows why.

'I heard about your daughter.'

Bert Kippax looks at his wine bottle, as if suddenly interested in the label. 'Did you now?'

'You never found out what happened to her?'

'No. But she's dead. I'm sure of that.' The man stands. His fly is undone, and he's wearing two different shoes. 'Got to take a leak. Watch my bottle.' He walks off towards the toilet, a little stiff but otherwise steady.

Ivan's phone rings. He's thinking it must be Nell returning his call, but then he sees the number and it's as if the Riverina sun has turned dim. The country code is +31. The Netherlands. The Hague.

'Ivan Lucic,' he says, trying to keep his voice even.

'Ivan?'

'Who is this?' He'd thought it might be a lawyer, or perhaps a journalist, not this frail-sounding thinness.

'It's Zlatko. Your father.'

Ivan says nothing, knows not what to say.

'Ivan, I am coming home.'

'No. Not to me,' says Ivan, and he hangs up.

He stares, seeing nothing, a chill running through him. His father. In prison for almost thirty years. Crimes against humanity. A killer. How could they ever let him free? Coming back to haunt his son.

He sits there. Time goes by. His phone rings, but he barely hears it. It rings again. Only after it finishes does it occur to him to see who it was.

Nell. As he stares at the screen, a message appears, an SMS. *Where r u?*

He turns off his phone, closes it down. Around him, the clear-sky day continues on carelessly, but he is no longer part of it. He leaves his food, his hunger gone, and staggers inside. Where he hears the siren song and sees the Medusa lights of the gaming lounge.

chapter twenty-four

1994

SUMMER WAS TILTING TOWARDS AUTUMN, AND THE ACADEMIC YEAR LOOMED, although Davis realised there was no obligation for him to return to Melbourne. He was a student still, but the tether to the Parkville campus had grown longer and looser. As an honours-by-thesis student, he would be expected to run his own race, meeting only occasionally with his supervisor. He wondered if he should even bother finding a new place to live there. The Victorian capital might be home to his university and closer to Yuwonderie, but New South Wales was where his story lay: the land titles, the legislation, the water flowing down from the alps. All in New South Wales, all controlled from Sydney, maybe with Canberra at the margins. It was true that in the early 1920s federal parliament still sat in the southern capital, but all the records from those days had long ago been transferred to Canberra. And the real story, the gist of it, must be here in Yuwonderie itself, if only he could lay his hands on it.

Sitting in the beer garden at the Coachman's Arms with Otto and Craven, Davis mentioned that he might spend the year at Three Wells Station after all.

'Sensible move,' said Craven.

'Now you're twenty-one, we need to sign you up to the Canal Club,' said Otto. 'Full membership.'

Davis laughed. 'Seriously? And the taxidermist too?'

Otto frowned. 'What does that mean?'

'It's a bit stuffy. Like being mounted in a museum.'

'Don't be disrespectful,' said Otto, smirking as he said it.

'Reciprocal rights,' said Craven. 'Handy. The Savage Club in Melbourne. Pioneers or Universities in Sydney. You could have stayed at one when you went to Sydney with Lucy.'

Davis thought of the hotel in Manly, the ferry, the walks on the beach. Being with Lucy had made him feel alive; the prospect of joining the Canal Club was as inviting as arthritis. 'I don't know. Maybe.'

'You'll need to become a member soon enough,' said Otto. 'Comes with the territory. I joined as soon as I could. Craven joined last year. Once we're all members, we can liven it up a bit. We'll be on the board before you know it. You can lead the way.'

'Me? Why me?' asked Davis, and then understood the implication. He would be the first of his generation to head one of the Seven families, or so his friends assumed. He still hadn't told them of his decision to renounce his inheritance. 'If you say so,' he said, kicking that particular can down the road. If he was handing his inheritance to Krystal, then there was no imperative for him to become a member of the Canal Club, certainly no urgency. He smiled as it occurred to him that they would be forced to change the men-only rule, allow Krystal to become a full member. It might make an interesting postscript to his thesis.

He was spending less time at the Yuwonderie Irrigation Scheme Company. The basement room had lost its appeal since the fight with Lucy in Sydney. They'd patched it up, but the drive home had been marked more by civility than fun. A fortnight passed before they fully reconciled, before they slept together once more. Nevertheless, he felt he'd exhausted the company's archives. If there were some buried vein of information to be found there, he'd failed to locate it. He could always return to it if he discovered new information elsewhere. It wasn't as if it was going anywhere.

And despite their rapprochement, he had to admit to himself that Lucy's allure had faded. The frisson had gone. He wondered if that were the case with all relationships: that initial rush weakening day by day, month by month. Something similar had happened with the American girl he'd dated at university. Perhaps that was why Otto seemed to have a new partner every month or two. Maybe it was why Craven was reluctant to have a girlfriend at all—he knew what lay ahead.

So Davis began to drift in the summer haze as he waited for the arrival of the photocopies from the Land Office in Sydney. And he was happy when the distraction of the annual Bandaville Bachelors' and Spinsters' Ball inserted itself into the social calendar. Such balls, originally created for unmarried youth to meet with prospective partners, had long ago transitioned into boozy and bacchanalian nights, full of Bundaberg rum and casual sex. Bandaville, seventy kilometres west of Yuwonderie and in the middle of nowhere, was famous for its ball, at least in Yuwonderie and the MIA. The town was not really a town, more of a hamlet, perhaps not even that. It was a settlement without a river and without a future. It sat at a crossroad: a modest pub, a once-a-month church, two houses, a community hall and an abandoned racecourse. The track had not seen a race in decades, but the clubhouse was still there, a kilometre from the pub, as were its stables and, across the car park, a working shearing shed, belonging not to the racecourse but to a neighbouring property. The three buildings combined were perfect. The shearing shed was at the heart of it, with the bands and the dancing, full of noise and revelry, while the clubhouse hosted the all-you-could-drink bar and the occasional tray of sausage rolls, party pies and reheated quiches. It was all class.

The Bandaville community hall across the road from the pub was not part of the ball precinct, but Otto and Craven, through a donation here and a quiet word there, had been able to secure it for the night's accommodation. It would still be camping, but indoors with an outside toilet and tank water. The rooms out the back of the pub were unobtainable at any price, reserved for the organising committee and the Melbourne band topping the bill.

Davis drove there in the Alfa, with Lucy at his side, and he felt some of the distance between them evaporate. She had done the right thing by him after all, keeping his secret that Krystal would inherit. He appreciated that. He was still to firmly commit, but as the month-long cooling-off period progressed, the less he could see his future as the laird of Three Wells Station, dining monthly at the Canal Club, growing old and fat and complacent alongside Otto and Craven and the rest of the establishment. He would have liked to share his thoughts with Lucy, but he didn't want to reignite the Manly argument.

They met the others at the Bandaville pub. The publican, for whom the ball generated more than half his annual income, had hired in backpackers from the irrigation districts for the weekend, setting up a barbecue and an outside bar, sheltered by trees and shade cloth. The place was already half full when Davis and Lucy arrived in the early afternoon, the first of their party, joined shortly after by Otto accompanied by Lucy's younger sister Jacinta in his father's Mercedes.

'She's too young,' whispered Lucy to Davis. 'Seventeen.'

'I was coming here at that age.'

'But with Otto? How old is he?'

'Twenty-three.'

'That doesn't worry you?'

Davis looked at Jacinta. She did look young and nervous. He was glad to see she was drinking water. 'You're right,' he said. 'We should keep an eye on her.'

Next to arrive was Athol, surprising Davis, for he was partnered by Stella, the policeman's daughter, who smiled at Davis's consternation. He'd only seen her once or twice at the Coachman's in the weeks since her storm-lashed twenty-first, and they hadn't spoken at all. But if she still held anything against him and Otto, she didn't show it.

They were followed by an even odder couple: Craven with Davis's sister Krystal, who had given the ball a miss these past few years.

'Don't look so surprised,' she said to him. 'I wanted to discover what's worse: this or the Canal Club.'

'I'm glad you're here,' he said, understanding her motive: making an effort to fit in, to embrace her community and comprehend it better. Or at least to present that impression. Assuming the mantle of landholder.

In the makeshift beer garden the sun was hot and the beer was at least cool, and before long there emerged that heady mixture of youth and alcohol and hormones and a sense of occasion. More and more people flocked in, and as the afternoon wore on, more and more of them were already dressed for the evening, the men in dinner suits, as often as not with scuffed brown RMs for footwear, just to indicate they weren't taking the dress-up or themselves too seriously. Some of the girls, though, had gone to considerable effort: hair done, make-up rigorously applied, body-hugging dresses. Champagne and giggling flowed among them like static electricity, even as the boys stuck to beers or rum, the laughter and chatter escalating, everyone up for a good time.

As the hour of the ball came closer, the small group, led in some unconscious but real way by Otto, peeled off and returned to the hall to change. There were about twenty of them, mostly friends of Otto's or otherwise connected with the Seven. Outside, car horns were blaring, the excitement gathering. The ball was set to start at six pm, but there was no real reason to get there early.

Before walking over, they gathered outside. A few chairs were taken from the hall, and they posed for a photograph: Davis at the front with Lucy, already a little tipsy, playfully draped across his knees; Stella sitting next to them, Athol behind with his hands on her shoulders; Otto standing with Jacinta, arm around her waist, on one side of Athol, with Krystal and Craven on the other, laughing at some private joke.

It was just an instant, people aligning, caught in the lens, frozen in time. One moment, Davis was aware only of Lucy squirming on his lap, then of Stella sitting next to him, and then the photo was taken and the moment had passed.

At the ball venue, the organising committee had decorated the shearing shed with bunting and hay bales and pictures painted on butcher's paper, superbly amateurish. The theme of this year's ball was the grape, the grain and the cane. And although pictures of all three adorned the walls, no one missed the reference: wine, beer and rum. Barley was grown in the YISC and the MIA on occasion, as were grapes, although the nearest sugarcane plantation was a thousand kilometres or more away. But Bundy was synonymous with a B&S, so there it was.

The first band was local, high school kids down from Hay, surprisingly good. All covers of course, Australian bands like Mental As Anything and Split Enz and the Sunnyboys, mixed in with Oasis and the Stones and a few old Beatles numbers. All mainstream, fashionably out of date, and known to all. People danced and drank, laughed and drank, and sang along as they drank.

The evening started going downhill when the main band began—or perhaps in the hour it took for them to get on stage after the high school band had finished their set to thunderous applause, finger-in-mouth whistling and hound-dog howling. Recorded music pumped a solid mix of mainstream contemporary, but most people went to the bar, drinking instead of dancing, outside under a string of coloured lightbulbs hung from the clubhouse awning. The high-pitched conversation from earlier in the evening dropped half an octave as people settled in for the evening. The first hijinks were underway, some drunks doing doughnuts in their utes at the centre of the old racecourse, and a couple of idiots taking turns to jump from the roof onto hay bales—straightforward leaps at first, then somersaults. Davis was just thinking that riding boots, corrugated iron and rum weren't the safest combination when a young cockie wearing torn jeans and a dinner jacket came sliding down the roof, arms flailing, before flying awkwardly through the air and landing half on the bales and half off. He screamed in pain, shoulder dislocated. His mates put him in a wheelbarrow and took him off towards the pub while onlookers cheered and he waved like royalty with his good hand, grinning like the village idiot.

Davis was drinking steadily, but not excessively. Three years at university in Melbourne, two of them in a residential college, had taught him the benefits of pacing. Lucy had strategically moved from heels to flats, in readiness for the main band and dancing, and had eased back on her own consumption. The real concern was Otto, who was becoming more and more voluble and less and less articulate.

'Ecstasy,' said Craven.

'Really?' Davis was surprised.

'Ecstasy and rum,' observed Craven dryly. 'What could possibly go wrong?'

What went wrong, first and foremost, was the main band. After taking forever to replace the high school group, they stalked onto the stage, dressed in black from head to toe with an attitude to match.

''Bout time!' shouted someone.

'Shut up and listen, cunt,' spat the lead singer, unsteady on his feet, living out his own personal biopic. The lead guitarist hit a power chord, the drummer pounded up a frenzy, the bass player stood bedazzled, apparently unaware he was expected to contribute, and the singer let out a banshee howl, thrust his pelvis forward in a statement of intent, then slouched back to an amp to suck on a cigarette and neck a bottle of bourbon. There was no melody, the beat was powerful yet erratic, the tuning indecisive, the arrogance appalling. Only the volume was world class; the bass—when it finally occurred to its practitioner to join in the musical melee—came pumping through Davis's guts, making him feel queasy. The singer wasn't so much singing as ululating, not a single word comprehensible, the sonic assault almost physical, any notion of a tune as distant as the nearest city. A couple of brave souls attempted to dance near the stage but were repelled by the sheer volume and lack of rhythm. People began to drain back out towards the clubhouse.

'Play something good, you arseholes!' shouted one unhappy punter as the song came to an end.

'Fuck you,' said the singer, comprehensible at last, raising his middle finger, while the guitarist mimed a masturbatory gesture above his forehead.

The volley of beer cans and bottles was immediate, fierce and prolonged, raining down on the stage like the mortars of Sarajevo. The singer stood uncomprehending, mouth aghast, biopic having lurched off-script, even while the guitarist smirked as if he had won a minor victory. The bass player, who had turned back to the drummer for a moment, perhaps seeking guidance as to the next song, copped a small bottle of Bailey's Irish Cream—thrown with drunken dexterity by a petite farm lass from Young—and went down like a sack of potatoes. The lead singer, his mojo back and feeling inspired, yelled his second and last distinguishable words into the mic: 'C'mon then. I'll have you!' He leapt from the stage to be knocked unconscious by the first local lad to get near him.

The steering committee, at least those members who were still sober, saw all this unfold from the back of the hall in much the same way the helmsman of the *Titanic* must have witnessed the iceberg: with an accelerating sense of dread. Fortunately, the committee secretary was made of sterner stuff, and she immediately ran out, hoping to intercept the high school band, who thankfully were eating sausages and enthusiastically underage drinking. A quick negotiation between the secretary and two of the mothers ensured the band would remain, with the promise they could have the rooms at the hotel that had previously been reserved for the Melbourne headliners. In return, one particularly generous mum offered to drive the lead singer and bass player to hospital in Hay, provided they travelled in the back of her ute.

Meanwhile, some order had been restored. The recorded music was back on, much to everyone's relief, and the dancers were happy to display their wares to more familiar and predictable tunes. The young man who'd delivered the haymaker that had put Jim Morrison out of action was at the bar, downing a never-ending round of shots. He lasted a good half-hour before he joined his victim in unconsciousness.

Otto, unfortunately, was still very much conscious, and feeling all loved up. He was lumbering around, touching up girls and generously informing them how fuckworthy they were. Craven was cringing, but trying his best to run interference for his friend and prevent him copping the same sort of haymaker that had felled the lead singer. Otto had already groped Jayce, forcing Krystal to step in—eyes rolling, tongue lashing and eyebrows excoriating—and tell him to tidy himself up, before she escorted his schoolgirl date back to the community hall. Lucy came and went, delivering

Davis a verbal swipe, at which point he realised he was either too drunk or too unobservant to comprehend why.

He decided he should go for a walk to clear his head, so he staggered out towards the stables to take a piss. 'Not there,' said some half-seen shape. 'People are fucking.'

He saw a tree, a lone survivor, out on the plain, its upper branches catching the coloured light from the clubhouse. He staggered towards it, then thought better of it. It wasn't compulsory to piss against something; the bare earth would suffice. He went far enough, out of the circle of light, a small concession to civility. And that's when he heard the voice.

'Get off me, you motherfucker.' The voice was female, assertive, with an air of panic. And then: 'No!'

Davis ran weaving towards it.

His eyes had adjusted, could see. It was Otto and a girl. Stella. The policeman's daughter. Otto had her by the arm; she was struggling to get loose.

'Otto! Let her go!' he yelled, urgency in his voice.

'Just playing,' said Otto. 'Just a joke.' But he didn't release her.

Davis approached them. Stella was still struggling, but looking at Davis.

'Now, Otto,' he said. '*Now.*'

'She likes me,' slurred Otto.

Davis closed the distance and punched his friend hard in the guts, hitting with force, enough to hurt. Otto dropped Stella's arm, emitted a sort of surprised groan, and then a grunt, and then started spewing. He tried to say something, but the vomit came again and again.

'Thank you,' said Stella. She straightened her dress and walked back towards the party.

'Jesus, Otto,' said Davis despairingly.

The big bloke just groaned again and collapsed into the dirt. Davis hoped he wasn't rolling in his own vomit.

'What's going on?'

Davis turned. Someone was approaching, but they were holding a torch, shining it in his eyes.

'Davis, is that you?'

He thought he recognised the voice now. 'Lucy?'

'Yeah. It's me.' Then: 'Is that Otto?' The torch's beam fell upon the fallen Lothario. 'What happened?'

'I hit him.'

'Jesus, you're a fucking idiot,' she said to Davis, venom in her voice. And she bent down and started tending to Otto.

'Right,' said Davis, thinking there wasn't much more he could do. 'Look after him.' He added: 'Careful of his hands—they wander.'

He headed back towards the shearing shed, where the high school band, feeding on their new-found and totally unexpected popularity, were starting to turn it around, riding the wave. On the bridge of the *Titanic*, the committee secretary had opened a bottle of champagne and was sharing it with the two remaining mothers.

From then on, the evening grew increasingly blurry for Davis. Later, he recalled encountering Stella in earnest conversation with Krystal.

'Thanks,' she said to him again.

'I'm just as drunk as he is,' said Davis, compelled by some unspoken code to defend his friend.

'That's not the problem,' said Stella.

Davis took the compliment and decided he needed another drink.

Craven was by the bar with Athol, their eyes sodden and hazy.

'You think this is all there is?' asked Craven. 'An endless series of small obliterations on the way to the big one?'

Athol and Davis exploded into laughter, partly in appreciation of Craven's ability to still conjure such an elegant and coherent sentence. Craven started laughing as well, before offering to fetch another round of obliteration from the bar.

'Heavy is the head that wears the crown,' said Athol.

'What is this? A profundity competition?'

'Nah, just you lot. The heirs. None of you look that happy about it.'

''Cos we're not,' said Davis. 'But don't tell a soul.'

Davis's last memory of that night was from many hours later. Back in the hall, rising to take yet another piss, his kidneys insistent on ridding his body of alcohol. The first light of the sun, dawn breaking. And Otto's father's Mercedes moving on its soft suspension, Lucy in the back seat, riding up and down like she might a rodeo bull.

chapter twenty-five

IVAN IS DREAMING. HE KNOWS HE'S DREAMING AND DOESN'T ATTEMPT TO WAKE up. He likes it here, in that half-state between sleep and consciousness, when the images and scenes spill into his waking mind. Going with the flow. He is walking along a beach and there are seagulls and he knows this is a good dream because the sky is blue and the sea is calm. Bad dreams are set at night, his father stalking through the gloom. Those are the nightmares when he forces himself awake. This is different, calmer. But just as he's thinking this, a breeze rises, and the sea becomes choppy. The seagulls are flapping and squawking. One of them is trying to tell him something, and he realises this is no ordinary seagull, but the embodiment of someone well-meaning, someone he knows. Who does he know who reminds him of a seagull? He can discern no identity in the bead-like eyes, just a radiating sense of concern. He wishes the other gulls would settle a little, stop squawking, give him a chance to hear.

There is movement on the horizon. A whale is waving. Waving or drowning? Surely a whale couldn't be drowning; that makes no sense. Now the whale is holding aloft a giant mobile phone. The phone is ringing, the familiar tone.

Ivan is awake. His phone is ringing. It's still night. He flips the cover: *Nell*. He answers, even as he checks the screen: twelve thirty in the morning.

'Nell?'

'Oh fuck. Alice,' she says, and in her words he hears fear and urgency and desperation.

He's fully awake now, consciousness surging as he leaps out of bed. 'Where are you?'

A flash catches his eye, pulling his gaze to the window. The sound of an explosion, the crump of the detonation followed by the sound of shattering glass. And the same sounds a split second later, coming through the phone, an asymmetrical stereo.

'Nell? *Nell!*'

There is no reply. The call has ended.

Through the window, Ivan can see birds rising above the darkened town, their harsh calls mixing with the shrill echo of car alarms.

Now he sees it, smoke, coming from up near Commonwealth Way. And there, a low orange aura. A fire. *Jesus. Nell.*

He gets his pants on, his boots, takes his phone, takes his gun. And runs. Out of his room, along the empty corridor, bounding down the stairs, through the empty lobby of the Progress Hotel and out the door. Running. Running up the ridge, running in desperation, running in denial, running as if it might turn back the clock, even by a few seconds.

He gets to Commonwealth Way, sprints along it, guided by the burgeoning glow. On the other side of the street he sees a group of people emerging from the Grandview, pointing. The fire is taking hold, and he's starting to realise where it's coming from.

He gets to McLean Street, turns right, and there it is. A solitary figure is standing, watching: Bert Kippax. But it's the building that captures Ivan's attention, the old shopfront, Athol Hasluck's accountancy practice on fire on the second floor. The downstairs is largely intact, but the windows on the second floor are all blown out, glass on the street, smoke rising, the orange aura growing stronger by the second.

'Must be a gas leak,' says Kippax. 'You called the firies?'

'Haven't you?'

'No phone, mate.'

Ivan dials triple zero, gives the handset to the former policeman. 'You tell 'em.'

Ivan sees a look of dawning horror on the man's face. 'You're not going in? There's no one in there.'

'How do you know that?'

'Middle of the night.'

'Get the firies, tell them there are two police officers inside.'

Ivan moves to the door, glass crunching under his boots. The entryway is shut, a glass door, the police tape removed. He smashes through it, using his gun. But there is no internal catch; the door is deadlocked. He pulls his gun, double-checks the old man is well clear. Fires, shooting away the locks, their brackets. *Nell.* He yanks at the door, kicks at it with fury and desperation. *Nell.* The door shivers, he kicks again, it caves. And he's inside.

There is not enough light. The building is on fire and there is not enough light. He can see the bottom of the stairs, but the top is lost in darkening smoke.

He races back to Kippax, wasting more precious seconds.

'On their way,' says Kippax.

Ivan seizes the phone without comment, re-enters the building, torch app on. There is smoke, curling but not orange, no flames, not here. He moves up the stairs, two steps at a time, entering the smoke, trying to keep low.

A corridor. He moves along to where it turns ninety degrees to the left. Now he can see the faintest glow, coming through the smoke. He ducks into a crouching run, under the worst of the fumes, towards the beckoning fire. He can already feel the heat on his face.

A door to the left. He holds up his phone torch: ATHOL HANCOCK, ACCOUNTANT, the door slightly ajar.

He pushes through into an outer office. Two desks, computers, nothing more. No sign of Nell. A door in the back of the room, rimmed with bright orange: the seat of the fire is there. He moves to it, knows he needs to open it, pass through. He looks about, sees a door to a small kitchen. He rushes in, strips off his t-shirt, soaks it, puts it back on. Seconds flowing, time wasting. *Nell.* He soaks a tea towel, wraps it around his face, a makeshift bandana.

Back to the door, down on the floor, sucking in lungsful of oxygen, hyperventilating, getting as much into himself as he can. Then he opens the door, feels the rush of heat, the fire angry, roaring with the inrush of oxygen, shouting at him to retreat. He pushes in. 'Nell!' he screams, but realises it's futile. Counterproductive: he risks coughing, risks asphyxiation. He sinks to the floor, gets in a couple of smoke-tainted breaths.

The billowing cloud has lost its monochrome and is infused with orange light, engorged with menace. He pockets the phone, light no longer needed. He can hear the fire, its appetite. It must be into the ceiling. He might have mere minutes. He might not have that.

Another doorway, door off its hinges, blown towards him. The site of the explosion.

His eyes are watering; he has to pause, cough into the make-shift bandana. He drops, starts crawling forward, trying to come in under the smoke, under the heat. Through the doorway, the wall to his right is close enough to touch, riddled with holes. Shrapnel. There in front of him, a dark shape on the floor. A person. He moves to it, purposeful. A woman. His heart surges, but it's not Nell. Alice Figtree. He feels the sticky dampness on the floor as he kneels beside her. Lifts his hand, smells blood. Fucking hell. He touches her throat, is almost surprised to feel a pulse.

He takes her feet, drags her out through one doorway, then another. Leaves her in the outer office, pausing only long enough to lie face down on the floor, breathing heavily, pulling oxygen into his lungs until he's dizzy with it.

Back through the doorways, flames now visible, smoke over-whelming. Some primal instinct is roaring inside his head: *Get back, get out.* Not without Nell. Onwards, around a desk. There. There she is! On her side, not moving. He gets to her, just as she coughs. Alive, but unconscious. It's enough. He takes her collar, stands, pulls her to relative safety, next to the unmoving Alice. Again he falls to the floor; again he draws air into his lungs, unable to see properly, eyes watering, unable to detect what injuries Nell has suffered. He takes some more breaths, coughing, wasting time, getting more oxygen into himself. Even at floor level, the air is choking with smoke. He can't stay here; he can't delay.

He hauls Nell out into the corridor and along to the head of the stairs, cool air being sucked up into the vortex of the fire, granting him some relief. He breathes deep as his coughing recedes. A fireman's hold, Nell over his shoulders, down the stairs, careful not to fall, using the banister, feeling his way as much as seeing it. Down the steps, out beneath the gathering smoke, out into the night, clear and cold. He lowers Nell onto the bitumen, starting to swoon, eyesight diminishing into a narrow tunnel. Coughing so much it hurts.

He makes the decision, almost too difficult to consider. He sucks air, runs back, a crouching trot, as if expecting to come under fire from an unseen enemy.

The old man is there, waving his arms, trying to stop him.

Ivan points back to Nell. 'Help her,' he says as he bustles past Kippax.

Inside, the bottom of the stairs, a last chance at clear air, knowing that he might have to go the whole way without breathing. Lungs full, he takes the stairs two at a time. He is running into hell. There is a groaning in the ceiling, a shriek heard above the roar of the fire. The corridor, dark just moments before, has started to pulse with heat and light, hard and dry, irradiating his skin. He can't see, there is too much smoke, he's guided by memory and touch and determination, along the corridor, through the outer door, onto his knees, like crawling into a volcano. Where is she? Has she moved? *Where is she?* He stumbles upon her, doesn't stop to think, takes her feet. He gets her into the corridor, but the urge to breathe is too great; he takes deep breaths just centimetres above the floorboards, but the smoke is too thick. The coughing comes again, robbing him of control, racking his chest with pain. A roar, a mighty din, the ceiling coming down inside the office. He must move; to stay here is to die. He drags her along the corridor, no time to think of protecting her trailing head. Behind them, the ceiling collapses, blasting him with a searing wave of heat, burning his neck. He changes position, takes her under her arms, pulls her round the corner towards the stairs. Almost there. He tries to stand, to lift Alice, but his vision starts to go and his knees buckle. He needs to leave her, save himself, but it is too late. He falls, consciousness waning. The sounds of a siren, somewhere in the distance. His last thought as consciousness loses its thread—at least Nell is safe.

Back in the dream, the sea has turned red. Lightning arcs across the sky. But the whale is still there, smiling at him. It raises a fin, gives a thumbs-up. How can a flipper give a thumbs-up? But he's sinking, sinking below the waves, and the dream fades to smoke-filled blackness.

chapter twenty-six

IVAN WAKES, OPENS HIS EYES, STARTS COUGHING ALMOST IMMEDIATELY, CAN'T stop. *Nell.* Uncontrollable. He sits up. He's in bed, a hospital room, lights dim. Another bed, empty. *Nell.* There's an oxygen monitor on his finger. He coughs again, throat full of phlegm. Looks around: a box of tissues next to the bed; he hawks up a ball of dark slime. His eyes feel as if someone has tipped sand into them. He drinks water from a glass beside the bed. The taste is of smoke, acrid and bitter. He desperately wants to clean his teeth. He takes off the oxygen monitor, gets out of bed, realises he's wearing blue cotton pyjamas, finds the discovery disturbing. How unconscious do you have to be for someone to strip you and redress you without you noticing it?

There's a face mask beside his bed. Has he been on supplementary oxygen?

He stands, tests his footing. All good. He doesn't feel swoony. Balance okay. Another bout of coughing, bringing up more phlegm. Can't be too serious; no nurses here to monitor him. *Nell.* Looks around. His pillow is dirty, smeared black. On the side table, next to the mask, his watch. Four forty in the morning. He listens: the whole place sounds dead, just the ticking of machines.

He leaves the room. A short corridor, a nurses' station at the end, an island of illumination. No one there. He goes into a toilet, takes a piss, flushes his mouth with cool water from the tap. His face in the mirror looks grim: his eyes are bloodshot and rimmed in red. Back in the corridor, a sign above the door declares it THE BLAXLAND WARD. The occupied rooms have names written on small whiteboards. He finds the one with DC NARELLE BUCHANAN written on it. *Nell*. He eases the door open, just a crack, then further.

She is on her back, tubes running from her nostrils, an intravenous drip leading into her arm. She looks peaceful, not stressed. There's an oxygen monitor on her finger, and her heartbeat registers on a silent screen. To Ivan's untrained eye the pulse looks strong, consistent.

He's standing, peering into the room, when the door opens from the inside, spilling light. There's the gasp of a nurse, a big bloke with a mullet. 'Sorry,' he says, just as Ivan does the same, an echo in the silence.

'Sergeant Lucic?' asks the nurse.

'Is it okay? Me here?' asks Ivan.

'Sure,' says the nurse. 'For a bit. Come in. Take a seat, let me check your vitals.'

The man moves to the bed, plucks the oxygen monitor from Nell's fingertip, puts it on Ivan's.

Ivan suppresses a cough as he sits.

'Ninety-six,' says the man. 'Very good.' He replaces the monitor on Nell's finger. 'You're almost back to normal.'

Ivan ignores the comment. 'Do you know what happened?'

'Firies got you out. Saved your life.'

'Alice Figtree?'

'You saved her and all. That's what the ambulance guys said.'

'Where is she?'

'Canberra. Airlifted. Intensive care.'

'She was burnt?'

'Stabbed. Lost a lot of blood.'

The memory comes rushing back: Alice in a pool of blood, the red liquid on his hands. Left for dead. He looks at his hands, darkness under his nails. He looks back at Nell. 'How is she?' asks Ivan. 'Not stabbed?'

'No. A blow to the back of the head. Quite a lump but doesn't need stitches.' The nurse looks at a monitor. 'She's good now. Out of danger. Still on oxygen, but the doctor says she should improve from here.'

Relief washes over Ivan. He realises he's been half holding his breath. He breathes out, initiating another round of coughing. His throat feels like his tonsils have been scraped with a metal file.

In the bed, Nell stirs slightly, and Ivan feels a ripple of guilt atop the tsunami he's already feeling.

The nurse takes his blood pressure. 'Big improvement. Strong pulse. They should discharge you in the morning.'

'Thank you,' says Ivan. And suddenly he begins to weep. 'Thank you,' he sobs.

The nurse seems to understand. 'Stay as long as you like. I'm just down the way. Let me know if you need anything.'

Ivan stares into Nell's closed eyes, takes her hand in his. 'I am so sorry,' he whispers. And he lets the tears come, stinging his eyes.

When he wakes sometime later, there is a blanket over him. He's still holding Nell's hand.

— —

Dawn light is seeping through the blinds the next time he wakes. He looks at Nell, no longer restful but moving her head in her sleep as if experiencing a bad dream. She withdraws her hand.

'It's okay, Nell,' he says, taking it again. 'I'm here.'

Her face reflects some internal struggle, but eventually her eyes flicker open.

'Ivan?' Her voice is just a rasp.

'I'm here. You're safe.'

She tries to clear her throat, grimaces as if in pain.

'I'll get the nurse,' he says.

But she shakes her head. 'Stay.'

So he does, watching as she takes in her surroundings, making no effort to lift her head from the pillow.

'Hospital?'

'Yes.'

'Yuwonderie?'

'Yes.'

'I'm okay?'

'Fine. They say you'll make a full recovery.'

She frowns. 'An explosion?'

'Yes. There was a fire. You got out in time. No burns.'

'You?' She tries to lift her head, but the effort is too much. She lowers it again, closes her eyes, breath coming steadily as sleep returns.

Ivan goes to fetch the nurse.

—

Later, with morning fully blossomed, Ivan is showered and changed, cough subsiding but eyes still stinging despite frequent drops. When he returns to Nell's room she is propped up on the pillows, alert. 'Morning,' she says, voice somehow formal.

'How are you?'

'My throat feels like I've been doing shots of hydrochloric acid.'

'You inhaled smoke. Passed out. But your oxygen levels are getting back to normal. No lasting damage.' He moves towards her bed, sits, goes to take her hand, but she withdraws it.

She looks directly at him, voice a throaty whisper. 'Where were you, Ivan?'

He doesn't answer, doesn't meet her gaze, stares down at his hands.

'I rang you, I texted you, nothing.'

He looks up at her, but the tears are too close, and he is unable to speak.

'Alice called. Said she'd found something important. Her voice was urgent. Excited. You didn't answer, so I went.' She coughs and tries to suppress it, pain on her face. 'The door was unlocked; I thought she'd left it open for me. I went in, up the stairs, found the office. There was someone on the floor, a body. It might have been Alice. I tried calling you. That's the last thing I remember.'

Ivan says, 'Someone flattened you. Knocked you out. You can't feel it?'

Nell explores the back of her head, winces as she locates the bandage.

'The doctor will need to check for residual concussion.'

'Alice?' she whispers.

'Canberra. Intensive care. Not the fire. Stabbed.'

'Jesus,' she says, before coughing once more, spitting phlegm into the bowl. 'Stabbed?' And she stares, her eyes telling the truth of it: she's lucky she was bashed, not knifed. 'How long have I been unconscious?'

Ivan smiles weakly. 'Just overnight. They gave you something to help you breathe more easily. You might feel a little woozy, but it should be wearing off by now.'

'Right.' She studies his face. He's scrubbed it clean, but he knows his eyes will still be red. 'You saved me?' she asks.

He draws a shuddering breath. 'We only just made it out.'

'You got there in the end.'

'Don't thank me. I should have been there with you.'

She frowns. 'Where were you?'

'Does it matter?'

'Ivan?'

He drops his head, knows he owes her the truth. 'The poker machines.'

She says nothing.

He lifts his eyes, sees the devastation on her face. The disappointment, the betrayal. 'I'm sorry, Nell. I really am.'

'After all this time,' she says.

Ivan is unable to match her gaze, looks away, considers telling her about his father. But he doesn't deserve sympathy; it can't excuse his actions.

Nell speaks. 'Alice said she'd found something in the filing cabinets, not the computer. She was preparing for the move. I went there to see what it was.'

Ivan wants to sigh. He'd told Alice to wait for Kevin, but there's no point in bringing that up now. 'The files are gone. Destroyed in the fire.' He pauses as a new thought comes to him. 'Someone knew. Knew we were going to shift the files to the station today.'

Now it's Nell who looks like she is about to cry. 'So they tried to kill her?'

Ivan meets her eyes, the slightest of affirmations.

'Was it you? Did you get her out?' asks Nell.

'Me and the firies.'

'So if we hadn't been there?'

Ivan doesn't respond, lets her work it through.

'We would have assumed she died in the fire?'

'Probably.'

Nell says nothing. There is nothing to say.

A doctor enters, a woman younger than the nurse, maybe just out of university, doing a bush placement to complete her qualifications. Her face is Indian, her accent private school.

'Lucky escape,' she says to Nell.

'Sounds like it,' says Nell, presenting an unconvincing smile.

The doctor is looking at her chart. 'No burns, no external injuries. Very good. Just the back of your head.' She moves to Nell. 'Lean forward a moment, please.' Nell complies, flinching as the doctor parts her hair and lifts the bandage. 'Not so bad. Will heal itself.'

'Thank you,' says Nell, in the way patients do.

'Headache?'

'No.'

'Any blurriness or double vision?'

'No.'

'Having trouble remembering events this morning?'

'No. Not this morning. Last night's a bit hazy.'

'Only to be expected.' The doctor turns to Ivan. 'Are you the husband?'

'No,' he says, 'I'm the sergeant.'

The doctor smiles knowingly. 'Perhaps you can give us a moment, then, while I examine the constable. I'm hoping I can discharge her this afternoon.'

Ivan leaves, and the doctor pulls the curtains around. He overhears her talking to Nell. 'He was here half the night,' she says. 'Holding your hand. Weeping.'

chapter twenty-seven

November 1914

My dearest Mother,

There is no easy way to write this: I am to have a child. I am awash with emotions—of joy and trepidation, of love and fear, of regret and anticipation. The world spins on and it is all I can do to keep my footing.

Do not be ashamed of me, Mother; do not judge me. Not you of all people, my greatest advocate, my greatest champion. Without you, I would have long ago lost that footing, been sent tumbling like so many of our people. The folk hereabouts attribute all that is good in me to my father, everything weak and vacillating in me to you and your mother in turn. But you and I know the truth of it; it is not just my literacy and my learning I owe to you: it is everything.

Jack is gone, two months ago, off to war, and the news of our child is chasing him across the ocean in a wave of letters. I have received two from him, such treasures. Both were from Albany, down at the bottom of Western Australia, already half a world away, where the recruits gathered before embarking for England. He says there is an air of excitement, a confidence that they are doing the right thing, that they will make Australia proud, raise our flag among those of the great nations of Europe. He says he promised me his droving days were over, but that I must allow him this one last adventure before we settle. I read his words and I can hear his voice; I close my eyes and I can see his smile through my tears.

And I am here, alone, and I am pregnant. So far knowledge of my condition has not spread beyond Castle View, but already I feel the judgement that awaits me, the steely condemnation of Augustine Chaulker and his ilk. I shall bear it as best I can, my head held high. For Jack and I would have been married by now, if only. Those are the words that haunt me, day and night. *If only.* I hope they won't be my epitaph.

Elaine is home from school for summer, and she has been wonderful, so kind and supportive, although I can see her regrets and her concern for me, no matter how hard she attempts to disguise them. Mrs Titchfield is still coming to terms with the news and has not yet acknowledged the fact, while Horace is silently scandalised. Why is it that the men are the most judgemental, as if they play no part in the process?

Elaine has suggested I stay close, but I can see that Horace would prefer me gone. I don't believe him callous; it is more than he assesses everything through the same prism: will it advance the scheme or hinder it? It was he who first suggested I move to the Marneys' property, Jolimont. I have already been spending two days per week there, cleaning and maintaining the place now that Jack and Noel have both gone to war. As my time grows closer, as my condition becomes evident, I will live there.

For the moment, I can still ride Penny, and I am beginning to enjoy the experience, the freedom it grants me, but already the doctor has warned me that physical exertion might damage the child, that women are not intended to straddle a horse. He said I should not tax myself, that I should confine myself to the indoors. I laughed when I heard it, thinking of how our sisters never took to bed rest. Then again, they weren't riding horses, so I must obey. Perhaps I might take a servant for myself. The idea sits uncomfortably with me, but I must become accustomed to my new station in life. I feel sometimes this is what troubles Horace the most—not that I am to bear a child out of wedlock, but that I will in future be elevated onto the same social plane.

I write to Jack every day. Those small envelopes trying to find him, somewhere in the enormity of the world, in Europe or Africa or England. They carry my hopes with them; our hopes. Wish them godspeed, those tenuous links of paper and ink, like notes in a bottle, thrown into indifferent seas.

I know him now, Mother, and I know he will be delighted to be a father. We spoke of it, our desire to marry, to have a family. This is what he wants; it is simply arriving early, in a different order. I can imagine your concerns: that this is a sweet-talking of a rogue, putting a child in me and then gallivanting off on the great adventure. But he has set it out in black and white, his intentions clear in his last will and testament. It chills me to think that a man so young and vital has signed such a document, but many of the local men have done so, those with wives and children, demonstrating that beneath the bravado and displays of confidence they have a deeper understanding of what they may confront. He declares that should anything happen to him, then everything should come to me. It is not as if he possesses a lot, just the little shack and parcel of land by Corkhills Creek, but the sentiment is clear. We shall marry. I am convinced of that, Mother: we shall marry.

I am hoping that by the time he arrives in Europe, the war will be over. Horace says it will be done by Christmas, or at latest Easter, expressing more frustration than joy when he does so, afraid he might miss his chance. If Horace wants the fighting elongated, I pray for the opposite, that it be done by the time Jack arrives, that he re-embarks forthwith and returns home. The five years will soon be up and he can divorce. All will be set right.

Your loving daughter,
Bessie

chapter twenty-eight

THERE IS NO MORE JOGGING FOR IVAN, NO RELISHING THE CLEAR SKY AND WARM morning breeze. It's not just his lungs, the residual cough, the lack of sleep: it's the remorse. It engulfs him, weighs upon him. A memory returns of the poker machine, the electronic leer of the Golden Dragon as he hits the play button again and again and again, a staccato haemorrhaging of money and soul and self-awareness. *Clack-bing, clack-bing, clack-bing.* He trembles with the memory, cringes from it. He sits outside the Lone Dog Café, drinking coffee without taste. *Chap doesn't look crash hot,* the owner tells himself as he delivers the coffee. Plodder calls for the third time in an hour, and Ivan again reassures him that Nell will make a full recovery.

'That's not the point, and you know it,' says Plodder, newly assertive, the care and concern of the previous calls replaced by a simmering anger. 'Someone flattened her, left her to die. The door to the street was open when she got there. They went down and locked it. Locked her and Figtree inside. We need to get those cunts. *You* need to get those cunts. Whatever you need,

266

you've got it. More foot soldiers, more forensics, the Dog Squad. Tactical response.'

Ivan is taken aback by the aggression he hears in the voice of his typically unflappable boss. 'Not yet. I don't want to ignite a media shitshow. The local sergeant is pretty canny. Good team.'

'McTosh? Spoke to him this morning. Reckons we should put you up for a bravery award.'

'No. Not that.' Ivan feels the blood run from his face. 'I should have been with her, should have been there.'

'You ran into a burning building. The brass are excited.'

'What does that mean?'

'They love handing out gongs, a made-for-TV ceremony.'

'No, sir, please. I don't deserve it. I don't want it.'

Plodder laughs. 'It's not about you, son. Image of the force and all that. Good press.'

Ivan breathes out. 'I was gambling, sir. Playing the pokies when I should have been with Nell.'

The laughter stops abruptly, replaced by a long and damning silence, Plodder joining the dots. 'I read the story in the *Herald*. Your father.'

And now it's Ivan who falls silent. 'Yes,' is all he can finally manage.

'You need time off to get it sorted?'

'Now? No. That's the last thing I need.'

'Go near the poker machines again and you won't get a choice.'

'I wouldn't deserve one.'

'You want to talk about it?'

Ivan doesn't know what there is to talk about. 'No, sir. I need to focus.'

A pause, in which Ivan can almost hear the mental cogs whirring down the line from Sydney. 'Okay. The priority right now is catching the scum. Pull out all stops. But when it's done, we need to address this. Counselling. Whatever it takes.'

'Yes, sir,' he replies, contrite.

Call completed, Ivan finds he can't sit still. He drains the last of his coffee and walks towards the fire scene.

There are clusters of townspeople, pointing and speaking softly. Again, Bert Kippax is there, standing apart, staring up at the blackened windows, a brown paper bag in his hand, the shape of a bottle.

'What did you see?' asks Ivan.

'You. Saving their lives.'

'But not who torched the place?'

'No. Nothing.' The former policeman unscrews the top of the wine bottle, thinks better of it and screws it back on. 'One thing, though, from last night. I went past earlier. Remember seeing the light on upstairs. Assumed someone had left it on by mistake.'

'What time?'

'Not long after sunset,' says the old man.

Ivan looks at the building. The fire crews have done a good job, stopping the blaze before the entire building could collapse in on itself. The internet cafe appears more or less intact, but the upstairs is gutted; smoke still wafts and water still drips and a large section of the roof has gone. People stare and whisper, a couple pointing him out. The story of his escape, him and Nell and Alice, will already be common knowledge. Ivan returns his attention to the building. He knows looks can be deceptive, that the damage must be extensive, that the building is probably beyond saving. Perhaps they will keep the facade, the Art Deco too precious to lose. The Seven can fund it, adorn it with another plaque. As good as new.

He'd love to get inside, poke about, but knows it will be unsafe, knows that any evidence will almost certainly be destroyed. Evidence of the arson, evidence of whoever tried to kill Alice Figtree, whoever bashed Nell, the evidence that got Athol Hasluck killed. All of it gone.

'I asked around,' says Bert. 'The bloke dossing out the back. Not a bloke. Woman called Kazza. Last name unknown. Thought it was safer sleeping there than in a park with a bunch of boozed-up blokes.'

'Know where I can find her?' asks Ivan.

Bert shakes his head. 'No one has seen her. Not for days.' He turns to Ivan. 'Maybe she did see something. Has done a runner.'

'Be good to find her.'

'Not easy if she's left town.'

They're still standing there when Ernst McTosh arrives. He joins them, offering Bert a nod of recognition.

'McTosh,' says Bert and moves away, leaving the two sergeants looking at the building.

'Close call,' says McTosh.

'Yep.'

'How's the lass?'

'Should make a full recovery. She'll be discharged today.'

'Glad to hear it.' McTosh looks at the charred ruins, concern clearly weighing on him. 'Alice Figtree. She was stabbed?'

'I believe so.'

'Same weapon as Hasluck?'

'Too early to tell. We'll be checking.'

'She's not local. Not originally. Parents live on a farm in Victoria. But I've been out to Three Wells Station, broke the news to her wife.'

Ivan regards McTosh, sees the strain on the man's face, knows the toll it can take. 'Thank you. She have anything relevant to say?'

'Not really. Said they had dinner together last night, then Alice went into work to prepare the files. Said they were being transferred to the police station today. Is that right?'

'Yes. We were worried they weren't safe here.'

McTosh turns back to the building, as if it might tell him something. 'So they were important?'

'Someone thought so.'

'Shit,' says McTosh. 'Wish you'd told me. I could have had someone guard it.'

'Hindsight, Ernst. Wonderful thing.'

'Come, I'll show you what we know,' says the sergeant.

He leads the way, down the lane to the alley behind the accountancy practice. Smoke smoulders from the ruins. McTosh lifts the police tape, lets Ivan duck under, then leads him up the flight of concrete stairs, the rear exit.

'Here,' says McTosh at the top of the stairs, indicating the security grille on the back door. It's been jemmied off, the hinges twisted and broken. 'Look but don't touch,' says McTosh.

Ivan examines the scene. 'Take a bit of force.'

'Aye. A bit of muscle. One bloke, possibly two. Crowbars, cold chisel.'

'Different from last Saturday night. No forced entry back then.'

McTosh grimaces. 'This is brazen, all right. But this alley, late at night, no one around—pretty good odds of getting away with it undetected.'

'Any ideas who could have done this?'

McTosh looks at him, as if surprised by the question. 'None.'

Ivan thinks of what he saw upstairs the previous night, files strewn everywhere. Breaking into the filing cabinets would have been child's play compared to levering the security door open.

'CCTV?' he asks.

'Yeah, we've already picked up the files from the store across the road, same as before. They had them waiting for us. It'll give us an exact time for the explosion. The fire brigade got the call at twelve thirty-eight am. We're accessing council footage from Commonwealth Way. Constable Simmonds is on it, but I can pull her off if you want your people to take over.'

'No, I'd be grateful if she stuck with it; she's done a thorough job so far. Local knowledge will be an advantage, knowing how to meld the different camera angles together.'

'Done,' says McTosh.

'Twelve thirty-eight. So the fire was set when? Twelve fifteen? Twelve twenty? Them breaking in not long after midnight. Seems on the early side to me. If I were breaking in, intent on arson, I'd be doing it at four in the morning. After Alice Figtree had left. After the lights went out.'

McTosh frowns. 'What's your point?'

'They knew she was in there.'

'Premeditated?' The horror on the sergeant's face is evident. 'And Constable Buchanan?'

Ivan thinks of the locked door. 'I reckon they were already inside when she arrived. Caught them by surprise. Anything more to see around here?'

'No. Not safe to enter.'

'Okay. Thanks,' says Ivan. 'I'd like to go and speak to Alice Figtree's wife. Can you give me directions?'

'Sure, but you'll have to be quick. She'll be heading to Canberra to be with Alice.'

——

The Heartwood property is not Art Deco or Italianate or anything else from the twentieth or twenty-first century. It's a mid-nineteenth-century colonial homestead, picture perfect, two storeys, large verandahs, with a stone tower at its centre, sitting in an island of green parkland amid the brown and sun-scorched earth beyond the Spur, five kilometres outside the boundary of the irrigation scheme. It's as if the days of the squattocracy never ended. Perhaps they haven't. There is a Mercedes SUV parked at the bottom of the stairs, as if carelessly discarded on the sweep of the circular drive.

He climbs the steps, walks across the wide verandah, raps at the door using a heavy iron knocker.

The woman who answers looks practical, hair short with streaks of grey, jeans, an old shirt, an expensive-looking linen jacket. Ivan can see in her face the echo of the B&S photograph. Like his, her eyes are red, not from smoke but tears.

He shows his badge, identifies himself.

'I'm afraid I was just leaving, Sergeant,' she says. 'Flying to Canberra.' She doesn't bother to offer her name, perhaps assuming he should know it. There is a leather overnight bag by her feet.

'You're Krystal Heartwood?'

She frowns. 'Of course.'

'Can I drop you at the airport?' he asks. 'Talk on the way?'

'We have our own airstrip, just over the rise.' Her voice is resonant, an actor's voice. It softens a little as she says, 'I'm told you saved her life.'

'I did what I could.'

'I don't much like police. But under the circumstances I can give you fifteen minutes, then I'll need to be off or I risk losing my landing slot in Canberra.'

'You'll fly yourself?'

'Yes. Come in.'

Inside, the sitting room is a skilful mix of the nineteenth century and the contemporary. The furnishings are light, and the art on the walls is modern. Ivan realises it has been rendered with some taste, beyond his ability to appreciate it.

'Why don't you like police?' he asks.

She looks him over, as if sizing him up. 'When my brother was murdered, they treated it as a missing persons case.'

'Including Bert Kippax?'

She shakes her head. 'I don't blame him; he lived in hope. Bert wasn't the problem. But please sit down, we don't have long.'

'Just you and Alice here?'

'For now,' she says, taking a seat opposite him. 'But we're seldom alone. It's a large place. Needs people in it. We run artists' residencies. Subsidise them.' She glances at her phone, checking the time. 'I want to help, Sergeant Lucic. Ask me whatever you like. I want you to apprehend whoever it was who did this to Alice.'

Her face is resolute, only her overly formal words suggesting the effort she is making.

Ivan decides not to insist on recording the conversation. 'Thank you. I believe Sergeant McTosh informed you that your wife was stabbed?'

'He did. Yes.'

'We think she was attacked because she's been helping our investigation into Athol Hasluck's death. There's no proof, but it's a fair assumption. We feel responsible.'

Krystal nods. 'Yes. She said you thought there might be some danger involved.'

'Was she concerned?'

A deep breath. 'No. She thought you were overreacting. I guess you were right.'

'She was examining Mr Hasluck's records, trying to establish if they might indicate those with a motive to kill him.'

'So I understand.'

'I last spoke to her yesterday, but Ernst McTosh said you and she had dinner together here before she returned to the office last night.'

'No. We ate in town.'

'My mistake. Did you talk about the case at all?'

'We did indeed. She was excited. Thought that the records might well hold some clue. She'd been working through digital files here at Three Wells and had already discovered Athol was in serious debt, and had then found he was overcommitted to that harebrained scheme to extract water from thin air, that he was overly influenced by Craven Allsop and his financial plays in the 'water market. The poor man had become so desperate that he'd raided his own trust account.'

'So she was sympathetic to Athol Hasluck's plight.'

'She's a very empathetic person. People say she's had a humanising effect on me.' Krystal offers a strained smile, as if remembering an instruction from her partner.

'Athol Hasluck also bought land—unirrigated land—not so far from here.'

'Yes. One investment that might make sense.'

Ivan is surprised. 'How?'

'Mr Hasluck was involved in local politics. You've discovered that, I assume?'

'Yes. Go on.'

'Do you know about the inland freight line? There's been quite the kerfuffle about it lately.'

'The railway?' Ivan has heard its benefits touted back in Dubbo: a 1700-kilometre, multibillion-dollar freight line linking Melbourne and Brisbane, traversing the agricultural hinterland of south-eastern Australia. 'What about it?'

'There are plans for a branch line to come down through Yuwonderie. Otto Titchfield has been engaged in a great deal of political horsetrading to secure it. Refrigerated produce from the Yuwonderie Wholesalers shipped directly to ports and airports. It would enable us to sell straight into Asia at a competitive price, making us less dependent on the Melbourne markets. We've all been backing him.'

'We?'

'The Seven. I'm sure you've heard of us.'

'I have.'

'I'm on the board of the Wholesalers, and the Irrigation Scheme Company.'

Ivan can't help himself. 'And the Canal Club?'

'No, thanks.' She smiles, a passing flicker. 'Just a member. Got the rules changed to admit women, once I became a family head. They're still not so fond of lesbians, though.'

'You were talking about the inland rail and Athol buying land.'

'The branch line is approved in principle and the route close to being finalised.'

Ivan can see where this is heading. 'You think Athol gained some inside knowledge about where the line will go. Bought the land, planning to sell at a profit when the government announces the route. Name his price.'

'Nothing so simple.' Krystal smiles again and gives a wry shake of her head. 'Governments have been playing this game since settlement. They pass legislation, acquire the land compulsorily, pay fair value. Still a good deal for him. We reckon he might have got most of his half a million back; not all, but he'd still have ninety per cent of the land.'

Ivan is confused. 'What then?'

'The land is mostly flat here, as you've probably noticed. A rail line, by necessity, has to be raised above the surrounding plain to avoid being flooded. Consider that. It is in effect a giant dam wall being built across the landscape, capable of diverting or blocking the flow of water. If it were built along the correct alignment, the one Alice and I have deduced is the most likely, the one Athol believed is about to be confirmed, it would run close to the western boundary of the land Athol bought. It would capture significant flow coming down off the far side of the Castle.' She raises an eyebrow, as if amused by Ivan's reaction.

'Like free irrigation?'

'Not as reliable, but enough for wheat in a wet year or to carry a good number of sheep in a relatively dry year.'

'Making the land worth . . . ?' asks Ivan, inflection rising.

'Two and a half, maybe three million. Plus whatever the government pays for the rail corridor.'

'Insider trading?'

'Possibly.'

'And would that upset anyone enough to commit murder?'

She laughs, and Ivan glimpses the woman Krystal Heartwood might be in normal times: a less severe, more convivial person. 'No. Among the Seven, such practice is more likely to be celebrated. And remember, Athol Hasluck was from one of the Seven families. And the money the Seven are likely to reap should the rail line come through is considerable, dwarfing any windfall of Athol's. No, it would have been seen as a feather in his cap.'

'What about the people who sold him the land?'

'You think it unethical?'

'Not me. Them. Could they have sought retribution?'

'No. Alice and I took a look. He bought it from a large agrobusiness investment fund. Scottish, based in Edinburgh.'

Ivan discards that line of inquiry, but he's starting to feel unsettled. He's been working on the assumption Athol Hasluck was in debt and desperate as a consequence. Now he can feel the ground moving under his feet: Athol was within weeks of making millions. Alice was meant to have been helping the police investigation, and yet she had told him none of this. He looks at

Krystal, senses she's assessing him as if aware of the discomfort she's causing. 'When is the decision on the track alignment due to be made?' he asks. 'Do you know?'

'Within the month.'

Ivan blinks. 'So he would have been able to sell the land, clear his debts?'

'That's what we were thinking.'

'Why didn't Alice mention this to us?'

'She intended to.'

'You're sure about that?'

'I've told you, haven't I? Why wouldn't she?'

Ivan stares. Something isn't sitting right. Athol had been in serious debt: so serious he bled his bank accounts dry and raided his trust account. And when he attempted to raise money—getting a refund from Toby Fairchild, borrowing money from Craven— he'd been rebuffed. So where did he get the money for the land from? Ivan thinks of the old photo, the partygoers at the B&S ball. 'You knew him, didn't you? Athol Hasluck?'

'Of course. He's from one of the Seven families. A younger son. We all know each other. All grew up together.'

'What did you make of him?'

'I always found him a very pleasant, well-meaning man. Rather boring, and not particularly intelligent, but sincere and unpretentious. I thought accountancy the perfect profession for him.'

Ivan hears the dismissal in the tone, the hauteur that comes with being the head of one of the families. He looks around the room, sees the wealth: it's not demonstrative, not there to impress, but it's there all the same. Suddenly something occurs to him. 'Why was Alice working there? With Athol?'

'Good question.'

'She didn't need the money,' says Ivan, pressing the point. 'And there's plenty to do out here, I imagine, if you have a steady flow of artists coming through. So why go and work there?'

Krystal Heartwood says nothing, as if waiting for him to draw his own conclusion. A clock chimes and is answered by another, deeper in the house. She looks at her phone once more.

'She was investigating Athol Hasluck's affairs even before he was murdered,' asserts Ivan.

'No. Not that.'

'What then?' Ivan is almost whispering. He remembers what Craven Allsop said: *Alice and Krystal are more interested in what happened in 1994 than what happened last weekend.* 'Does this have anything to do with your brother? Was Alice looking for evidence related to his murder?'

The look on Krystal's face is one of strange intensity. 'My brother has been dead for thirty years.'

And now Ivan wishes he was recording the interview. 'Answer the question please, Ms Heartwood.'

But she doesn't; not straight away. She looks out through the window, back again. 'Athol came to me. Seeking money. I wasn't much interested. So then he dangled something in front of me, something I had never heard before.' She leans forward in her chair, as if to emphasise her point. 'He'd been to a professional conference on the Gold Coast. Said he'd encountered an old accountant, now retired, who'd had a lot to drink at the conference dinner. This man claimed to have done some work for one of the firms down at the fruit and vegetable markets in Melbourne. Decades ago. This man said he'd heard my brother and Stella had been murdered to silence them. That they had discovered something untoward at Yuwonderie Wholesalers.'

Ivan blinks. 'Such as?'

'The man didn't say, but Athol believed him. You probably don't know this, but Athol dated Stella briefly, before she started going out with Davis. He knew Stella had worked at the Wholesalers.'

Ivan recalls once more the photograph from the B&S ball, Athol standing behind Stella, hands on her shoulders. Something shifts in his mind. 'Go on.'

Krystal sighs. 'I know what you're thinking—that it's all in the past. But I found myself dwelling on the murder. I'm sure you've seen the reports. My brother was shot in the back of the head. Executed. I'd always thought it was something to do with the money that was stolen from the safe here, but I began to think I was wrong, that his death resulted from something Stella had discovered. It started to haunt me. Alice never knew my brother, but she knew how important he was to me. She could see I was obsessing, so she suggested she team up with Athol to see if they could get to the bottom of his killing.'

'And he was agreeable?'

'When I lent him the money to buy his land he was.'

Ivan's mind is whirring. 'So Alice told us he was in debt, but he wasn't, was he?'

'He most certainly was. If the branch line goes ahead, he would have been saved, but that's by no means guaranteed. Otto Titchfield doesn't always get his way.' Krystal leans forward, giving her words even more weight. 'Everything Alice told you was true. He was seriously in debt. He had invested unwisely in water and air. She didn't mislead you.'

Ivan can feel his anger rise. 'She didn't tell us about the land.'

'She didn't know.'

'What?'

'About the loan to Athol.'

'Why ever not?'

'He insisted.' She shrugs. 'I didn't know he was in debt. He kept that from us both. Alice only discovered that after he was killed. So when I lent him the money, it was a simple proposition: he got the land, and he and Alice investigated this claim about Davis and Stella.'

Ivan remembers the tremor in Alice's voice as she told them about uncovering Athol's debts, and later finding his investments in Riverina Water Traders and Air Stills of Australia. Either she was a brilliant actor, or Krystal Heartwood was telling the truth.

'That's one thing, but she also didn't tell us about her and Athol investigating Yuwonderie Wholesalers. The story about the old accountant and the Melbourne fruit and veg market. She must have known about it.'

'They'd made no progress with that. None at all. I can't see that getting him killed.'

Ivan shakes his head, anger reasserting itself. 'That's not the point.'

Krystal bites her lip. 'She was protecting me.'

'What? How?'

'I stole documents. From the Wholesalers. I'm on the board. She didn't want to tell you, because she didn't want me arrested and ejected from the board. Not to mention being ostracised by the Seven.' She spreads her hands wide. 'Those accounts were what she and Athol had been working through. But she told me again at dinner last night that there was nothing there. They'd found nothing; nothing at all. It was Athol's accounts that she was excited about.'

'Do you have a copy of them? Did Alice back them up?'

Krystal glances again at her phone. 'I'll see what I can find, but I'm sorry, I need to leave.'

Ivan frowns. He's not done yet. 'Can I ride with you? Talk on the way to the airstrip?'

'Sure. But I'll need to leave the car there for when I get back. It's about a kilometre and a half. An easy return walk.' She smiles. 'Wait out by the car. I'll just check the doors, set the alarm.'

Ivan does as suggested, using the opportunity to take in the house and the gardens. The trees are tall and mature; some must be a hundred years old or more. They're the trees of England: poplars and oaks and ashes and birches, even a few willows by a wide pond. A statement of water, of heritage, of wealth. It can't possibly be that Krystal and Alice live here alone; there must be gardeners, maids, farm managers and workers. A genuine estate. Genuine privilege; genuine entitlement.

Krystal joins him, handing over a portable hard drive. 'On her desk. I think it's what you're after.'

Once they're in the Mercedes, Krystal behind the wheel, she starts talking again, unprompted, as if she finds it easier to look through the windscreen than into his eyes. 'One day Davis was with us, and then he was gone. Our grandfather was still alive then; he spent a fortune on private investigators. Nothing. I always thought my brother would be found, that he and Stella Kippax had run off together. I couldn't handle the alternative.' She pauses, concentrating as they rattle over a cattle grid. 'I always thought he was out there; that he wouldn't leave me alone in the world. When his body was found, I felt an overwhelming sense of guilt, as if I had let him down. He was a remarkable person, so charismatic, so dynamic. It seemed inconceivable that he was dead.'

They're following a farm track up a low rise, an echo of the Spur. She points to a hillock. 'That's where he's buried, among the family graves. I don't know why, but I still find it hard to go there.'

Ivan can see an iron fence on the crest of the rise, some gravestones sheltering under a lone oak tree.

'Do you think Athol might have found something that he didn't tell Alice?' Ivan asks. 'Something he could exploit? You said yourself that the rail line might not go ahead. He was desperate to make money.'

She nods, and now there is a wetness in her eyes. 'It's possible.'

Ivan looks again to the small graveyard up on the rise. It seems lonely, without grandeur, marooned in the drylands.

They top the rise and Ivan can see the airstrip, with a hangar at one end and a farm truck waiting. There is a plane, twin props, larger than he had imagined, a man next to it. The manager, preparing it for the flight.

'If he did find something, it might have been what killed him. And the murderers assumed that Alice shared his knowledge,' Ivan summarises.

They reach the hangar and Krystal stops the car, lets the engine run, stares unseeing out the windscreen, a single tear on her cheek. She turns to Ivan. 'Last night, at dinner, Alice said she might have something, something she wanted to look into. That was the first and only time she said anything like that. That's why she was returning to the office.'

'What was she checking?'

'She didn't say. But she said it might prove useful to you.'

'To me?'

'To the investigation.'

'Do you know what it was?'

Krystal doesn't speak, merely shakes her head, lips pressed together into a thin line. 'I wish I'd asked.'

'It can't have been the documents you stole,' he says, wanting to comfort her. 'She already had those. If she needed to be in the office, she must have been checking something against the client files. The paper files in the filing cabinets.'

'They were destroyed in the fire?'

'Yes,' says Ivan.

Krystal sighs deeply, nods. 'I am sorry, Sergeant. We should have trusted you. I should have trusted you.'

After the plane has gone, a dot disappearing into the blue, Ivan doesn't walk straight back to the house. He climbs to the graveyard under the solitary oak and looks at the headstones, lonely yet united. He finds that of Davis Heartwood standing a little apart from those of his forebears. Ivan is surprised by how weathered it is, edged with small cracks and lichen. Dead thirty years; how could his murder possibly be relevant?

chapter twenty-nine

1994

AT THE COACHMAN'S ARMS TWO DAYS LATER, OTTO WAS FULL OF APOLOGIES: for getting a skinful, for 'upsetting' Stella, for stepping out of line. 'To be honest, I don't remember much of it.'

'Eccies,' said Craven. 'Idiot.'

'So what's the story with Lucy and you?' asked Davis.

Otto almost choked on his beer. Craven looked bewildered.

'She tell you about that, then?' said Otto, once he'd recovered.

'Not in so many words,' said Davis.

'I dunno,' said Otto. 'She seems to fancy me.' His face is as guile-free as ever. 'I feel bad about it.'

'Shit happens, Otto,' said Davis.

'You're okay with it?'

'I don't own her,' Davis said, a little testiness creeping in.

'That's very mature of you,' said Otto. 'She really is a firecracker.'

'Oh, please,' said Craven, eyes rolling.

Davis stopped listening. Lucy was over at the other side of the bar with her little sister Jacinta and Athol, apparently chatting happily, except that he could see her stealing a look in their direction at regular periods. He waved, just to let her know he could see her, and she waved back, looking unsure how to interpret his gesture.

'Spoke to the old man last night,' said Otto. 'He's a bit upset.'

'You're not the first to go off the rails at a B&S,' said Davis, unsure why he should even placate his friend.

'Not with me—with you,' said Otto, a smirk creeping across his face.

'Sorry, what?' Davis thought about how he'd punched Otto in the stomach, wondered if somehow Otto's father had got wind of the incident.

'Your research,' said Craven. 'My grandfather said the same thing.'

Davis frowned. 'I had lunch with your family heads, Jessop and Van Dyke, at the Canal Club. They were enthusiastic. Wanted to fund a book. Glossy photos, the works.' But even as he spoke, he felt an uncomfortable shifting in his stomach. 'A proper editor.'

Craven laughed. 'They're worried you might emphasise the wrong areas. You know them. Used to controlling everything.'

Davis looked across at Lucy, but she no longer met his gaze, apparently engrossed in a conversation with the other two.

'Lucy. She told you what we found in Sydney?'

Otto looked blank. 'No. Not me.'

'Craven?'

Craven shook his head. 'She might have let something slip, but that's not the point. That's not what's got the old men worried.' He lowered his head, whispered conspiratorially. 'We're going to be running this show one day. You'll be on the board of the company, of the Wholesalers, the Land Trust. The board of the *Wonder*, the Progress Association, and whatever else you want to stick your finger in. The Canal Club. They don't want you to undermine their legacy.'

Davis had grown very still. 'What are you saying?'

'Strength in unity,' said Craven.

'Don't shit in your own nest,' Otto boomed, none of Craven's hushed tones.

Craven continued, trying to finesse the blunt assertions of Otto Titchfield. 'It's a matter of perception,' he said. 'This whole district, everything to do with it, is one integrated project. People are invested in it, financially and emotionally. They believe in it. It's their lives, their futures. The small landholders and the towns-people, the shop owners and rural workers. They all have a stake in it; they all profit from it. As long as the money keeps rolling in, and they believe in the unity and dedication of the community's leaders, then everyone's a winner.'

'The Seven,' said Davis, half a question, half a statement.

'Who else?' said Otto.

'It's not just us as individuals,' added Craven. 'It's the standing of our families.'

'You believe that?'

'Don't you?'

'I'm not trying to undermine any of it,' said Davis. 'Tell your families to relax. It's just an honours thesis. No one's going to read it.' He kept his voice calm, but inside he was seething. Not at the family heads, but at Lucy. She must have told the ruling clique of his research. He had half a mind to walk over and confront her, but he refrained. She still hadn't told them of his intention to renounce his inheritance; she had at least kept that a secret. Maybe she hadn't meant to talk about his research; maybe the smooth-talking Hilary Housego at the Irrigation Company had wheedled it out of her. So his anger bubbled, without an obvious outlet. He couldn't believe how readily Otto and Craven had adopted their families' stance. Suddenly the pub felt claustrophobic. 'Excuse me a moment,' he said, taking his drink and heading outside to the beer garden.

The sun was still up, and it was still hot, the concrete paving reflecting the heat. Not many people, just a few smokers. Fine by him. He'd finish his drink, then leave. He sat with his back to the interior, under the shade of a small awning. He breathed, reminding himself he was under no obligation to stay here, that he could leave Yuwonderie anytime he liked.

Gradually, his anger subsided, replaced by a growing determination not to be intimidated. If the Seven pushed him, he'd push back, find out what was making them so sensitive, find out what really happened during the formative years of the scheme. Whatever it was, it couldn't be so bad. Craven was right: they were just used to getting their own way. All the people involved were long dead, the district prosperous. And if it caused a little embarrassment, so what? He'd be gone anyway, off to do his PhD or travel the world. Whatever. But not with Lucy, that much was clear.

Of course, he wouldn't be entirely gone. He couldn't ever fully escape Yuwonderie, because his family would still be here. His grandfather and Krystal would have to wear any opprobrium that he left behind. Craven had said as much. It was a sobering thought. His grandfather had dedicated his life to Three Wells Station, spent every day overseeing it. What grief might it cause him to have his standing eroded in his fading years? And Krystal, unequipped as yet, her management degree not even started? She could inherit at any time, he realised, be required to sit on all those boards that Craven mentioned, with all those canny, scheming old men. How unfair would it be if she were handicapped from the outset by his ruminations?

He stopped, mid-thought. What had Craven said, in among the Irrigation Scheme Company board, and the Wholesalers board and the newspaper board and all the rest? The Land Trust . . . What was that?

'Hello.' It was Stella Kippax, standing next to his table, glass of white wine in her hand. 'You're looking thoughtful.'

'Happens on occasion.'

'I just wanted to thank you. For Saturday night. Otto.'

'He was out of line.'

'He holding it against you?'

'Not that I can see.'

'Right.' She looked a little undecided, and then: 'Can I join you?'

'Please,' said Davis. 'I'd be glad of the company.' Which was only half a lie.

Stella made her way to the far side of the table, sat facing him, took a sip of her wine, then fell into silence. Davis quite liked that. It was a contrast to Lucy's bird-like chattiness.

'I told my father,' said Stella eventually. 'About what happened.'

'What did he say?'

'To forget it. No harm done.'

'Was there?'

Stella looked at him. 'Yeah. There was. He had his hands all over me, forced his tongue into my mouth, scared me shitless. If it wasn't for you, who knows how it might have ended.' There was a crack in her voice. 'I couldn't believe it was happening. It came out of nowhere.'

'You want me to be a witness?' asked Davis.

Her eyes narrowed as she studied him. 'You wouldn't do that. Betray a friend.'

'I punched him in the guts, didn't I?'

'You're Seven. That's what Dad said. "You can't win against the Seven."'

The assertion annoyed Davis. 'Doesn't mean we don't know right from wrong.'

'Maybe.' She took another sip of her wine, appraising him over the rim of the glass. 'Self-interest usually comes first. Not just with the Seven. Way of the world.'

'That's pretty cynical.'

'But accurate, don't you think?' She shook her head, sighed. 'Sorry, Davis, I didn't come over here to criticise you. But soon enough, you'll inherit your estate. You'll be part of it. Nothing will change.'

'I won't inherit—my sister will,' said Davis, the words out of his mouth before he could consider them.

Stella said nothing, just looked at him across the table.

'She's older than me,' said Davis.

'The estates always go to the eldest son. That's what I heard.'

'Not anymore.' And then: 'Please don't tell anyone. It hasn't been finalised. Not yet. I shouldn't have said anything.'

'Why would your grandfather decide to do that? Did Krystal persuade him?'

'It was my decision.'

Stella squinted, as if attempting to discern his motivation.

'But you're right, it is self-interest,' said Davis. 'I don't want to be a farmer, run an estate. Or sit on the boards of the Irrigation Scheme Company and the Wholesalers and the Land Trust, whatever that is.'

'You'll give it all up?'

'I won't starve.'

'What *do* you want, then?'

And Davis smiled. 'I wish I knew.'

They sat and talked after that, speaking of her, not of him, as if she too enjoyed having someone she could confide in. He learnt she'd only arrived in Yuwonderie three years ago, when her father was posted to the town, after Davis had already left for university. She told him she'd been forced to repeat her final year at school, then spent the last two working and saving. Even so, Davis wondered why he hadn't noticed her before, with her clear skin and calm eyes, her assured manner, her measured voice and lively intelligence. She said she had a job at the Wholesalers, packing fruit at first, but she had now secured an office job.

'I'm saving for university. That's the dream. Not a lot for me here.'

'Studying what?'

'I'm thinking literature or history. Maybe peg on a teaching qualification. Or become a librarian.'

'Where would you study?'

'Not sure. Melbourne; maybe Canberra. Somewhere regional would be cheaper, but I'd like to go somewhere a bit more dynamic.'

'Sounds like your mind is made up. Why the delay?'

She smiled at that. 'Money. I've been saving up. Now I've worked two years, I can get Austudy.'

'Your dad won't help?'

'He'll do what he can. He's let me live at home rent-free. I've saved heaps.'

Towards closing time, when Davis went to the bar for more drinks, he saw Otto and Lucy together, the big bloke's arm around the small woman's waist. It didn't bother Davis as much as he thought it should.

chapter thirty

AT THE POLICE STATION, THE UPSTAIRS ROOM IS FILLING UP. CRIME SCENE investigator Carole Nguyen is here and so is Detective Senior Constable Kevin Nackangara, freshly arrived from Dubbo. He's setting up his laptop, connecting it to a large monitor. Blake Ness is sitting to one side, intently examining full-colour close-ups on his laptop. There is an urgency here, a sense of unity and purpose; their colleague is in hospital, a woman is fighting for her life in intensive care in Canberra and a killer is on the loose.

An impromptu meeting begins without Ivan even convening it. He starts by briefing them on Nell, telling them he's seen her and that she's fine and expected to be discharged from hospital at any time. He then informs them of the new development: that Athol and Krystal were investigating the accounts of the Yuwonderie Wholesalers, that it was most likely something in the client files that led to the arson attack and the attempt on Alice Figtree's life, and that Athol was likely to make a killing on the land he'd bought out past the Spur.

'Are they safe?' asks Kevin. 'Alice Figtree? Krystal Heartwood?'

'I called Plodder. He's putting security into the hospital. Federal police.'

There's a pause in the discussion, a quiet acknowledgement that there is danger lurking.

Carole speaks. 'I still don't have a location for Athol Hasluck's murder. No blood at the canal and none in his office; I checked it thoroughly before the fire. Collected some fibres, but they're meaningless without something to compare them to. No fingerprints that match anything on the database.'

'The divers?' Ivan asks. 'They still up at the Hawkesbury?'

'Just arrived. We'll hear from them later today or tomorrow.'

'Anything else?'

'I've just come back from Athol Hasluck's office with Blake. It's structurally precarious, so I couldn't get full access. But there are obvious signs of break and enter, and clear signs of arson. The place was deliberately torched. No attempt to disguise it.'

'And the records that were kept there?' asks Ivan.

'Destroyed. Nothing left.'

'This isn't just arson,' says Ivan, addressing the group as a whole. 'A witness, a former copper, saw a light on in the office earlier in the evening. So the perpetrators knew Alice was there, broke in, attacked her—probably with a knife—but then Nell surprised them. So they clobbered her. They then locked the door to the street and torched the place to destroy the documents and incinerate the two of them. It would have left no evidence of murder.'

'Why was Nell there?' asks Kevin, a tremor in his voice.

Ivan feels his breath catch, the guilt returning. 'Alice rang her, saying she'd found something.' Ivan finds it difficult to meet their eyes. 'I should have been there. I wasn't.'

There's silence.

'We really need to get across any CCTV. McTosh has Constable Simmonds on it, but we need to be in control, to supervise. Kevin?'

'On it,' says Kevin.

'There's this,' says Blake. He passes his laptop to Ivan. There's a full-frame photo, a gash in white flesh, the brown stain of pre-op antiseptic. 'From Canberra. Alice Figtree, before surgery. Knifed.'

'And?'

'Spoke to the surgeon. She said there was millimetres in it. A bee's tit to the left and Alice would have died on the spot. They're sending through more photographs, but I'm not sure we can be any more definitive.'

'Of what?' asks Carole.

'The blade. Looks like the same sort that killed Athol Hasluck. And a very similar location. One thrust. Practically identical.'

'Same perpetrator?'

'Or a very unlikely coincidence.'

Again the frisson runs around the group, the knowledge that someone dangerous is on the loose. 'I'm going to visit Nell again, see if she's ready to leave,' says Ivan. 'Kevin, when you're set up, go through the hard drive Krystal Heartwood gave me, see what you can glean from the files Alice was checking. She found something there that caused her to go into the practice. That's the priority. Supervise the CCTV, but let the locals do the grunt work.' Kevin nods his understanding, and Ivan addresses the team. 'One more thing. There was a murder here thirty years ago. Two young people disappeared: Stella Kippax and Davis Heartwood, Krystal's younger brother. It was treated as a missing persons case until the body of Heartwood was discovered in a shallow grave many years later. Stella has never been found. Krystal Heartwood says Athol and Alice were attempting to revisit the case—that's why they were trying to examine Yuwonderie Wholesalers. Nell's already pulled the files and had a look, but can you make sure we've got everything? She can start back on them when she's up to it.'

— —

The day is blazing as he arrives at Yuwonderie Hospital, the air-conditioning losing the battle inside the century-old building. Nell is looking better, cheered at the prospect of being discharged. Her oxygen levels are back to normal, and she says the coughing is growing less persistent. She has showered and dressed and is sitting on her bed, laptop open. Apart from her red-rimmed eyes, she looks practically back to normal. Ivan suspects she looks better than he does; she's certainly had more sleep.

'Any news of Alice?' It's the first thing she asks.

'Out of surgery. Still in intensive care. Induced coma.'

'She'll make it?'

'Should do. Provided there's no unexpected complications.'

Nell says nothing.

'You're looking better,' says Ivan.

'Feeling better,' she says. 'I'll be out of here in no time. They're just waiting on the results from a last set of tests.'

'Fantastic,' he says. 'Meantime, we've made progress.'

'Tell me.'

He recounts his visit to Three Wells Station and Krystal Heartwood's revelation that Athol Hasluck probably wasn't facing financial ruin after all, that his land purchase made sense even if it was based on insider information.

Nell looks into Ivan's eyes. 'She knew that Athol wasn't teetering on bankruptcy?'

'She maintains that she didn't know he was in debt. Not until after he was dead. That's not why she lent him the money.' He explains Athol's claim that the murder of Davis Heartwood was somehow connected to the Wholesalers, that he and Alice were supposedly investigating the company. That Krystal had stolen documents, so Alice hadn't confided in the police.

Nell is already shaking her head before he's finished. 'Fuck, Ivan. What if we find that, intentionally or unintentionally, Alice was the one who triggered all of this? That she was the one who found something that got Athol killed in the first place?'

It's Ivan's turn to shake his head. 'No. She would have told us. And if she didn't, now that she's fighting for her life, Krystal would have told us.' He takes a breath. 'If she found something, it wasn't until last night.'

She stares back at him for a moment, considering. 'I agree. But if she and Krystal Heartwood have been playing some double game, or withholding information, then we need to nail their arses. Fuck the Seven—I could have died.'

And now Ivan is nodding fervently, glad to see his partner has lost none of her feistiness. 'You have my total support. If they've misled us, we'll prosecute them and I'll own the mistake of bringing Alice on board. But for now, we need them onside. Krystal was helpful this morning. And once Alice has regained consciousness, she should be able to tell us what she found. And, with any luck, who attacked the two of you.'

'Let's hope she can.' Nell doesn't sound entirely convinced.

'I spoke to Plodder. He's fully briefed. He's backing us.'

'Good,' says Nell, her tone noncommittal.

'You sure you're all right?'

'No, I'm not,' she says, looking him in the eye. 'I almost died while you were playing the poker machines. Remember?'

That deflates him.

'What about you?' she asks. 'You all right?'

'My father called me,' he says, the words coming before he has time to consider them. 'Spoke to me on the phone. He's been released.'

She says nothing, but her eyes are on him, searching.

'He's coming back to Australia. He wants to meet me.'

'Fuck,' she says. And her brow is creased with concern.

'I should have told you.'

'That's what drove you to the pokies?'

'I guess.'

'Does Plodder know?'

'About my father? He does. It's in the paper. And I told him about the pokies.'

'What will you do? About your father?'

'Don't know.'

She sits and considers that, staring at the screen of her laptop. Eventually she looks up. 'Let me know if I can help.'

He feels a sense of relief. 'Nell, the pokies—it was a one-off. An aberration. Won't happen again.'

'Prove it.'

——

Ivan is walking back through the hospital's reception, chastened by his meeting with Nell, when his attention is seized by the blare of an approaching siren. An ambulance pulls up, the siren falls silent. It takes him a moment to register it, he's so preoccupied. It's a country hospital: the emergency entrance and the main entrance are the same thing. He stands back, not wanting to get in the way. The paramedics remove a gurney from the back, a man strapped in, unconscious, face bloodied and swollen. It's the shock of blond hair that captures Ivan's attention, makes him approach. Toby Fairchild.

Ivan steps over as the paramedics move to wheel the patient through the doors. It's Fairchild all right, lying there, hairpiece awry. Hairpiece. It's a wig, come away somewhat, showing the bristle of a shaved head below. The mouth is slightly open, the glimmering dental work no longer evident.

Ivan flashes his badge. 'His teeth?'

The older of the two ambulance officers takes in his badge, answers the question. 'Wearing a prosthetic,' he says, picking up on Ivan's curiosity. 'Like an actor. We took it out to help him breathe.'

'Holy shit,' says Ivan. He shakes Fairchild. 'Wake up.'

'Go easy,' says the ambulance officer.

'I won't hurt him,' says Ivan, and gives Fairchild a harder shake.

The eyes flicker open for just a moment, see Ivan and close again. But it's enough. One eye is blue, but the other is brown, the coloured contact lost.

'Well, I'll be fucked,' says Ivan, and starts to laugh. He gets out his phone, opens the MobiPol app, double-checks, still laughing.

'What is it?' asks the younger officer, confused by Ivan's glee at the plight of the injured man.

Ignoring him, Ivan studies the patient, satisfied by what the app has confirmed. He leans in close, face next to the apparently unconscious man. 'Hello, Harley. Bad news, I'm afraid. You're under arrest.'

'Jeez, who is he?' asks the younger officer.

'Dangerous?' asks the older one.

'Not for long,' says Ivan. 'His name is Harley Snouch. Been on the run these past five years. A con man and worse.'

There's a groan from the gurney.

'Wheel him in, let's get him checked out,' says Ivan. 'But I'll be right with you,' he adds, more for the benefit of their patient than for the paramedics.

The officers wheel Harley inside. Ivan follows, ringing McTosh as he walks.

'That you, Ivan?'

'Yes. I need a constable down here at the hospital. I've arrested a man, Harley Snouch, aka Toby Fairchild from Air Stills. There are warrants out for his arrest. He's getting treated, but I need him watched. He'll do a runner first chance he gets.'

'Who is he?'

'A con man. Not the first time I've met him.'

'You got it,' says McTosh. 'Someone will be there in five.'

Ivan catches up with the ambulance officers after they've delivered their patient and are heading back out. 'What happened to him?' he asks them.

'Not sure. Bashed, by the look of it. We got the call, found him bleeding and disorientated.'

'Where abouts?'

'Up on the Castle. Just sitting there in the car park, semi-conscious. Probably concussed.'

'This is the car park of Air Stills of Australia?'

'That's the place.'

'How bad is he?'

'Difficult to say. He's conscious again. Vital signs are good. Breathing okay once we sorted out the teeth; they'd come loose. Insists he's fine, wants to be discharged. Getting vocal about it.'

'I bet he is.'

The paramedic smiles. 'Chances are he's okay, but there's a possibility it's more serious. Bleeding on the brain, a fractured skull. They have X-ray and ultrasound here. If he deteriorates, he'll be off to Wagga or Griffith for CAT scans and MRIs and the rest. Airlifted to Canberra if he gets worse.'

'He say what happened?'

'No. We asked, but he said he didn't know. That can happen with concussion: short-term memory loss.'

'You sound sceptical,' Ivan observes.

'A bit. Not sure why. Just something in his manner. Like he was being cagey. Didn't want to come with us at first.'

'Anyone else up there?'

'Not that we could see.'

'And the call?'

'No idea. The dispatchers might know.'

'Right. Thanks.'

Ivan walks back into the casualty section, where Harley is trying to talk his way out of treatment. He glares at Ivan, then submits to the doctor's ministrations as Ivan stands guard.

Ivan feels the jubilation of having arrested Snouch start to dissipate as he begins working through the implications. Snouch was in
disguise, pretending to be someone he wasn't, promoting a scheme
extracting water from thin air. There can be only one conclusion:
Air Stills is one immense scam, staggering in its audacity. One
Ivan hadn't seen through. His last remnants of satisfaction are
replaced, first by shame at his own gullibility, and then by anger.
Snouch tried to play him, extract money, revelling in the challenge
of putting one over the police. And almost succeeding.

Ivan suppresses thoughts of vengeance, telling himself that the
confidence play isn't what matters. The death of Athol Hasluck
matters, the stabbing of Alice Figtree matters, the bashing of Nell
matters. Finding the killer or killers matters. Compared to that,
the fate of the grifter must come a distant second.

So who bashed Snouch? Someone who'd discovered that he
was running a fraud, had cheated them out of their money? That
seems the most likely.

Or was the assault of Snouch somehow connected with the
death of Athol Hasluck and the attack on Alice Figtree?

The door to Casualty swings opens. McTosh strides through,
shadowed by a constable, a young man, who listens intently as
Ivan briefs him. 'Don't let him out of your sight,' Ivan concludes.

McTosh waits for his subordinate to move towards Snouch,
before addressing Ivan urgently: 'Come on. There's been a tip-off.
Air Stills of Australia.'

'What kind of tip-off?' asks Ivan.

'A knife.'

chapter thirty-one

July 1915

Dearest Mother,

I miss you so much. To have you here for the birth, for those first precarious weeks, was everything. Without your love and reassurance, I am sure I would have been lost. Do not worry about the slurs; they mean nothing to me and so they should mean nothing to you. Horace is a fool and will always be, but I am distressed that Elaine felt obliged to remain silent.

We should all learn from Joseph. He is such a wonderful boy, so lively and jolly. Nothing seems to daunt him. He grows chubbier day by day. He feeds so well, sleeps so well, but when he is awake, he most surely informs the world of the fact. I have heard of difficult babies, colicky and teething and unable to sleep, and sickly babies, always beset by some cold or sniffle or worse, but Joseph is happy and he is healthy. He gurgles away to himself, as if speaking some private language, chortling at some joke he alone understands. I do so hope he grows and prospers; it gnaws at my heart, the thought that he may not.

I am happy enough here by myself at Corkhills Creek, but I yearn for the return of Jack. Much as I adore Joseph, days pass without me uttering a word to an adult, or hearing one in return. There is kind Mr Morris, the old rabbiter whom you met. He drops by every now and then when he's passing, just to make sure I am well and give me a bunny or two. Sometimes he will bring an old newspaper, for despite his rough appearance he is quite the reader. I scour the papers for news from Gallipoli. They say the campaign continues to go well, but I can't see it. Our forces have barely progressed in months and have captured little territory. I had been under the impression that gaining ground was the whole aim, or maybe I understand battleground strategy even less than I comprehend cricket.

One benefit of this apparent stalemate is that mail from Gallipoli grows more reliable. The post comes through weekly, often with more than one letter. Jack has written a new will, acknowledging Joseph as his heir should anything happen to me. It is a strange comfort that, despite what confronts him, he continues to think of us. The document has been lodged with the lawyer in Narrandera. I try to put it out of my mind, dreaming instead of his homecoming. I can't count the days—for who can know when he will return—so instead I count the days until the five years will have passed. Less than a year remains now. What a bittersweet wedding anniversary that will prove to be.

Joseph remains blond-haired and his blue eyes have only recently shaded to the lightest hazel. He looks for all the world like a little Britisher, and I am glad. Is that so very wrong of me, such a betrayal of you and your mother and all who went before? I feel it is. And yet I know from my own experience that if it allows him easier passage through this world then I must be pleased. Nevertheless, I am determined that he knows there is not just Irish blood running through his veins. Is that not the future of Australia? That we all mix together, that our differences become our strengths? The more you can visit, the more you can teach him, and put him into contact with our men and our elders.

I know the mission is your home, that you feel safe there, but you must know you are always welcome here. I was sorry to hear of the problems there and the character of the new overseer, but I am sure everything will work out. And it is not so very far, an easy day's ride. When Jack is back, he can teach Joseph to ride, and all three of us can travel down to visit. And Jack will welcome you here. You will see: he's a good man. I don't know why you doubt it.

And now I must sign off, for Joseph is awake. It has already taken me three attempts and two days to write this slim missive. I never appreciated how much time I had until he arrived!

Your loving daughter,
Bessie

chapter thirty-two

IVAN EXPLAINS AS McTOSH DRIVES THEM UP THE CASTLE TO AIR STILLS. 'TOBY Fairchild's true name is Harley Snouch. I encountered him about five years ago, during the drought, out at a one-horse town called Riversend.'

'The case with the homicidal priest? The one that journalist wrote a book about?'

'That's the one.'

'Never read the book, but I remember the media circus. Sounded mental.' A note of sympathy in McTosh's voice. 'Heard it's going to be a miniseries.'

'I won't be watching,' says Ivan curtly.

'Who's playing you?' asks McTosh, sympathy replaced by humour.

Ivan snorts. 'I was a bit player, at best.'

The redhead sergeant turns serious. 'I remember the story of the priest and the dead backpackers, but not Harley Snouch.'

'Another bit player. But a nasty piece of work. Narcissist. Didn't give a shit about anyone except himself. Fooled a lot of people. Hurt a lot of people. Shot through before we could jail him.'

'What's he wanted for?'

'Fraud, larceny, drugs. He'll do a runner first chance he gets.'

There's a moment's silence as they continue to ascend, the view over the drylands revealing itself. Ivan can see Three Wells Station, the homestead surrounded by its verdant parklands.

'He was good,' says Ivan, returning to the conversation. 'Fooled me. The wig and the contacts and the teeth. Oscar-winning.'

'So what's he up to?'

'A giant scam.' And Ivan details the long con, how Snouch suckered investors. 'I reckon we've got him just in time. He was finalising a share offering this Friday. He was dangling the prospect of a stock market listing or a corporate takeover in the new year or both. I reckon he'd have been off come Saturday, and we'd never have seen him again.'

'How much?' asks McTosh.

'Millions,' says Ivan.

'Shit,' says the sergeant, glowering.

Ivan can understand his sensitivity: a massive fraud taking place on his watch, the Yuwonderie police oblivious. Not that Ivan is in any position to judge the local man.

'Plenty of motive to kill Athol Hasluck and attack Alice Figtree if they discovered his scam,' says McTosh.

'Maybe. What did the tip-off say?'

'A two-second call. "Murder weapon is at Air Stills." That's it.'

Ivan frowns. 'Crime Stoppers?'

'No. Direct to the station.'

'Man or woman?'

'Man.'

'Same person who called the ambos?'

'Don't know.'

McTosh slows the car; there are a couple of lycra-clad cyclists, riding two abreast up the steep gradient. 'Seriously. In this fucking heat,' says McTosh, touching his horn and, when that doesn't work, his siren. The cyclists pull into single file, and he accelerates past. 'That wasn't so hard, was it?' he asks rhetorically. One of the cyclists flips Ivan the bird as they pass. He ignores it, grateful for the car's air-conditioning.

'Okay. I'll buy him killing Athol, that he needed to shut him up,' says McTosh. 'But burning down the practice, knifing Alice Figtree? Why? Any incriminating evidence there wouldn't matter, not once he had his money and was gone.'

Ivan is starting to wish he'd driven up by himself; this is his investigation, not McTosh's. 'Maybe.'

'So who beat up Fairchild—Snouch—whatever you want to call him?'

'At a guess, someone else who twigged that he was conning them.'

'How is that connected to the murder weapon?'

Ivan sighs. 'Let's not get ahead of ourselves.'

McTosh eases the car through the now wide-open gates to Air Stills of Australia. He follows the access road around and parks outside the office, next to the technician's van, the logo of the smiling water drop on its doors, and Toby Fairchild's Range Rover. Ivan gets out and gives the upmarket SUV a quick once-over: someone has keyed it, and one of the tyres has been slashed. The wind is blowing strongly up here, taking the edge off the heat; the twin windmills are belting around, feeding power into the machinery shed. Ivan can't help but feel a sense of admiration: this must be one of the most elaborate confidence plays in history.

The office door is ajar, banging softly in the wind. Ivan pulls his gun, enters; McTosh follows him in.

There's no one there. The digital display on the wall lists the temperature as thirty-four degrees, the wind gusting at forty kilometres an hour, relative humidity at fifty-three per cent, litres per hour at sixteen. Convincing, until you know it isn't. He checks the laptop on the desk; still on, but it's gone into sleep mode. He reholsters his gun, puts on latex gloves, is careful not to touch the keypad, just taps one of the more obscure keys with a pencil. The screen comes to life, demanding a password.

The filing cabinets are unlocked. The top two drawers of the first are full of glossy brochures and other printed materials: advertising bumph and sales pamphlets, nothing remotely incriminating. The bottom drawer is empty. He opens the top drawer of the second cabinet and smiles when he sees a cash box, key still in the top. He opens it, but it's empty. His smile vanishes.

'Let's have a look in the shed,' he says.

'You don't imagine that this could be for real, do you?'

Ivan frowns at McTosh. 'What do you mean?'

'Okay, he's a crim. But what say he came across this amazing technology, bumped off the inventor and stole it. Or the inventor is down in Melbourne, unaware that he's going to rip them off along with everyone else.'

Ivan looks at him sceptically. 'No.'

'Nothing wrong with spitballing options.'

'Nothing wrong with collecting facts. Come on.'

They move towards the shed, then stop. There is the sound of hammer blows, metal on metal, coming from inside. Ivan holds a finger to his lips, signalling silence. He unclips his gun but this time he doesn't draw it. He looks at McTosh again and the sergeant nods, indicating his comprehension. 'Must be Ponds—the technician,' Ivan says quietly.

He eases the door open. The space is well illuminated: light flooding in through skylights, complemented by low-hanging banks of LEDs. As he enters, Ivan is again impressed by the scale and cost of the con. Over to one side, he can see the tech in his lab coat, working away at a bench, unaware of Ivan's entrance.

McTosh has followed him in. Ivan points to the man, and McTosh nods. The sergeant draws his gun, holding it by his side, crab-walking away from Ivan, providing cover.

Ivan approaches the bench. 'Dr Ponds?' he says clearly.

The man spins around, as if caught doing something illicit. There's an instrument suitcase on the bench. Ponds seems to be filling it.

'You . . . you shouldn't be in here,' he asserts, a half-stammer.

'We're the police,' says Ivan. 'Investigating a crime.'

'You need the boss's permission.'

'He's in hospital. Under arrest.'

'What?'

Ivan takes the opportunity to step forward, hand on the grip of his gun. He can see this has caught the technician's attention. 'Dr Ponds, please step away from the bench and raise your hands. My colleague will search you for weapons.'

'Are you serious?'

'Please do as you're told, then we can all relax.'

The scientist shuffles forward, hands raised. Ivan removes his gun from the holster as McTosh replaces his own. There is fear on Ponds's face.

McTosh frisks the scientist. 'All clear,' he says.

'All right, you can drop the hands,' says Ivan, holstering his weapon.

'What's this about Dr Fairchild in hospital?' asks Ponds.

'Lost your glasses,' notes Ivan, ignoring the man's question. 'You seemed almost blind without them yesterday.'

'Here . . .' The man returns to the workbench, fetches some wire-framed glasses, puts them on. 'That's better,' he says. 'I'm short-sighted. Take them off for close work.'

Ivan doesn't believe him. 'We know Toby Fairchild is a fake. Real name Harley Snouch. Someone has bashed him, put him in hospital.'

'Bashed? Is he okay?'

'Happened up here, not so long ago,' says McTosh. 'Where were you?'

'I only arrived half an hour ago. From Wagga. I needed to pick up some components.'

'That your van outside?' asks Ivan.

'Company's.'

'You won't mind if my colleague checks the rego, then?'

The man shrugs. 'Go for your life. Nothing to do with me.'

'Oh, I think it absolutely has something to do with you,' says Ivan, watching as Ernst McTosh heads outside to check the licence plate. Ivan places his hand back on the grip of his gun to empha-sise the point, causing a shiver to run through Ponds.

McTosh takes less than a minute. He returns, holding his phone. 'Checks out. Registered to Air Stills of Australia.'

'There you go,' says Ponds. 'All above board.' But his voice is wavering, and there is sweat on his upper lip.

'Driver's licence,' says Ivan.

Ponds stares, like a rabbit in a spotlight. 'I think I left my wallet in Wagga.'

'How inconvenient for you,' says Ivan dryly. 'Ernst, could you check his licence, please? Quentin Ponds.'

McTosh taps at his phone, then looks up. 'Nope. No licence for a Quentin Ponds. Nothing close.'

'It's a Victorian licence; we're Melbourne-based,' says Ponds, but Ivan can hear desperation in his voice.

'Oh, for fuck's sake,' says McTosh. He walks up to him. 'Hands up, idiot.'

Ivan draws his gun again, more to intimidate than from necessity.

The man, looking cornered, quickly raises his hands. 'This is illegal,' he says.

'Bullshit,' says McTosh. He reaches into the man's pocket, withdrawing a wallet, holding it up for Ivan to see. He steps back, and Ivan lowers his gun. McTosh flicks through the wallet, withdraws a licence. 'Terry Zappia,' he says. 'Fifty-three Goldfields Street, Tamworth.' He runs the licence through his phone app. 'Outstanding speeding fine, Terry.'

'It's not due yet,' says Terry.

'Possibly not your biggest concern,' says McTosh, with a smile that wouldn't go astray on a hyena.

Ivan shakes his head. 'Listen, Terry, there are two ways this can go. Fairchild is under arrest—for past offences and, soon enough, for a shit ton of new ones. He's not talking his way out of this and neither are you. But based on past form, he will shift as much blame on to you as he possibly can. You realise that, right?'

Terry's brows are knitted, the sweat on his upper lip is beading, and his mouth is pursed.

Ivan continues. 'Now it just so happens that I am a homicide detective, not Fraud Squad. Investigating the murder of a local accountant, Athol Hasluck. You know anything about that?'

Terry seems confused. 'Yeah, I heard some blokes talking about it. Nothing to do with me, though. Surely not with Toby.'

'That's yet to be established. But what I'm saying is, I'm interested in catching killers not con men. Understand?'

Terry looks like he comprehends very little.

'We received a report about a knife up here. You see a knife, Terry?'

Now he looks like he understands plenty. 'I had nothing to do with it.'

'Where is it?'

Another hesitation, but Ivan knows he has him.

'Here.' And the man opens a drawer in the workbench.

Ivan retrieves a cloth wrapped in a plastic bag. And inside the cloth, a knife, spattered with what looks like dried blood.

'It was in the car park, near his car,' says Terry. 'There was no sign of him. I thought maybe he had been killed.'

Ivan flicks his head towards the half-filled suitcase. 'You were leaving?'

'Wouldn't you?' asks Terry.

Ivan just shakes his head.

'What's on offer?' asks Terry. 'Can you give me immunity?'

Ivan feels McTosh's eyes upon him; the local policeman will know that such deals are well beyond his authority. Ivan frames his words carefully. 'Do you have any information directly relevant to the murder of Athol Hasluck?'

The man looks surprised. 'No. None. I told you that.'

'Okay, so I can only talk leniency if it involves my investigation. I can't speak on behalf of the Fraud Squad.'

McTosh backs him up. 'Reality check, Terry. You're not walking away from this. We're going to arrest you and take you into custody. But if you start helping us now, that's something your lawyers can use to argue for a lesser penalty in future. We can tell the Fraud Squad you're being cooperative, and they may want to cut a deal.'

Ivan gives it time, letting the alternatives play out in Terry's mind, seeing the emotions on the man's face, witnessing the moment when he caves.

Terry removes his glasses, places them back on the bench. 'What do you need to know?'

'Did you ever see Fairchild with Athol Hasluck?'

'No.' The answer is clear and immediate.

'Did Fairchild ever mention Hasluck?'

'No. But he never mentioned any of the marks.'

Ivan searches the man's face, can't think of a reason to disbelieve him. 'What do you know of the financial scheme behind all this?'

'Almost nothing. We set this place up to attract investment. Fairchild's plan was to get as much funding as possible, then just walk away with the loot.'

'You know when?'

'There was a big capital raising closing this Friday. That was it. Then he'd vanish.'

'And you?'

'Take my cut. Go back to Tamworth. Lay low.'

'So what's the deal? Cash in hand? Shares in the company?'

'Cash. I'm not stupid.'

'Why you?' asks Ivan.

'I'm an electrician,' says Terry, gesturing about him. 'I rigged all of this up.'

Ivan thinks he catches the vestiges of pride in the electrician's voice. He gestures towards the stainless-steel demonstration unit, still humming away. 'All this?'

'Yep, I made it.' Terry gives a little laugh. 'Funny thing is, the technology works. Just not well enough to make money.'

McTosh is frowning. 'You're saying this thing actually makes water?'

Terry smiles. 'It does. I'll show you.'

'Not sure that's necessary,' says Ivan.

'I'd like to see,' says McTosh, throwing him a glare, and Ivan realises he's trying to humour Terry, to win him over.

Ivan shrugs. 'Why not?'

'Okay. Let's disconnect it first,' says Terry. 'We don't want any accidents.'

Ivan can see McTosh come alert, just as he has himself. 'Accidents?' Ivan asks, trying to keep his voice even.

'The electricity supply, coming off the solar panels. Direct current. Can be nasty if you don't know what you're doing.'

The man's voice is unwavering; to Ivan it doesn't sound as if he understands the implications of what he's saying.

'How nasty?'

'Potentially fatal.'

chapter thirty-three

1994

DAVIS DECIDED HE COULD NO LONGER WORK IN THE BASEMENT ROOM AT THE Irrigation Scheme Company, not after seeing Lucy and Otto together at the Coachman's Arms the night before. He had exhausted the archives and outstayed his welcome. When he arrived after lunch to collect the last of his notebooks, he found all the files gone and Lucy was nowhere to be seen, the room returned to its original state. He felt bad about that, and wasn't sure why. After all, it had been her decision to dump him and take up with Otto. Still, he wished he'd handled it better; Yuwonderie was a small town.

He gave his key back to Hilary Housego.

'Perhaps it's for the best,' Housego said sagely. 'I trust it was of some assistance?'

'Yes. Some excellent background information.'

Housego smiled. 'No revelations, then?'

'Your secrets are safe with me,' Davis joked. When he saw Housego wasn't smiling, he added, 'No. No revelations.'

Back at Three Wells Station, Davis set himself up in the library, a downstairs room lined with bookshelves, with a couple of well-worn armchairs, each flanked by a marble-topped occasional table on one side and a reading lamp on the other. One chair boasted a leather ottoman, the other an antique smoker's stand complete with polished brass ashtray. The faint smell of tobacco lingered, or perhaps that was his imagination. The room was tidy and dust-free—the weekly cleaner saw to that—but to Davis it seemed like a museum exhibit.

He worked on a roll-top desk beneath the window. He couldn't recall his grandfather ever using the library; Clemence preferred an office in one of the converted outbuildings, next to the farm manager's. However, Davis could remember his father working silently at the desk, his back to the room. Davis would sneak in, climb onto one of the armchairs, feet dangling, and read, careful not to disturb his father. It's where he had discovered his love for books, maybe his attraction to history. It felt right, him returning here, promoted from the armchair to the desk. And when he rolled up its top, he found his father's manual typewriter sitting there, as if waiting for him. It was like an omen, and he hoped his father would have been proud of him and not upset that he intended to surrender his inheritance to his sister. Nevertheless, he reluctantly pushed the old machine aside and set up his new PowerBook laptop.

He also removed two framed pictures from either side of the window: a landscape painting from a generation or two before— the Castle, lit by a setting sun above a darkened panorama of low trees—and a fading black-and-white photograph of an early gathering at Three Wells Station. He replaced them with corkboards, and on them pinned the printed maps from the Land Office: 1912, before the scheme; 1917, the land carved up between the Seven, and the boundary of the irrigated area defined; and 1924, with the plans finalised: the canals set out, the smallholdings delineated, the grid of the town established.

He studied the first map, the one from 1912. The district before the scheme. He took it back down and, as accurately as he could, he traced the boundaries of the scheme from the 1924 map onto it. Comparing the two, he could see how much the landholdings had changed during the intervening dozen years. Not just the emergence of the town and the creation of the smallholdings, but also how the major pre-scheme ownership had changed. In 1912, there were nine properties within the boundaries of the future scheme, with their identifying numbers. By 1924, there were seven major estates, a patchwork of two or three hundred small-to-medium farms, plus a single title covering the centre of the town. The reference numbers on some of the holdings had changed; he remembered that the titles system meant that each time a property was divided or consolidated, new title documents were created.

First there were nine, and then there were seven. And someone owned most of the land in the town centre. What had happened? The maps didn't reveal who owned each property; instead they used identifying numbers, correlating to the title folios held in Sydney. Hopefully the copies he had ordered would arrive soon. He would need them to work out who owned what land, and who had bought and sold, and on what date.

The 1924 map indicated the town was covered by one consolidated title, whereas he'd always assumed, if he'd thought of it at all, that the various properties lining the main street were owned by different shopkeepers and landlords. Superficially, they were all so different—the newsagent and the unisex hairdresser and the clothing boutiques and the pubs—but the buildings that housed them displayed a remarkable architectural consistency. He'd always attributed that to the town being planned. Now he saw it differently.

He remembered Craven mentioning the Land Trust the night before at the Coachman's Arms, his suggestion that Davis would end up on the board.

He walked down to the entry hall, looked up the number for Riverina Water Traders in the yellow pages and dialled it. He asked for Craven.

'Hi, mate, what's up?' asked his friend.

'Working away on this thesis of mine. Remember last night at the pub, you mentioned the Land Trust? Is that the company that owns all the land in town?'

'Hasn't your grandfather filled you in?'

'Only in general terms.' Which was true, as far as it went. 'And it's owned by the Seven, right?'

'Sure. A company we control.'

'Do you know if, when it was set up, the land had water rights connected?'

Craven paused for a moment. It was almost as if Davis could hear his thoughts in the static on the line. 'Is this for your thesis?'

'That's right. From the first steps to create the scheme up to the 1930s. Looks like the Land Trust was operating from the get-go.'

'Yeah,' his friend said at last. 'The trust still owns permanent water rights. Originally connected to the land. Leases them out each year to the highest bidder.'

'Smart,' said Davis.

'Dual income streams. Rent and water.'

'Killing it. Thanks, mate.'

Returning to the library, he pondered the map. He wondered if the smallholders knew about the trust owning water rights, if they were in any way resentful. In the 1920s, it probably wasn't a big issue. Back then, water was free and pretty much unlimited. No one ever imagined it becoming scarce. And trading it wouldn't have been possible until the temporary water market opened up in the 1980s. Only after that would the Land Trust have started to generate income from it. If nothing else, it demonstrated a remarkable prescience by the founders. Or luck. Or maybe the original intention wasn't about income but security, just in case there was some drought-induced shortage.

Davis wondered if that was one of the things the Seven would like to remain undeclared, would prefer their hand-picked editor to exclude from their new coffee-table history.

He thought about that. Each landholder owned a stake in the Yuwonderie Irrigation Scheme Company, based on their holdings. The Seven dominated, of course, but the Land Trust would also participate, controlling votes, reinforcing the power of the elite families. Maybe this was something else the canny old men at the Canal Club wanted to keep to themselves.

His thoughts were interrupted by a knock at the door. It opened before he could respond: Krystal, with a knowing grin on her face. 'Phone,' she said.

'Who is it?'

'Didn't say. A girl.' And the smile broadened.

The phone sat on a purpose-built table in the corridor, with a rotary dial and no privacy.

'Hello, this is Davis,' he said.

'Stella Kippax.'

'Oh. Stella. Hi.'

'Wondered if you'd be up for a coffee. Or a drink.'

'When?'

'Today. Now, if you're free.'

Davis checked his watch. It was already three in the afternoon. A coffee seemed unlikely. A drink would be possible, but the thought of running into Otto and Craven, or Lucy, at the Coachman's Arms put him off. 'What about pizza?' he suggested. 'Paulo's, six thirty?'

Down the line he heard a laugh from Stella. He wasn't sure how to interpret it, wished he could see her face. 'Sounds good,' she said, a playfulness in her voice.

'My shout,' he added, thinking of her savings plan.

'No chance,' she said. 'See you at six thirty.' And she hung up.

'Well?' asked Krystal, making her presence known.

Davis shrugged. 'Pizza,' he said.

'Stella,' she said, elongating the syllables, voice teasing, before expressing her approval. 'I like her. She's ballsy.'

Davis thought about asking his sister what she knew of the policeman's daughter, but a shyness held him back. He told himself it was just pizza.

— —

Before leaving Three Wells, Davis showered and started to dress in the unofficial uniform of the young landowner: riding boots, moleskins, blue chambray shirt. But the day was hot, and he had second thoughts, changing into some lightweight cotton pants, a linen shirt and deck shoes. He hesitated over the deck shoes. He considered swapping them out for Docs, but didn't want to come across as too try-hard. He opted for sandals.

There was nothing special about Paulo's. The red-and-white checked table coverings were plastic, and the prints adorning the walls were already fading: the Coliseum, the Duomo, a gondolier. But the pizzas were good.

Stella was there waiting when he arrived. She was inside, near the window. She didn't stand but her face was open and welcoming enough. If she was wearing make-up, it wasn't obvious to Davis, except perhaps for a little eyeliner or mascara. He liked her crimped hair, the way it framed her face.

'Hi,' he said. 'Thanks for accepting the invitation.'

They made small talk: the weather; how pineapple didn't belong on pizzas but olives did; when and where chilli was appropriate. They ordered drinks, then food. And then she made her pitch. 'Last night you said you weren't like Otto and Craven and the rest, that you weren't all the same.'

'Did I?'

'You want to prove it?'

He smiled, shook his head. 'No, I don't want to prove anything.'

'Empty words then?'

'Stella, tell me what you want. Don't try to goad me into it.'

She laughed at that. 'Good call,' she said. 'Maybe you're not like the others. Maybe you're smarter.'

'Don't be so sure.'

And still she hedged, or so it seemed to Davis. 'Are you really going ahead with it?' she asked. 'Renouncing your claim on Three Wells Station?'

He looked about before answering. 'That's my intention. But please don't mention it to anyone. Not until my sister and grandfather and I have worked it through.'

'Takes guts,' said Stella. 'I'm impressed.'

Davis felt uncomfortable with the focus on his choice. 'What is it, Stella? What do you want?'

Now she became serious, the lightness gone from her voice. 'You're researching the origins of the scheme. I heard you were running into some resistance from the Seven.'

He was unsure how to respond. He couldn't see why he should tell her anything. The pizza arrived, breaking the impasse.

'You've got them worried,' she said, helping herself to a slice.

Davis started on a piece of pepperoni with his cutlery, saw she was using her hands and followed suit. He wasn't convinced he should talk about it, but the inspiration of his discoveries was still with him, and the temptation to share them with someone, someone smart, someone independent of the Seven, was hard to resist. That and the crimp of her hair and those intelligent blue eyes. 'They're just a bit protective, that's all,' he said.

'Protective of what?'

'Their status, I guess.'

'What have you found?' she asked.

'Nothing important. Quite a lot of land changed hands early on in the scheme, but I haven't found anything that would cause consternation or embarrassment. Not anymore.'

She watched him as they ate. It occurred to Davis that Stella was the one who'd called him; it seemed unlikely she merely wanted to inquire after his research. Now he looked for it, he could see she was only acting at being relaxed, that there was a tension in her, as if she were holding something back.

She came to a decision, or so it appeared. 'Remember I told you I was working at the Wholesalers?'

'Uh-huh,' he said through a mouthful of pepperoni.

'There's something wrong there.'

And now he could see the nervousness in her eyes. He swallowed his food. 'Wrong? How?'

'The paperwork doesn't always make sense. Consignment numbers don't always match.'

'What does that mean?'

'Produce comes in from the farms. Quite a bit from the MIA as well as Yuwonderie. It's a big operation, always in motion. Fruit and vegies and grapes coming in, getting sorted, graded, dispatched. For the most part, it remains in the original boxes, the ones carrying the brands of the individual farms, but sometimes it's combined with those of other farmers when there's a bulk order—from the big operators in Melbourne, say, or the super-markets. Other times, when a big landholder—one of the Seven, for example—delivers in bulk, then it's split into smaller consignments. Just what you'd imagine.'

Davis frowned. 'Fruit in, fruit out. Isn't that how it's meant to work?'

'Sure. It's efficient. Very little wastage. They're big on that.'

'So what's the problem?'

'I thought more was going out than coming in, but I double-checked and the paperwork matches up.'

Davis still couldn't see the point. 'Sorry, I'm confused. What's the issue?'

Stella shook her head. 'There's not enough trucks.'

'What?'

'I can't work out how they're delivering all the produce to Sydney and Melbourne.'

Davis thought about it for a moment. 'Maybe they aren't. Maybe they take it as far as the nearest railhead, ship it the rest of the way by train. Or maybe the big supermarkets or distribution centres send their own trucks.'

'Not according to the paperwork.'

He considered what she was saying. 'Maybe some of the big growers, some of the Seven, drive the produce directly from their properties to Melbourne or Sydney or the distribution centres. On paper, it passes through the Wholesalers, but in practice it goes direct.'

Stella frowned. 'Why would they do that?'

'More efficient. No need to unload, store, reload. Less spoilage.'

'So why put the paperwork through the Wholesalers?'

The answer comes to Davis almost immediately. 'So the Seven can't be accused of undercutting the smallholders. The Wholesalers gets its cut. Everyone remains on equal footing.'

Stella stared at him. 'Shit. I feel like an idiot. I should have thought of that.'

'Doesn't mean I'm right,' said Davis, not wanting to hurt her feelings. 'Just saying it's plausible.'

'Could you find out?'

'Me? How?'

'You're one of them. Your grandfather will have shares, sit on the boards. He must know where your own produce goes.'

'I guess I can ask.'

'If I were to show you the documents, would that help?' she asked.

'Help what?'

'Help find out what's going on. Help your research.'

'My research doesn't cover the Wholesalers,' he said. 'It's too recent.' But Davis saw the disappointment in her eyes, and he was discovering he did like those eyes. Not as sparkly as Lucy's, not as much mascara, but something else. Intelligence. And curiosity. And sincerity. 'But sure. I'd like to see them. Find out what's going on.'

After they'd finished dinner, they emerged from Paulo's into a day not yet done. The sun was still clear of the horizon, the temperature still high. Davis felt reluctant to say goodbye. 'Wouldn't mind a drink,' he said. 'Not sure about the pub, though.'

She smiled teasingly. 'Worried about your reputation?'

'Worried about my friends.'

She looked at him, as if considering. 'I like the look of that little car of yours. We should go for a drive.'

He looked back at her, and something moved between them.

'Maybe get a bottle of something,' she said. 'Head up the Castle—watch the sun set.'

chapter thirty-four

IVAN ASKS McTOSH TO DROP HIM AT THE HOSPITAL. HE'S ON A HIGH, DESPITE his fatigue, the excitement of the investigation overcoming the lingering effects of his overnight vigil at Nell's bedside. If he's interpreted events correctly, someone has attempted to frame Snouch for the murder of Athol Hasluck and the attempt on the life of Alice Figtree. Whoever it was, they went to Air Stills to plant the knife but were discovered by Snouch. So they bashed him. Ivan needs to convince the con man to identify them.

Inside the foyer, he runs into the nurse from the night before, the big guy with the mullet.

'Your friend, she's already checked out,' says the nurse.

'Thanks, but it's not her I'm here to see,' says Ivan, bustling past.

He finds Snouch in a private room, the young police officer sitting inside, slouched in a plastic chair and scrolling through his phone. Bored witless, by the look of him. Snouch looks haggard, like a deflated balloon. The hairpiece has gone, so has the remaining coloured contact lens, so have the artificial teeth. And so too has the act. His lip curls when Ivan enters. 'Not talking,' is all he says.

'Constable, give us a minute, please,' Ivan says to the uniformed officer. 'Get yourself a coffee.'

The young bloke doesn't have to be told twice.

'Still not talking,' says Snouch.

Ivan takes the recently vacated chair. Snouch won't meet his gaze. 'Murder, Harley. Attempted murder. Athol Hasluck knifed. Alice Figtree knifed. A police officer assaulted and left to die.'

Snouch shakes his head.

'Knifed with this.' Ivan holds up the evidence bag.

Snouch steals a look. 'Nothing to do with me.'

'I believe you.'

Snouch cracks a lopsided smile, as if half of his face is considering cooperation and the other half is steadfast in its refusal.

Ivan pushes his advantage. 'I don't give a shit about Air Stills, Harley. All I care about is murder. And this weapon was found at your property.'

Still Snouch says nothing.

'Good fit, too. Athol Hasluck was a big investor, ploughed a lot of money into your little scheme. Found out that you were pulling a scam. Tried to get his money out, but you refused. Then he tried to blackmail you out of it; give him his money or he would blow the whistle. So you killed him, to shut him up. Convincing motive. Don't reckon I'd have any trouble selling that to a jury. Piece of cake, given your history.'

Snouch grunts, smile gone, mouth drawn as tight as a miser's purse string.

Ivan leans in. 'Clever of them. Two birds with one stone. Get you arrested, so you can't shoot through with their money. And frame you for the murder. Neat.'

CHRIS HAMMER

'I was in Melbourne. I told you.'

Ivan spreads his hands in a gesture of understanding. 'I told you: I believe you. I don't think you killed anyone. But I need a defendant, and right now you fit the bill.'

Ivan can see he has Snouch's attention: the con man steals another look at the evidence bag. 'What do you want?' he growls.

'Who beat you up? Who planted the knife?'

Snouch shakes his head. 'Balaclava.'

'Why would you want to protect them?'

'Wearing a balaclava.'

'So just one person, then?' asks Ivan, but gets no response. 'Vehicle?'

'Didn't see.'

Ivan looks him in the eye. 'A Murderer, Harley. A killer. If I don't get him, there's a fair chance he'll come back for you. You're a loose end. Think about it.'

'Nah.' Another shake of his head and he closes his eyes.

——

Ivan is just leaving the hospital when his phone rings. An unlisted number.

'Yes?' he answers, voice noncommittal.

'Morning, Ivan.'

He recognises the voice, can't quite place it.

'Who is this?'

'Your old pal Nathan Phelan.'

Ivan stops walking. Stops breathing. Nathan 'Feral' Phelan, the scourge from Professional Standards, the man charged with policing the police, keeping the force free from corruption and

330

other evils. And, from Ivan's experience, an utterly untrustworthy maverick, an operator, a collector of influence and secrets and leverage—with the power to end a career. Ivan can imagine his face, the pleasure he would take in unsettling Ivan, his crooked smirk, his gloating eyes. 'Nathan. So nice to hear from you.'

'You think?'

Ivan collects himself. 'What?'

'You shitting me?' says Phelan. 'You must have some sort of death wish, son. Do I need to spell it out?'

'Might help,' says Ivan. He knows Phelan is trying to provoke him, that the man takes joy in the sport, and that Ivan needs to remain calm and cautious.

'A woman is on the edge of death, a machine breathing for her in Canberra Hospital. Major surgery. Intensive care. Months of rehab at best. Alice Figtree. Remember her? Knifing victim. Knifed because you recruited her, had her doing unauthorised police work. Could that possibly be correct?'

Ivan thinks quickly. Plodder had authorised it, but he's not about to drop his boss in it. 'She was assisting the investigation; what of it?'

'And you invited her to work inside the secure area of a police station, without clearance. And why? Because you think you can circumvent proper process and have her trawl through the papers of Athol Hasluck's clients without seeking a warrant? In what world do you think any of that is defensible? In what world would that evidence be admissible?'

'Nathan, there's a killer on the loose here. I want to catch them before they kill again. And I'm within days, maybe even hours, of making an arrest.' He is surprised by his own passion. 'You hinder me, and it will be on your head if someone else dies.'

'That a threat?'

'Statement of fact.'

'So the ends justify the means? Recruiting Alice Figtree and putting her in danger?'

'That's why I wanted to move her into the station. For her own safety.'

'That worked well.'

For half a moment, Ivan considers telling Phelan the truth, that he didn't want to expand the investigation into other squads, but holds back. For all he knows, it would simply be supplying ammunition to be used against him. Instead, Ivan tries appealing to the man's better nature on the outside chance he has one. 'Nathan, we're making real progress here. Just this morning, I've arrested a fugitive, a man named Harley Snouch, a known criminal, on outstanding warrants. We've stopped a multimillion-dollar fraud. We have seized a bloodstained knife found on his premises, very likely the weapon used against both Athol Hasluck and Alice Figtree. Snouch has a clear motive for wanting Hasluck dead and for the arson attack his premises. We're collecting CCTV footage and forensics. We'll be in a position to charge him as early as tomorrow.' Ivan pauses. 'Give me some space, Nathan. Don't be seen as responsible for a killer getting away.'

'So what are you saying? That if I pull you off the case, I'll endanger his prosecution?'

'You'll endanger the public. And the reputation of the New South Wales Police Force. I don't want to end up explaining that to a parliamentary committee.'

Ivan is thinking he might have swayed the investigator when Phelan changes tack, voice low, words stiletto sharp. 'I heard your partner almost died while you were glassy-eyed ga-ga in a pokie den.'

Ivan stares unseeing at an inflated Santa, bobbing in the breeze. The hole in his stomach is widening; he's unable to find the words to defend himself.

There's a bitter little laugh. 'I could suspend you for that alone.'

Ivan searches for something to say, some retort, and again comes up empty.

'Keep your badge, keep your gun—for now,' says Phelan. 'Think of this as a courtesy call. Letting you know where you stand. You've got your forty-eight hours. Charge Snouch and wrap it up, or I'll be down there in person and you'll be on gardening leave. Spending time with your dear old dad.'

And the phone goes dead.

Ivan finds himself panting and forces himself to take a deep breath.

He walks up the slope towards Commonwealth Way in a daze, insensible to the sweltering sun. He crosses the main street and heads down the ridge towards the police station, but keeps going until he reaches the town canal. He takes a seat on a bench in the shade of a willow tree, his thought processes gradually re-engaging.

Why isn't Phelan pushing his advantage? Why hasn't he suspended Ivan now he has the chance? He calls Plodder.

'Ivan.'

'I've just had Feral Phelan on the phone.'

'I know. He spoke to me as well.'

'What did you tell him?'

'As little as possible, of course.' Plodder sighs. 'I didn't have much choice, under the circumstances. Not with Alice Figtree fighting for her life. You realise that her relatives could go us for millions, for involving her and putting her in danger.'

'She was more than willing.'

'That's hardly the point.'

'She was already investigating. Before Athol Hasluck died, before we arrived.'

'What?'

'She deliberately got herself employed by Athol Hasluck so they could run an investigation into some corporate shenanigans down here. Alleged shenanigans. All tied to a murder here, thirty years ago.'

'How do you know that?'

'Her wife told me. And without Alice, we would have lost vital evidence. Before she was attacked, she secured digital copies of many of Athol Hasluck's files. Otherwise, they would have been lost in the fire as well.'

There's a pause. 'Who is aware of that?'

'Just me and her wife, plus the team here: Nell, Kevin, Carole and Blake.'

'Good. Let's keep it that way.'

Ivan frowns. It's not the response he was expecting. 'You're pushing back?'

'Of course I'm pushing back.'

'The brass supporting you?'

'The brass is doing what the brass does best: sitting on the fence, protecting its arse.'

Ivan is finding it marginally easier to breathe. 'So how does it play out from here?'

'Simple. Solve the case. Meanwhile, I'm trying to get to the bottom of where this has come from. Seems to me the shit is raining down all right, but it's coming from on high.'

'What does that mean?'

'Politics, that's what it means.'

'Jesus. I hate politics.'

'I reckon that's why Phelan is involved. Not acting of his own volition; someone has persuaded him. But I don't think he's gunning for you. Not yet.'

'Funny way of showing it.'

'He hasn't gone down there, hasn't suspended you. You're still in charge of the investigation.'

'What are you saying? That Phelan's on our side?'

'Hardly that,' says Plodder. 'More like he's withholding his judgement. Like the brass. Waiting to see which way the wind blows.'

'Well, that's something, I guess. He tell you about Harley Snouch?'

There's a laugh down the line. 'I know of it, put it that way. Good result, Ivan. Not the main game, but one more scumbag off the streets. Lot to like about that.'

'I told Phelan that Snouch might be a good fit for Hasluck and Figtree,' says Ivan. 'To get him off my back.'

'Quick thinking. Lot of people would be happy if you charged Snouch. Lot of powerful people.'

'But not you?'

'Not you either, I hope,' says Plodder. 'One thing about Phelan: he likes running his own race. He doesn't like getting pushed around any more than the rest of us. If he's going to come after you, it will be on his own terms.'

'Is that meant to make me feel better?'

Plodder laughs. 'No.'

—

Ivan returns to the hotel, wanting some time to himself, thinking he might steal a power nap. He was awake half the night, sitting with Nell in the hospital. The resistance of Snouch and the phone call from Phelan have sapped him.

But no sooner has he closed his eyes than there's a knock at the door. He considers drawing his gun, decides he's being paranoid.

'Yes?'

'It's McTosh.'

'What do you want?'

'To talk.'

For just a moment, Ivan imagines McTosh has come to kill him. But that makes no sense. He opens the door but doesn't invite the ginger sergeant in.

'Thought I should clear the air,' says McTosh.

'Clear away.'

'It wasn't me. I didn't rat you out to Professional Standards.'

'You spoke to Phelan?'

'He called me, aye.' McTosh offers a grimace. 'To be honest, he seemed to know more about what was going on than I did.'

'So why come here?'

'I didn't want you thinking it was me, or my crew. There's just the six of us, and I trust them. None of them alerted Phelan. I spoke to him when he called, but I didn't say anything to incriminate you.'

'Alice Figtree working out of the police station without clearance?'

'He already knew.'

Ivan senses there is more the local man wants to say. 'Come in, Ernst. Take a seat.'

McTosh enters, takes the one chair, while Ivan sits on the bed.

'This town. It's more feudal than democratic,' says McTosh.

'The Seven?' asks Ivan, hearing his own thoughts echoed in McTosh's assertion.

'Aye,' says McTosh. 'When I was posted here, promoted, I was put on notice by the regional commander. To respect the lay of the land, to work with the community, not against it.'

Ivan thinks he knows what the sergeant is driving at. 'I understand. I worked in a country town myself, first couple of years in uniform. The Central West.'

'Then you know what it's like. Letting them off with a warning if they're speeding, not breath-testing their kids, answering their calls.'

'What are you trying to tell me, Ernst?'

McTosh takes a deep breath, as if girding himself. 'I've been briefing Otto Titchfield. Informally. Ever since Athol Hasluck's body was found in his canal. Keeping him across the investigation. He rings me from time to time; I tell him.'

Ivan feels a flare of anger. 'Just him?'

McTosh grimaces. 'I've also spoken to Nigel Blaxland and Craven Allsop and Krystal Heartwood. They all feel entitled to call whenever they want. My fault; I've encouraged it in the past, been amenable.' He shakes his head. 'It didn't occur to me at first that I might be doing anything wrong. I'm sure I haven't told them anything sensitive.'

'So why tell me this now?'

'Feral Phelan. Someone has been feeding him information, but it wasn't me. At least not directly.'

Ivan feels his anger subside. McTosh didn't have to come here, make this confession. 'You think it's them? The Seven?'

'Who else? They carry a lot of clout in Sydney.'

'So why would they want to impede the investigation?' asks Ivan. 'You think they have something to hide?'

'I wouldn't go that far. These are people who are used to controlling events. Maybe they think if Snouch was charged, then life would return to normal.'

Ivan shakes his head. 'That's not going to happen.' Then he smiles for the first time since McTosh arrived. 'Keep talking to them, Ernst. Just don't tell them anything important.' And Ivan's smile grows further. 'Tell them I intend to charge Snouch with murder.'

chapter thirty-five

September 1915

Mother,

The most terrible news has arrived. The letters that have so sustained me have now betrayed me. Noel Marney is dead, wounded on the battlefield, with Jack in the trenches less than a mile away. They managed to get Noel to the beach, across to a hospital ship, but it was too late. Nothing could be done. Jack heard of the injury, but not of his brother's death later that day. There was a telegram prepared, but there was confusion over where to send it, so it sat on a clerk's desk. It was word of mouth that took the news to Jack some days later, and he wrote to tell me immediately. It broke my heart, for I have never seen two brothers so close. Noel Marney was such a fine man; there was not a drop of rancour in him. I can picture him now, barrel-chested and ready with a laugh, his moustache an implement of humour, mischief in his eyes. He was a brother, a friend and almost a father to Jack, the rock upon which his life was built after their parents died. I had pictured Noel as an uncle to Joseph, a godfather. Now their paths will not cross; they will never know each other. The thought saddens me beyond description.

I fear for Jack, now more than ever, all alone, lost amid the battlefields of the north. In the past, he always attempted to cheer me, to paint the struggle with optimism, but even before Noel's demise the gloom was infiltrating his letters. Comrades dead, wounded, diseased, going mad. No King, no country. No God. No end in sight, just the senseless, everlasting war. I worry for him—not just for his life and physical safety, but for his soul; I fear that it might be crushed, so diminished that it never regains its vitality.

Elaine visited, to console me, for Jack had written to the Titchfields as well, informed them of Noel's death. She assures me Jack is not alone, no matter how horrible the conditions; that they are all comrades, bonded to each other. I pray that she is right.

Horace rode over too, and he was very kind, very considerate. He admired Joseph and said he could see a little of his uncle in him, assuring us he would not want for anything. But for all of his sentiment, Horace is a practical man, and for all occasions there is a practical solution, even in the face of death. He has suggested that I now move from our little cottage and take up residence in the main house at Jolimont. He has good reason, and I know it makes sense, for Jack will now be master of all the family lands, and the estate will encompass the family's larger holdings and not just this little bush block at Corkhills Creek. Horace says with me in the main house, he might hire a worker to put in the cottage. It is a sensible plan, although he might struggle to find a good man with so many at war. Be that as it may, it encourages me that Horace wants me at Jolimont; I had thought him pleased to have me and Joseph hidden away out of sight.

Still, I wonder about Horace sometimes, that he is still here and Jack is still there. At first, he seemed so keen to go, fearful that he might miss the great adventure, but that attitude has ebbed over the months. Part of me resents him, yet another part of me is grateful that not all the good men of this country are gone, feeding themselves into that pitiless maw. Elaine excuses her brother, says his presence is vital to protect the interests of his family and all our families, but I can't see what it is he does that Elaine could not do. She is at least as capable as him, probably more. Certainly she is a better listener, a more perceptive judge of character. But when I suggested this to her, she simply laughed. 'I can do the books,' she said, 'write the letters for him to sign. I already do. But I can't sit in the clubs of Sydney and Melbourne, smoke the cigars and drink the port. For that we need Horace. There is no escaping the fact.' And Jack has made it clear he is relieved that Horace is here to attend to our interests and secure our future by progressing the irrigation project. I assured Horace that Jack and I remained totally committed to his scheme, just as Noel always was. I told him that it means everything to Jack, that it gives him something to hold on to, to believe in, a beacon to lead him home. Horace seemed glad to hear it.

He visited again today, bringing Elaine with him. It is always such a joy to see her. She is already Joseph's unofficial aunt. When Jack returns and we marry, we should formalise it and make her the boy's godmother. That thought brings me joy, but also a tinge of sadness, for Noel would have been such a wonderful godfather. And now we have lost him, and whatever cousins he might have fathered for Joseph. This war is stealing not one generation, but entire generations to come.

This time, Horace brought legal papers with him from McLeans, the lawyers at Narrandera, confirming that all the Marney lands will pass to Jack, that we will not be confined to our little pocket of bush. Elaine will return later in the week with some men to assist the move to the large house. It is a grim job; I do not look forward to supplanting Noel at Jolimont. I still can't believe he has gone, and the idea of settling in the main house feels like trespass.

And yet I must make it a home for Joseph, and to welcome Jack upon his return, so that he can take his proper place in the affairs of the district. Nevertheless, I will be sad to leave this little cottage, where Joseph entered the world. It is full of Jack, full of his memories; it is where we were truly together.

Horace tells me plans for the scheme are progressing well. He has coined a name for it: the Yuwonderie Irrigation Scheme. He pumped out his chest with pride, telling me that 'Yuwonderie' is an Aboriginal word meaning 'plentiful waters'. Of course, I was tempted to correct him, to demand to know where he had found this word, tell him that I had never heard of it and accuse him of making it up. But just in time I remembered Jack's counsel: that I should choose my battles with Horace and men like him; that I needed to conserve my energy for the struggles that matter.

I am so sorry to hear that the situation at the mission has deteriorated even further. It used to be such a wonderful place, so productive. Why didn't you tell me more of it while you were here with us? This new manager sounds awful—but worse than that is this new policy of evicting anyone whose skin is judged too light. If that be the policy, how can you possibly escape it?

You must come and live here. Joseph is such a joy. He puts everything in his mouth. Such a curious boy; I fear he takes after his father, that one day I shall lose him to the droving. Come, Mother, do!

Your loving daughter,
Bessie

PS Mother, wonderful news. I was about to seal the envelope when, quite unexpectedly, Elaine rode up. She is engaged! She will marry Douglas Heartwood, from one of the local grazing families, younger brother to the owner William and another supporter of irrigation. I am extremely happy for her, for I have met Douglas. He is a shy man, very polite, very deferential. A cultured and decent man. Her vivacity will bring him out of himself. He is the younger son, with two elder brothers, so he can expect no inheritance, but this does not worry Elaine in the least. She says Douglas is the most educated and intelligent man she has ever met, and one of the most considerate. She says, perhaps a little boastfully, that equipped with an allowance from his family's estate at Three Wells Station, combined with her dowry from Castle View, he will be well equipped to make his way in the world. But even her elation must be tempered at such a time; they have announced their betrothal as Douglas plans to enlist, following one of his brothers. He too is heading to war. The district is emptying.

chapter thirty-six

ONCE McTOSH LEAVES, IVAN MAKES A SECOND ATTEMPT AT STEALING A FEW moments of sleep before dinner. But he's too tired, too wired, too restless, unable to subdue random and ill-disciplined thoughts. He's feeling thin, extenuated. Even as he drifts towards sleep, his mind won't let him, conjuring up images of fire, of Nell helpless, of his father. That's enough to jerk him upright, fully awake. So he showers, the water cold, trying to conjure an artificial freshness.

He leaves the hotel, heading towards the restaurant, and there is Nell walking from the police station. For a moment she doesn't see him. She looks unscathed, moving with her normal ease, self-contained and confident. He stands and watches, elated that she's okay even as the guilt returns. She finally notices him and waves. He extends one hand in welcome as she approaches. 'All good?'

She hesitates, then replies. 'All good.'

They walk the last fifty metres to the restaurant side by side.

'I heard about Phelan,' she says.

'Plodder thinks Otto Titchfield sicked him onto us.'

She nods. 'Sounds about right.'

8

The team is meeting at a newly refurbished woodfired pizza place that Blake has found called Paulo's Emporium. Inside, it's cooled by air-conditioning and warmed by the aroma of food. Ivan realises sleep isn't the only thing he's been missing.

The others are already there: Kevin, Carole and Blake. They stand; hands are shaken.

'I'm starving,' says Blake.

Carole laughs.

A waitress organises drinks, they order food, and then they ease into business, Ivan feeling more comfortable in the familiar mantle of responsibility. He explains why he's arrested Harley Snouch, recounting the story of Riversend, the investigation into murdered backpackers and his first encounter with the con man. It's a suitable appetiser: they already know about Snouch being bashed.

The pizza arrives, and they busy themselves with serving slices and doling out salad.

'The knife,' says Carole, returning to the investigation. 'There is residual blood but not enough to extract a sample for my portable sequencer. I'm sending it to the Sydney lab to extract the DNA. But it's a good fit for Athol Hasluck's killing and consistent with Alice Figtree's injury.'

'No fingerprints?' asks Kevin, voice suggesting he already knows the answer.

'No. But one thing: it's not an ordinary kitchen knife. More professional. A filleting knife, very sharp. The sort favoured by a hunter or a fisher.'

Blake speaks, mouth half full. 'A single knife thrust, from below, up under the rib cage.'

'A surprise attack?'

'Possibly. No defensive cuts on the hands of either Athol or Alice.'

'Someone known to the victim?' asks Nell.

'Possibly,' Blake repeats.

'Hopefully Alice can identify them,' says Carole.

Ivan sighs, an element of frustration in the expression. 'Induced coma. Apparently, the surgery was extremely delicate and they want to prevent any movement. Might be a couple of days before they bring her out of it.'

'Jesus,' says Nell.

They sit in silence, conversation stifled. Ivan imagines the brutality of the attack, the violence of it, the premeditation. The ruthlessness.

The waitress, alerted by their silence, bustles across, asks if all is well. They smile, and Blake compliments her on the food.

'Any luck with the divers?' Ivan asks Carole. 'We've got the knife, so I'm assuming they haven't found a weapon.'

'No,' says Carole. 'Visibility is poor, but otherwise it's an easy job for them. Limited search area, negligible flow, no danger, nothing likely to be washed away. They've been through with metal detectors.'

'Nothing?'

'Just some old car keys. Been there for years.'

Ivan is about to take a bite of pizza, but he lowers the slice back to his plate. 'What sort of car?'

'Alfa Romeo. Classic car. Why?'

Ivan is shaking his head. There can't be a connection. Surely not. Nevertheless, he turns to Kevin. 'This morning I mentioned that cold case from thirty years ago—Davis Heartwood.'

'Yeah, the file was on Nell's desk. Haven't had much chance to get into it.'

Nell chips in. 'Davis drove an Alfa. When he went missing, it was found parked in the main street here, keys gone.'

'Can you find out if the keys match?' Ivan asks Kevin.

'Sure. Try my best.'

Ivan manages a mouthful of pizza before asking him, 'Where are we up to with the CCTV?'

'Making progress. We've been through the vision from the electrical goods shop on the other side of McLean Street from the practice. Only two people entered through the front door: Alice Figtree at eight forty-five Wednesday evening, and Nell just after midnight. Then, within about five minutes'—he swallows—'an explosion, an orange flare.' Kevin takes a deep breath, continues. 'The information you had, that there was a light on upstairs at the practice, visible from the street, is accurate. It came on almost as soon as Alice entered.' He steals a glance at Nell, then returns his gaze to Ivan. 'The fire starts, and a few minutes later a man appears, standing in the street, watching. You come running, give him something. You know the rest.'

'Bert Kippax,' says Ivan. 'I gave him my phone. He called the firies.'

Carole addresses her colleagues. 'As you know, there are clear signs of forced entry at the top of the stairs in the back alleyway. Maybe someone acting alone, maybe not. They were wearing gloves. The fire was deliberately lit.'

'Left me for dead,' says Nell, reaching for a slice of pizza. 'Fuckers.'

Ivan regards her, amazed at how unperturbed she seems. 'Entered and exited through the back,' he summarises. 'We already know there's no CCTV out there.'

'No,' says Kevin. 'But we've picked up a man on the main street. Mainly it's the timing. About twenty minutes before the fire walking in the direction of Athol's, then hurrying back in the opposite direction, just minutes before the cross-street camera catches the explosion. It's blurry, but the man is silhouetted against the shopfront. A large person, definitely male. He seems to be looking at his hand.'

'Blatant,' says Blake to no one in particular.

'Identifiable?' asks Ivan.

'Not easily. Low-res image. He's wearing a hoodie and glasses.'

'Could it be Harley Snouch?' asks Nell.

'Doubt it. Snouch isn't that big. Nor is Terry Zappia. I've sent it to the techs for enhancement, but it seems unlikely they'll be able to extract anything more definitive. But it gives us a timeframe; we're checking other cameras.'

'Okay. What else?' Ivan asks the table.

Carole responds. 'I had a quick look around at Air Stills. It's been taped off, and McTosh has posted one of his constables there to ensure it's not disturbed. But it doesn't look like a murder scene. Not to me. I'll head back first thing and double-check; either I'll find traces of blood or the chemicals they've used to clean it up, or I won't. Same with the electricity outlets. Same with the two vehicles, the Range Rover and the technician's van; I'll check if they were used to transport the body.'

'So what's the connection with Air Stills?' asks Nell. 'The killers tried to plant the knife there, implicate Snouch. Why?' She looks to Ivan. 'It feels clumsy to me. Ham-fisted.'

'Maybe it was an investor,' says Kevin. 'Someone who lost money investing through Athol, realised they were getting scammed, and killed Athol. Thought they'd get back at Snouch.'

'Get him arrested,' says Blake. 'So when the scam gets exposed, he's already in custody.'

'Do we have access to the Air Stills accounts yet?' Ivan asks Carole. 'Those computers in the office up there?'

She shakes her head. 'Zappia knew the password to one login, but that held nothing important. There is a second login, but either we'll need to get the password from Snouch, or get a warrant and get some techs in to crack it.'

'Can we get that underway, please?' asks Ivan. 'Even if we don't think Snouch is a killer, we need to cast as wide a net as possible.'

'These mum and dad investors,' asks Nell. 'How much do you think he ripped off altogether?'

'At least ten million,' says Kevin.

Ivan stares at him. 'How do you know that? I thought the client files were destroyed.'

'They are. But we have the digital copies of Athol's bank accounts, thanks to Alice. On the hard drive Krystal Heartwood gave you. There was money constantly moving in and out of his trust accounts to Air Stills. Simultaneously, money would go into his own account. An identifying code, the amount and the description: "Commission. Five per cent." He received about half a million in commissions over the past year. That's five per cent of ten million.'

'What did he do with it?'

'Most of it appears to have gone straight back into Air Stills, and the rest into Riverina Water Traders.'

'Was he getting any sort of commission from the traders?'

'Yep. Not nearly as much.'

'So these codes on the commissions, you think they're identifying the accounts of Athol's clients?'

'That would be a fair assumption.'

'Surely that changes the complexion, though,' says Nell. 'From what you say, Athol was confident he could sell his land and recoup all the losses he had made through investing in Air Stills, and any losses from trading water. But his financial-planning clients would still be taken for millions. His reputation would be shredded, and chances are they'd sue him.'

'Only if he had finally realised that Snouch was a fraud,' says Ivan. 'According to Snouch, he was still interested in investing more.'

Nell frowns. 'Can we trust Snouch?'

'No, never,' says Ivan. 'But the point stands. Athol could have died thinking his clients were set to collect big time.'

Carole interjects. 'Let me get this straight. The client files detailing the tax affairs and investments of individuals have all been destroyed, but we have some visibility of money flowing in and out of Athol's personal and business accounts, including the trust account?'

'Correct,' says Kevin. 'So I can confirm he received money from Krystal Heartwood and that he then spent it on buying land.'

'What else can you see?' asks Ivan.

'As well as his accounts, I can see those accounts where Athol was a signatory. He appeared to have power of attorney for a couple of clients, or at least was authorised to run accounts on his clients' behalf. There are signs he was skimming some of those as well.' Kevin pauses, as if to be sure of what he's about to say. 'But not the Country First account and not the Watermen's Foundation. From what I can see, there's no sign Athol touched either.'

'But he could have, if he'd wanted to?' asks Ivan.

'I believe so,' says Kevin. 'He was a signatory to both accounts.'

'Watermen's,' says Ivan. 'What's the balance?'

'Maybe fifty thousand dollars.'

'So not enough to get Athol out of debt or to buy the land,' Nell suggests. 'Maybe that's why he never touched it. Not worth it.'

Ivan is frowning. 'Fifty thousand,' he says. 'As of when?'

'As of now,' says Kevin, smiling as if he knows where Ivan is heading.

'But that's just a snapshot. Can you see how much has been distributed over the past year or two?'

'Sure, easy enough. But I'll tell you right now, it's a lot more than fifty thousand.'

'Ballpark?'

'Millions.'

'What? And he never touched it?'

'I'll double-check.'

Ivan's frowning. This all means something, he knows it, but he just can't put a finger on it. 'Do one other thing. Draw me up a list of the major donors. Let's find out where the money is coming from.' He looks around the table. 'No one can know we are doing this, okay? It's a political slush fund. If word gets out, the blowback could be devastating.'

'Feral Phelan,' says Nell. 'He's been sniffing around.'

Ivan can see the chilling effect the mention of the Professional Standards investigator has on his colleague.

The waitress reappears, clearing away their empty plates as the group sits in silence. Blake orders dessert while Kevin and Carole ask for coffee. Ivan is thinking coffee is the last thing he needs. That's when the door opens and in bustles Ernst McTosh.

'Good feed?' asks the sergeant.

'Fills the gap,' says Ivan. 'Take a seat. What have you got?'

McTosh sits, declines the offer of wine. 'We've got the voice recordings from the triple-zero calls. The one that called the fire brigade to Athol Hasluck's practice and the one that called the ambulance for Toby Fairchild—Harley Snouch. And the one to the station with the tip-off about the knife at Air Stills.'

He pulls out his phone, taps with his finger. 'Here,' he says, adjusting the volume so they can all hear it. 'The firies.'

'*Fire brigade. It's urgent.*'

'*What's the location, please?*'

'*Yuwonderie. Right in town.*'

'*Nearest cross streets?*'

'*Commonwealth and McLean. I'd get a move on.*'

Ivan gives a wry smile. 'That's my phone,' he says. 'Bert Kippax calling it in.'

'Here's the tip-off about the knife,' says McTosh, tapping at his screen.

'*Murder weapon is at Air Stills.*' It's a man's voice, low and gruff and to the point.

'Unidentified number,' says McTosh. 'Could be almost anyone.' He taps at the phone again. 'And here's the ambulance call, for Snouch.'

'That the ambulance? Good. There's a man, badly injured. Very badly. In the car park, at Air Stills of Australia. On the road up the Castle in Yuwonderie.'

'What's—'

'Send an ambulance. He's dying.'

And the call cuts out.

'Different person,' says McTosh. 'Younger. Higher pitch.'

But Ivan is no longer listening, he is just staring into space. 'I know that voice,' he says.

chapter thirty-seven

1994

THE NEXT MORNING, THE DOCUMENTS ARRIVED FROM THE LAND OFFICE IN SYDNEY, a solid wad of photocopies wrapped in brown paper inside an Australia Post envelope. Even before the parcel was opened, it felt substantial. This was primary source material: real research. Davis loved it: this was new, this was original, no matter that the documents themselves were old.

He began with the 1912 map, removing it once again from the corkboard. It was the 'before' map, the most simple, marked with his own crudely drawn pencil boundary to delineate the shape of the future system. That pencilled perimeter contained just nine titles. He turned to the photocopies, and one by one matched the numbers on the map with the names on the title documents. Carefully, he wrote the names on the map: Titchfield, Allsop, Chaulker, Hasluck, Horsham, Blaxland, Heartwood, Marney and Pratt.

A quick comparison of the 1912 map with its 1924 counterpart immediately told him something useful and possibly important:

the land upon which the Yuwonderie township was now built, the land now owned by the Land Trust, was owned in 1912 by a man called Noel Marney. Who was he? What had happened to him?

Davis removed the 1917 map from the corkboard and started working through the changes, as recorded in the title documents, writing the names of the owners onto it with pencil.

The property belonging to the Chaulkers in 1912 was transferred in its entirety to the McLeans in 1916. The records revealed it was a sale, but not the price. That made Davis smile: the McLeans, such integral members of the Seven, were in fact latecomers, buying into the land just before the scheme won government support. The McLeans had bet big on it going ahead; the Chaulkers had taken the safer route and sold out.

Next, the Pratts. In 1917 ownership of their land passed from Mr Melville Pratt (deceased) to Mrs Melville Pratt. Given the date, Davis wondered if Mrs Pratt had just become a war widow. Whatever her circumstances, she disposed of her property the next year, selling to the Allsops and the Haslucks. Perhaps there had been no children. Perhaps there had been many children.

Which left Davis to explore the Marneys and their holdings, much of it now owned by the Land Trust. He found the record, the photocopy of the original ledger with its spidery cursive, the property called Jolimont, and moved to the second last entry in the folio. In 1916, just weeks after the Chaulkers sold to the McLeans, the Marneys transferred ownership to three buyers: the Titchfields, Allsops and McLeans. Then the last entry a few months later: the land divided into three.

He examined the 1917 map, the three separate holdings clearly marked, then at the 1924 version, with them consolidated into one.

He rifled through the papers, finding the extract covering the new holding, established in 1918, but its first entry merely listed the owner of the consolidated holding as The Yuwonderie Land Trust Company Pty Ltd, and not who owned the Trust. He stared down at the photocopies: there was no more information to be gleaned.

He studied the maps once more, and didn't know whether to feel elated or dejected. He now knew who bought what and who sold when, but still didn't have any real idea why.

But one thing was clear: the old men at the Canal Club had misled him. They'd said the property owned by the Marneys, Pratts and Chaulkers was not suitable for irrigation, that it was too far out or too high. And yet the records were clear: prior to 1916, all three families owned valuable land right in the heart of what—just a few years later—became the Yuwonderie Irrigation Scheme. Why were Van Dyke Allsop and Jessop Titchfield so keen to disguise that truth? Were they lying, or were they simply mistaken?

— —

That evening at dinner, Davis's grandfather Clemence was looking none too pleased. Krystal had decided it was time Davis started cooking. Earlier in the week, before the evening with Stella and the arrival of the Land Office documents, he'd confided in her that he was at a loose end. Krystal was already immersing herself in the family's affairs, spending long hours with station manager Flax Fairfield. So she put him to work. Davis was up for it. He'd spent his third year in Melbourne in a group house, so he knew the basics. Nevertheless, Davis attributed his grandfather's grim mood, when he sat down to dinner on the verandah, to the spaghetti bolognaise.

'Wonders will never cease,' Clemence said with a sigh, looking at the food and distributing the wine.

Davis thought of biting back, having never seen his grandfather cook anything in his life beyond an occasional barbecue, but thought better of it.

'I had lunch at the Canal Club today,' said Clemence, once the wine was poured.

Davis and Krystal looked up from their meals, caught each other's eye. They had both detected the weight in the words.

'You never go there,' said Krystal.

'Don't much like the food,' said the old man, before reappraising the spaghetti. 'Or the company. On this occasion I didn't have much choice. It seems they've got wind of our intentions.'

Krystal turned to Davis. 'You dick!'

'Language,' said Clemence.

'I'm sorry,' said Davis. 'I must have mentioned it to Lucy Fielder in Sydney.'

Krystal was about to retort, but Clemence held one hand up. 'What's done is done.' And then, to Davis, 'Have you had second thoughts?'

'No. Krystal should inherit.'

His sister eased back in her chair, pacified.

Clemence continued. 'I told them we were seriously considering it, and left it there.'

'How did they react?' Krystal asked her grandfather.

'Mixed. Hayseed McLean seemed to find it amusing, but Van Dyke Allsop was seething. His eldest grandchild is a girl, Agatha.'

'I haven't seen her for years,' said Davis, thinking of Craven, and the unintended consequences his decision might have on his friend.

'Working in London,' said Clemence.

'Most competitive person I ever met,' said Krystal. 'Utterly ruthless on the hockey field.'

'She'll fit right in,' observed Clemence.

'And the others?' asked Davis.

'Hard to say. Parker Hasluck inquired about Krystal. Her qualities. Seemed genuinely intrigued. Dear old Montgomery Horsham's main concern was the club—that it might have to entertain female members. Seemed quite put out by the idea. Kept muttering about the last bastion. I think he spends most of his afternoons there,' said Clemence, chuckling.

'What about Jessop Titchfield?' asked Davis.

Clemence became serious. 'Yes. Interesting. Not so concerned about Krystal. More concerned about you.'

'Me?' said Davis. 'Why?'

'Your research thesis. Said he hoped you weren't going to go slumming.'

'What does that mean?'

'I think he was referring to journalism.'

Davis laughed. 'That's the last thing on my mind.'

'Pity,' said the old man. 'But he'll be glad to hear it. Kept issuing euphemisms. "Let sleeping dogs lie." "What's past is past." That sort of thing.' He twirled some spaghetti on his fork. 'You've got them spooked, Davis. What have you found?'

'Nothing to get upset about. All I've discovered so far is that when the idea for the system was originally floated, there were about twelve local grazing families interested, which was whittled down to about nine, then seven. Some dropped out because their land didn't lie within the boundaries of the scheme.'

'Some?' asked Clemence.

'Three of the families did own extensive property within the scheme's boundaries; they sold out before the canals went in.'

His grandfather considered this. 'They were bought out by the Seven?'

'That's what the documents indicate.'

'Nothing unusual. That's the history of Australian agriculture, right there.'

'How do you mean?' asked Krystal.

'It's Darwinian. Survival of the fittest,' said Clemence. 'Successful farmers get bigger, buy paddocks from their less-successful neighbours. Economies of scale take over, technology, capital reserves, the weak farmers drop out, the big ones get bigger. It's the way of things. All those soldier-settlers with their square-mile blocks—how were they ever going to survive?'

'So why are they so sensitive about it, if it's commonplace?' asked Davis. 'Van Dyke Allsop and Jessop Titchfield deliberately misled me when I had lunch with them. What could they know that you don't?'

'Good question,' said the old man, twirling more spaghetti but not raising it to his mouth. 'I don't know. And that bothers me. I should have been more attentive.'

'The Land Trust,' said Davis. 'Tell me about that.'

'It's the company that owns the land the town is built on.'

'We're shareholders?' asked Krystal.

Her grandfather shook his head. 'Not of any significance. A few token shares, bought at some time in the past, just so we get the annual reports. The main holders are the ones who owned that land at the time the town was built on it. They subdivided and sold off some residential blocks, but retained the commercial area. Lease it out to the shopkeepers.'

'The Titchfields, the Allsops and the McLeans,' said Davis, looking at his grandfather. 'That land is raised, right in the middle of the scheme. It was always going to be the site for the town. It's on the ridge running out from the Castle along Commonwealth Way, too high for water to flow.'

'The obvious place,' Krystal concurred.

'They weren't the original owners of the land,' added Davis. 'It was a family called Marney.'

'Really?' said Krystal. 'You think that's what's making them gun-shy?'

'Why would it?' asked Davis, but his grandfather wasn't responding, apparently deep in thought. The brother and sister exchanged another look and returned to their meals. The patriarch would speak when he was ready and not before.

After a bit more spaghetti and a throwaway compliment—'It really is very good, Davis'—the old man spoke. 'It's about time you two knew a bit more about the Seven and the scheme. Particularly you, Krystal.'

He paused, as if rehearsing his lines in his head, looked down, looked back up.

'Everyone talks about the Seven as if we're a single unit, as if the families are equals, as if we are joined at the hip—all for one, one for all—and that uppermost in our minds is the welfare of the town and the small landholders and not just of ourselves. But that's not quite right; we're not all equal. There are the inner families and the outer families. The Allsops, Titchfields and McLeans are the inner; the Heartwoods, Horshams and Blaxlands are the outer; and the Haslucks are somewhere in between. The inner families control the Land Trust, they collect a considerable amount of rent.'

'And water,' added Davis. 'It's never been agricultural land, but it had permanent water attached when the scheme was set up.'

'There you go,' said Clemence. 'I'd never thought of that.'

'So the inner families are richer?' asked Krystal.

'Generally speaking,' said Clemence, sounding quite blasé. 'And it's not just the Land Trust. They used their wealth to take a controlling shareholding in the Wholesalers when it was set up in the 1960s.'

'I thought that was a type of cooperative?' said Davis.

'Yes. All landholders in the scheme own a share, originally determined by the size of their block. So the Seven own a clear majority of shares because we owned most of the land. But the Land Trust also owns shares. And there were further shares created at the beginning, not connected to land, for those who actually financed the set-up.'

'The Seven?' asked Davis, before correcting himself. 'The inner Seven.'

Krystal laughed. 'So us Heartwoods are kind of second-class citizens then,' she said flippantly.

Clemence rewarded her with a glare. 'No. Never let them tell you that,' he said, pride in his voice. 'Our family is the only one of the Seven whose fate isn't entirely beholden to the scheme.' The old man stares down at his spaghetti, thinks better of it and reaches instead for his wine. He continues once he's refilled his glass. 'When the scheme was being finalised all those years ago, there was a kind of gold rush mentality about it. There had been a terrible drought. Four or five years. Devastating. All the outlying graziers were keen to sell up, keen to buy into the scheme instead. The promise of limitless, reliable water. Free water, or so they thought back then. They all wanted in, but the drought had drained a lot of them. They had no money, just debt. But my grandfather was a canny old coot, a contrarian. Everyone thought he was crazy— something I suspect he encouraged. We already held a sizeable amount of land inside the scheme, so we were in the box seat; we didn't need to sell our outside land. We could have, of course, joined the rush, possibly bought more inside. Become one of the inner three, and a major shareholder in the Land Trust. But he didn't want all his eggs in one basket, so he did the opposite: subdivided and sold some of our holdings inside at inflated prices and bought up dryland farms outside at bargain basement prices. Trebled the size of our holdings, left us with a foot in each camp. So when the rains came back, we had vast holdings outside the system. And when drought returned, we could use our irrigated land to grow feed for the grazing properties if necessary.'

Krystal looked at Davis, then to their grandfather. 'Is that why we've always kept this place, the homestead, out of town, out here in the drylands?'

'Clever girl,' said Clemence, rewarding her with a beatific smile. 'It's a statement. A reminder to ourselves and to others that we stand apart—or we can if we need to.'

'And you keep shares not only in the Irrigation Scheme Company but also in the Land Trust and the Wholesalers. So you get all the information, know what's going down,' Krystal noted.

'I'm even on the board of the Canal Club, pretentious relic that it is.'

'You never go there,' said Krystal.

'Irritates the hell out of them,' said Clemence, a twinkle in his eye.

'I see,' said Krystal, laughing.

Davis felt the same: they had never before heard their grandfather disparage the town's institutions. He really was confiding in them, treating them almost as equals.

'The one institution I'm not part of is the Water Traders. Private company, controlled by the Allsops. Flax trades water through it. I'm in two minds about that. I'd like an insight into the inner workings, but I'm not sure I would have the stomach for it. The Allsops have set it up, but I suspect some of the others are shareholders. The inner families.'

'What do you mean you wouldn't have the stomach for it?' asked Davis.

'Buying and selling water. Playing with people's livelihoods.'

Davis thought of Lucy's father, permanent entitlements gone, temporary entitlements unaffordable, trees and vines dying. Suddenly it became clear to him: the real reason the inner families were so concerned with his investigations. 'They're buying up permanent water, driving irrigators into bankruptcy, then buying the land at rock-bottom prices. No one else wants it, unless they have water.'

The old man appraised his grandson, nodded in approval. 'That's my suspicion. Well done, Davis.' He raised his glass in a mock toast, then placed it back on the table without drinking.

'But that would be very hard to prove. Almost impossible. Tread carefully.'

'But I'm not researching any of that,' said Davis. 'My thesis will end in the 1930s, fifty years before water trading.' He looked to Krystal, but she was considering her spaghetti, the sauce starting to congeal.

She put her fork down. 'You've got the documents, but none of the horse trading.'

'No. None of the behind-the-scenes negotiations between the families, if that's what you mean.'

Their grandfather stood, then, saying nothing, he entered the house proper, before emerging with a dusty bottle of port and three glasses. He raised his eyebrows, a question, and the brother and sister nodded. Clemence poured three glasses. Davis again checked his sister's reaction, but she looked as perplexed as he felt.

Finally Clemence spoke. 'Krystal has a point. What you need aren't the official records but an insight into what people were actually thinking. Not companies and corporations. People.' And he raised his eyebrows once more and smiled at Davis. 'What you really need is access to our family records. My grandfather's diaries and my grandmother's correspondence.'

Davis blinked. 'They exist?'

'I believe so. We're just like the rest of the Seven in that regard. Full of our own self-importance. Diaries are in the library, where you're working. Not sure about the correspondence. Up in the attic, probably, if the mice and possums and silverfish haven't devoured it.'

Davis said nothing, just considered the port, its age, its provenance.

'But be careful, Davis. And don't go off half-cocked. Talk to Krystal and me before you make anything public. Understood?' Clemence sipped his port. 'One thing about this game, running estates, simultaneously competing and cooperating with your neighbours: you have to think strategically.'

'Of course,' said Davis, although he felt the last comment was directed more to his sister than to himself.

chapter thirty-eight

THE SUN IS SETTING WHEN IVAN AND NELL GET TO THE LAST HOUSE ON THE LAST street in the last suburb in eastern Yuwonderie: Eggs Bright's house. There is none of Yuwonderie's Art Deco flair here, just a small house, cladding coming away, dead grass sprouting from the guttering. The lawn has either died, leaving bald patches, or become overgrown with weeds. There's a dog on a chain, barking with vicious intent.

It continues growling as Ivan and Nell walk up to the enclosed verandah and bang on the flyscreen door. Somewhere inside a television is blaring, volume loud enough to be heard above the dog. Ivan can see the reflected flickering of its colour inside the darkened house.

Ivan knocks again, knowing he won't be heard over the blare of the television and the dog. He yells, but there is still no response. He tries the flyscreen door, finds it open, and they proceed across the verandah to the front door proper. It's wide open. 'Hello!' he yells. 'Anyone here?'

A soporific woman comes to the door; her hair is mussed and she's wearing a nightgown, her upper arms exposed and wobbly. She has a black eye and a swollen lip.

'He's at the pub,' she says. 'I ain't got no money.'

Ivan pulls out his badge, offers it almost apologetically. 'Detective Sergeant Ivan Lucic. This is Detective Constable Nell Buchanan.'

That wakes the woman up; he can see it in her eyes: fight or flight. Neither is an option, so she curls her lip instead. Defiance, the sort that every police officer from Perth to Paddington is familiar with. She walks past him to the screen door, yells in a powerful and well-practised voice, 'Shut the fuck up!' And the dog does, issuing a low whimper. The woman returns her attention to Ivan. 'I told you, he's at the pub.'

'We're not looking for your partner. We want to talk to Benedict.'

'Eggs? What's he done?' Surprise joins defiance in the woman's voice.

'Nothing. He's not in any trouble.'

'What then?'

'Might have witnessed something.'

The woman becomes alert, sensing danger. 'He's no dobber.'

'Can we talk to him, please?'

'He's not here.'

'You were asleep.'

'You deaf? He's not here.'

Nell intervenes. 'Mrs Bright, we're concerned for Benedict's safety. It's important we find him.'

The eyes shift again, a sign of knowledge, of fear. She looks to Ivan for confirmation, sees some truth in him. 'Try the shack.'

'The shack?'

'His grandfather's old place. Other side of the Castle, down by the anabranch.'

Ivan recalls the view from the Castle, Eggs's geography lesson, the sweep of scrubland by the waterway. 'Big area.'

'Take the Hay Road. Get to the scrub, about ten k's out of town. Turn off to the left, dirt track, just before the Corkhills Creek Bridge.'

'Thank you,' says Ivan.

'We'll look out for him,' says Nell.

'Sure you will,' she says. 'Now piss off.' She kicks out the wedge beneath the door and closes it. As if on cue, the dog starts up again, yelping and straining at its chain, and not falling silent even when they return to the car and drive away; they can still hear it barking in the distance.

Ivan is driving.

'Corkhills Creek,' says Nell.

'What about it?'

'It's where the body of Davis Heartwood was found.'

They drive in silence back through Yuwonderie. The last rays of the sun are catching the peak of the Castle, but at ground level the streetlights are already taking up the slack. There are people out and about on Commonwealth Way, but soon the two of them are driving on deserted streets, past the wetlands, birds swooping down from the Castle to roost. They pass a house where the Christmas lights are up, an electric Santa waving to no one.

By the time they get to Corkhills Creek, the sunset is receding into a darkening glow behind them, and when they leave the bitumen and ease onto a rough four-wheel track, the darkness starts to crowd in under the trees. Nell has her phone out, checking the satellite view on Google Maps. She shows it to Ivan. 'Looks like there might be a track through there.'

It's not so clear, but Ivan goes with it. It's a fire track or a fishers' track, unformed and ungraded, dipping down onto the flood plain, winding its way through the scrub, forking and re-forming. Through the four-wheel drive's open window, there is just the sound of the engine and the call of an owl.

They see the glow to the left before they see the shack itself. The track forks, and Ivan navigates his way to the rough cottage, a fire burning in a ring of river stones outside. There is no one to be seen, just the fire.

They park the car, check inside.

Still no one.

'Heard us coming, done a runner,' says Nell. 'Don't blame him.'

Ivan yells into the darkness. 'Eggs! It's Ivan! Detective Lucic!'

He waits, but there is no response. He's thinking of leaving a note when his phone pings. A message from Eggs. *That you?*

The signal is strong, even out here in the scrub; there's good coverage from the top of the Castle.

He shows it to Nell before typing his response. *Yes. By the shack. Corkhills Creek.*

Nell pulls her gun, fades away into the dark. Ivan nods to himself, appreciative of his partner's instincts.

A shape emerges from behind the shack. Eggs. There's a flash, torchlight washing across Ivan's face.

'You alone?' Eggs asks.

'My partner is with me,' Ivan answers; the boy must surely have seen her.

'Why is she hiding?'

'In case it wasn't you.'

Eggs is still. 'It's serious, isn't it?'

'Starting to escalate,' replies Ivan.

'Shit.'

The young man is just a silhouette; Ivan can't really make out his face.

'She can come out if she likes,' says Eggs. 'Or she can stay there. Keep guard.'

The youth walks to the fire, sits down.

Ivan follows, sits opposite him. And it's only now, with the fire-light on Eggs's face, that Ivan sees it: evidence of fresh violence. 'Shit,' he says. 'You all right?'

'I've survived worse.'

'Thanks for calling the ambulance. For Toby Fairchild. At Air Stills.'

The lad looks away into the darkness, saying nothing.

'They record triple-zero calls.'

'So?'

'So thank you.' He smiles. 'You're not in any trouble.'

'Then why raise it? Why come here?'

'I need to know what you saw.'

The young man looks away again.

'What were you doing at Air Stills?' Ivan asks. 'It's fenced off.'

The lad shrugs. 'Just wanted to check it out.'

'You'll have to do better than that,' says Ivan.

'Will I? Says who?' The words are defiant, but not the emotion behind them. Rather than defiance, it's as if Eggs is exploring a problem, asking for advice.

'Toby Fairchild isn't his real name,' Ivan tells him, hoping that by volunteering information he might receive some in return. It's worked in the past. 'Real name is Harley Snouch. We've arrested him on outstanding warrants.'

'What for?'

'Various offences. Dating back years.' Ivan pitches his voice as if he's confiding, letting Eggs in on an intriguing story. 'You wouldn't believe it if I told you. He's a grifter. Air Stills is one humungous con, a massive scam.'

'Yeah, I know.'

Ivan's heart almost misses a beat. 'You do?'

'Athol Hasluck told me.'

'What?' Ivan's mind races to catch up. So much in those four words that he barely knows where to start. He keeps his voice as even as possible, as if what the boy has said is totally unremarkable. 'When did he tell you that?'

'Day before he died. Said he'd just worked it out that morning.'

'You know who killed him?'

The boy looks at Ivan, then away into the darkness. 'No.'

'When I spoke to you that time up on the Castle, you said you didn't know him.'

Eggs sighs. 'I lied.'

'Why?'

'Wanted to stay out of it.' He hangs his head, studies the fire. 'His body, in the canal. There for me to find. A warning to me to shut up.'

'A warning to you?'

'Maybe.'

'So why tell me now, that you knew Athol?'

'They tried to kill Alice Figtree.'

Ivan considers the damage to the lad's face. The more his eyes adapt to the low light, the more he sees. Bruising. Cuts. Abrasions. 'Your mum's partner?'

'Yeah. Complete arsehole.'

'What's his name?'

'Toxteth McGrath. Known as Toxic. A fucking understatement.'

'Eggs, anything you can tell us about Athol Hasluck could be a great help.'

'Not sure I know much.'

'I think you might. What you just said before, that Athol knew Fairchild was a scammer, we didn't know that, haven't been able to substantiate it.'

'How's that important?'

'It would be a clear motive for murder. Harley Snouch, or someone else set to profit from his scheme, could have killed him to shut him up.'

'That's what I figured. That's why I didn't tell you I knew Athol. I didn't want to be next.'

'So explain it to me. What was your relationship with him?'

Eggs shakes his head. 'Not sure I should tell you. I could still be in danger.'

'Was it personal?'

'How do you mean?'

'Romantic?'

Eggs bursts out laughing, letting the tension out for a moment. 'No. I'm not gay and he certainly wasn't.'

'How do you know that?'

'He was married, wasn't he? Had a wife.'

'That's not exactly definitive. You'd be aware of that.'

'Sure. But I never saw any sign of it.'

'So how did you know him?'

'We played cricket for the same club. I knew he was an accountant and told him I was interested in studying economics at uni. He said I could do some work experience if I liked. He couldn't pay, but could show me a few things.'

'And did you?'

'Sure. I wasn't so interested in the bookkeeping side, but he knew a fair bit about the economy and investing.' Eggs gives a little chuckle. 'He was interested in this.' Eggs gestures around him, to the shack and the dark. 'Interested in buying it.'

'What did you say?'

'It's Mum's. But if she sold it, then Toxic would take the money.'

'You didn't tell her?'

'No.' He looks at the fire.

'So you talked to Athol about economics. He offered you work experience. He offered to buy this land. I don't get how any of that would put you in danger.'

'Athol offered me paid work.'

'What sort of work?'

'Research. That's what he called it.' Eggs looks up from the fire. 'Ever since I was old enough, I've worked part-time at the Wholesalers, saving for university.'

Ivan nods. 'That's why you still live at home, despite Toxteth. So you can save money.'

'He hates the idea that I want to go to uni.'

'You figured a few more weeks and you'd be out of here.'

'Yeah. Gone for good.'

'So what were you doing for Athol?'

'Like I said, I worked at the Wholesalers. He wanted me to access some records for him.'

'And did you?'

'No, I was trying, but I didn't manage to get my hands on any.' He shrugs. 'I was packing fruit.'

'What sort of records?'

'Financial transactions, shipping details. What was coming in and what was going out. Buyers and sellers.'

'Who else knew about this?'

'I'm not sure, but I figure Alice Figtree might have done.'

'Anyone else?'

'Pete Allsop. Some of it.'

'The boy you were waterskiing with?'

'Yeah. His dad is Craven Allsop. They're Seven. Craven is a second son, but rich. Maybe richer than his sister. Runs Riverina Water Traders. Chairman of the Wholesalers.'

'Why did you tell Pete?'

'He's working at the Wholesalers too. Summer job.'

'And he knew Athol was after the records?'

'No. Not that. I didn't mention Athol or Alice or any of that. I just dropped it casually one day. Pete's doing economics and finance down at Melbourne Uni, and I'm keen on doing the same. I said I'd love to see the books at the Wholesalers, see how they compare with the public balance sheets. Made it a bit of a joke.'

'Did he bite?'

'Sort of. Said it would be interesting, seeing how the Seven worked from the inside. Behind the facade of philanthropy and civic spirit.'

'What did he mean by that?'

Eggs gives a small laugh. 'Whether they're ripping off the smallholders.' He grimaces. 'He thought it was funny.'

'You reckon that's what Athol was interested in as well?'

'I don't know. He didn't tell me.'

'Would you have objected if he did?'

'Me? No. Pete might be right, but I don't know. Most small landholders seem to do okay.'

'Not your mum, from what I saw tonight.'

'She's not a landholder. Welfare.'

'Her boyfriend?'

'A fucking parasite.'

'Doesn't work either?'

'Only when he feels like it. He's a welder. Earns plenty when he gets off his arse, but even then, he pisses it all up against the wall.'

'A drinker?'

'And a gambler.'

Ivan considers that, thinks of his own father and his drinking, thinks of himself and his gambling. 'So he hits you. You and your mum.'

'If I complain, he'll only beat her harder.'

'You tried? Told the local cops?'

Eggs shakes his head, gazes into the fire. 'No.'

Ivan stares up into the sky, first stars visible. He can see a jet, flying at altitude, heading to Perth or Adelaide. He considers Eggs's situation before he speaks again. 'I told you at the canal that my father bashed me. Not my mum's boyfriend, not a step-father. My own father. Would come home drunk, beat my mum. A fucking monster. I didn't tell anyone, not for years.'

'Did you leave?'

'He did. I was too young.'

'Where is he now?' asks Eggs.

'Doesn't matter. I never want anything to do with him again.'

Eggs looks at the fire, says nothing.

Ivan keeps talking, isn't sure why. 'It's why I became a cop.'

'To stop people like him?'

'I guess. And the cops were the only ones who gave a shit. When someone finally told them what was going on. They were good to me, good to my mum. Tried to convince her it wasn't her fault, got her to take out restraining orders. Didn't do any good, but even so.'

'How is she now?'

'Dead. A long time.'

'His fault?'

'Yeah. He didn't kill her, but he might as well have done.'

'That's tough,' says Eggs.

'If I can help your mum, I will,' says Ivan.

'Thanks.' But there is no enthusiasm in the youth's voice, as if he doesn't believe anything can change.

'So what were you doing at Air Stills this morning, when you found Fairchild bashed?'

'Looking for evidence.'

'Of what?'

'That it was a scam. Like Athol claimed. Stupid of me.'

'What did you find?'

'Nothing. I didn't get a chance.'

Suddenly Ivan understands. 'You didn't just discover him bashed, did you? You witnessed it.'

Eggs says nothing for a long while. Finally he relents. 'Yeah. Yeah, I did.'

'Who?'

'Who do you think?'

'Toxteth McGrath.'

'Yeah. It was him. The bastard.'

'You're not going home,' says Ivan. 'Not until we arrest him.'

chapter thirty-nine

October 1915

My dearest Elaine,

I must apologise. I spoke entirely too rashly, my emotions taking hold where my more rational self should properly have held sway. You have been my best and only friend since I arrived in the district nigh on two years ago, and I should never have treated you with such incivility. With Jack away, you have been my sole support. Joey cannot yet form words, but I feel he is asking for you, the way he looks towards the door each time he hears some unusual noise. It is another twist to the dagger in my heart.

It feels so strange, to write to you like this, so formal, instead of mounting Penny and riding over. But I feel it is better; this way I can consider my words and make my intentions plain.

Surely you must understand. My guests are not just itinerants: they are my kin, my cousins, my mother's family. They may not behave like me, their manners and speech foreign to your ears, but how could I turn them away in their hour of need? What would become of them? The brothers are not here of their own volition. The mission is governed by a new policy and has begun evicting those with lighter complexions, telling them to find their own way in the world. Walter is a skilled horseman and a good worker. He would have enlisted, and might yet, if his brother Billy was any older. But Billy is just fifteen and Walter will not abandon him.

What harm can they do to anyone? They simply reside on our land while they plan their next move. They have moved from Jolimont now down to the cottage by Corkhills Creek, out of sight, where they might shelter and help me maintain the property. Even today, despite this late cold snap, the two of them are out attending to the fences. Come spring proper, and they can help with the shearing. The misconception that our people are work-shy could not be further from the truth. You must know that the suggestion of Horace's, that Walter might spear a neighbour's sheep, is beyond ludicrous in this day and age. Please don't think me ignorant of how their presence will grate with some of the landholders of the district; I have lived my whole life with this.

I do hope everything is progressing well towards your marriage. Please assure Douglas Heartwood and his family that I have nothing but the greatest respect for him and for them. I know him to be a fair and honest man. I do look forward to the day when he and Jack are friends, neighbours and shareholders in the irrigation company, when you and I are ladies of the district. I can't believe Horace's assertion that the presence of my cousins may somehow endanger support for the scheme. They are at Corkhills; that block does not even lie within its proposed boundaries.

I have written to Jack, setting out the situation as fairly and objectively as I might, so he can weigh all sides of the debate. I will most certainly abide by any decision he makes; it is his land, after all. No doubt Horace has written as well; let Jack be the arbiter. But I do want to assure you of one thing—and, through you, to reassure Horace: Jack and I are unwavering in our commitment to the project. I have communicated the progress that Horace has made, and Jack's responses are full of praise and optimism.

I can see now, from the new maps, plans and designs Horace has shared, that the Marney lands will play a pivotal role. Indeed, it is hard to envisage how the scheme could be developed without our participation. Horace can be confident we will do everything within our power to advance it. I feel it is all that keeps Jack sane, his vision of this future for Joseph and whatever siblings we may be blessed with upon his return, when the world is at peace and we can work together to build a better one. Let us lift our eyes to the promise of the future, rather than dwell on the tribulations of the past.

But for now, I have told the brothers that they may continue to shelter at Corkhills Creek.

You are my finest friend, Elaine, my only friend. Please let us be reconciled. Just give the word, and I will ride over to see you. We have so much to share. But before I do, I must journey down to see my mother. She is seriously unwell. She has said nothing to me, so it is only through the brothers that I know of it. They tell me this is why the new superintendent has permitted her to stay on at the mission.

And so I have a mighty favour to ask. Would you care for Joseph while I am gone? It will just be for a day or two. He is too small to tolerate such a trip on horseback, and he does love you so. Perhaps it will give you a little practice for when you are wed and start a family of your own with Douglas. I know it is a lot to ask, that Horace won't approve, but it may be my last chance to see my mother.

Your adoring friend,
Bessie

chapter forty

THE HOTEL IS NO RESORT. ONCE, THE DROVERS REST WOULD HAVE OVERLOOKED Lake Yuwonderie; now it overlooks the wetlands, and a row of black-light bug zappers are aligned near the entrance to counter incoming mosquitoes. It's a working man's pub, the decor unchanged since the lake was filled in, the seats ripped and the carpet threadbare, an island of need in the postcard prosperity of Yuwonderie, its patrons willing to ignore the shabbiness in return for cut-price schooners. The Canal Club and the Drovers Rest are the bookends of Yuwonderie, the elite and the dregs, but Ivan almost welcomes the pub's atmosphere. The uniform tidiness of the town has been getting under his skin; this feels authentic. The bikers drinking around a pool table certainly appear authentic. There is no sign of Toxic McGrath, not the way Eggs described him: almost two metres tall, tats all over his arms, a lazy eye and a mullet like a doormat.

Ivan walks towards the bar, Nell right behind him, one eye on the bikers. There's no need to badge the barmaid; she pegged him the moment he walked through the door.

'Not drinking, I'm thinking,' she says.

'Toxteth McGrath. Seen him?'

The barmaid smiles. 'You gonna arrest him?'

'That's the plan.'

'Be my guest. In the VIP suite.' She points. And her smile grows wider. 'You just made my day.'

Ivan and Nell exchange a glance. The VIP lounge. The state-wide euphemism for the pokies room. No windows, no clocks, no distractions.

Nell smiles encouragingly. 'You've got this.'

He nods, feels grateful for her show of confidence.

They enter under a flashing neon sign and past a rubber plant so covered in grime that it can't possibly be real. Ivan feels his heart accelerating. It's all so familiar, but seen through clear eyes: the thick carpet to soak up distractions and spilt drinks; the almost soundless air; the closed fug of the space: beer and body odour, old hamburgers and illicit cigarettes. The smell of desperation. And dominating all: the glowing, flashing, mesmeric machines, dancing lights alive, casting their spell amid the gloom.

No one looks up as they enter, the players' attention attached, umbilical-like, to the machines. There's an old lady, purse clutched in a talon-like hand, mouth ajar, a little drool escaping. Further along a fat man, perched half on, half off his stool, glasses slipping down to the end of a greasy nose, a forgotten schooner going flat by the side of the machine. And at the end of the row, Toxic McGrath, oblivious to their presence, eyes staring blankly as his finger punches the button, again and again and again, in a rhythm like a heartbeat, the pace steady regardless of what the machine is showing.

Ivan can't move, not for a moment. He'd been expecting a fight. He'd come to fell a giant, a man full of spite and anger and bitterness, a latter-day version of his own father. He wasn't expecting this: this hollowed-out spectre, so entranced by the technology, so hypnotised by the lights, that he doesn't even sense the police. And in that moment, Ivan sees himself as he must appear when he enters that same trance, when he falls under the same spell. A word enters his mind, irrefutable: pathetic.

He steps forward. The steam has gone out of him, the urge to wreak revenge on this man who has done to Eggs what his own father once did to him. But as he moves, Toxic notices him at last. He turns his head, looks at Ivan, one eye wandering, a sneer spreading across his face. He looks to Nell for a fraction of a second, dismisses her, before turning back to Ivan. 'The fuck do you want?'

'Toxteth McGrath?'

The man doesn't answer, just swivels slowly and stands. He's big, a good fifteen centimetres taller than Ivan, his shoulders bulging. One hand is bandaged.

'You're under arrest,' says Ivan, almost gently.

'The fuck I am.'

Ivan doesn't reply, just moves closer to McGrath, reaching for him.

The man explodes into action, unforeseen and quick. His money has gone into gambling, not alcohol. He hits Ivan, left fist to the guts, right fist following, his bandaged hand no impediment. He keeps moving in with the momentum, charging Ivan, picking him up and hurling him into a wall. Ivan can't believe it, the strength of the man, like a beast, roaring like one too. The breath goes out of him; he's winded. McGrath stands over him, holds up a fist the size of a sledgehammer. 'You're fucking lucky I'm too smart to mark you. Don't come near me again.'

And the big man heads towards the exit. The exit where Nell is standing, legs spread, arms across her chest. Ivan can't breathe, can't move, his eyes wide. She should have drawn her gun.

Toxteth says nothing, just extends a hand to brush her aside. Ivan watches, spellbound, as Toxteth goes to pass her. Watches as Nell takes his hand, twists it, using her weight for leverage, wrenching it up behind him, shoving it up high, all in an instant, all before the man can react. Ivan hears something pop, then McGrath's shriek as Nell turns him, then the sound of his face smashing into the poker machine, shattering the visage of the Aztec god. Then nothing for half a second, just Nell breathing hard. And then lights and bells and whistles of joy. The sound of magic, the promised land, come at last to the gambling pit of the Drovers Rest. The old woman and the fat man, not distracted by the fight, turn to witness the miracle. McGrath's head has won the jackpot.

Nell looks down at Ivan, still on the floor. 'Don't you fucking dare.'

chapter forty-one

1994

IN THE BOOK-LINED LIBRARY IN THE GRAND HOUSE BUILT BY HIS FOREBEARS AT the heart of his great estate, Clemence Heartwood pointed and his grandson Davis pulled books from one of the highest shelves, standing atop a small ladder.

'Never thought to read them,' said Clemence. 'Never thought it wise to.'

Davis said nothing, concentrating on extracting the diaries, passing them down to his grandfather. They were leather-bound and filled the entire shelf.

'I think my own father put them up there; thought they looked impressive,' said Clemence. 'Like those politicians on television with bookshelves lined with Hansards and Senate debates.'

Once the books were assembled and Clemence had left him, Davis sat examining the pile. Forty volumes, one for each year, starting in 1901, when William Heartwood, aged twenty-six, inherited the land from his father, through to 1940, when he died, aged sixty-five, caught in the London Blitz. The diaries appeared uniform despite covering four decades: all the same size, all the same thickness, all bound in thin Morocco leather, all with marbled page edges. They were a little smaller than the modern A4, complying to some imperial standard. William must have ordered them, or had them made bespoke, when he inherited Three Wells Station—a statement of intent if ever there was one. Davis wondered if his great-great-grandfather had ordered more, if there were blank books somewhere, up in the attic or elsewhere. Davis wondered if he were to order such books to record the rest of his life, how many he would have made. Three score and ten, minus twenty-one? Forty-nine? That seemed neither too pessimistic nor too arrogant. If it were him inheriting the estate, maybe such a uniform collection would be appropriate, but now surely he would be better buying one each year, diaries in all shapes and sizes, the more diverse the better, reflecting life as it came.

Davis opened the first volume reverentially, breathing in the musty smell, careful not to damage the spine. The leather binding had dried, and he could hear its small creaks of protest. Ninety-three years old; ninety-three years since his great-great-grandfather had dipped his nib into an inkwell and put pen to paper. Davis wondered how long it had been since anyone had looked upon these words, since anyone had opened the diaries. Had they ever been reviewed since they were written, by the author or anyone else? Inside, an embossed mark, inked separately with a stamp. *Ex Libris: William Goldstone Heartwood*. The pages themselves were in good condition: thick paper, good stock. He wondered if he could commission someone to restore the binding, to make the leather supple again. He could place them on a lower shelf in the library, make them more present, more accessible. Rehabilitate them. A parting gift to his grandfather and sister.

He started at the first volume, the first entry. The writing was steady and clear, the lettering a simple copperplate, elegant but with the flourishes stripped back. It gave him an insight into a slower age, when writing wasn't hurriedly scribbled or typed on a keyboard, when thoughts were allowed to mature before being committed to the page. Davis imagined William, aged twenty-six, sitting in this very room, writing by candlelight or kerosene lantern, a well-educated young gentleman, a graduate of Oxford.

The first entry was dated 11 May 1901.

The world is changing and yet it has not: of a sudden, Australia is a country and the Queen is dead and a new century is upon us, yet the drought continues, as bad this century as the last, contemptuous of calendars. My life is changed, however, that is definite, responsibility thrust upon me. I am called home to the great constant: Three Wells Station. My father is dead, unexpectedly so. A riding accident. I suspect he was drunk, but no one will speak ill of the dead and confirm it. I must refrain from asking lest I appear ghoulish. Not that it matters, for sober or drunk, the end result is the same. He was returning from the neighbours, at night, after cards. By all accounts he was in high spirits. It is unclear if the fall killed him, or the cold. His horse returned by itself, and Mother roused the workers to search. They did all they could but he wasn't found until morning, and by then it was too late.

His death could not come at a worse time. The drought is never-ending. The Federation drought, they are calling it.

Not even the black fellows can recall it ever being so bad. The Murrumbidgee has slowed to a trickle and started to dry up altogether, a river in name only, the water gathering in brackish ponds, the fish dying. Of our seven wells, only the original three are still providing water, barely enough for the homestead. God alone knows how we might fare if they too run dry.

Mother is beside herself, anxious that she not be seen in public until proper clothes arrive: the obligatory black of widowhood. Even in grief we must respect the forms of society. It seems cruel; she seems mad.

Above all, she is insistent on my own marriage proceeding, that the estate demands it, that my father would have wanted it. She talks of stability and legacy and dynasty, and him, barely cold in his grave. And so Mary and I have set the date for September; let us pray for spring rains to bless it.

I am not sure how I feel about all of this. It has happened, and is still happening, too quickly for me. Oxford seems like a dream now, a green dream, whereas all there is here is the brown reality of bare earth and the white of animal bones. I wish I had appreciated it more while I was there. Friends for life, we swore, but now I realise there is a good chance I will never see my colleagues again. And if I do, it will be on some fleeting visit, where we will sit and drink and laugh like old times, but we will be reminiscing about life rather than living it anew. Those days have passed me by, and I barely saw them receding.

I should not be ungrateful, I know. I must make the most of my lot and be thankful for it, to be heir to all of this, to Three Wells, to stand on our little hill, up by Pa's grave, and to know that almost as far as the eye can see the land is ours. Blessed indeed.

And yet it seemed so barren on that hill, left so exposed by this relentless drought, that I sought an oak sapling in the garden, grown from a fallen acorn, and planted it up there to provide him with shelter, a small reminder of England.

It is not that I don't want it. I do. But I thought it would not come to me for many years yet. That I had more time. Father was always so strong and hearty; it is still difficult to believe him dead. I do wonder if I can ever be half the farmer he was, the way he mastered it all, from knowing when a horse needed shodding to what crops to plant to how to secure the best deal for our wool. I feel I have so much to learn. Too much. He must have developed strategies for coping with the drought. If only he had shared them; if only I had thought to ask.

But now I must develop my own strategies. I must take good care of my mother and assist her in her grief and her recovery. I must foster my younger siblings. I must put thoughts of travel and learning and fellowship away. I must commit to it; duty demands it.

Davis was bewitched. He'd feared the diaries would be little more than the individualised version of the Yuwonderie Irrigation Scheme Company records: arid accounts of day-to-day life, of sales and transactions, lists of meals and people met and crops planted and sheep shorn. Instead, he had found a young man pouring his thoughts onto the page; a young man who, unlike Davis, was unable to sidestep destiny.

Davis moved through the pages, scanning paragraphs, reading snatches here and there, before finding the entry for 15 September 1901, a Sunday.

I am married a week now, and find myself entirely satisfied to be so. Mary and I were obliged to attend church this morning, the new lord and lady of Three Wells Station, paraded for the people of the district, high and low. Oh, how people clucked and gathered and blessed us. And all the old women swarming Mary, wanting to touch her, knowing what she had known, unable to mention it but wanting to share in it all the same, eyes wide and mouths wider. And the same for me, the men with their knowing looks and suggestively arched eyebrows, a little proud and a little jealous. And us, dressed in our finery, and all the time knowing what lay beneath. If I heard the sermon, I can't recall a single word.

Mary is happy and I am happy. I knew that I loved her, that she loved me, that marriage was inevitable. But now, instead of trepidation, I rejoice in it. It is true: we are one. It is like Three Wells Station; until I was delivered mastery, I wasn't sure that I should want it, or that I could master it. And so it is with marriage. And now I have found it, the longing for England, for the world, has been washed away. Our life is here; our future is here. We are blessed!

Davis decided he liked his great-great-grandfather and his stream-of-consciousness writing dressed up in Victorian formality. He read on, eager to learn more of his ancestor, until the sheer weight of forty years piled on the desk overwhelmed him and he decided he should focus on his research. Guided by the timeline already established by the Land Office maps and the documents from the company, he began to skip forward, searching for mentions of the scheme. He knew that the first company, the South Murrumbidgee Irrigation Company—the precursor of the YISC—was established in 1914. He moved through to 1913, by which time William would have been around thirty-eight, in his prime, confident of his place in the world. By then Mary had given birth to five children, four of them still living. The hand holding the pen had grown steadier, the language less florid, the copperplate less elaborate. Where there had been emotion, now there were more measured ruminations on the weather and land clearing and crop prices, hunting parties to combat dingoes and wild dogs. Davis moved back and forth through the pages, looking for some relevant entry. He didn't find it until the next volume, 1914.

Horace Titchfield and Noel Marney are agitating for those of us south of the Murrumbidgee to be incorporated into the proposed Murrumbidgee Irrigation Area. I heartily support their efforts. How dare this woeful government neglect us so, considering how much we have done for colony, state and commonwealth? If the federal government can push for this irrigation scheme north of the river, and convince Macquarie Street to partner in it, why can't the New South Wales government convince the national government to extend it south of the river? Titchfield and Marney have written to me, requesting I declare my formal backing, saying we are all bound to profit—if only we can gain

access to the guaranteed water from the new mountain dams.
I have written back, agreeing wholeheartedly. I did not wait
for the post; I had a man ride across with my reply.

And two weeks later:

Titchfield proposes a meeting, so that all the landed families of
the district might gather together and make common cause. We
will meet at the Marney homestead, Jolimont, on Saturday of
the coming week. Marney is promising a festival for the chil-
dren, entertainments for the womenfolk, while the family heads
lock ourselves away and talk strategy.

It is an exciting development, and we will attend with our
minds open.

Davis put the diary down. The Marneys. There they were again.
And not sitting at the periphery, but at the heart of affairs, driving
advances. How could they have been so instrumental in instigating
the scheme, then sell out in 1917 when it was reaching fruition?

He moved forward through the pages, finding William's record
of the day of the meeting.

It was a most interesting day at Marney's. Augustine Chaulker
was upset by the presence of alcohol, and it was left to me,
of all people, to pacify him. Fortunately, a representative of
Southern Cross windmills was passing through and Marney had
invited him to show off the latest designs. That caught Chaulker's
attention, and the thought of water, and not the demon drink,
seemed to calm him down. I sometimes wonder how it is we
will come together in this project: our temperaments and beliefs

are so disparate. Yet clearly it is in all our interests. No one has forgotten the Federation drought, and we all fear its return.

Marney and Titchfield reported they had been to Sydney to make representations to the Minister. They say he and his officials were impressed by the maps and the engineer's reports and the surveys, and they were swayed that a gravity-fed irrigation scheme south of the river would be viable. But Marney and Titchfield say that, in private, dining with the Minister away from his officials, he was candid, revealing the sticking point isn't the technical feasibility, but the financial structures and the politics. The government is afraid that the perception of public money being spent to enable private gain is an insurmountable obstacle, and the budget to establish the MIA is already stretched. His suggestion was to propose the scheme as separate from the MIA, a scheme privately funded in its entirety. He said such a scheme might win legislative support, but that was the limit the government could commit to at this stage.

Marney was still upset by this, even days later. He felt we were being fobbed off, or worse. He expressed a new fear: that now we had done their work for them and demonstrated the scheme is feasible, the government might move against us, compulsorily acquiring our land and then auctioning it off, leaving us all landless. He said this is what has happened north of the river.

Titchfield was more measured. He said that regardless of the government's motivations, it was now clear that the only way forward was for us to pursue an entirely private scheme. He suggested the government was doing us a favour. If we funded it, then we would reap the benefits. And if we acted quickly, then that might act as a bulwark against compulsory acquisition.

That was the real purpose of the meeting, I see now: to galvanise us landowners, and to formalise our intent. Whereas in the past we contributed funds on an ad hoc basis to commission surveys and engineer's reports, all aimed at winning government support, now Titchfield and Marney proposed the formation of a company. Shares would be allocated according to the amount of land likely to fall within the boundaries of the scheme, with an initial financial investment scaled accordingly.

Marney was madly enthusiastic, saying guaranteed water would be the making of us. Titchfield was again more measured, saying we should take it one step at a time: form the company, work through the prospective costs in more detail, secure the required legislation.

I spoke in support of Titchfield and his step-by-step approach. I said I wanted the scheme to proceed, but only if the sums added up. I said there was no point in advancing any further until we had won an assurance from the government that we would have access to the Murrumbidgee's water, including that to be stored in the new dam, Burrinjuck, under construction up by Wee Jasper.

I said it was important to keep the initial capital contribution small, just enough to produce a proper feasibility study. Not to commit too much, too early.

I would like to think that between the enthusiasm of Marney, the knowledge of Titchfield and my natural caution, we combined to win over the others. And so the South

Murrumbidgee Irrigation Company will be formed. Titchfield
will have a solicitor in Narrandera draw up the required papers.

Here it was, Davis saw, the very start of the scheme, the moment
the founders' intent was crystallised into the precursor company: at
a meeting at the Marneys' homestead. He looked at the 1912 map.
The Marneys' land lay at the very centre of the future scheme.
He wondered where the homestead Jolimont had been sited; he
had never heard of it. Probably somewhere up on the ridge, where
Commonwealth Way now ran.

As the afternoon wore on, Davis dug deeper, scouring the diaries
for developments, moving on through the rest of 1914. But apart
from the formation of the company and commissioning of feasibility studies, there was little else recorded. Strangely, there was
no mention of the looming war, as if this had not yet traversed the
globe, or had not penetrated so far inland, or had simply not been
of interest to William Heartwood. There were some references to
progress on the feasibility study and frustration with the government, but nothing fundamental.

And then the war did come, breaking over the pages of the
diary like a wave. They were suddenly filled with nothing else.
Here, William came across as more of a dispassionate observer,
reporting the patriotic fervour, the rush to join in lest it be over
and done with by the time the troops got there.

The Marney lads have gone, so too Will Horsham and Ellory
Pratt. My brother Tyce has enlisted and Douglas is champing at
the bit. It feels as if the place is emptying out. Thank goodness,

Horace Titchfield is still here, advancing the scheme—not that I expect him to make much progress, with everyone so preoccupied. And so uncertain of the future. I have a bad feeling about this war. I am not so sure it will be over by Christmas, and I am not so confident that all our lads will return.

Davis finished the 1914 volume and took a break for afternoon tea, finding Krystal in the kitchen, dressed in dusty overalls and wearing a shower cap. 'Mulesing sheep?' he asked playfully.

'Helping you, thank you very much.'

'How's that?'

'Grandfather has dispatched me to the attic, fossicking around for records. Reckons he's too old. Have you been up there lately? There are great hoards of stuff, like the sacking of Rome. Tea chests and trunks, boxes and suitcases. Like the entire family history has been preserved. We could open a museum.'

'Wow. Thanks. Need a hand?'

'No. I'm happy up there. Quite a trove,' she said cheerfully. 'You've really put a spark into Clemence. Suddenly the old chap seems invested in your research.'

Davis laughed. 'I think they tried to put him in his place down at the Canal Club.'

Krystal echoed his laughter. 'Jesus. Good luck with that.'

Back in the library, he kept moving through the diaries. At one stage, William devised a plan to trap rabbits and supply their pelts, free of charge, to make the slouch hats that by then were synonymous with Australia's soldiers. All the other landholders joined in, and it was declared a huge success. William wrote:

I am pleased with the result, that in some small way it might assist the war effort. But even more pleasing is how it demonstrates what we can achieve when we band together and act in unison, putting aside our petty differences and working towards a common goal. I feel it bodes well for the irrigation scheme.

A few weeks later, another entry: Horace Titchfield declaring his intention to leverage the spirit of community and run for state parliament, seeking the financial backing of the district; William Heartwood discussing the prospect, reluctantly deciding to support his neighbour.

And then, dated September 1915, news from the war.

Such a terrible loss: Noel Marney, killed in action at Gallipoli. Not even on his horse; they don't use them. Not in combat, but an artillery shell, late at night, an unexpected bombardment. A terrible loss. He was a wonderful man, so energetic, so responsible for one so young. Visionary in his quest to better the district. And now his property must fall to his brother Jack, himself somewhere on the frontline. May God protect him.

That's it, thought Davis. That's what happened to the Marneys. They weren't cheated or swindled or diddled, not by their neighbours. But by war. By fate.

He rushed through now, wanting to find out. Had Jack Marney survived or not? Instead his eyes, scanning for the name, came across another entry.

Augustine Chaulker is most upset. He says the treatment of Bessie Walker is unconscionable. He wants no part of it and has

declared he will not profit from it. He will sell his land rather
than participate in the irrigation scheme. He calls it unholy and
despoiled. He has sought my advice, and has completely reversed
his decision. Whereas earlier he thought my intention to retain
dryland holdings was ill-advised, now he wants to do the same.

Davis was taken by surprise. What treatment of Bessie Walker? Who was she? He hadn't even seen her name before. Was this the secret he was looking for? He scanned back through the pages, all the way to the death of Noel Marney. There was no mention of Bessie Walker or how she had been treated.

His search was interrupted by Krystal. 'I need a hand.'

'What is it?'

'William Goldstone Heartwood. Found a trunk full of his papers in the attic. Too awkward for me to carry down on my own.'

'Shit. Really?'

'All sorts of stuff. Letters, photo albums, memorabilia. His degree. Surveys. Share certificates. It's a historian's wet dream.'

'Show me the way.'

'And your mates called. Craven and Otto. They need a third for waterskiing.'

chapter forty-two

THEY WORK INTO THE NIGHT, THE LURE OF IMMINENT SUCCESS DRIVING THEM
on, the sense of momentum, of purpose, of justice. There is no
fatigue now, no struggle to stay awake. They've hit the pivot and
gone past it: Ivan is no longer driving the investigation; it's driving
him. McTosh has called in his entire team, despite the late hour.
The detectives from Dubbo, the uniformed officers of Yuwonderie
and the technical experts from Sydney are united. They have their
man; now all they have to do is prove it.

Toxteth McGrath is in the holding cell, under arrest; Ivan gets
him hauled into an interview room, two burly locals doing the
honours, Nell supervising with arms crossed and a superior smile.
McGrath is kept awkwardly cuffed, his injured arm in a sling.

'You'll wear this,' he mutters darkly as Ivan and Nell enter.
'Police brutality.'

Nell scoffs. 'You resisted arrest, you assaulted a police officer,
you were attempting to escape custody.'

'Prove it.'

'There are two CCTV cameras in the pokies room,' says Ivan. 'Both working. Both recording.' What he doesn't relay is the glee with which the barmaid made them copies. The USB drive is in the evidence locker, the vision uploaded onto the police network.

'Makes good watching,' says Nell. 'We can release the vision, if you want to mount a public defence.'

There is no comprehensible response, just a grunt, and Ivan knows why: the hard man isn't keen to have the world see his head being put through the front of a poker machine by a young woman half his size.

Ivan lays down the ground rules. 'We're giving you a chance here. Confess and it will be noted. Demonstrate remorse and it will be noted. Bullshit us and it will be noted.'

Toxic glares, all pent-up anger, a bag of resentment and grievance and bile. If there's any decency in there, Ivan can't see it. 'A lawyer,' says the hard man. 'Not a word without a lawyer.'

'Anyone in mind?' taunts Ivan. 'You want us to call them?'

'On their way, mate. You won't know what hit you.'

'Is that it?'

'Not another word.'

Ivan pulls out a plastic evidence bag stuffed full of cash. More than two thousand dollars, found on Toxic when they arrested him. 'Want to tell us where you got this from?'

The man says nothing, but can't help stealing a glance at the money.

'Take a good look, pal. It'll be the last time you ever see it unless you start talking.'

But Toxic McGrath just shakes his head.

They return him to his holding cell.

Back upstairs in the detectives room, Kevin is waiting. 'Sorry about this, but the phone tracking is useless.'

'Really?'

'No triangulation. Whole district covered by one tower on top of the Castle. All I can do is confirm he was in the district at the relevant times.'

'Press hard,' says Ivan. 'He wasn't working alone. He might have wielded the knife, but he was acting at someone's behest.'

A phone call. It's Feral Phelan, and Ivan instantly becomes defensive.

'A heads-up,' says Feral. 'All sorts of shit is coming down the line. I'm starting to get a lot of pressure.'

'Shit from where?'

'From on high. Wanted to warn you.'

Ivan feels wrong-footed, disorientated by Phelan's assistance. 'Why?'

'So I don't get left to clean up the mess.'

Ivan doesn't know what to say. 'Thanks,' is the best he can summon.

'Everything by the book,' advises Phelan, 'or they'll have me on to you.'

Ivan is still processing that message when his mobile lights up again. Plodder Packenham. 'Boss.'

'Ivan, what's happening?'

'Just arrested a man for murder. I was about to call you.'

'Yes. Toxteth McGrath. Nasty piece of work.'

As always, it seems his superior is ahead of him.

'Carole Nguyen is at his welding shop,' says Ivan. 'Looking for evidence to tie him to Athol Hasluck's murder and the attack on Alice Figtree.'

'Sterling work,' says Plodder. 'But that's not the reason I'm calling. Don't want you getting blindsided.'

'What is it?'

'Martin Scarsden. The journo. Remember him?'

'How could I forget?' Leaking information to Scarsden was how Ivan had ended up banished to Dubbo in the first place.

'Just had a call from him. You know the sort: a reporter rings at the last possible moment for a comment, when they've already written the article and are about to publish. So they can say they have sought both sides of the story.'

'What story?'

'Athol Hasluck. Alice Figtree.'

'Shit. I haven't said a word to him.'

'I know. But you should. Call him, Ivan.'

Ivan pauses. It's like the world is playing tricks on him: first Phelan, now Plodder. 'Really?'

'Yes. Tell him you have Toxteth. See if you can find out what he knows.'

'Didn't he tell you?'

'No.'

'How could he ask you for a comment then?'

'Cagey bugger. Do your best.'

Ivan calls Martin Scarsden; the journalist's number is still in his phone's contact list.

'You've got a gall,' says the reporter, answering after the second ring, anger in his voice.

'*I've* got a gall?' retorts Ivan. 'You're running a story on my case and you don't even pay me the courtesy of telling me.'

'Don't give me that shit.'

Now Ivan is confused as well as offended. He reels it back. 'What is it, Martin? What's got up your nose?'

'You don't know?'

'I didn't even know you were writing a story until five minutes ago, when Plodder Packenham told me.'

'Seriously?'

'What's going on?'

'We're copping it from all sides. Threats of defamation, threats of contempt. We're being injuncted in the Supreme Court.'

Ivan looks at his watch. 'At midnight?'

'Tell me about it.'

'Who by?'

'That's it: we don't know. Bunch of lawyers in very expensive suits. It's not you lot, is it?'

'The police? No way. You'd recognise the lawyers.'

'Well, someone's trying to stop us.'

'Any ideas?' asks Ivan.

'Best guess would be Otto Titchfield. For a so-called independent, he sure has a lot of sway with the government.'

'So what's the story? The one you can't publish?'

Silence. The reporter considering his options. 'What do I get in return?'

'I've just arrested someone. We'll charge him first thing with the murder of Athol Hasluck.'

'Shit. Congratulations. Who is it?'

'You don't know?'

'No.'

'So what's the story you're running if not that?'

Silence.

'I'll give you the perp's name, everything I can,' says Ivan. 'An exclusive. Won't talk to your competitors.'

'Okay,' says Scarsden. 'But I can't hold the story. If we beat the injunction, we'll have to publish before the lawyers close us down again.'

'Understood.'

'Our story is that the murder of Athol Hasluck and the attempted murder of Alice Figtree are linked.'

'No shit. That all you got?'

'Let me finish. The story is that the murder of Athol Hasluck and the attack on Alice Figtree are linked to the murder of Davis Heartwood and the disappearance of Stella Kippax thirty years ago.'

For a beat, Ivan is lost for words. But only for a beat. 'Who told you that?'

'Sources.'

'Give me a break.'

'Sorry, can't say.'

'Fuck, Martin. Don't jeopardise our investigation.'

'We can't hold it or we'll cop another injunction.'

'Okay. Here's the offer,' says Ivan. 'I give you everything on this killer we have in custody. Bloke called Toxteth McGrath. Known locally as Toxic McGrath. You can publish that, and we'll stonewall the rest of the media. Your exclusive. And another story for tomorrow. A beauty. One you'll love. Then, by the day after tomorrow, if we haven't got what we need, you're free to go.'

'What other story?'

'Toxic isn't the only bloke I've arrested today. You remember Harley Snouch?'

There's a sharp intake of breath, and Ivan can only smile. Snouch is technically the journalist's father-in-law. And he knows that Scarsden hates him.

'He's in your cell?'

'And, mate, the story. What a screamer. He's been running one of the most audacious stings in the history of Australia. Or anywhere. Fleeced scores of life savings, more than ten million dollars. Was within days of getting away with it. There's a book in it. A movie. And it could be all yours.'

There's a long silence. It seems to go on forever.

'Okay, deal,' says Scarsden. 'We run the Toxteth McGrath story asap. Online—it's too late for the paper. And then tomorrow, while everyone is busy chasing our tail, I'll write up Snouch for Saturday's paper. Front page. And we hold the exclusive linking Hasluck and Figtree to Heartwood and Kippax until Sunday or Monday.'

'Thanks, Martin. I'll see you get everything you need. But tell me, what's the link with Davis Heartwood and Stella Kippax?'

Scarsden sounds sincere when he responds. 'I still can't tell you. It's not me: it's my sources. I promised them. Nothing until it goes to print.'

After the call, Ivan fills in Nell and Kevin, explains the rationale, the concerns of Plodder and Phelan, the deal he's struck with Scarsden, the journalist's assertion that the recent violence is linked back to Davis Heartwood and Stella Kippax.

'What connection?' asks Kevin. 'I've been through that file. So has Nell.'

'Scarsden has found one, that's all that matters now,' says Ivan. 'And where Scarsden goes, the others will follow. We'll get flooded with media. And because of that, our investigation will instantly become massively important to the brass and the pollies. All eyes will be on us, and they'll be pressuring Plodder and Feral Phelan. Plodder we can trust; Phelan we can't. We need to work quickly, get to whoever is pulling Toxteth's strings.'

Nell just shakes her head as if in disbelief.

He calls Plodder Packenham, tells him what he knows, tells him what he's done.

chapter forty-three

December 1915

Oh Mumma,

Jack is dead. Jack is dead. My eyes are rivers and yet they can't drain the quagmire of my grief. He is dead. Killed in the war to end all wars. My dreams are shredded, our hopes destroyed. Only Joey, innocent and oblivious, gives me reason to raise myself from my bed.

The telegram came, and it was not even addressed to me. An insult delivered without knowledge is worse than an insult delivered with spite. The unknowing callousness of it, the impersonal wreckage. The language impersonal, the same words used in ten thousand telegrams. It said nothing of him, his soul, this brave knight.

I had started the preparations for Christmas, bringing a casuarina sapling up from Corkhills, the nearest approximation I could find to a pine hereabouts. And now it stands in the corner, undecorated. It will be Joseph's first Christmas, and what a bleak gift it is that the world has given him.

But that is not the worst of it. For the telegram has come, but the will has gone. Jack's will, the one bequeathing the land to me, and through me to Joey, to be held in trust for him by me until his majority. It is beyond comprehension. Horace arrived with a lawyer, this McLean, all fob watch and waistcoat, full of bluster. He looked me straight in the eye, claimed he had never received the will from Jack, that it was most likely an error in the mail, that such things were commonplace in times of war. His face was hard as he said it, not a glimmer of sympathy or understanding. Was that the true man I saw, or had he steeled himself in preparation for our meeting? For then he told me that the previous will, the one bequeathing me the cottage by Corkhills Creek, was somehow not properly formed. He used legalistic words, so that I struggled to comprehend them; he made no attempt to put them in plain English. He then expressed his sympathies and his condolences with the same utter lack of emotion, all politeness and propriety, and departed. He didn't even do me the courtesy of explaining the implications. He simply took his leave, and it was left to Horace to explain.

He said he will journey to Sydney on my behalf, to plead my case with Maybelle, to learn if she is in any state to comprehend the situation. I asked him why—why this was necessary. And he explained to me what the lawyer should have done: that in the absence of a legally binding will, the law dictated that Maybelle should inherit, that the law saw her as Jack's widow.

I do think him a good man at heart. His obsession is with the irrigation scheme, of course, and no doubt he sees the deaths of Noel and Jack as an impediment, given how strongly the brothers championed its development. I made sure that Horace knew of my ongoing commitment before he departed, knew that I wanted

Joseph to prosper from the work of his father and his uncle, that he might live to see their dreams come to fruition. Who knows what Horace might do to secure its future, but in this matter, knowing my enduring support for it, I am sure he will do his best. I wrote him a letter, authorising him to act on my behalf.

I have no idea of Maybelle's state of mind, whether she has the faculty to understand what it is that Horace will put before her, if she will ever be rid of her demons and be able to return to civil life. I suggested that, if so, she might have the cottage. After all, Jack originally restored it for her, so perhaps she would be happy there, or perhaps the memories are too painful. I left the idea with Horace.

They do not bring the bodies back, Mother. I did not realise. They bury them where they fall. Horace told me Jack would have full military honours, be laid to rest alongside his comrades; that they would march through Heaven's gates in unison, into glory. It was a comforting vision, but now Horace has gone and I am an empty vessel, with only Joseph to give me purpose and fill my days.

The newspaper tells me that they have left Gallipoli now, that they've abandoned it to the Turks. They report that not a life was lost in the evacuation, as if this in itself is some sort of victory. Not for those left behind, not for those bereaved at home.

I am sorry to burden you with such news at this time, but I thought it better that you heard it from me than through some wandering cousin. I hope the new medicine is working as it should and that you are feeling somewhat better. Do have a happy Christmas, despite everything.

Your loving daughter,
Bessie

chapter forty-four

IT'S ALMOST TWO BY THE TIME IVAN GETS TO BED AND, UTTERLY SPENT, HE falls into a sleep too deep for dreaming. And yet he still wakes before seven; there is too much happening and he can't afford to miss any of it. Five hours sleep. It will have to be enough. He wanders into the bathroom, splashes water on his face, drinks water even as he craves coffee. He gets his phone, checks the *Sydney Morning Herald*'s app.

POLITICAL LINKS IN YUWONDERIE MURDER
By Martin Scarsden
Police have achieved a major breakthrough, arresting a man in connection to the murder of Riverina accountant Athol Hasluck in the irrigation town of Yuwonderie in the state's south.

Toxteth Thomas McGrath is expected to be charged later today for his part in the knifing murder of Mr Hasluck last Saturday.

Mr Hasluck's body was found dumped in an irrigation canal on the property of state MP and leader of the Country First party, Otto Titchfield.

Police are expected to allege Mr McGrath drugged, electrocuted and knifed his victim before driving the body to Mr Titchfield's property and dumping it in a canal.

It remains unclear why the alleged killer dumped the body there, and at this stage the *Herald* is unaware of any allegation of wrongdoing by Mr Titchfield . . .

Ivan reads on, feeling a sense of relief. Scarsden has honoured their deal. The rest of the article appears to be filler, containing nothing new, reporting the fire at the accountancy practice and Alice Figtree fighting for her life in Canberra Hospital. Until the last line.

Beginning Monday: 'Crime in the Canals'—a major Martin Scarsden investigation.

That puts Ivan on edge; he can imagine rival media companies tolling up, preparing to send their own reporters to Yuwonderie. What is it that Scarsden uncovered? He knows the journalist won't tell him; reporters never do. What is the link between the contemporary case and the murder of Davis Heartwood and disappearance of his girlfriend Stella Kippax? How has Scarsden found a connection, while Ivan and his team, based here on the ground in Yuwonderie, have not? One thing he does know: Scarsden has a good track record. And he doesn't make things up.

Ivan showers, gets dressed, walks towards the police station along Titchfield Street. The town is starting to irritate him. It's too neat, too perfect, the buildings too well maintained, the lawn on the nature strips always mown to a regulation height, the palm trees on Commonwealth Way evenly spaced, all a uniform size. Like a movie set, an invented reality with the same Christmas decorations found from one end of the town to the other, erected by some central committee rather than individual businesses. He misses the haphazard nature of regular towns, with their vacant blocks and empty buildings, their potholed streets and their hodgepodge pubs, their war memorials and stray dogs and absence of self-congratulatory plaques. Where the homeless aren't kept out of sight in back alleys.

He stops by the Lone Dog Café and picks up a coffee. Even the quality of his flat white is unreasonably good, more Lygon Street than black stump. Maybe it's not the town that irks him: maybe it's the knowledge it will soon be crawling with media, come not to laud him and his team for catching a killer but to position themselves for whatever bombshell Scarsden is about to splash all over the *Sydney Morning Herald*. At best, Ivan has a day and a half to beat him to it.

At the station, he reviews the reports on Davis Heartwood's death. For the life of him, he can't see the relevance. There are no obvious similarities. Davis's body was found fifteen years after he disappeared, buried in a shallow grave. The cause of death was evident: two bullets to the head, one in the side, one in the back, execution-style. By contrast, Athol Hasluck was drugged and tortured, stabbed and electrocuted, his body left where Toxic McGrath knew it would be found.

He tries calling Scarsden, unsure what he wants to say, but the phone rings out. Too early in the day for a journalist.

Nell arrives, handing him a second coffee. 'You look ordinary,' she says.

'Thanks,' he says.

'Big day.'

'Let's hope so.'

— —

At nine they enter the interview room to find Toxic McGrath seated beside a petite young woman with thick blonde hair, a severe fringe cut at eyebrow level giving it the appearance of a battle helmet. McGrath's solicitor. She looks too young for the job, until she stands and locks eyes with Ivan. He's been told that his gaze can be unnerving; now he's on the receiving end. There's a confidence about her, a self-possession, the sort that comes with experience. He's the first to break eye contact. Her clothes are expensive, her watch understated, but not so much as to ever be mistaken for cheap. And when she smiles at Ivan he can see the fine lines around her mouth and eyes, suggesting her apparent youth might have taken a sizeable chunk out of her credit card. 'Ilsa Jones,' she says. 'Representing Mr McGrath.'

Ivan introduces himself and Nell. 'Which firm, Ms Jones?'

'Halleson Parkes Cummins.' She rolls the name off her tongue as if the words themselves are an intimidation.

And they are. HPC. Sydney-based, big end of town. Commercial as well as criminal.

'That was quick,' he says, wondering how she could have travelled here so early in the day.

'Chartered plane?' asks Nell, obviously thinking along the same lines.

'Private jet,' says Jones, taking her seat. 'Shall we commence?'

Beside her, Toxic McGrath is grinning like a loon, like he's won the lottery or something, as if the Aztec god jackpot has found its way into his pocket after all. But his head is still as rough as ever, his teeth yellow and intermittent, his wayward eye as bloodshot as its mate. He's a man who's spent too much time in the sun or too much time in the front bar, his skin a tapestry woven from broken capillaries. His left hand has a new bandage.

Nell starts the video recorder; Ivan goes through the formalities. Then, before he can speak, Ilsa asserts herself. 'For clarification, my client is under arrest but has not yet been charged. Is that correct?'

'It is, Ms Jones. He will be formally charged later this morning with a number of offences: resisting arrest, assaulting a police officer, damage to private property.'

'We will be applying for bail.'

'As is your right.'

'And will you be opposing it?'

'We will present our position to the magistrate,' says Ivan. 'Now, as this is a police interview, perhaps the police might ask some questions?'

Ilsa Jones smiles. Her teeth are perfect: symmetrical, glowing and unblemished. They remind Ivan of the buildings along Commonwealth Way.

'Mr McGrath, where were you on the evening of last Saturday?' he asks.

'Excuse me?' interjects his solicitor. 'How can that be relevant to the charges you just outlined, concerning an alleged altercation last night?'

Ivan sighs. Ilsa has an impressive smile and an irritating manner. 'We are homicide detectives, Ms Jones. We investigate murders.'

'That was not made clear—'

Nell speaks over her. 'Well, it's clear now. And if you didn't know it already, why have you flown here on a private jet to represent a man facing low-grade assault charges?'

Ilsa's smile has been replaced with steel. 'I am not the one under examination here, and my client is entitled to legal representation.'

'Who's paying your bill?'

Ilsa frowns. 'I am under no obligation to reveal that.'

'You don't know,' says Nell.

The solicitor offers a faux smile that comes about as close to her eyes as Hobart is to the equator.

'Shall we continue?' Ivan asks the lawyer, before returning his attention to Toxic. 'Where were you between ten pm and two am on the night Athol Hasluck died?'

'Probably at the pub. Then home.'

'We'll check CCTV, track your phone. You know that, don't you?'

The question is designed to put pressure on Toxteth, but it has no apparent effect. 'Go for your life,' he says with a knowing smirk.

'Nasty burn,' says Nell. 'On your hand,' she adds, for the record.

'Who said it was burnt?' says Toxteth.

'The doctor who patched you up at the hospital,' says Nell.

Ilsa Jones shifts in her seat.

'On the hot plate. At home.'

'Do a lot of cooking then?' asks Nell. 'Vindaloo? Croquembouche?'

Toxteth sneers; he doesn't like being mocked, not by a girl, not by a girl who put his head through a poker machine and dislocated his arm. 'Bitch,' he spits.

'Hot plates leave a pretty distinctive burn,' says Nell. 'A searing. Want to show us?'

Toxteth says nothing. Nell lets it go.

'Speaking of fires,' says Ivan, 'where were you on Wednesday night, around midnight?'

'You tell me.'

'Answer the question,' says Ivan. 'Where were you?'

'Griffith.'

'You sure?'

'Positive.'

Nell again, tag teaming. 'That's interesting, because we have images of you on CCTV in close proximity to Athol Hasluck's practice.'

'Bullshit.'

'What were you doing in Griffith?' asks Ivan.

'Playing cards. At the club there. Monthly game.' He offers an ugly leer. 'That's where I won the money you bastards stole from me.'

'Like gambling, do you?' asks Ivan.

Toxic stares right back at him. 'Yeah. I do. And unlike you, I'm good at it.'

'That's right,' says Ivan. 'You hit the jackpot last night.'

It's a good comeback, but Toxteth's comment has sowed a seed of doubt in Ivan's mind: how does this thug know about his gambling problem?

Nell jumps in again. 'We'll need the names of those you were playing cards with in Griffith.'

'Not a problem.'

The interview lasts another forty minutes, but at its completion Toxic is still smiling and Ilsa Jones is still looking bulletproof.

Afterwards, Ivan and Nell review the interview upstairs.

'You look worried,' says Nell.

'Too right, I'm worried,' says Ivan. 'High-powered lawyer, down on a private jet. That's money and clout.'

'The Seven?'

'Could be. And playing cards in Griffith? Too tight. Someone will have driven his phone there, witnesses signed up.'

'So the arson: premeditated?'

'I'd say so.' Ivan rubs at his neck, feels the tension there. 'The alibi. The lawyer. McGrath wasn't working alone. I reckon he's just a pawn.'

'But the CCTV looks like him—the large man.'

'Too blurry. It's not definitive. Not against the sworn statement of three or four witnesses in Griffith.'

'Can we charge him?' asks Nell.

Ivan thinks ruefully of Martin Scarsden's article. 'Not with murder. Not yet.'

'But we can charge him with the assault last night, hold him on that.'

'Unless the magistrate bails him.'

'Surely not. Not if we set out the murder investigation.'

Ivan shakes his head. 'He's got a very capable lawyer. And I suspect he won't have any trouble posting bail, no matter how high the amount.'

'Does it matter?'

'I reckon if he gets bailed, we'll never see him again.'

'Can we argue that to the magistrate? Flight risk?'

'We can try.'

'Shit.' Nell casts about, as if looking for an answer. 'Is there nothing else we can hold him on?'

Ivan gestures his frustration. 'Not unless Carole can find something incriminating at his workshop.'

'I'll see if there's anything in the system. Any intel. Bloke like that's going to have a past. What about you?'

'Hospital. I'll have another crack at Snouch.'

'He's downstairs. In the cells.'

'Even better.' Ivan massages his neck again. 'Let's not charge McGrath this morning. Hold him until this afternoon. See if you can move the magistrate back until as near to close of business as you can get. See if there is anything in his past that we can use to keep him in custody.'

—— ——

Ivan decides to talk to Snouch in his cell, not the interview room, explaining it's off the record. 'I'm worried about you, Harley.'

'I'm touched. Last time we spoke you threatened to frame me for murder. Or have you forgotten that?'

'It's not me you have to worry about.'

'Tell me something I don't know.'

'I've arrested the bloke who bashed you. Toxteth McGrath, known as Toxic. A real charmer. I have a witness.'

Snouch frowns. 'He was wearing a balaclava.'

Eggs hadn't made any reference to Toxteth wearing a balaclava or a ski mask. Why is Snouch protecting him? 'He's in the cell next door. The bloke who planted the knife. The bloke who's going to try to shift the blame on to you. I won't have to frame you for murder; he'll do it for me.'

Snouch remains silent, the muscle in his jaw tight and flexing, as if he's willing his mouth to stay shut.

'He's just the hired muscle, Harley. Working for someone.'

Snouch says nothing, the muscles in his jaw flexing once more. He breaks eye contact, stares down at the table.

Ivan pushes hard. 'Sooner or later, we're going to work out who it was, and they'll suspect someone ratted them out. So this is your chance. You tell us; we'll spread the word that it was Toxic who talked. Otherwise, they'll think it was you.' Ivan gives it a beat, sees that his words are penetrating. 'Last chance, Harley. Tell me now or you're dog meat.'

But Snouch is shaking his head. 'No. I'm going to jail. I know that. But I'm still not talking. Because if I do, one day, when I'm minding my own business, someone I won't even see will slide up behind me and shiv me in the guts. That's how it ends. My only chance is if McGrath and me both refuse to talk. Otherwise we're both for the high jump. Here's hoping he's smart enough to work that out. You don't mess with these people.'

And Ivan sees something in the man's eyes he never expected. Fear. 'What people, Harley?'

'You work it out, genius.'

The hairs on Ivan's neck start to rise. It can't be the Seven. Not Otto Titchfield, for all his political sway. Snouch isn't scared of them; just the opposite. He set up in Yuwonderie precisely because he believed them ripe for the picking. And Ivan thinks of Davis Heartwood, executed, mafia-style. And he thinks of

Ilsa Jones, flying in on a private jet. And he thinks of Martin Scarsden, finding a link between murders thirty years apart.

'Why haven't they killed you yet?' he whispers, but Snouch turns away. He's said enough.

Ivan leaves the cell. He texts Martin Scarsden. *Ilsa Jones from Halleson Parkes Cummins. Who's paying her bills?* And then, after a deep breath: *Is my team in danger?*

Next, he rings Plodder Packenham and asks the same question.

chapter forty-five

1994

DAVIS DIDN'T MUCH FEEL LIKE WATERSKIING. HE WOULD HAVE PREFERRED TO stay in the library at Three Wells Station, delving into his great-great-grandfather's diaries and rummaging through the trunk of documents Krystal had discovered in the attic. But he felt he owed his friends an explanation. Word was out, he knew that. His grandfather had been summoned to the Canal Club, his last will and testament openly discussed. By now, the news would have spread across the district.

Davis rang Stella, told her he was heading to Castle View to see his mates, suggested she should come along, that afterwards they could all go to the Coachman's Arms to celebrate his decision. She agreed. Davis hoped his friends would see Krystal's inheritance that way: as something to be celebrated. Nevertheless, he felt some trepidation as he edged the Alfa gently through the open gate and along the canal-side track. The surface was smoother than last time; Otto must have put a grader over it. It would enable the truck to go faster, and the skiing would be all the more exhilarating. It was a good idea, Davis thought.

The others were waiting. Otto and Craven and, Davis was a little surprised to see, Lucy. He was glad she was there. With Stella coming, the reconfiguration of the group's relationships could be confirmed. They could all go to the pub together, reconcile, and he could take them through his decision to step aside from Three Wells Station in favour of his sister.

The first inkling he had that something was wrong was when he stepped from his car, dressed in board shorts, sandals and a t-shirt. Otto was in jeans, a cotton shirt and riding boots; Craven was still in his office clothes. Lucy was leaning on Otto's truck wearing a summer dress and a hard-faced scowl.

'Hey, guys,' said Davis. 'We doing this?'

'Hey, buddy,' said Otto. He walked over to Davis and punched him in the stomach, catching him completely by surprise. Davis collapsed to the ground, winded, straining for breath.

'That's for the B&S,' said Otto, leaning over him. 'Cunt.' He spat, not at Davis but into the dirt beside him.

From his position on the ground, Davis could only stare up at Otto towering over him. He could see Craven, head down, clearly uncomfortable, and Lucy frowning but meeting his gaze.

Otto kicked him in the ribs, the pain a searing edge. 'And that's for everything else.'

'What?' Davis managed, a wheeze more than a word.

'What the fuck do you think?' said Otto. 'Craven is meant to be your friend. You ever think of him?'

'What?' Davis managed again, the single word painful to utter.

'Your mate, fuck face. You're not the only one with a big sister.'

Davis looked at Craven, saw the hurt in his eyes. His sister, two years older. Agatha Allsop. 'Not my fault,' he gasped.

'Of course it's your fault,' said Otto. 'You want to blow the whole show up.' And here he stole a glance at Lucy, who looked at him then back to Davis, her eyebrows raised as if challenging him to deny it. 'The scheme relies on unity. The Seven's unity, our unity, for seventy years—and you want to piss all over that heritage. And for what? A shitty little piece of paper from a shitty little university.'

'I want nothing more than Yuwonderie to prosper,' said Davis, breath back, but still on the ground. 'My family is just as committed to it as yours; our fate hangs on it just as much as yours.'

'Oh, fuck off. We both know that's not true. The Heartwoods own more land outside the scheme than in it.'

'You should have told me,' said Craven, speaking for the first time, his voice filled more with sorrow than anger. 'Agatha wants the lot.'

Davis shook his head. 'Your grandparents are still alive. Your parents. It's all in the distant future.'

'Easy for you to say,' said Otto, shaping to land another blow, Davis raising his arms defensively. Otto backed off, laughing. 'Not so brave now.'

Davis turned to Craven. 'I'm sorry. I am. I wanted to tell you, but my grandfather said we should keep it under wraps until we were sure we wanted to go through with it.'

'You still could have talked it over with us, trusted us,' said Craven. 'We would have understood. We all carry the same expectations.' And then he looked to the ground. 'Or we did.'

'If you want to do us a favour, you should just fuck off,' said Otto. 'Drop your stupid research project and do something else. Give her half a chance.' He spat into the dirt again. ''Cos as of now, you've got none.'

Davis had had enough. He wasn't just about to walk off, tail between his legs. He hadn't been raised to be a victim. He eased up onto his knees and, when he saw Otto wasn't about to hit him again, onto his feet. 'What's it to you, Otto?' he said. 'You're the only son.'

'Don't you ever listen, you dumb cunt? This whole structure, it's the Seven. Together. Always has been, always will be. Don't expect you can fuck over Craven and me, and we'll think nothing of it.' He stepped forward again, then lowered his fist. 'I would never betray my friends.' And this time there was a sadness to his voice. He must have heard it too, and immediately tried to cover it. He strode across to Davis's Alfa, wrenched the keys out of the ignition where Davis had left them. 'Glad you've got your boardies on,' he said, and threw the keys into the canal. 'Have a nice swim. We're off to the pub.'

And Davis was left to watch them go: Otto with his chest puffed out, like some cowboy from a movie, dispensing rough justice, vindicated and righteous; Craven, face creased with a kind of despair but following all the same; and Lucy, with a smirk on her lips and flint in her eyes.

As he watched the truck head back to the highway, Davis started to cry. Otto was a bully and an oaf, Craven was weak and vacillating, but they had been his friends for as long as he could remember, united by a common destiny. And however wrong and unjust their reaction, he couldn't escape the fact: he was the one who had broken their bond.

That's how Stella found him when she drove up a few minutes later in her ancient Corolla: covered in dust, nose bleeding, tears on his cheeks. She said nothing, just leant in and held him. He laid his head on her shoulder and gave a last sob. 'I fucked it up,' he said.

'I doubt that,' she said softly. 'C'mon. Let's go to the lake. Swim out to the pontoon. Wash off all the dirt and misery.'

'My keys,' he said. 'Otto chucked them in the canal.'

Stella stood and examined the waterway, brown and still. 'Muddy as hell. You got a spare set?'

'At home.'

'Let's go get them. Then we can have that swim.'

chapter forty-six

BACK UPSTAIRS, AND IVAN GOES STRAIGHT TO KEVIN.

'What are you up to?'

'Telephone tracking, warrant applications, preparing the charges for the magistrate.'

'When are we scheduled?'

'Four this afternoon.'

'Do we have any access to Harley Snouch's files yet?'

'No. Carole had a closer look, reckons it could take experts days or weeks to crack it.'

Ivan waves Nell over, so the three of them are together at Kevin's desk. 'I just spoke to Snouch. He intimated very nasty people are involved. Probably the people who ordered the killing of Athol Hasluck and attacked Alice. He must have had some dealings with them.'

'What are you thinking?' asks Nell.

Ivan takes a breath; saying it out loud makes it real. 'The Calabrian mafia. The 'Ndrangheta. They've always had strong links to Griffith, ever since the days of Robert Trimbole and Donald

Mackay.' He takes another breath, sees the understanding and apprehension in their eyes.

'Toxteth McGrath,' says Nell. 'His alibi for the night of the fire. In Griffith, playing cards at a social club.'

Kevin is doubtful. 'He doesn't look like mafia to me.'

'No. Just local muscle,' says Ivan. 'But that lawyer, Ilsa Jones, down from Sydney on a private jet—he's not paying her bills, that's for sure.'

'Can we turn him?' asks Nell. 'Offer him some inducement?'

Ivan shakes his head. 'He and Snouch both know informing would be a death sentence. I reckon that's Ilsa's real mission down here: not to defend them but to threaten them.'

'There is one thing . . .' Kevin trails off, but both Ivan and Nell have swivelled, eyes upon him.

'What?' they demand in unison.

'Athol's accounts. You said he tried and failed to get back his investment from Snouch, right?'

'Correct.'

'Well, someone got their money back. There's a deposit into the trust account from Air Stills.'

'You sure?'

Kevin turns to his monitor, opens up a spreadsheet. 'The trust account. Money flowing in from investors, flowing out into investments. A lot to Air Stills; a lot to this company, RWT Holdings. But look here: the flow to Air Stills is reversed.'

Ivan and Nell lean in. There are two payments from Air Stills to the trust account: the first for $200,000, the second for $150,000. Both were made in the week before Athol Hasluck died.

'And look here.' Kevin scrolls back through the accounts. 'A deposit from RWT Holdings for two hundred thousand dollars six months ago, and another hundred thousand a fortnight ago, followed shortly after by money flowing to Air Stills, minus the five per cent commission.' He looks to Ivan and smiles. 'Three hundred thousand invested, three hundred and fifty thousand withdrawn. They extracted a premium from Snouch.'

'They discovered it was a scam,' says Ivan, thinking out loud.

'Looks like it.'

'Who is RWT Holdings?' asks Nell.

'Riverina Water Traders,' says Kevin.

Ivan stares, blinks. 'Craven Allsop.'

Before Ivan can say anything more, Nell's phone rings and, almost immediately, Ivan's own handset starts vibrating. He checks the screen, then takes the call. It's Carole Nguyen.

'I think this is it,' she says, and Ivan can hear the exhilaration in her voice. 'McGrath's welding workshop. There are arc welding electrodes. Explains the burns on Athol's body. I think I've found where he was tied up. Traces of blood, buckets of bleach used, recently and liberally, but with that much blood it's hard to eliminate it all. Plus we've found the cable that might have electrocuted him.'

Ivan feels the thrill of the pieces coming together. 'Tortured there. Murdered there. Body dumped in the canal.'

'It all fits. We're impounding McGrath's work truck, seeing if he used it to move the body. Also, you need to check his employment record. See if he ever worked in an abattoir. He's got some of the gear. Mesh gauntlet, knives, whetstones.'

'Any knives missing? Any knives that might be the murder weapon?'

'Yes. Blake is here. He reckons the one planted up on the hill might have come from here. One of a set.'

'You're a champion, Carole. Get us a summary of what you've found to put before the magistrate.'

'One more thing. I found it sitting on top of a toolbox. A receipt, dated Monday. Toxteth McGrath invested ten thousand dollars in Air Stills of Australia.'

'The day after Athol's body was found?'

'Correct.'

Ivan laughs. 'Explains why Toxic bashed Snouch yesterday then. Must have found out it was a con. Went and got his money back, then planted the knife for good measure. Still had some of the cash on him when we arrested him.'

Ivan congratulates the forensics expert once more and ends the call. He turns back to Kevin and Nell, who are staring at him with expectation, and fills them in. 'That's it. We charge Toxic McGrath with murder; we oppose bail. Let's see Ilsa Jones wriggle him out of this one.'

Kevin looks elated, but not Nell. Her eyebrows are weighted with concern, as if she has heard something troubling.

'What is it?' he asks.

'The other call. Canberra. Alice Figtree is doing okay, stabilised after the surgery. Still in intensive care. But they want to give her at least one more day, possibly two, before waking her up.'

'And?'

'And Krystal Heartwood has left the country.'

'What?'

430

'Flew to Norfolk Island from Canberra late yesterday. A three- or four-hour trip. Refuelled. Logged a flight plan to return to Canberra. Took off from Norfolk this morning, didn't arrive.'

Ivan is having trouble assimilating this new information.

'What are you saying? She crashed?'

'Doubt it. Her plane's twin engine, long range. Has the legs to get back to Australia. Or New Caledonia, Vanuatu, Tonga, Fiji, New Zealand. Not just the capitals—remote islands, World War Two airstrips without towers or radar. Without customs and immigration.'

'Shit. She's on the run.'

'Looks like it,' says Nell. 'With all the money and resources of Three Wells Station backing her.'

Ivan looks from one face to another, realising that the investigation has now gone so far past the tipping point that it's not just driving him: he's struggling to keep up. 'Well, let's go get Craven Allsop before he runs too.'

chapter forty-seven

July 1916

My dearest Elaine,

We are at the mission, Joey and me. It is bitterly cold of late, and my mother will not last much longer. They have at least granted her this final kindness, to allow her to die here, to be buried here, before the mission is closed for good and the property sold. They have shut my mother's school, where she taught all these years, imparting her knowledge and her love to her people, equipping them for this new world. But if it saddens me, she seems content at last, at peace. I am glad I made the effort to bring Joey; she absolutely adores him, and his mere presence brightens her day and lightens her load. I still can't believe this may be the last time I see her. We have been welcomed here, but it is clear we can't stay, that we must move on when that terrible day arrives.

It is Joseph's first birthday next week, and what a bittersweet occasion that conspires to. He is starting to walk, and has his first words. He brightens our days, a small beacon signalling the way to a more promising future. I wish you could see him; he is changing and growing so quickly now; every day there is something new.

I am sorry I will not make it to your wedding. I am sure you understand; I need to be here, with my mother. I dare not leave her now. Besides, I am not sure I could control my emotions should I attend. I apologise that I cannot even send you a decent gift, just this token, when you have been so kind: you who have been my voice when no one else stood by us. Douglas Heartwood is a very fine man indeed, educated and gentle and generous of heart. I know you will be happy with him; I will never forget his kindness towards myself and Joseph. He and his brother William were under no obligation to consider our welfare in their land dealings. (I do think William's decision to buy all that unwanted land falling outside the scheme is an astute strategy, to avoid tying your family's fortune too closely with those of the other foundation families.)

I will always be grateful to Douglas for making representations on our behalf and delivering us ownership of the cottage and that little parcel of scrub by Corkhills Creek. It means absolutely everything to me. Jack has gone, and I will never see him again this side of the grave, but whenever I am there, in that little cottage where we were first alone together, where we first discovered each other, I will feel that he is still with me, that his spirit lives on and that he is watching over our son.

I know there have been times when our relationship has been tested, but this news that you and Douglas have been able to secure Jack's cottage for Joseph and myself is confirmation that it will endure. I know that it lies on the 'wrong' side of the Spur, that it can never be irrigated, that it is too small and too dry for cropping and too flood-prone for fencing, but I find comfort in that, in being able to keep it more or less as Jack and I knew it in those few weeks we had together. It will remain bush, in its natural state, when so much of the land will be changed beyond recognition.

Between nursing my mother and attending to Joseph, I have been rugging up and taking long walks by the Murrumbidgee, that wonderful river, trying to reconcile all that has happened to me. I don't blame Maybelle for selling the land. The law is clear; it belonged to her. What can she know of missing wills, of backroom conspiracies and avaricious alliances? I hope the money serves her well and buys her some relief from her affliction. As to those who have purchased it, I do hope they will make the most of it, that the scheme succeeds every bit as much as Noel and Jack and myself intended, if not for them, at least for all the honest people who have subscribed to the dream.

I see Horace has succeeded in being selected to represent the Liberal Party in parliament. How proud of himself he must be. But he need not bother canvassing my vote; he knows I am not yet of voting age, just as I am not yet seen as an adult in the eyes of the law.

I have been making plans as I take my walks along the river. It is not easy, as all futures must necessarily start with the death of my mother. But she is reconciled to it, so I must be stoic. I have been offered a position as a governess up near Cootamundra. A prominent family there, the Goodmans, have heard of my abilities and offered me employment. I am indebted to your mother for providing me with the most marvellous reference. I did not always see eye to eye with her, as you know, but at the end, when I was down on my luck, she saw to it that I might have a future after all—and, more importantly, that Joseph might as well. Most marvellous of all, the

Goodmans will pay me a decent wage. Please don't tell her, but it is significantly more than Mrs Titchfield gave me, and I won't have to clean or cook or wait upon their table. My duties are almost exclusively to care for and educate the children. My plan is to work there until they enter boarding school. I am hoping I might save enough that one day, when Joseph is grown and has entered the world in his own right, I might return to that cottage by Corkhills Creek and start a little school of my own.

I look forward to that day so very much, when you and I might be neighbours once more. The idea fills me with a kind of gratification. You don't know what a joy and relief it is; you gifting me this land, you and Douglas. It proves there are decent people in the world, that not everyone is angling to advance their status and maximise their possessions.

But now I have one last favour to ask of you, and it is a mighty one. Having been visited so often by death these past few months, with Noel and Jack and my mother, I have come to realise that it may come to me much sooner than I could ever imagine. God willing, I will live into my dotage, but for Joseph's sake I must consider that I may not. And so I find myself writing my own will, for I have learnt the bitter lesson of how important such documents can be. I will name Joseph my heir, of course, and he should inherit our cottage by Corkhills Creek and all else that I own. You may recall we once discussed how you might become his godmother? I know this must have been on your mind when you acquired the cottage and Jack's land for me. So please promise me this: that should I die before Joseph attains his majority, you and Douglas will be his guardians, and you will support and house him, cherish and love him, until he can make his own way. Can you find it in your heart to promise me you will fulfil this most important duty?

Forever your friend and servant,
Bessie

chapter forty-eight

THEY TAKE THE FOUR-WHEEL DRIVE TO THE RIVERINA WATER TRADERS, JUST IN
case they need to arrest Craven Allsop. But when they arrive
at the offices on Titchfield Street, they're told he's not in today.
Instead he's at the Wholesalers, wearing his other hat, chairman
of the board.

Ivan drives, negotiating one roundabout then another, dropping down the slope towards the railway line. The Wholesalers
looms before them, a single giant warehouse, the size of a football stadium.

It's fenced off, razor wire and security cameras ostentatious in
their surveillance, floodlights ready to keep the trucks moving
twenty-four seven. There are two entrances: one for trucks, another
for cars, both with boom gates.

Ivan follows a ute up to the car entrance. The driver in front
swipes a pass; the gate opens. When it's Ivan's turn, he presses the
intercom button.

'Help you?' asks a disembodied voice.

Ivan holds his badge up to the camera lens above the intercom button. 'Detective Sergeant Ivan Lucic and Detective Constable Narelle Buchanan.'

'Right you are,' says the voice. 'Come through. Follow the markings to the right, travel counterclockwise. Come to security, park right outside. I'll meet you there.'

Ivan says thanks, and the barrier tilts up.

Inside the fence, Ivan is reminded of an airport tarmac: an expanse of concrete and bitumen with roads marked in paint. To the left, an entire side of the barn-like building consists of loading docks: produce in, produce out. There must be a good twenty docks.

Around the corner of the building, the security office is unmissable: a demountable, with a two-metre-high yellow-and-black stripe painted around its exterior wall, like oversized police tape, branded with the word SECURITY.

Ivan parks. Out of the car, the heat is overwhelming, the tree-less expanse of pavement baking in the sun. Inside the sliding doors, the air-conditioning roars, creating more noise than relief.

There's a counter, someone making an inquiry, but they don't have to wait. A beefy-looking bloke approaches wearing a white shirt with epaulets. He's big, part Islander, around fifty, sporting a paunch, a buzz cut and a couple of well-worn tats on the biceps protruding from his short-sleeved shirt. His belt supports a gun, a two-way radio, assorted leather pouches and several bunches of keys that wouldn't look out of place in Alcatraz.

'Morning, officers,' he says. 'Merv Morrel. Twenty years, Victorian police.' His handshake is formidable.

'G'day, Merv,' says Ivan, keeping his accent broad and flexing his fingers. 'We appreciate your help. We'd like to see Craven Allsop.'

'The big kahuna, hey? I'm guessing you don't have an appointment?'

'No, but it's urgent.'

'If you say so,' says Merv. 'Strictly speaking, I should ring ahead, get it cleared, but why don't I just walk you over, let you sort it out?'

'Thanks. That's decent of you.'

'Any excuse to get out of the office.'

They follow the big man out the door and into the heat. It's lifting up off the tarmac, somehow more daunting than the sun itself. The air curls and shimmers, curdling the distance. Merv wades through it, like a sumo wrestler in a uniform. He's whistling a jaunty tune, but Ivan can't identify it. Ivan checks out the gun on the guard's belt, a huge thing, some sort of magnum. Perfectly legal for a security guard, but Ivan wonders at the size of it in a place that ships nothing more dangerous than avocadoes and table grapes.

Merv leads them to a door in the warehouse, unmarked and rendered tiny by the scale of the building. He takes a card attached to his belt with an extendable elastic and swipes. He opens the door for them, and they enter a featureless corridor with a cement floor and LED lighting.

'Back way,' says Merv once they are inside. He guides them along further, whistling once more, turning left and arriving at twin lifts. 'Allsop's on the top floor,' he says. 'Always the way, right?' The lift arrives and Merv does the honours, punching the button for the seventh floor.

'Quite the operation,' says Nell, making small talk as the lift rises up and up.

'Goldmine,' says Merv. 'Everything within a hundred-kilometre radius comes through here.'

The lift stops, and Merv holds the door open. They enter a glassed-in space. Through the floor-to-ceiling windows, Ivan can see down across the warehouse operations: derricks and cranes and trucks and sorting bins and conveyor belts, people reduced to Barbie doll dimensions. He guesses he's standing at the top of an administration block contained within the larger structure.

Merv leads them away from the view, swiping them through another security door and into a reception area. There are no windows, but skylights flood the place with light. The air is cool and scented; the air-conditioning is silent.

'Morning, Jenny,' Merv says to a receptionist. 'A couple of detectives here to see Mr Allsop. No appointment.'

Jenny smiles. 'I'll show them through. Paul can help.' And for the benefit of the detectives, she adds, 'That's Mr Allsop's executive assistant.'

'All good,' says Merv. 'Give me a ring when you want me to escort them out.'

Merv heads back the way they came, whistling once more. Ivan looks at Nell and she meets his gaze. He wonders if she's thinking the same as him: the scale of the operation is much larger than he imagined. From the top of the Castle, the Wholesalers had looked large, but not this large. So much money.

Jenny takes them through a glass door into a small meeting area, kitchen and toilets off to one side, then swipes them through a beautifully panelled door into an outer office. There are two unoccupied desks.

'Oh, I'm sorry,' says Jenny. 'I forgot. Paul has the day off. Unusual.'

'How so?' asks Ivan.

'Mr Allsop is only here one day a week.'

'But he's in today?'

'I saw him enter earlier.'

Ivan knocks on Allsop's door, an impressive-looking thing, bearing an inlay reading CHAIRMAN. There is no response.

He tries again, saying to Jenny, 'You sure he's here?'

'I didn't see him leave.'

Nell draws her gun. Ivan does the same, then tries the door, pushes it open, moves through.

Craven Allsop is at his desk, framed by a window overseeing the factory floor. Dead, gun still in his hand, brains spattered across the mahogany.

The receptionist screams.

chapter forty-nine

1994

DAVIS FELT ELATED. THE ARGUMENT WITH OTTO AND CRAVEN STILL SMARTED, but it was completely overshadowed by Stella. They had returned to Three Wells Station in her old Corolla to fetch his spare keys, Krystal concerned at first by his injuries, and then beaming benignly at seeing them together. They'd gone back to the canal, collected his car and driven to Lake Yuwonderie, plunging in, washing off the dirt and the blood. Swimming out to the pontoon. And suddenly kissing. As if it was always meant to be.

Next morning he was back in the library, flushed with emotion and residual hormones, the memory of the evening beside the lake fresh in his mind. After sex, they'd talked, a rambling exchange of thoughts and ideas and emotions, a touching of minds and beliefs, simultaneously an exploration and a synthesis. She had still been offended on his behalf at the aggression of Otto and Craven, but he had said to forget it. It strengthened his resolve; he wanted to leave the town, leave Three Wells Station to Krystal, forge a new reality

442

somewhere far away. And so they had talked about the future. She wanted to leave Yuwonderie, and he had to leave. They might as well go together. She would go to university and he would accompany her.

'I want to work part-time,' she had said. 'I don't want to be dependent on your money.'

'I understand,' he said, 'but it will be cheaper if we're together.'

'Before we go, we should get back at those bastards,' she said.

'What's the point? Let it be.'

This morning she had returned to work at the Wholesalers, while he had the trunk to go through, hauled down from the attic and sitting on the library floor. It was as Krystal had described, a rummage sale of items, the lingering smell of naphthalene and age. Party invitations, postcards and photographs; pennants, sashes and streamers; books, pamphlets and half-a-dozen 78 rpm records. He picked up a photo album, and something fell from its pages. A large print, faded shades of grey. A group of people, well dressed, standing in front of two elegant roadsters, the fashions sturdy and formal, a large house in the background framed by trees. He flipped it over. *Jolimont. Feb 1914.* Davis turned back to the image. Looked again, wondering who was who. Jolimont: the Marneys' homestead. He searched the diary. Sure enough, the meeting at Jolimont, where the seven families, or the nine, or however many were there, had committed to forming the South Murrumbidgee Irrigation Company, the day the scheme moved from being an abstract proposal and the first concrete steps towards reality were taken. Did they have any concept what they were starting?

Davis opened the album: pictures of William Heartwood at school, at Oxford, dressed in ridiculous neck-to-knees by a river, standing with arms folded beside a rowing shell, the men with moustaches, waxed and black, appearing simultaneously old and young. He studied a studio portrait of William, imagined he saw a resemblance to Clemence. Another photo, formal, in another studio, William and Mary in their wedding finery. The images brought them to life. Another wedding: William's youngest brother Douglas, his bride Elaine fair-haired and beaming.

Lifting a leather-bound book from the trunk, he caught sight of a bundle of letters, the envelopes more or less consistent, tied together with a faded ribbon, once red, now mottled pink. Letters. Like a diary, full of words, full of insights. He untied the ribbon, examined the top envelope.

Mrs Elizabeth Walker
Worthington Point Mission
New South Wales

The address caught Davis's attention. A hundred years ago, there had been an Aboriginal mission at Worthington Point. There was a date stamp on the envelope identifying the year: *1912.* He turned it over, and there was the name of the sender.

Miss Bessie Walker
Castle View
Via Narrandera

Bessie Walker. His mind jumped back to William Heartwood's diary, the entry he had read the day before. What had it said? That Augustine Chaulker had been so appalled by the treatment of Bessie Walker that he preferred selling his land to being party to it. To what? Davis held the letter closer. What has he found? He looked again at the address: written from Castle View. The Titchfields' home. And he started to read.

My dearest Mother,
So I have arrived and am found acceptable . . .

Two and a half hours later, having read the last letter, Davis was in tears, sitting on the library floor, mourning the fate of a woman he had never known: Bessie Walker, cheated out of her rightful legacy.

He was still there when Stella came rushing into the library, all alive and excited, sweating from the heat of the day, breathing hard. She stopped at the sight of him. 'What is it? What's wrong?'

Davis held up the letters. 'I know what happened. How they got the land the town is built on. They cheated the rightful owner. Stole it. The McLeans, supported by the Titchfields and Allsops.'

'Right.' Stella's expression was somehow uncertain, but not her voice. Her voice sounded very certain. 'They're still criminals. To this day.'

Davis blinked. 'How do you mean?'

'I went back through those files I told you about. The consignments coming in, going out, with not enough trucks. I double-checked.'

'Wasn't that just some of the Seven trucking direct but running the accounts through the Wholesalers?'

'No.' And now Stella seemed almost beside herself, as if fearful of what she was about to say. 'All the ghost consignments, they're from outside the scheme, not from the Seven at all. From the MIA.'

'Ghost consignments?'

'They're not real, Davis. Don't you see? There's no fruit and vegetables. Only the money is real. Coming into the Wholesalers from the markets in Melbourne, going back to the growers around Griffith, the Wholesalers keeping their commission.'

'Why would they do that?'

'It's money laundering. Organised crime. Think about it. The Italian mafia. Active at the Melbourne markets, active in Griffith. Washing their dirty money up through the Wholesalers, a respectable multimillion-dollar business, then sending it through to the growers. Who then, I assume, return it to the people who sent it from Melbourne in the first place.'

'Holy fuck,' said Davis, the enormity of it dawning on him. 'And the management at the Wholesalers—they know?'

'At some level they must.'

'Jesus, Stella. This is playing with fire.'

'I know,' she said, eyes wide. And then: 'I have documents.'

Davis couldn't believe her. 'You what?'

'Documents. In my car. I took them.' She looked at him, eyes still wide, but now the excitement was being overtaken with fear, with the magnitude of what she had done. 'I didn't know what they were. Only after I went through them.'

'Fuck me. We need to return them. They could kill you.'

——

Fifteen minutes later, they were back at the Wholesalers, driving separate cars, Davis tailing Stella. He watched as her Corolla went through the gates and then he kept driving, not wanting to attract attention, returning to Commonwealth Way and parking outside the Coachman's Arms. His stomach was a churning vat of nerves and fear. There was a ringing in his ears, a tension headache creeping up from his neck. He couldn't believe it. The mafia? How had they got their talons into Yuwonderie? How had the Seven ever allowed it? Enabled it? No one here needed money. The smallholders, maybe, but not the Seven. He thought of the Wholesalers. He knew it had a reputation as highly efficient and highly profitable, paying good returns for shareholders, securing good deals for growers, good enough to attract business from neighbouring schemes like the MIA. Was that how the business kept its high margins and competitive edge? By underpinning itself with tainted money? The implications were enormous. Did his grandfather have some inkling? Was that why Clemence stayed away from the Canal Club? Why the Heartwoods remained outside the irrigation zone, lived at Three Wells Station?

And all the time Davis was thinking, he was staring straight ahead, waiting to catch sight of Stella's Corolla, to know she was safe. He got out of his car, no longer able to sit still, and began to pace, glancing at his watch, checking that it hadn't stopped working, oblivious to the heat of the day.

A friendly-looking man with a nice smile approached him, well dressed in a casual sort of way. Chinos and a short-sleeved shirt and rather elegant shoes. And a small but lethal-looking gun pointing right at Davis's chest.

Davis looked about him. The street looked normal. The town looked normal. Even the man looked normal. Only the gun insisted on imposing a conflicting reality.

'Mr Heartwood?' the man said, voice pleasant and non-confrontational. 'I wonder if you would join us?'

Davis turned. A large car with tinted windows had materialised behind his sports car. A Holden Statesman.

'I'm not sure I want to do that,' he said politely, as if declining a cup of tea.

'A natural response,' said the man, nodding in comprehension, voice like treacle. 'But your girlfriend is inside the car. And it would be better to join her than to be shot down in the street like a dog.' The man's smile didn't reach his eyes.

Again, Davis looked around, desperate now; why wasn't anyone noticing what was happening?

'Get in, please,' said the man. 'We need to establish what you have learnt.' And he smiled his reassuring smile and pressed the barrel of the gun hard against Davis's heart. 'Get in or you both die.'

Davis got in.

The man hadn't lied. Stella was in the back seat, constrained by the seatbelt, tape across her mouth, cable ties holding her wrists together. He could see the panic in her eyes.

There was a burly man in the front seat, tattoos on his arms. Davis recognised him: Lucy Fielder's father. And by the look of hatred in his eyes, the man recognised Davis in return. He smiled, a gap-toothed leer. From the front seat, he levelled a sawn-off shotgun at Davis: a dirty and battered gun, nothing like the well-dressed man's pristine pistol.

'Seatbelt, please,' said the first man, voice still gentle.

Davis clicked the belt on.

'Hands out.'

Davis stared at the shotgun and complied.

The man leant in through the door and locked his wrists together with cable ties, then secured them to the lap belt with two more ties, ensuring Davis couldn't raise his hands. Lucy's father handed the man a roll of tape. Davis shook his head, but it didn't make any difference. The man smiled, apologised, and placed a strip across his mouth.

Then the man closed the door, walked around and got in the driver's seat. He turned and addressed Davis and Stella. 'We will drive out of town. Then we will talk. It is important for me to understand what it is you have discovered. You won't be harmed.' He nodded to Lucy's father, who kept the gun on them.

They drove north. Around the fountain of water and plenty, and out over the town canal.

Davis looked across at Stella, her eyes full of fear and apology and love, and wished he could at least hold her hand or speak a few words of comfort. But all they had was eye contact and words unspoken.

As they left town, the car sped up. The driver lit a cigarette, humming between tokes. The melody soon lost its clarity and became tuneless. Or so it seemed to Davis.

He wondered if they were heading towards Griffith, but as they approached the Murrumbidgee, the driver turned left, tracking the river west. Davis could see the Castle passing to his left. Once they were past, the sedan slowed, turning right as if to cross the river. Lucy's father was leaning forward, searching for a turn-off. There was a sign: CORKHILLS CREEK. 'There,' he said, pointing.

The driver braked, and the car left the highway, turning onto a dirt road. They bounced along a little way, the man slowing to a crawl. This was not a vehicle for bush tracks.

Another turn-off, a smaller track, scrubby trees scratching at the windows. They were on the flood plain now, going so slow they could have walked faster, the car's suspension still bottoming out. It pushed through some tea-trees into a clearing lined with casuarinas.

They stopped. The polite man got out, opened Davis's door. In the front seat, Lucy's father still had the shotgun raised, was pointing it at Stella.

'Thank you for your cooperation, Mr Heartwood. Let's get you out.' The man leant in. He had a sturdy pair of scissors, more like silver-plated wire-cutters. He clipped the cable tie that ran through the seatbelt and quickly stood back. 'Release your seatbelt and get out.' Davis found he could do it, even while his wrists remained bound together.

The man had his pistol out once again, and held it just a metre from Davis's head. 'The girl,' he said, and Lucy's father released Stella. The man stepped behind Davis, touched the gun to his spine. 'Walk forward; I will guide you. Take it slowly, so that you don't trip.'

Davis felt a surge of panic. This was not what the man had said would happen. Who could they be meeting out here in the scrub? He wanted to yell, but the tape was still across his mouth and he dared not lift his bound hands to remove it. He could hear nothing but the sound of birds, maybe the river, wind in the casuarinas like a sigh. Somewhere, too far away to be of help, someone operating a chainsaw.

The gun barrel ground into his backbone, and he walked.

He thought of running, but could not see how. Lucy's father was behind Stella with the shotgun.

'Okay, you can stop,' said the polite man. 'Please kneel.'

Davis didn't, so the man kicked behind his knee, sent him stumbling, then hit him in the back of the head with the gun. 'Please do as I say.' The voice was no longer so pleasant; there was a chill in it. Beside him, Davis could hear Stella sobbing through her gag. Lucy's father pushed her down onto her knees.

The polite man said, 'This is not an easy day. Not for any of us. But we need to kill you. It is unfortunate, but it is decided.'

Davis tried to protest through the gag, but the man cut him off, speaking gently as if soothing a child. 'It is not my decision. You cannot persuade me. Stay still.'

Davis was having trouble breathing, his entire body tense, expectant.

But instead of a bullet, Lucy's father came around and ripped the gags from their mouths: first Stella's, then his.

'Why?' asked Davis. 'Why do this?'

From behind, the man's voice was flat. 'This is not a movie. I don't explain. I just kill.'

'So why haven't you?' asked Stella.

'Ah, the smart one. In any couple, there is always the smart one, and the one who only thinks he is smart. I am glad we have that sorted.'

Davis looked at Stella, and she looked at him with fear and sorrow. 'I am so sorry,' Davis said.

'Before I kill you, I need to know exactly what it was you saw in those documents,' said the polite man, stepping around so they could see his face as he addressed Stella. 'You tell me, you die quickly. Painlessly.' And now the polite veneer was gone, and Davis could see the underlying madness. The pleasure of it, the power. 'But if you lie or delay, then you can watch while I do terrible things to Mr Heartwood. Despicable things.' The man leered, teeth exposed, as if he was hoping Stella would lie or delay.

'He doesn't know,' said Stella. 'I took them. He had no time to read them.'

'You know what they were?' asked the man.

'Yes,' said Stella, almost collapsing. 'The records of produce arriving. The shipping times. What was received and when. And then what was shipped out. What time, where they were headed. That's all.'

'So why did you take them?'

Stella shook her head, but answered. 'I thought there were discrepancies. There were too many deliveries, too many dispatches, but not enough trucks.'

The man sighed. 'Where were the discrepancies?'

'I don't know. That's why I took all of them.'

The man nodded. 'Yes. I can see that makes sense.'

'You're going to do it here, not deeper in the woods?' asked Davis.

'Here's good,' said the man. Then to Stella: 'Thank you.' He didn't raise his voice. He had the manner of a snake charmer, a mesmerist.

She bowed her head.

'I'm so sorry,' said Davis again.

452

'I love you,' said Stella.

'And I love you.'

The man walked around so he was standing behind them. He sighed. 'Such a pity,' he said.

Davis wanted to say something else. There was so much to say; there should have been a lifetime in which to say it. But he didn't have time—not before the gun fired.

chapter fifty

NELL COMFORTS THE RECEPTIONIST, JENNY, GUIDING HER BACK TO HER OWN office. Ivan stays a little longer, careful not to touch anything, trying to breathe through his nose and avoid the worst of the smell. His training kicks in, the objective investigator attempting to view the body of Craven Allsop as a piece of evidence, an 'it', not the 'he' it so recently was. Ivan has seen many murder scenes in person and plenty of suicides, studied many more. He'll leave it to the experts to determine for certain, but by the time he closes the office door behind him, he's convinced it was suicide, even without a note.

They wait in silence in the outer office for Merv to return, for a colleague to care for Jenny, for Carole and Blake to arrive. Nell is doing her best for the distraught receptionist. Ivan should be asking her questions, but he's distracted. He came here thinking Craven was his best chance to break open the larger case, establish the link between organised crime, the bashing of Snouch, the murder of Athol, the destruction of the practice and the stabbing of Alice. Now he has to consider that Craven was more than that: that he was the one running Toxteth McGrath. The middle man between mob and muscle. Who realised if Ivan and Nell didn't get him, then the 'Ndrangheta would. He scowls as he imagines the relief Allsop's suicide would bring to Ilsa Jones's employers.

Merv arrives with a second security guard, both wide-eyed and clearly shaken. An ashen-faced woman enters hesitantly and ushers Jenny away. Ivan imagines the warehouse floor, the news hurtling through like a sand-storm across a desert.

Nell keeps her voice low. 'She says she saw no one else enter or exit.'

'No.' Ivan sighs. 'Looks like it was self-inflicted.'

'In too deep,' she says, shaking her head.

'But why here?' asks Ivan. 'If the money was flowing through Water Traders, why come over here?' He's thinking of Athol and Alice investigating the Wholesalers, Davis Heartwood's execution, Martin Scarsden's investigation linking the killings. Krystal Heartwood on the run.

Nell shrugs. 'Does it matter?'

'Not for Craven. Not anymore.'

—

When they get back to the police station it's almost empty, just Constable Simmonds staffing the reception desk and Kevin working at his laptop in the detectives room. They left Blake and Carole at the Wholesalers, and McTosh has most of his crew over there as well. Kevin hears them enter, stops what he's doing and stands, demeanour solemn. 'I heard,' he says.

'Yeah,' says Nell. 'Half an hour earlier and we might have saved him.'

Ivan slumps into his chair, places his head in his hands, closing his eyes, trying to think, trying to make the connections.

'I got something,' says Kevin.

'Does it change anything?' asks Nell.

'Maybe everything,' says Kevin softly.

Ivan's eyes are open, he's sitting upright, exchanging a glance with Nell. 'Tell us,' he says.

'It's all there,' says Kevin. 'I went back through Athol's accounts to see if I could identify dark money, but there was nothing. Nothing in his private accounts; the only mafia money going through his trust account was that money Craven Allsop directed through Riverina Water Traders, the money you already know about.'

Ivan frowns. 'What's the significance of that?'

'Suggests that Athol was a cleanskin. Not actively or knowingly washing money for organised crime.'

'Fair call. Go on.'

'So I left the trust account and moved to the single biggest bank account Athol administered: the Watermen's Foundation. Otto Titchfield's slush fund. And right away, there are a whole bunch of big donors. They leap out at you. The Seven, all of them. Plus donations from the Wholesalers, the Yuwonderie Land Trust, the Irrigation Scheme Company. Sizeable donations from mining corporations, from agribusinesses, from transport companies, from a regional airline. That's what catches your eye. The big donations. But it's not the big donations that hold the key: it's the small ones. And only if you know what to look for.'

'Which is what, exactly?' asks Nell.

'Griffith.'

'Griffith?'

'There are lots of little donations from individuals. Farmers, small businesses, that sort of thing. I can see the names, the account numbers and the BSB numbers identifying the bank branch. Most are from Yuwonderie, some are from further afield, but a significant amount are from Griffith.'

'I'll be damned,' whispers Ivan, starting to understand what Kevin is saying.

Nell has come alert, shifting her weight from leg to leg as if preparing for a martial arts bout.

Kevin continues. 'There are dozens of these accounts. Donating a hundred dollars here, a thousand there . . . Not regular payments, seemingly at random—but coming out of the same accounts. They're all there, hiding in plain sight, overshadowed by the big donations.'

'So deliberately disguising them?' asks Ivan.

'Over time, it adds up to tens of thousands of dollars per year from each account. But there is no legal requirement for them to be declared to the Electoral Commission. The commission wouldn't even be able to see them. The individual donations are too small, and they're hidden behind the Watermen's Foundation.'

'Kind of genius,' says Nell.

'Dark money,' says Kevin, 'never declared.'

'Let's be clear here,' says Ivan. 'These donations, they're coming from accounts completely separate from the two big payments flowing from Riverina Water Traders into Air Stills and back?'

'Absolutely. Nothing to do with the Water Traders and nothing to do with Air Stills.'

Ivan understands. 'These accounts—who owns them?'

CHRIS HAMMER

'I've only had a cursory look, but I'd say legitimate businesses and residents. Farmers, small businesses. Upstanding citizens. Many of Italian extraction. Coerced to wash the money through their accounts. Maybe they get a small commission; maybe they don't.'

'Fuck me.' Ivan swallows. 'I don't know what's worse: where the money's coming from or where it's going: the Calabrian mafia funnelling money into a political party.'

'Buying influence,' says Nell.

'Otto Titchfield,' says Kevin. 'Country First.'

Ivan blinks. What sort of hornets' nest have they sunk their boot into? 'This account you're looking at, the Watermen's Foundation: Athol Hasluck could see everything you're seeing?'

'Of course—but, like me, only if he were looking.'

'We need to haul in Otto Titchfield,' says Nell softly, voice solemn.

'Shit,' says Ivan, aware of the gravity of her suggestion. He considers ringing Plodder. It'd be the smart move: cover his arse, protect his team.

'I say we do it,' says Nell, as if sensing his hesitation.

Ivan is still weighing up his options, is about to speak, when his desk phone rings. It's Constable Simmonds, the sole uniformed police officer still at the station, downstairs staffing the reception. 'I think you need to come down here, sir,' she says.

chapter fifty-one

DOWNSTAIRS, THE RECEPTION AREA IS DESERTED APART FROM CONSTABLE Simmonds. 'Outside,' she says.

And outside, standing on the footpath, next to Ivan and Nell's four-wheel drive, is Bert Kippax with his brown paper bag. Ivan is wondering if it's more of a prop than a dependency: the man looks steady as a rock.

'What?' says Ivan impatiently.

'Someone you should meet,' says Bert.

'Not a good time,' says Ivan.

'Worth your while,' says Bert.

Ivan hears the conviction in the former policeman's voice. 'Who?' he asks.

'Kazza,' replies Bert. 'I tracked her down.'

— —

Ivan rings Nell, tells her to brief Plodder and ascertain Otto Titchfield's whereabouts, but to take no action until he returns.

459

Then he drives Bert to an agreed meeting place inside the wetlands. They park the car and Bert leads the way along one of the walking tracks. The sun is setting; there are ducks and ibises and a young mum with a toddler learning to ride a tricycle.

'Where is she?' asks Ivan.

'Come on,' says Bert. 'She's scared shitless. Took me forever to convince her.'

They enter the wetlands along one of the paths Ivan remembers from jogging. He's starting to wonder how wise this is, to come alone without back-up. He rests his hand on the grip of his gun, still clipped into his holster. If Bert notices, he doesn't say anything.

They reach a fork in the path. 'Down that way's a hide,' says Bert, pointing. 'Wait for her there. I'll stay here, make sure you're not disturbed.'

'How long?'

'No time. She'll have seen us. Seen we're alone.'

'Right,' says Ivan.

He follows the path, enters the hide. It's nothing more than four walls, unlined weatherboard with a tin roof and a dirt floor, a plaque acknowledging the generosity of the Seven, a second commemorating the boating accident that killed three of them. There are empty chip packets and some discarded alcopop bottles. Ivan looks out through the viewing gap: the water shimmering, but no birds.

'Hello,' says a voice behind him.

Ivan turns. It's a woman, about sixty. She's clean, dressed in a loose t-shirt, jeans, sandals. It's only on closer inspection that he sees the suggestions of a life lived tough: the self-administered haircut, a chipped tooth, another missing, a scratch on the lens of her glasses. 'Kazza?' he asks.

'Karen. Karen Montgomery-Bell.' She cracks a nervous smile. 'Fancy name. All my mum ever gave me.'

'Thank you for coming forward,' says Ivan.

She takes a shuddering breath. 'I'm frightened,' she says.

'I understand,' says Ivan. 'But tell me what you know and I'll do everything I can to protect you. I'm hoping that no one needs to know your name or what you tell me.'

'Can you promise me that?'

'No. But if you help us identify criminals, we'll search for other evidence we can use to convict them.'

'There a reward?'

'Sorry, no. Not at this stage.'

'Hmph. That's what Bert said.' She sighs, looks at her hands. 'There were two of them,' she says abruptly. 'They walked him out with his hands tied.'

Ivan blinks, realising she wants it over and done with. 'Last Saturday night. You were in the alleyway behind Athol Hasluck's practice?'

'I was.'

'You were going to sleep there for the night. In that alcove behind the Lone Dog Café.'

'One of my regular spots. I could see everything from there.'

'Tell me.'

'There were two of them: one big, one small. They went up the stairs, knocked on the door. Went inside.'

Ivan interjects. 'Before you go on, tell me—they knocked, but was the door open or did someone let them in?'

Kazza frowns, then smiles. 'No. Someone let them in.'

'That's useful. And then?'

'I thought it was a bit suss. So I crept up, got closer, hid behind a garbage skip. A few minutes later they came out. I knew straight away something was wrong. The big guy, at the back, he had his hands on the man in front of him, kind of guiding him. It was Athol Hasluck; his hands were tied behind him. I realised that they were abducting him.'

'You knew him?'

'No, but I heard what happened to him.'

'So you couldn't be a hundred per cent sure it was Athol Hasluck?'

Kazza frowns. 'Who else could it be?'

'Fair point,' says Ivan. 'Can you describe them? The large man guiding him?'

'Absolute giant. Huge. Ugly face. A mullet.'

Ivan pulls out his phone, finds the mug shot of Toxteth McGrath, shows it to Kazza. 'Him?'

'That's the bloke.'

'And his accomplice, the smaller man: can you describe him?' asks Ivan, even as he searches the phone for a picture of Craven Allsop.

'Wasn't a man.'

'What?'

'The other one. The one in charge. It was a woman.'

'Jesus,' says Ivan, 'I should have realised.' Krystal Heartwood, in her private plane, fleeing the country. He swipes through the photos, brings up the thirty-year-old photo from the B&S ball. It will have to do. He zooms in as best he can, shows Kazza the image of Krystal laughing with her old friend Craven Allsop. 'It's a dated photo, but could that possibly be the woman you saw?'

'You kidding? That's Krystal Heartwood.'

'You know her?'

'She helps out at Vinnies and at the refuge. Bit reserved, but good-hearted.'

'Can you describe the woman you saw?'

'Hang on. Show me that photo again?'

Ivan shows her the phone.

'That one.' She's pointing to Jacinta Hasluck. 'Or maybe that one.' Lucy Titchfield.

'Fuck me,' says Ivan. Lucretia Titchfield. The founder and president of the Watermen's Foundation. The Foundation's account with millions passing through it. The account that Athol Hasluck dared not touch, despite his desperate need for money.

chapter fifty-two

Mr Charles Goodman Esq.
Tundridge Waters
Via Cootamundra
New South Wales

To Mrs Elaine Heartwood
Three Wells Station
Via Yuwonderie
New South Wales

September 1924

My dear Mrs Heartwood,

It is my sad, sorry and unfortunate duty to inform you of terrible
news. Your dear friend, Mrs Bessie Marney, has been killed in a

most unfortunate accident. She was riding her mare Penny when the horse caught her by surprise and threw her to the ground. A farm worker saw the incident; they believe the horse was spooked by a snake. In any case, your friend did not suffer. One moment she was riding care free, the next her neck was broken.

Her death has caused great sorrow among our family and within our wider community. Bessie was a most valued citizen of our little town, not least for her work as a teacher these past few years. We will always cherish her memory.

Mrs Marney, as she styled herself and we were pleased to call her, was unfailingly kind, generous and dedicated, first as the governess on our property, then as the assistant at our little school, and finally as the teacher herself. She led a virtuous and exemplary life.

We will arrange her burial here in our churchyard. If you wish to attend the funeral, it will be held next Wednesday at eleven in the morning at St James' Catholic Church. I do hope this letter might reach you in time. Should you wish to attend, please telegraph me. I would be honoured to fetch you in my automobile.

We have studied Bessie's papers and have found her will, as well as much of the correspondence between the two of you and the letters she once sent to her mother. Her savings will pass to her son Joseph, as fine a boy as you might ever encounter. He has mischief in his eye but goodness in his heart, and more intelligence than most adults. He is a credit to his mother, a testament to her love and sacrifice. As I am sure you are aware as the boy's godmother, and as stipulated in Bessie's will, his care now falls to you. If it would be of assistance, I could bring Joseph to you at Three Wells Station if you are unable to make your way here next week.

I have discussed this matter with my wife. If, for any reason, you are unable to take Joseph, rest assured he would be welcome to live with us.

Please let me know your wishes.

With the kindest regards and our deepest sympathies,
Charles Goodman

chapter fifty-three

IN THE END, IT'S ERNST McTOSH WHO ARRESTS LUCY TITCHFIELD AS SHE'S fleeing Yuwonderie, wearing dark glasses and a cheap blonde wig, the disguise undermined by her car: a late-model Bentley worth half a million dollars, registered in her name. But it's Ivan who gets to interview her.

Night has fallen, and the cells at the Yuwonderie police station are beyond capacity: Harley Snouch and Terry Zappia and Toxteth McGrath and now Lucretia Titchfield. To free up enough space to keep them separated, McTosh is forced to release a pair of itinerant break-and-enter merchants, sending them on their way with a boot up the arse. The two low-level crims find the street outside almost as packed as the cells inside: the metropolitan media is beginning to arrive, crowding the entrance, alerted by that morning's story by Martin Scarsden. The journalists pap the burglars as they leave, firing questions, just in case they are somehow relevant. The crims run for cover, scampering along to the Drovers Rest in need of beers and a bit of time to process exactly just what has happened to them.

Ivan and Nell enter the interview room to find Lucy Titchfield waiting, looking even more shrunken. Sitting next to her is a local solicitor, filling in until her Sydney lawyer arrives. Ivan wants to break her before that can happen. He sits, gets the formalities out of the way as soon as possible, then goes in hard.

'Your accomplice, Toxteth McGrath, says he witnessed you murdering Athol Hasluck, and that he was there when you knifed Alice Figtree.'

Lucy Titchfield looks him directly in the eye, full of defiance. 'I deny that. Categorically.'

'He claims you paid him in cash. That he acted entirely at your behest.'

'I deny it.'

'So did he when we arrested him last night. Now he's had a change of heart. He has a most impressive lawyer. Ilsa Jones. She's persuaded him to make a clean breast of it. Or at least to shift the blame entirely on to you.' He lets that hang in the air just a moment. 'She's not representing you?'

'Our family lawyers are on their way.'

'Toxic is going to say whatever they tell him to say—you know that, right?' Now he thinks he can see the first cracks in her defiance. 'Easy enough for him. He can claim ignorance of the motivation behind the killings. Claim he knew nothing about the Watermen's Foundation. The millions washing through it. The mob and their money.'

She winces at the words. 'I need to confer with my lawyer,' she says. 'In private.'

—-—

It's a full two hours before Ivan returns to the interview room. A lawyer was on the way from Sydney, and then they weren't, Otto Titchfield vetoing Lucy's access to the family firm, deciding to distance himself from his own wife.

Plodder Packenham is involved, the commissioner, the Australian Federal Police, the Australian Criminal Intelligence Commission and, eventually, the state and federal attorneys-general. The feds want to cut some sort of deal, a reduced sentence and guarantees of prison protection, if Lucy Titchfield is willing to inform on organised crime, but the state government is pushing back, asserting there can be no clemency for premeditated murder. Nevertheless, the next time he enters the interview room, it's not Nell who accompanies him: it's Chloe Fortnight, a middle-aged woman with a disarming manner, her clothes rumpled and her smile friendly, eyeglasses hanging from her neck on a granny chain. She'd look at home running a school canteen. She's also an Australian Federal Police inspector, a barrister, a PhD and an adjunct professor, but no one is telling Lucy Titchfield that. The inspector's expertise is organised crime. And yet, despite her qualifications, she defers to Ivan. It's his interview. He's glad to see Lucy is still represented by the same local solicitor.

'I'm willing to negotiate,' says Lucy.

'I'm not,' says Ivan.

Beside him, Inspector Fortnight shifts in her seat and coughs softly, signalling her disagreement.

Ivan continues, unperturbed. 'No negotiations, no deals. It's homicide. You will be prosecuted to the full extent of the law. Your only hope of a reduced sentence is through full cooperation. Confess to the murder of Athol Hasluck and the attempted murder of Alice Figtree. It's in your interest not to go to open trial, where you can be cross-examined over your motives, the operation of the Watermen's Foundation and your cultivation of dirty money.'

Lucy looks at Fortnight, back to Ivan. 'No trial?'

'A trial. But if you plead guilty, the judge can move straight to sentencing. No evidence aired in open court.'

'Understand this,' says Chloe Fortnight, unable to remain silent any longer. 'We will do our best to protect you. We will do our utmost to keep any statements you make here out of the public domain. Like you, we do not want the allegations against the syndicate ventilated in open court. But we can only do that if you are honest and open with us.'

Lucy sighs, almost as if she is bored. 'I understand.' And then: 'There's no coming back. Craven understood that.' She takes a deep breath. 'I killed Athol Hasluck. I tried to kill Alice Figtree.'

'Why?' asks Ivan.

'Athol realised the true nature of the Watermen's Foundation.'

'Which was?'

'To extend our power and influence—my power and influence—through the state's power elite. By using the money to fund the campaigns of Country First and like-minded politicians, both independents and those from other parties.'

'But it wasn't just that,' says Ivan. 'Athol realised the source of some of that money. The mob. That's why you killed him.'

'Yes. He'd happily rubber-stamped the accounts year after year. God knows what made him look more closely after all that time. I never thought he was that smart.'

'He tried to blackmail you?'

'Yes.'

'How much?'

She smiles weakly. 'Not just money. He wanted preselection. For Otto's state seat.'

Ivan nods. 'Ambitious, then.'

'Same as Craven. Second-son syndrome. Spares.' She offers the same weak smile. 'Never knew how lucky they were.'

'What does that mean?'

Lucy scoffs, and Ivan can hear the derision as she answers. 'They were still part of the Seven. Not outsiders like Jacinta and me. Our father abandoned us, left us with nothing, just shot through without saying a word. I know you think I'm shit, but people always did.'

Chloe Fortnight inserts herself into the interview again. 'What role did Craven Allsop play?'

She raises a shoulder, a dismissive shrug. 'Everything and nothing. We were always close. Similar outlook. Knew if we wanted to be on an equal standing with the family heads, we needed to take it for ourselves, establish our own wealth and our own power bases.' She gives a little laugh, as if at some fond memory. 'When I first set up Watermen's and convinced Otto to break with the Nats and go it alone, I had no intention of taking dark money. I barely knew it existed. There was plenty of capital to be sourced from fossil fuel companies, agribusinesses and the like, all lining up to buy influence. It was Craven who had the contacts, sent their money in our direction.'

Again, it's Fortnight who asks the follow-up, her interest in organised crime evident. 'Do you know what his relationship with them entailed?'

'Not the details of it, no. But I think it was all about money laundering.'

'Through the Water Traders?' asks Ivan.

'Through the Wholesalers. The same farmers who donate to Watermen's sell their produce through the Wholesalers.'

Chloe Fortnight leans back in her chair. 'Makes sense.'

But Ivan isn't leaning back; he's leaning forward. 'Athol Hasluck,' he says. 'You tortured him first. He told you about the accounts, Watermen's, how he had figured out what was happening.'

'I didn't torture him. That was that thug Toxic. By the time I got there it was too late, Athol was already half dead. Toxic had gone at him with a welding iron. I was forced to kill him. Use the knife.'

'That's a lie,' says Ivan. 'You were there from the start.'

She says nothing, her mouth withdrawing to a straight line, clamped shut.

Ivan silently berates himself; just when she's been talking. He tries to soften the blow. 'It wasn't premeditated, though, was it? You found the knife there, among Toxic's equipment. Opportunistic.'

Lucy grabs the lifeline like a drowning woman. 'That's right. I had no plan to kill him. We just went too far.'

'I believe you,' he says, giving the smallest of pauses. 'But why dump his body on your own property? Draw attention to yourself?'

'Isn't it obvious?'

'To warn off Otto.'

She smiles. 'He needed to be put in his place. I think Craven had accidentally let something slip, assumed he knew more than he did.'

'So Otto never knew about the dark money going into the Watermen's account?'

'That moron? Never.'

Chloe Fortnight smiles at that and asks her own question. 'And the murder of Athol Hasluck, the attempt on Alice Figtree, the assault on Detective Constable Buchanan, the bashing of Harley Snouch, the arson on McLean Street—that was all your own doing, you and Toxteth? The mob never knew what was going on?'

Lucy shrugs. 'I wasn't operating under their instructions, if that's what you mean.'

chapter fifty-four

THAT NIGHT, THEY CELEBRATE. IVAN AND NELL, CAROLE AND BLAKE, KEVIN AND McTosh. They've formally charged Lucretia Titchfield and Toxteth McGrath with a panoply of crimes, including the murder of Athol Hasluck and the attempt on Alice Figtree. They eat pizza at Paulo's for a second consecutive night, drink wine and beer, and even Kevin—normally a teetotaller in public—joins in a champagne toast, cheering loudly as Ivan reads out a herogram from Plodder and a little less loudly at one from the police minister. And as they eat and drink and talk, outside the modest rural restaurant events swirl and grow, as if the Dubbo Homicide Squad sits in the eye of a cyclone.

In Sydney, Otto Titchfield rises in parliament, announcing his intention to resign immediately and stating he will not contest the forthcoming election, citing family concerns and the need to look after his children. But news of his wife's arrest has beaten him to it, and as he stands to speak, there's a rush of MPs, staffers and journalists into the chamber and its galleries to bear witness to the downfall of a political maverick, like the crowd at a public hanging.

In Melbourne, undercover operatives, armed with information seized from the Yuwonderie Wholesalers, are preparing dawn raids on a select number of stores within the sprawling Victorian fruit and vegetable markets, while their counterparts in New South Wales are applying for search warrants, targeting various farms and small businesses around Griffith and further afield.

At the Yuwonderie police station, lawyers representing Harley Snouch are attempting to negotiate leniency for their client in return for information.

But for a precious hour or two, the team at Paulo's remains largely oblivious to the events they have set in motion, upending lives and cutting a swathe through Yuwonderie and beyond. They celebrate, bonded by satisfaction and vindication. Only as they leave the restaurant and the media descend, thrusting microphones and papping photographs, do they feel the winds of the tornado, begin to appreciate the scale of what they have unleashed.

It will be a big day tomorrow, and Ivan is hoping to get some respite at the hotel, a solid sleep before returning to the police station. He and Nell are ascending the stairs, laughing and talking, buoyed by their success, when a figure steps out of the shadows. Ivan senses Nell tense next to him, her martial arts training kicking in.

But he recognises the man almost immediately. Martin Scarsden.

'Hello, Ivan,' says the investigative reporter, raising an eyebrow and tilting his head towards Nell. 'Going to introduce me?'

'I can't talk, Martin. Not now.'

The reporter ignores him, addressing Nell. 'I'm Martin Scarsden. Not armed, not a threat.' He turns back to Ivan. 'We're holding the

Air Stills story for now. Far too good to waste, given tomorrow's coverage is going to be wall-to-wall Lucy and Otto Titchfield. Probably go next week. *The World's Greatest Scam: Money from Thin Air.*'

'You came here to tell us that?'

'No. To thank you. It's one hell of a yarn.' Scarsden is grinning. 'And there's someone I want you to meet.'

'And who's that?'

'My source. Davis Heartwood.'

— —

They travel out to Three Wells Station in separate cars. Nell is driving, following the red tail-lights of Scarsden's Subaru. They talk on the way, recounting what they know: the disappearance of Davis and Stella back in 1994, and the discovery of his body fifteen years later, the corpse identified by DNA.

'How is it all connected?' asks Nell.

'I think we're about to find out.'

Three Wells Station is as impressive by night as it was during the day. The moon is not yet up, and the sky is a swathe of starlight, the Milky Way stretched out above them, a reminder of their insignificance.

Davis Heartwood himself answers the door, instantly recognisable from the photo taken at the long-ago B&S ball. His hair is still a thick mop of blond, a few grey strands intruding at the temples, and his eyes are clear and acute, a sky blue. There are wrinkles around his eyes, but he has aged well. So too has Stella Kippax, who rises to meet them as they enter the sitting room. And in a corner chair, nursing a glass of wine, is Stella's father, Bert Kippax. He doesn't rise, just offers a silent toast and a sheepish grin.

Martin moves across, greeting the former policeman with familiarity and pouring himself a glass of wine.

'Thank you for coming,' says Davis.

'Your sister?' asks Ivan.

'Dropped us here, then flew back to Canberra to be with her wife. They'll bring Alice out of the coma tomorrow morning.'

'What's the latest?' asks Nell.

'They're now saying a full recovery.'

'Krystal,' says Ivan. 'She flew you here. From somewhere in the Pacific?'

'New Zealand.'

'So she knew. All along.'

'Of course. She flew us out thirty years ago.'

Ivan looks at Bert and Martin watching on in interest, grinning, as if they have front-row seats.

Nell isn't smiling. 'The body. Your body. The one discovered by the river,' she says to Davis.

'The one buried up there on the hill in your family cemetery,' adds Ivan.

Davis looks at Stella, then back to Nell. 'A mafia hit man was sent to kill us.' He describes their abduction back in 1994, the drive to Corkhills Creek, their imminent execution.

Ivan has no doubt Davis is telling the truth. As the story unfolds, the emotions that run across his face match Stella's, as if synchronised. The same emotions at the same time: horror, shock, despair. In his corner, Bert Kippax is no longer smiling.

'So what saved you?' asks Ivan.

'An old man who lived in a shack down there. Joseph Marney. He was a sniper in the Second World War: a marksman. He saw what was happening and shot the hit man before he could shoot us.'

'Why? Why side with you?'

'He remembered me,' says Davis, an edge of emotion touching his voice. 'He used to work here. Lived on the property. An employee, but almost part of the family. His mother had been the best friend of a member of my family, Elaine Heartwood. She cared for him after his mother died. He said the Heartwoods had always been good to him and his family.'

'But the DNA?' asks Nell. She and Ivan turn in unison to look to Bert Kippax.

'Yes. It was me. I swapped out the sample.'

'You knew they were alive?'

'Of course.'

'So who else knew?' Nell asks. 'Who was in on this conspiracy?'

Davis doesn't speak, as if weighing the words, so it's Stella who answers. 'My father. Davis's sister and his grandfather. Joseph Marney. More recently Alice Figtree.' She pauses just a moment, glances at her father, who nods. She turns back to the detectives. 'And Patrick Fielder.'

Ivan frowns. 'Fielder? A relative of Lucy Titchfield and Jacinta Hasluck?'

'Their father. He was there, acting as muscle for the hit man.'

'Take us through it,' says Ivan.

'We will. But please, take a seat,' says Davis.

Ivan looks at Nell, who shrugs. They sit, and Davis and Stella follow suit.

Davis leans forward, gesturing with his hands. 'We buried the hit man down there by Corkhills Creek. Joseph Marney had a shovel, Fielder dug the grave. But we couldn't shoot him, not in cold blood. We're not killers. It became clear that he was desperate for cash, had only been brought in to help the killer at the last minute. He became more cooperative once he realised the assassin must have planned on killing him as well. So we cut a deal. Or, rather, my grandfather Clemence Heartwood did.'

He offers some wine; Ivan and Nell both decline the offer, and Davis continues.

'Krystal got us out. Flew us to a small airport on an outlying island in Vanuatu. This was all back before September 11; borders and passport controls were less rigorous back then. My grandfather had plenty of money, plenty of clout, plenty of connections. He got us new identities, new passports. A month or so later we flew into New Zealand and have lived there ever since.

'Meanwhile, my grandfather organised for Fielder to disappear. It wasn't hard: Fielder realised the mafia would be after him. Bert and Joseph Marney found the killer's Italian passport in the back of the car. His name was Giancarlo Pasquali. Grandfather had it doctored, replaced the photo with Fielder's. All possible back then, before biometric passports. He gave Fielder two hundred and fifty thousand dollars in cash and bought him a one-way ticket to Rome, via Singapore. Fielder drove the killer's car to Melbourne Airport, caught the flight, bailed out at Singapore. Clemence reported the money missing, claiming that a safe in the library had been plundered. If the mafia went looking for Pasquali, they would have concluded he had taken the money and run.'

Ivan glances at Bert Kippax, who just shrugs.

'Fielder died about a year later,' says Stella. 'He was already sick. I think that's why he was helping the hit man. He was desperate.'

'Did they get any of the money? Lucy and Jacinta?'

Stella shakes her head. 'No. He was a bastard all right.'

'My grandfather bought their land. Thought it might help. There was no water left. Overly generous, but I'm not sure they ever saw it that way. Not Lucy, at any rate.'

Ivan looks from one to the other. 'You still haven't explained why. Why did the mafia want to kill you?'

Davis defers to Stella.

'I was working at the Wholesalers,' she says. 'I thought there was something amiss with the shipping records. I took some papers, so Davis and I could work out what it was. Before we could do anything that man Pasquali abducted us at gunpoint.'

'You know what it was?'

'We think so. We believe organised crime was washing money through the Wholesalers.' She explains the ghost shipments and the fake invoices, the money flowing from the Victorian markets through the Wholesalers to individual farmers and then back to the mafia.

'Brilliant,' says Ivan. 'But why run? Why didn't you go to the police?'

'We were shit scared,' says Stella. 'Someone was trying to kill us and we didn't fully understand why.'

'We tried,' says Bert Kippax, speaking up. 'Once they were safe. But we couldn't guarantee their safety. And all the evidence of the ghost shipments had been destroyed by then.'

'How?'

'This was 1994. The board of the Wholesalers decided they needed to fully computerise. Lots of companies were back then. They hired Craven Allsop to digitise their records. Which he did, shredding anything incriminating along the way.'

'Craven Allsop?' says Ivan. 'Even back then?'

Davis sighs, shrugs. 'I'd just destroyed his world, me handing the inheritance of Three Wells Station to Krystal. His elder sister became heir to the Allsop fortune, and suddenly he needed money and a job. He was destroying evidence, but he was also there when the Wholesalers stopped laundering the mob's money.'

'You sure about that?'

'So my grandfather believed. He got himself back onto the board.'

'Clemence Heartwood? He died, though,' says Nell. 'In that boating accident. Before the lake was converted back into wetlands.'

Ivan sees the reaction in Davis and Stella, their identical look of concern, doubt where they have been so self-assured. Ivan makes the leap. 'It wasn't an accident, was it?'

'We were in New Zealand,' says Davis.

Ivan looks to Bert Kippax, still as a rock. Next to him, Martin Scarsden is sitting meerkat-straight. This is news to the reporter.

'What happened?' whispers Nell.

Bert drains his wine glass, refills it and explains. 'Clemence. He wasn't about to forgive,' says the former policeman. 'The two of us quietly investigated.' He glances at Scarsden, frowns, but continues anyway. 'I was talking to a contact in the federal police, trying to work out who it was that had alerted the mafia about Stella and the documents. Anyway, a couple of years later, this guy comes back to me out of the blue. A mafia capo had turned informer, revealed

481

a lot of stuff. This grass knew about the money-laundering game, said it was a sweet thing while it was working. He confirmed it was no longer operating, but he named two members of the Seven, the ones who'd set it up, the ones who knew about it.'

'Let me guess,' says Ivan. 'Van Dyke Allsop and Jessop Titchfield.'

'Yes. Craven's and Otto's grandfathers, family heads.'

Ivan turns back to Davis. 'So your grandfather killed them? And himself?'

For the first time, Davis looks truly distraught. 'He was a fine man, my grandfather. A wonderful man. But he was old and he was tough and he was dying. He didn't tell us, not even Krystal, who was here. Pancreatic cancer, not long to live. So it was a final act. He desperately wanted to clear out the Wholesalers, reform the irrigation scheme, bring it back to its original purpose, give Krystal an untainted future. After everything, he still believed in it. He acted alone. Invited Allsop and Titchfield to go fishing, blew up the boat.'

Ivan nods, thinking he understands. He turns to Bert. 'You covered it up. Declared it an accident—premeditated murder.'

Bert examines his wine glass before answering. 'You can charge me if you like. But I had no foreknowledge of his plans. Afterwards, once I figured out what had happened, I wasn't prepared to risk the discovery of Davis and Stella. That same source in the AFP, he advised me against it. They were settled in New Zealand with kids of their own.'

'You resigned not long after,' says Nell. 'Is that why?'

'Yeah. It was. Covering up for Joseph Marney and Fielder was one thing. Swapping the DNA was necessary. But yes, covering up a premeditated murder, that was it for me.' He smiles. 'Even though part of me couldn't help applauding Clemence.'

Ivan turns back to Davis. 'All this to keep your existence secret. To protect you. And yet here you are, no longer hiding. Why now?'

'Athol,' says Davis.

'Athol was the catalyst,' says Stella. 'He was in New Zealand for some professional conference. Christchurch. We almost never went to town, but that day we did. I was taking our daughter to a doctor's appointment, and I ran straight into him, rounding a corner. Face to face. And before either of us could say a word, Davis came around the same corner. So Athol knew it was us; it was undeniable.'

'And you told him what you'd found?'

'Yes.' She looks at her partner. 'We'd started talking about coming back. Our youngest, Bessie, was turning twenty-one, and Josh, our eldest, is almost thirty. They know the whole story. We've discussed it with them, now they're old enough. Krystal and Alice won't have children, so Three Wells will pass to Josh. He needs to come back here, start learning the ropes.'

'You trusted Athol?'

'Stupid of me, I know. But I always liked him. We'd gone out together briefly, before I met Davis. He was always sincere and honest back then. I thought we could trust him.' She swallows. 'I asked him about the Wholesalers. If it was still clean. He had no idea what I was talking about. So I explained. I guess he started checking the accounts, working out the flow of money. That chance meeting in New Zealand; it set this whole awful chain of events in motion.' She looks to Davis, then back to the detectives. 'We had no idea about Athol's debts.'

'And we needed to tell him something,' adds Davis. 'Give him some reason to keep our secret a little longer.'

'Alice?' asks Nell.

The distress is clear on Davis's face. 'She went to work with Athol. To help him. To work out if the danger had passed, whether the Wholesalers was still clean or if the mafia had come back. But Alice was starting to worry; she could sense that something was wrong.'

'That was the real reason why Krystal lent him the money to buy his land, wasn't it? To keep him onside, to stop him from revealing your secret.'

'Yes.'

'And when he died?'

'We were scared. Really scared. So we called off our return.'

'And then Alice discovered he was in debt.'

'The photo. The one in his diary of the B&S ball,' says Nell. 'It was planted, wasn't it?'

Davis shakes his head. 'No. Alice found it among his papers. Put it in his diary. He must have been trying to work out what really happened back then.' Davis looks to his wife. 'We discussed it. Thought it wouldn't hurt to have you looking at the connections between the Seven.'

'You think he talked to Craven?'

'Yes. He must have asked Craven about the Wholesalers. Younger sons of the Seven. The old boys' network.'

Silence falls on the table. Everyone is sombre, except for Martin Scarsden, who looks like he's hit the jackpot at the Drovers Rest.

chapter fifty-five

ONE MONTH LATER

DAVIS HEARTWOOD LOOKS DOWN AT HIS GRAVE AND FEELS A SHIVER ROLL UP HIS spine. It should have been amusing coming here, some sort of anecdote made real. But seeing the headstone, weathered over the years and bearing his epitaph, makes the trauma of that day real again, the knowledge that he was within seconds of death, within seconds of this really being his grave. *In memory of our beautiful boy. Davis Douglas Heartwood. 1972–1994. In destiny's arms.* He wonders at the inscription, who thought of it; his sister, he imagines. A necessary charade. He is again humbled by her emotional strength: that she was able to carry it off, even knowing he was alive. But he's pleased he's come to see it; the police are due out in the coming week to exhume the body, to confirm the hit man's real identity. The polite man with the nice smile and the pristine pistol.

He turns back to the other graves, sheltering in the shade of a gnarled oak. His own is slightly separated from the rest. His grandfather's plot is here, in among those of his family, the style similar to Davis's own, just a little more weathered. How strange that is, he thinks. *Clemence William Heartwood. A good and honest man*. True, thinks Davis. An honest man, who helped perpetuate the lie of his grandson's death. And who murdered Van Dyke Allsop and Jessop Titchfield in cold blood. Beyond the law now.

There are other graves, too. Elaine Mary Heartwood, nee Titchfield, long dead and buried next to her husband Douglas, but brought to life somehow through the letters of Bessie Walker. He wonders about Bessie, where she lies: in a Cootamundra church-yard, according to long-ago correspondence. Another life well lived, a life cut short. But her son is here, his grave in a place of honour, neither segregated nor assimilated, the style quite different. *Here lies Joseph Marney, a proud Wiradjuri man—a friend to all. 1915–1997.* Davis thinks again of the letters of Joseph's mother, of her struggles. He thinks she would be pleased that her son rests here, not so very far from Elaine and Douglas Heartwood; not so far from Clemence.

And she would be pleased that her great-grandson, Benedict Marney Bright, should be able to visit his grandfather here. And that Eggs still loves the little shack by Corkhills Creek, where she and Jack Marney first bound themselves to each other. And no doubt she would be pleased that all these years later the young man would be able to attend university and live in Davis's old college, courtesy of the bursary that he and Stella and Krystal and Alice have bestowed upon Eggs.

Davis ponders again the threads of history winding their way through this landscape and its people, through his family. Then he turns and walks down the hill, back to the banquet that is being prepared, and to his family and guests. He and Stella and their two adult children, Josh and Bessie, together with Krystal and Alice, the latter now approaching full health. Stella's father Bert is coming, released on bail, awaiting the pleasure of the prosecutor's office. And Eggs and his mother. And Martin Scarsden and his wife Mandalay and their handful of a boy, Liam, and the three police officers, Ivan Lucic and Nell Buchanan and Kevin Nackangara. It could be quite a lunch: he and Krystal have been into the cellar, hunting out the house wine, Heartwood Estate, finding a case of 1994, perhaps a good year after all.

chapter fifty-six

IVAN REMAINS SILENT, STARING STRAIGHT AHEAD THROUGH THE WINDSCREEN
as Nell pulls up outside the nursing home, the white noise of
Sydney's west all around them.

'Ivan. We've arrived.'

He turns to her, blinks, becoming aware of their location.

'I'll wait out here. Find somewhere to park.' She touches his
arm. 'Ring when you're done.'

He nods, unable to find the correct words. Sees her smiling
encouragement. 'Thanks,' he manages.

He climbs out of the Mazda, Nell's private car. It's late morning,
the sun hard upon him, no respite on the concrete drive. He takes
a breath, walks towards the entrance of the Sunland Retirement
Home.

Inside, one of the nursing staff leads him into a small lounge.
The smell is a discomforting melange of air freshener and boiled
cabbage, with undertones of body odour and old bowels. He's
familiar enough with the smells of death; these must be the
precursors.

He doesn't recognise his father when they wheel him in, not at first. He'd been such a large man, always towering over Ivan, full of anger and energy. This is just a shadow, shrunken into the chair, his eyebrows and nostril hairs run amok, his hair, once thick and dark, now grey and sparse. The whites of his eyes are no longer white but tinged with yellow. The irises are still the same rich brown, though, brimming with intelligence beneath the hooded lids.

'You came,' says his father, the deep voice now reedy and thin.

'I came.' Ivan stares at his father unapologetically, trying to reconcile the fearful memory with this husk. He studies the old man's face, pallid and splotchy, with a jaundiced sheen. 'What do you want?'

'To see you.' Zlatko extends a trembling hand, skin like rice paper, the veins showing through.

'You've seen me,' says Ivan, voice hard and even, examining the hand but not taking it.

'Forgiveness,' says his father.

Ivan finds himself shaking his head, but stills it before speaking, looking his father in the eye in a way he would never have dared as a child. 'I forgive you for what you did to me, but not for what you did to Mum. Never that. And not for what you did to those poor people in that village. That is beyond forgiveness.'

Ivan sees the eyebrows fall in doubt and, maybe, a hint of anger. It's enough. 'Goodbye, Dad.' And he turns and leaves without looking back.

Outside, he just stares into the day, trying to breathe, a subterranean well of tears threatening to surface. He's still standing there when Nell's car pulls up, having negotiated the driveway. The door opens, and he climbs in.

She says nothing for a period, giving him space, turning the car around, getting back onto the road. Eventually he looks across to her.

She takes it as a cue. 'How was it?'

He shakes his head. 'He was so big when I was a kid. So angry, so powerful. And now, it's like a puff of wind would blow him away.'

'You talked?'

'Enough.'

She frowns, concentrating on driving, changing lanes and crossing an intersection, before making another attempt. 'I'm here, if you want to talk. You know that.'

He looks at her, sees the concern in her eyes, even as she's focused on the road. And he finds himself recounting the final exchange between father and son. And feels the better for it, and grateful to her.

'Where to?' she asks when he is done. 'You want to eat before we leave? Coffee?'

'Dubbo. I've had enough of Sydney.'

He waits a good ten minutes, until they are onto the freeway, before he speaks again. 'I'm selling my apartment. Don't get down here enough anymore.'

She doesn't respond, not with words, but he can see the thoughts playing out on her face.

The Blue Mountains are in the distance, hovering above Penrith in the heat, the barrier to the hinterland. 'Can't see myself living here again. Time to move on.'

Nell smiles, nods. 'Good call.'

'Thought I might buy up there. Dubbo. More affordable than here, that's for sure.'

Her smile broadens. 'You want a hand? Looking at houses?'

And for the first time all day, he finds a smile emerging. 'Yes. I'd like that.'

Author's note and acknowledgements

YUWONDERIE IS NOT A REAL PLACE; DON'T EXPECT TO FIND IT ON A MAP. THE district described, south of the Murrumbidgee River, is the location of the real-life Coleambally Irrigation Area, developed by the government in the 1950s.

The privately developed Yuwonderie Scheme and the Seven families are fictitious. However, some characteristics of Yuwonderie township are borrowed from Leeton, designed by Walter Burley Griffin and Marion Mahony Griffin (the couple who designed Canberra). Leeton hosts an annual Art Deco festival.

Bessie Marney's story is not based on a real person or events. That said, the mission where her mother lives has some parallels with the Warangesda mission at Darlington Point. Warangesda Station was closed in 1924 and its remaining Indigenous residents evicted, as government policy moved towards assimilation.

I pay respect to the Wiradjuri people, the traditional owners of the lands of the Riverina, and acknowledge the deep injustices perpetrated against them over many decades.

Water trading is real. There is a widespread belief among farmers that they are being cheated by water barons, hedge funds and screen jockeys.

Shamefully, the opacity of political donations is also a reality. Over the years, hundreds of millions of dollars in political donations in Australia have been hidden from public scrutiny. It is entirely possible for nefarious individuals and organisations to donate large amounts to parties and politicians without detection.

The Calabrian mafia, the 'Ndrangheta, has been present in Australia for more than a hundred years, with a well-documented presence in regional areas such as Griffith.

The Peltier effect, spruiked by Harley Snouch, is real.

There are many people to thank, starting with everyone at my Australian publishers Allen & Unwin.

I am particularly indebted to the amazing editorial team that I've had the great good fortune to work with on all my novels: Jane Palfreyman, Ali Lavau, Christa Munns and Kate Goldsworthy. How could I go wrong? And a special thanks to A&U's former head of publishing Tom Gilliatt, who so effectively supported the first five books.

Big thanks to publicist Bella Breden and marketing wizard Sarah Barrett.

I am so fortunate to be published in the UK by the wonderful team at Wildfire, notably Jack Butler, Alex Clarke and Caitlin Raynor.

And a shout-out to the foreign language publishers—and their dedicated translators. Thank you!

I remain totally indebted to agents Grace Heifetz of Left Bank Literary Australia and Felicity Blunt of Curtis Brown UK. Just brilliant. And welcome to Peter Steinberg at UTA in New York.

The maps have become a real feature of my books, and thanks once again to Aleksander Potočnik for his wonderful imagining of Yuwonderie. Luke Causby has created yet another eye-catching cover for Australia—thank you. Gratitude to friends and photographers Mike Bowers and Robert Owen-Jones for author portraits over the years.

Thanks also to audiobook narrators Dorje Swallow and Lockie Chapman—what skills!

And a huge thanks to all the brilliant booksellers—we authors would be nothing without you.

And, as always, my gratitude and love to Tomoko, Elena and Cameron.